Erin reached back to make a blind grab at the child. A sharp set of baby teeth attached themselves to her pinky and sunk in with all the tenacity of a pit bull. Pain shot up her arm and exploded in the back of her neck.

A slight pull at the wheel forced her attention back to the road—except the road had turned into a white nothingness and the nose of the car was at an odd angle to where the road should have been.

They hung, as if suspended, in midair. Erin let go of the wheel and relaxed; the realization that she was going to die came as a relief. No fear. No remorse.

In the split second before the huge white mouth swallowed them whole, she hoped she would be forgiven. . . .

By Echo Heron
Published by Ivy Books:

INTENSIVE CARE: The Story of a Nurse
MERCY
CONDITION CRITICAL: The Story of a Nurse Continues

PULSE
PANIC
PARADOX

Books published by The Ballantine Publishing Group
are available at quantity discounts on bulk purchases
for premium, educational, fund-raising, and special
sales use. For details, please call 1-800-733-3000.

PARADOX

Echo Heron

IVY BOOKS • NEW YORK

An Ivy Book
Published by The Ballantine Publishing Group
Copyright © 1998 by Echo Heron

www.randomhouse.com/BB/

Library of Congress Catalog Card Number: 98-96475

ISBN 0-8041-1459-5

Manufactured in the United States of America

First Edition: November 1998

10   9   8   7   6   5   4   3   2   1

ACKNOWLEDGMENTS

For their advice and continued support, I wish to thank the following collection of wonderful and caring people:

Ken Holmes, Coroner, Colette Trembly, Dr. Richard Lavine, J. Patrick Heron, Esq., Frank Langben, Linda Stone, R.N., Tom Meadoff, M.D., Glen and Petula Dvorak-Justice, Nora Bianchi, Elinor and Franco Mazzucchelli, Elliott Chernin, Simon Heron, Rinelle Shay, Jill Sproul, R.N., Dr. Glen Justice and Janey Justice, Laura Gasparis Vonfrolio, R.N., Louis Mendez, Leona Nevler, Dominick Abel, Eleanor Boylan, Storm Salato, R.N., Catherine Barnes, R.N., Scott Jones and Kellie Moore, Mary C. Bianchi, Kaye Manly-Hayes, R.N., Art Coolidge, Ed Schoon, Kurt Helm, Kelly Pratt, Laura Gray, R.N., and Martha DeLaney.

ACKNOWLEDGMENTS

DEDICATION

For the life term gang:
Janey O'Hara Justice, Colette Coutant Trembly, Mary Catherine Bianchi, Kathleen Coffey Heron, Storm L. Salato, Mari M. Salato, and Catherine Murray Barnes.

ONE

THE THREE-YEAR-OLD SUCKED HER THUMB AND stared out the car window. For as far as she could see, there was nothing but thick, white fog—fertile ground for bogeymen.

"Mommy?" It came out a whimpery mumble.

As if startled by the presence of the child, the woman's gray eyes snapped to the rearview mirror. Her grave expression did not change. "What?"

"Where's Daddy and Butchie?"

"Butchie should be back there with you, and Daddy is asleep."

Erin returned her gaze to the road in time to see the side of the mountain coming at her. Reflexively tugging at the wheel, the car jumped back onto the black pavement but not before a jutting rock scraped the rear fender. Erin searched beyond the headlights for some break in the fog. The child tugged at the too-tight seatbelt and began to whine in earnest, her voice climbing the decibel scale.

"Where's my daddy and Butchie?"

"They're in sleepyman's land, baby," Erin said as tenderly as she could. The front right tire went off the narrow road and her eyes again returned to the rearview mirror, searching for something behind them. "Just like you should be. Now lay your head back and make believe you're inside a big bowl of whipped cream. Make believe we're . . ."

"I want my daddy!" the child's voice quivered and rose.

"Baby, you need to relax now. Try to . . ."

"I waaant my daaaadddy!" The high-pitched wail cut through Erin's head like a knife; there was no shriek in the world like that of an agitated three-year-old. To emphasize her point, the child kicked the back of the seat and pushed on the seatbelt

1

button so that the veins in her forehead stuck out blue and pulsing.

Erin's hands tightened on the steering wheel. "We're going to Daddy right now, darling. Stay quiet and we'll . . ."

"No! I want my daddy *now*!" The ear-piercing scream that followed pulled Erin's eyes to the rearview mirror in time to see the head of curly light brown hair slide under the shoulder strap toward the floor.

"I want my . . ."

Erin reached back to make a blind grab at the child. A sharp set of baby teeth attached themselves to her pinky and sunk in with all the tenacity of a pit bull. Pain shot up her arm and exploded in the back of her neck.

A slight pull in the wheel forced her attention back to the road—except the road had turned to white nothingness and the nose of the car was at an odd angle to where the road should have been.

They hung, as if suspended, in midair. Erin let go of the wheel and relaxed; the realization that she was going to die came as a relief. No fear. No remorse.

In the split second before the huge white mouth swallowed them whole, she hoped she would be forgiven.

Paramedic/fireman Jelco "Jellyroll" Love hated the fog and he hated the section of Highway 1 between Mill Valley and Stinson Beach. Twisting narrow curves set on the tops of sheer three- to four-hundred-foot cliffs—most without guardrails. It was, he had decided years before, the California Highway Commission's contribution to population control.

Jellyroll lifted the face shield of his flame hood and adjusted the breathing mask on the bridge of his nose. He also hated Detroit's newer compact cars: they burned faster and hotter because of the plastics and synthetics—the kind that gave off toxins which killed humans much faster than the old Naugahyde.

His mouth went dry as he neared the vehicle. This one was truly foul; despite the protection of his bunker gear, he could still feel the heat of the flames. The hose came alive in the hands of the fireman next to him and the car was instantly engulfed in a snowbank of high-protein foam.

As soon as it began to disperse, he held his breath and looked inside. Even after twenty years of gruesome sights, he still found burned human remains hard to stomach.

What Jellyroll Love saw went beyond being hard to stomach. This time the sight of the small charred thing in the back would fuel his worst nightmares until the day he died.

The forearms and lower legs were gone—burned away to points. The skull was exactly that: an ebony skull with a hole through one side where the brain had bubbled and burst through. Inside the tiny rib cage was a black crusted lump through which a dark red ooze bubbled. The liver. Possibly the heart. It was hard to tell now.

There was nothing of the driver to be seen. Not so much as the remains of a shoe. Making the car their start point, the crew headed outward in different directions to search for the ejected driver and any other passengers.

Ten minutes later, he found a woman propped against a rock not two hundred feet away. Her skin was drained of color—all except her hands and wrists, which appeared to have sustained a combination of second- and third-degree burns. He guessed her to be between twenty-eight and thirty-four. The left front of her jacket hung in smoldering shreds at her side. As if it were an extension of the jacket, her hair on that side was singed, and her left foot was bare and crisscrossed with cuts and scrapes. On the right, both her coat and her hair were intact. The right foot was securely tied into a sturdy walking boot covered with mud.

Jellyroll shouted for help and knelt beside the woman, staring into her gray eyes. Taking less than four seconds, he let his fingers travel over the cold flesh of her neck, searching for her carotid pulse. It was rapid, slightly irregular, but strong enough. He flashed the light in her eyes ("Pupils reactive and of normal size" he would note later in his initial trauma assessment. He would not, however, try to describe the eerie, catatonic-like expression.) and asked if she were okay. She continued to stare, the large eyes unblinking in a pale-as-death face. Classic shock. In a way he was glad; at least she wasn't screaming—not now, anyway.

Jellyroll pictured it all in his head: The mother ejected from the car with the first impact, the child still trapped inside. Mom coming to and running toward the fireball that had been her car. He could hear the woman's tortured screams as she tried to reach into the roaring inferno for her child, and was forced back. Maybe she'd tried again, or maybe she'd gone unconscious for a time, crawling away from the heat, going into shock.

"We're going to help you. Are you experiencing pain anywhere?"

Nothing. Not even an attempt to answer.

He ran his hands gently over the sides and back of her head, checked her ears for fluid or blood. He found a large swollen lump on the left side of her head. A concussion for sure.

"Can you tell me your name, ma'am?"

Not so much as a blink answered him.

He rapidly checked the reflexes in her legs, unlaced the one boot, checked pulses in both feet. The bare foot had some deep scrapes on the toes, and one on the bottom, but as far as he could see, no tendons were cut.

Four of them moved her onto the longboard as if she were a Dresden china doll and instituted c-spine precautions with belts, head rolls, and lots of tape. He was worried about her head injury.

"Does your head hurt, ma'am?"

No answer.

"You got any tingling in your hands or feet?"

She blinked. Things were looking up.

The med box came: one of the men poured sterile water over her burns and wrapped her hands and forearms in sterile gauze while another got a blood pressure, which proved to be low, but not load-and-go low. Kirby, the young rookie of the set, made a joke about having her back home in time for dinner. Nobody but Kirby laughed.

Jellyroll placed an oxygen cannula in her nose and the electrodes on her bare chest, apologizing continually for his cold hands and trying to cover her naked breasts with what was left of her blouse. Thanking God that the burns did not extend much past her wrists, he searched along her inner arms for any large vein. Shock was bad that way; when you needed intravenous access the most, the veins, even the large ones, collapsed from lack of volume or constricted to spider threads due to adrenaline overload. On the other hand, he was glad she was in shock—she wouldn't feel the pain.

Once the IV was running, he touched his hood as if it were the brim of a cowboy hat. "My name is Jelco Love. I'm a paramedic. Can you tell me your name?"

The woman blinked, opened her mouth, closed it, and continued to stare expressionless, uncomprehending.

Her blood pressure was still low, but the monitor showed a corresponding sinus tachycardia. He palpated her abdomen, which was soft and flat. He listened to her lungs and found them clear, although the breaths were shallow and rapid. Without thinking, Jellyroll leaned forward, close enough that his nose almost touched hers. He told her to open her mouth. She did.

He wrote "Fol. com." on the palm of his hand—shorthand for "follows commands." With the wooden tongue depressor wedged between her front teeth, he applied pressure until she opened wider. The penlight found some blood from a small gash on her tongue, and a chipped left incisor. He didn't smell anything like alcohol or the fruity acetone odor of ketoacidosis.

He looked at his watch: time to load and go. He did another blood pressure check, then they lifted her and began their long ascent of the steep hill. Two steps into the climb, she tried to sit up, weakly attacking the straps that held her immobile with hands that were now two huge balls of white gauze. Her eyes strained to see down to where the burned shell of the car sat in the night fog.

Jellyroll thought she was looking for the child. "It's okay, ma'am. Everything is taken care of. What's your name?"

"What happened?" she asked in that muzzy, accident-victim way.

He hadn't expected such a low, husky voice. It could have been smoke inhalation, but he thought it was probably her natural voice. "Your vehicle went off the side of the road and you were thrown out. Do you remember what happened?"

"I don't remember," she said, as if the idea scared her.

"What's your name?" Jellyroll asked.

Her mouth opened and closed. She'd gone back to staring.

Later, when the nightmares about this night came, it wouldn't be only the charred remains in the back of the car that haunted him; it would be that stare. He found it more than disconcerting.

After a while, she muttered, "I don't know."

Post-traumatic stress amnesia. He shuddered and laughed to cover the movement. "Well, that's okay, ma'am; there's some days I can't remember mine either. Don't worry. It'll come back to you."

"The car," she said, making weak attempts to get off the stretcher. "In the car. I don't . . . What is it?"

"Do you remember who was in the car with you?" he asked, praying she wouldn't. His eyes sought out the med box in case she did.

She closed her eyes and tried to lick her lips. "Don't . . . remember."

They'd reached the road. Jellyroll was glad; even though the woman was light, his quadriceps were throbbing. It was at times like this that he cursed himself for selling his mountain bike.

"Are you married, ma'am?" he asked. It seemed like a strange question, considering all the ones he could have— should have asked. There had been no rings on her fingers, he remembered, and no purse or any form of identification had been found.

"I . . ." She grimaced, tried to shake her head and couldn't because of the tape holding it to the backboard. "I don't remember."

He let it go while they slid her into the back of the rig and climbed in behind her.

His partner, Paramedic Hinds, made radio contact with Ellis Hospital trauma base. He gave an ETA of twenty minutes, which seemed overly optimistic to Jelco Love, considering the fog and the condition of the roads. He told Hinds to change the ETA to forty minutes and try not to drive like a cowboy. The patient was stable—no need to risk everybody's life and limbs.

The woman's eyes opened wide and looked around slowly as if in wonder. "What happened?" she asked like someone half-asleep—or drugged. Trauma trance.

Jellyroll stopped listening to her lungs. "You've been in a car accident out on Highway One about three miles from Stinson Beach. You're in an ambulance. We're taking you to a hospital."

She seemed to draw back and study him, then the inside of the van. "You aren't . . . ?" She let the question die. When she opened her eyes again, he could see they were teary.

"What's your name?" he asked, gently brushing a chip of drying mud from her cheek. Despite the singed hair and the dirt, he was not blind to the fact that the person on the stretcher was a woman. Solidly built, *and* pretty—just his type.

"What happened?" she asked again in that absentminded way trauma victims had.

Jelco Love looked at Hinds and shook his head. It would be a waste of breath to keep repeating his answer. She would continue to ask the same question over and over again. If she was unable to remember her own name, he doubted her short-term memory would be any better. It was a blessing at this point.

"You don't worry about that right now, ma'am. We'll have you in the ER in no time. You're going to be okay." Jellyroll looked out the front of the cab into the solid wall of fog. With a pinch of apprehension, he wondered how Hinds could see to drive.

He looked back at his patient and studied her. What the hell was a woman with a baby doing driving on a night and a road like this? Jellyroll decided that she must not have been familiar with the roads or the fog.

One of her bandaged hands moved slowly out between the straps and came to rest on his knee. It looked, Jellyroll thought, like a defenseless animal lying there.

"I'm scared," she whispered, staring into his eyes. "I can't think." She was pleading. The survivors always did.

Jelco had a wild urge to tell her he'd take care of her, take her home and nurse her until she was recovered. Sure. Balding, forty-three-year-old bachelor with car payments, student loans but no PC and no toys, living in a pool-less, hot-tub-less one-room studio in the low-rent district of San Rafael? Get real. What else could he offer her except daily blood pressure checks and a decent splint?

He adjusted the IV rate and bent close, feeling for another carotid pulse. It was still around 110, but stronger. He thought she had a little more color in her face.

"You shouldn't be scared," he lied. "I—we won't let anything happen to you."

At least, he thought, not yet.

TWO

ADELE MONSARRAT, R.N., SAT ON HER COUCH WEARing men's Jockey shorts and a sleeveless undershirt. She took a swig of warm beer, belched, scooped an indecent amount of bean dip onto a corn chip, and stuffed it into her mouth. Wild cheering blared from the TV as the Dallas Cowboys and the San Francisco 49ers went after each other on the ten-yard line, although neither viewer could have said exactly whose ten-yard line it was.

"So. *This* is what it feels like to be a guy, huh," Adele said to the best of her human friends, her coworker Cynthia O'Neil.

The mortician-turned-nurse scratched her crotch and straightened her boxer shorts around her thighs with all the modesty of a Theodore Dreiser novel. Opening her mouth, she crammed in a handful of Barbecue Flavored Corn Nuts. "What part do they think is fun?" she asked, "The beer, or watching a group of their gender peers do public physical bonding?"

Adele bit off the end of a large cigar, took too much, and violently spit the shreds of tobacco onto the floor where Nelson, a three-year-old black Labrador retriever and the best of her nonhuman friends, was on it immediately, sniffing the dark clump, hoping against hope it was some sort of low-flying treat. He backed away immediately, shaking his head until his ears flapped.

Unfamiliar with the rules of proper stogie smoking, Adele stuck the unbitten end in her mouth and put a match to the part she'd dentally mutilated. She could not bring herself to draw in the smoke. "I can't help you on that, Cyn," she said, trying to remember whose idea it had been to have a "Boys' Day" instead of a "Girls' Day" on their weekend off. If it had been Cynthia's, she'd have to think of a way to retaliate—maybe a day at the reptile petting zoo, forcing her friend to have close contact with a variety of lizards and snakes.

So far, the two "guys" had played basketball at Redwood High, gone to Easy Street Cafe for garden burgers with extra onion and vegetarian chili—extra beans and garlic—hung out at Java in Larkspur drinking iced designer coffees and making lewd remarks about guys' butts, chest sizes, and abundance or lack of hair, then gone back to Adele's and put an old 49ers video into the VCR.

During the first three quarters, including the halftime show, they'd hooted and hollered, yelling out things at random like, "JeSUS! What the HELL is that motherfucker thinking?" or "Interception!" "Fumble!" and "Time out, you son of a bitch!"— not having a clue what any of it meant, but breaking into hysterical, wheezy laughter every time. They'd leered at the players and made more obscene comments about how cute the uniforms were, and how they accentuated the bulges in the front of their breeches.

The announcement that there were two minutes left in the final quarter, with San Francisco in the lead by such-and-such points, caused Adele to brighten. "Hey, isn't this when guys start talking about 'serious chow'?"

Cynthia made a face and mimicked sticking her finger down her throat. "Yeah. They throw a six-pound block of cheap cheese into the microwave for nachos, and then put ten or twenty Manly Mouthful frozen Mexican-style entrees into the oven."

The younger nurse stared thoughtfully at Nelson, who yawned and licked his chops. "As soon as they cram those down, they do the farting contest thing, then they all go to the nearest park, play football pretending they're famous football stars, then some-one gets hurt and they come into the ER. After that, they all go to a bar, get drunk, call their current squeeze, and, like overtired little boys, go home, apologize for being six hours late, and get laid."

With the exception of the noise from the television, there was silence for several minutes while both women envisioned quite vividly men they had known engaging in flatulence competitions. The images were neither appealing nor romantic, but rather left them vaguely depressed. They were still ruminating on the windy scene when the phone rang. Adele grunted and swore, stuck the unlit cigar into her mouth, and lunged for the receiver.

"Yeah?" she growled loud and harsh, like a New York bookie, "Whadda ya want?" She hoped to God it was someone who would understand and readily forgive her—like her mother, or a telemarketer.

"Oh dear," said the high, thin voice. "I was looking for Nurse Monsarrat. I must have the wrong . . ."

Adele sucked wind through her back teeth. "Ah, hold on a minute," she said and instantly began mimicking the speech pattern of a Mafia plumber. "I'm, ahhh, da lady plumber. Adele, she's outside wit' da dawg. Hold a minute."

Adele put the phone down on the table then ran to the other end of the house, where she opened and slammed the door, and clopped noisily across the floor, thanking "Wanda" for coming to get her from the backyard. Pretending to be out of breath, she managed a cheery greeting in her normal voice.

"Ardel?" came the high, strangled voice of the nursing supervisor at Ellis Hospital. "This is Mattie Noel."

"Yes, Mrs. Noel?" Adele's stomach tightened automatically. They were going to ask her to come in on her day off and work Ward 8—the catch-all ward from the deepest pits of mangled healthcare Hell that specialized in the almost dead, the should-be dead and the would-be-better-off dead.

Across the room, Cynthia made her fingers into a cross and hissed. "Where are the wooden stakes?" she whispered urgently.

". . . terrible accident came in from Stinson Beach," Mrs. Noel was saying, "so now Ward Eight is understaffed and we're desperate for . . ."

"No," Adele said, closing her eyes. Her stomach was pouring out guilt and codependency acids, which were immediately relayed to her other vital organs. She began having stress angina.

"Only for four hours?" the supervisor begged. "Please, dear? Just to cover until we can get someone to come in and do a whole twelve-hour shift?"

"Four hours?" Adele repeated in a tiny voice.

Cynthia's eyes narrowed. "Just say no, Adele! You can do it, I know you can."

". . . new admit is the sweetest young woman, Ardel. Her

hands are burned terribly and she's got post-trauma amnesia. Can't remember a thing and . . ."

"Amnesia?" Adele repeated, the seeds of interest beginning to sprout and crawl like crabgrass as Mrs. Noel rushed through the rest of the details.

"Damn it, Del, say no!" Cynthia hissed resentfully. "This is your first day off in two weeks."

". . . there was nothing left of her baby. They found the charred remains in the . . ."

"A baby?!" Adele swallowed hard. "Oh, my God, that poor . . ."

"Oh for Christ's sake, Adele . . ." Cynthia paused, scowled, then, in spite of herself asked, "What baby?"

Impatiently Adele motioned Cynthia away, gripping the phone tighter. "What baby?" she asked.

"There was a baby strapped into the backseat who was burned to death. That's why we *need* you here, Ardel. This poor, poor woman needs you. You're the most senior and best R.N. we have. Don't you think she deserves the best in her hour of need?"

Adele quickly covered the mouthpiece and spoke in hushed, hurried tones to Cynthia. "A woman went over the cliffs by Stinson. She was thrown clear of the vehicle, but she burned her hands trying to pull her baby out of the backseat. She's suffering from post-trauma amnesia."

Cynthia was holding her breath, her eyes wide. "What happened to the baby?"

Adele shook her head sadly and, covering the mouthpiece, whispered, "Toasted."

Cynthia's hands flew to her mouth in horror. "Oh, my God!" Nelson whined as if in commiseration.

"Can we count on you, Ardel?" Mrs. Noel asked, her tone conjuring up pictures of apple pie and Uncle Sam superimposed on an American flag.

"Christ on a bike!" Adele said then pulled at her bottom lip. "Amnesia, huh?"

"It's a disaster, Ard—"

"Yeah, yeah. Okay. Give me twenty minutes . . . but you have to promise that I get the trauma case as my patient and I leave after four hours."

Mattie Noel grinned. Oh, these nurses, she thought; ask for an inch and they give you five miles. Even the Ward 8 nurses—deviates that they were—could be suckered in with the lightest application of guilt. She wouldn't need to go to the trouble of looking for anyone to come in early—this Arden or Ardel would work straight through until 3 or 4 A.M.

"Oh, and Arden?"

Wearily, Adele brought the phone back to her ear. Mrs. Noel had been calling her by various wrong names for fifteen years—it had long since ceased to irritate her.

"Ayuhn?"

"You wouldn't happen to know where Nurse O'Neil is, would you?"

"Nurse O'Neil?" Adele echoed, a nasty, vindictive smile beginning at the corners of her lips.

Cynthia shook her head vigorously, frantically mouthing, "No! No!"

Adele grinned wickedly. "Well, Mrs. Noel, I might be able to *find* her if you could throw some incentive my way."

Happy in the knowledge she wouldn't have to work Christmas Eve for the next five years, Adele whistled and gave the Beast—her 1978 Pontiac Grand LeMans station wagon—a loving pat, as though the shandrydan were a well-loved horse.

"Get in, Cynthia, my dear best friend," Adele said in a maple-sugar voice.

"Fuck you, Monsarrat," Cynthia said stubbornly, her breath visible as small white puffs in the freezing rain of November.

"Oh, come on," Adele encouraged. "At least we'll be suffering together."

Cynthia hitched up the borrowed scrub dress, which hung below the middle of her calf, and warily got into the car. "How the hell did I let you talk me into this? I'm giving up a romantic night with my landlord so *you* can have Christmas Eve off?"

Adele honked twice to Nelson, who was now barking in protest through the closed miniblinds in the front bay windows, and backed out of the driveway. "Stop complaining. Look at it as having been saved from a slimy, helmet-haired creep who only wants to get into your pants. Plus you got next Friday off.

All for four hours of easy work on evening shift? That sounds like some kind of deal to me."

"You call going into Ward Eight 'easy work'?" Cynthia asked in disgust. "Fifteen minutes' work on Ward Eight would make most grown men cry."

That was true enough. The forty-bed ward took all the over-flow patients from every unit in the hospital—medical, surgical, oncology, orthopedic, ICU, CCU, obstetrics and pediatrics thirteen years to adult. The nurses who regularly worked there were often thought of as altruistic to an unhealthy extreme, or masochistic psychos who were probably covered with tattoos under their uniforms. That Adele had worked Ward 8 for seventeen years officially qualified her for sainthood—or eccentricity.

"Hey," Adele said, as the top floor of the hospital came into view through the redwoods, "it's got to be easier than eating frozen dinners and watching a bunch of morons jump around after a pointy ball."

Evening shift was considered the social-hour shift. It was that time of the healthcare day when visitors came in, and the business of torturing the patients with tests and procedures was mostly put to rest for the night. The programs on the television were sporadically entertaining, and the nurses were generally more laid-back. The doctors avoided coming in at all costs, wanting to get in at least one unhurried meal with the family, who might or might not still recognize them.

There was a time when Adele lusted after evening shift, but she had put it off for the first ten years of her career because she wanted a social life. Now that she was divorced and the single parent of an emotionally challenged dog, she put it off because Nelson was afraid to be alone in the dark.

Once Nelson was gone, she told her supervisors, she would apply for work on swing shift. Unfortunately, while Nelson's mental health may have been somewhat debatable, his physical health was extraordinarily good. The vet once told her, in a funereal tone, that he thought Nelson would set a canine record for longevity. He mentioned something about doggie Alzheimer's, but didn't pursue the subject when he saw she was not amused.

In the Ward 8 nurses' lounge, Linda Rainer, one of the

regular Ward 8 R.N.'s, hiked her uniform skirt up to her waist, leaned over the sink to run cold water over a fresh bloodstain in the shape of a butterfly, and continued her story.

"So, the guy in eight-oh-four B waits until I get the IV in—six tries, mind you—all nicey-nicey and quiet as a mouse, right? Then, as I'm getting ready to secure the catheter with tape, I tell him to hold his arm very still so we don't lose the IV, and the next thing I know, he's screaming like a woman, scratching and biting, blood splattering everywhere." Linda scrubbed at the stain. "AIDS dementia. I tried to transfer him out to Psych, but no dice. He's restrained, but still dangerous. We're not admitting to the other bed." She blew the bangs out of her eyes, shook out the extra water from the hem of her uniform, and flopped down in the chair nearest Adele. With a sigh, she picked up her patient information cards and began the abbreviated "Alive and Breathing" report—a reserved right belonging to senior nurses only. Minor details that could easily be picked up from the chart were left out, leaving only the bare bones of pertinent information to be passed along. The resulting monologue had a sing-song rhythm of short sentences and nurses' jargon.

"Most of your patients you know already. Eight-eleven bed A is Mr. Cummings with his resolving MI. Four days out. Off lidocaine since three, and started on p.o. Pronestyl. Walked once in the room. Nothing new. Alive and breathing. He and his family need nutrition teaching. His daughter sneaked in a large pepperoni pizza. He devoured half of it before we caught him."

"How the hell did she sneak in a large . . ."

"She could carry a bicycle rack under her coat and nobody would know the difference," Linda said dryly.

"Eight-twelve B is Mrs. Habibi with her shingles. Alive and whining for pain meds. Still on massive doses of acyclovir. Nothing new. We're cutting down on her Demerol and swinging her over to Tylenol number three. If we try harder, we can probably ensure she'll be addicted by the time she gets discharged.

"Eight-ten bed A is Gloria Fowler with fever of unknown origin, six days post-op crainy. I changed her bed and bathed her. She's weighed. Nothing new. Alive and breathing on her own.

"Eight hundred bed A is a San Quentin prisoner with stab wound to chest and resulting pneumothorax, blunt trauma to abdomen, testicles, and kidneys. Alive and breathing. Still has some blood in his urine, but his blood work and I&O are fine. Had the rest of his chest tubes out today—dressings are dry. Mental abilities are that of a gerbil, but what can we expect with an IQ of fifty-one? He likes to watch cartoons and read comic books, which puts him a bit ahead of his guards, who don't understand the cartoons and can't read.

"Bed eight-fifteen A is our new Jane Doe. You know as much history as anybody. We got her up from ER thirty minutes ago. She's suffering from amnesia and has scattered first- and second-degree burns to right hand and thumb. Left hand, including digits, has scattered deep second-degree extending to a few centimeters above the wrist. She also has a concussion, a laceration on the left lateral knee, multiple bruises including the left rib cage; the left foot has some deep scrapes to dorsal and plantar surfaces. Hair is singed on the left side and she has some slight first-degree burns of her left neck and cheek. Chest, abdominal, and pelvic X-rays are all negative. Vitals are okay. Her labs are okay; electrolytes were a little screwy, but we're fixing those. Blood alcohol level is zero, and her drug screen is negative.

"She was hypotensive in the field, but she's up to one forty-six over ninety." Linda laid her head back on the couch. "But then again, you know how these MVA traumas are; they're either off the ceiling or vagal as hell and dropping out to zippo.

"Her specific gravity is low, so I increased her IV rate. You need to get an order for that from Dr. Murray. She's on her second liter of lactated ringers.

"Neuro-wise, she's not with us a hundred percent. She's got a major post-concussive headache and nausea. Neuro checks are Q one hour. CAT scan is negative. Dr. Murray is going to call in a neuro consult, but I haven't seen anybody yet.

"We're titrating morphine for the pain."

Adele nodded. "No respiratory involvement?"

Linda unwrapped and stuck a piece of gum into her mouth. "Not that I can hear."

"Any more details about the accident?"

"Nope. She was thrown clear of the car before it burned, which explains the concussion and the bruised ribs. Rescue One thinks she got the burns trying to get to the baby. That's all we know."

"And why wasn't she sent to a burn unit?"

The charge nurse chewed vigorously for a moment, her jaw popping loudly. "She's under ten percent body surface area, and Dr. Murray didn't think the burns were bad enough. He did the debriding himself in ER—he thinks there's enough dermis remaining on the left hand that it'll regenerate. If it doesn't, she'll have to go to St. Francis for a follow-up and grafts, but for now we play the waiting game. She's seven hundred and nineteen hundred hour dressing changes, but Murray doesn't want them touched until tomorrow. We've got both hands elevated—the left is splinted."

"What does she remember?"

Linda shook her head. "Nothing. Not even her name. I don't think anything was found either—no purse, no papers. Everything went up with the car."

Adele looked over her report sheet and the assortment of patient information cards. On Jane Doe's card, right under the notation that she'd received a tetanus shot in ER, was the red coded message NFP. Translated literally it meant "not for publication"—Ms. Doe was a "secret patient."

She wondered how long it would take for the woman and her child to be missed. A vision of the bereaved father and husband arriving on the ward in a state of grief madness made her hope the woman was still amnesic when and if this happened.

"Oh, by the way," said Linda, pushing herself to the edge of the couch, "do you know that you're scheduled to work until three A.M.?"

"Oh no, no no," Adele laughed. "I'm only here for four hours. I work day shift tomorrow; they wouldn't dare try to make me do a turnaround."

Linda pursed her lips and raised her eyebrows. It occurred to Adele that Mattie Noel might have suckered her in. It certainly wouldn't have been the first time management had diddled with her, making promises and not keeping them.

"You should have had them put it in writing, Adele," Linda chided. "It's the only reason I bought a fax machine. I make them write their promises and sign them. That way I have a leg to stand on when they threaten to take me to court for abandoning my patients."

"I'll call someone in on my own." Adele sniffed, realizing

that she probably wouldn't get Christmas Eve off either. Not that it bothered *her* to work the holidays, being seasonally impaired as she was, but Nelson, not to mention Martha Monsarrat, her mother, would be crushed. She supposed she'd better call her mother back before she made any plans that involved major numbers of people.

"Oh yeah?" Linda mused. "That should be interesting."

"Why do you say it like that? I can always get Denise or Marcella to . . ."

"You won't find a nurse for love or money to cover you tonight, girlfriend. Did you forget that the committee meeting for the nurses' protest march is tonight?"

"Oh, Christ on a bike," Adele said, closing her eyes and slumping her shoulders. "I spaced it. I was supposed to help with the banners and go over my speech."

The idea that she'd get only three hours of sleep before having to report for duty again didn't seem so bad when compared to how she felt about missing the committee meeting. It had already been predicted that the nurses' march on San Francisco City Hall, in the interest of patients' and nurses' rights and safety, would be the largest gathering of nurses in the history of northern California. She, along with other bedside working grunts, congressmen, senators, and several sympathetic union executives, had been asked to prepare a five-minute presentation supporting patient and nurse safety.

She set her jaw and resolved to wait until after she saw her patients before she spoke to Mrs. Noel—a worthwhile substitute for counting to ten.

The private room was dark except for the light coming under the door. Adele turned on the small five-amp lamp inside the med cabinet and waited for her eyes to adjust.

Jane Doe's left hand and arm dangled from the IV pole by a length of gauze, reminding her of a tiny body hung by the neck. The right hand lay elevated on two plump pillows.

Adele approached the bed.

The patient lay staring at the ceiling, her thin face covered with a fine mist of perspiration.

"Hi," Adele whispered softly. "I'm Adele Monsarrat, your nurse. Are you having pain?"

Jane Doe studied her, although she said nothing or gave any indication that she was actually seeing her.

"Are you in pain?" Adele repeated, instantly concerned that the woman's level of consciousness had decreased. "Do you want more pain medication?"

After a pause, the woman stirred. "Yes," she said slowly, her pale lips set in a thin, strained line.

"I'm going to turn on the light."

The woman groaned and shook her head in protest, moving her untied hand to cover her eyes. Gently, Adele put it back on the pillows.

"Please," Adele said in a hushed voice. "I need more light to do your assessment and give you some pain medicine. I'll turn it off as soon as I can."

The patient stared unhappily at Adele, her forehead puckered in a frown.

Adele angled the indirect overhead lamp as far away from the patient's face as she could and turned it on low.

Adele studied her patient, taking in what she could with her senses. The woman was cool, pale, and wet with perspiration. Her pupils were of equal size and dilated—probably because of the pain; her respirations were rapid and shallow, for the same reason; and the breath had the usual acrid, foul smell—that of a trauma victim who was NPO, *non per os,* "nothing by mouth."

"You've got really great eyes," Adele said as she pulled the bedside table closer and put the flow sheet and chart down.

"You, too," the woman mumbled. "They're gold."

Though she should have been used to it, it still made Adele self-conscious when people commented about her eyes. An aberration of nature, the golden irises never failed to make people do a double take or stop in their tracks. Her optometrist kept jumbo color photo enlargements of them on his office wall. It was, she told people she knew, rather like being a sideshow freak.

"Remember your name yet?" Adele asked, shining her penlight into each pupil, watching to see how quickly each constricted.

"No," the woman said flatly. "I don't remember anything."

"Okay. How about if you think of a name you do like? I'll be damned if I'm going to call you Jane Doe."

The woman smiled a little, closed her eyes, then shook her head. "You think of one."

Adele wrapped the blood pressure cuff around her upper arm. "Gray-eyed women should have classic names. Like Amelia, Eleanor, or Mathilde."

"Mathilde?" She pronounced it the way the French did: *Matild.* "I like it."

"Well, then, Mathilde it is for now. Are you having pain anywhere else besides your hands?"

"A headache." She went to touch her forehead, forgetting about her hands. "It hurts to breathe."

"You've got a concussion and a few bruised ribs." Adele drew up some morphine and injected it into the IV line. "Do you remember how this happened?"

"They said I was in a car that skidded off the road," the woman said without affect. "And that I was thrown out, and then the car burned. I tried to get something out of the car."

"Do you remember what it was in the car that you wanted?"

The frown returned. "I don't know. I can't . . ."

"Okay. Don't worry about it. I'm going to do a physical assessment on you. If I do anything that hurts you, don't hesitate to tell me."

Adele lifted the sheet off the woman's feet and checked her reflexes and the wounds on her left foot. "Push as hard as you can against my hands."

The woman did as she was told.

"Who's the president?" Adele asked.

The woman furrowed her brow trying to remember.

Adele hoped she wouldn't answer Lincoln or Eisenhower. "Don't tax yourself," she said after a minute. "What's ten minus seven?"

"Three."

"Seven times seven?"

"Forty-nine."

"One-fifth of forty-five?"

"Nine."

"Were you a math major in college?"

"I don't remember."

Adele made note of the time she gave the morphine and the quantity, then filled in the flow sheet a section at a time with the information she had gathered: Neuro, Cardiac, Pulmonary, Urinary, Gastrointestinal, Muscular-Skeletal, Psycho-social.

She remembered that Mrs. Habibi was waiting for her medications, but sat down in the chair next to the bed anyway.

The morphine worked its magic as the woman's eyes rolled lazily back into her head. The woman certainly wasn't accustomed to any kind of drugs.

"Mathilde?"

"Um."

"How does it feel not to remember anything?"

The gray eyes came front and center. "I don't remember," she said, then, after a pause, both of them giggled.

"Okay, well. I'll see you in a little while to do your neuro checks. I'll have to wake you up every half hour, so don't hate me, okay?"

The woman had fallen asleep, and the child she'd once been showed plainly in a face that was free of all the lines of care and worry. Adele imagined that the baby who had died must have resembled the woman. She cringed, first at the vision of the child enveloped by the flames, and then, at the moment in which the woman would realize the full meaning of her loss.

Before she left, Adele lifted the covers off her patient's feet and, taking the narrow left foot in hand, prudently examined the injuries again. Someone in ER had cleaned and treated the scrapes, but the legs had been left dirty.

The woman's legs were extremely muscular; obviously, she was an athlete or someone who worked out beyond the limit of simply keeping fit. A professional dancer, Adele thought. Perhaps a gymnast or a body builder.

Her fingers ran lightly over small clumps of a dried yellowish brown substance stuck to the ankles and the back of the calves. Maybe mud. Maybe diarrhea. Soaking a washcloth with warm soapy water, she wiped off one leg and smelled the cloth. The rich and heavy smell of earth filled her nose. Yellow clay mixed with dark mud.

There was something deeply satisfying about the task of washing away the dirt—something that reminded her of why she had gone into nursing in the first place.

* * *

When all the medications had been given, and all her patients were assessed and settled for at least the next thirty minutes, Adele sat in a corner near the nursing station watching the activity of Ward 8. In addition to herself, Linda, and Cynthia, a group of what were euphemistically referred to as "unlicensed assistive personnel," or UAPs, was working—young, tired-looking women and men whose eyes alone betrayed the uneasiness they felt at having responsibilities they were not qualified to take on. This growing corps of mostly non-English-speaking people almost never had any medical training except for one or two hours of hurried instruction on how to take vital signs, give injections of potentially lethal medications, and generally diddle around in critical care—where they had no business being.

Adele stretched and turned back to her stack of charts. It wasn't thirteen seconds later that a call bell went off. She could see that it was one of Cynthia's patients: a woman by the name of Fanny McKinney—a hag full of acid recriminations for any nurse who went near her.

Suddenly, the hall that had been bustling with personnel only a few seconds before was devoid of both nurse and UAP. Cynthia was at the end of the hall starting an IV on a new admission; Linda was making rounds with one of the physicians.

She looked at her watch. With seven minutes left until another round of neuro and vital signs on Mathilde, she heaved herself up, speaking in a dramatic intonation to the invisible nurse martyrs on the ceiling as she made her way toward Mrs. McKinney. "Ah, I lament. Onward I proceed into the depths of patient hell, letting compassion shield me from spittle, vomitus, and urine, healing those who shall not be healed, groveling at the bedside of those who have shat upon me. Thus I take up my stethoscope and thermometer to . . ."

"Can it, Monsarrat!" whined Tina, the surly ward clerk from day shift. "It's bad enough I have to work a double shift—I don't want to have to listen to some weird Shakespearean nurse shit too."

"Get this thing out from under me!" Mrs. McKinney yelled the moment she saw the black-haired nurse enter her room. She struggled to lift the bulky mass of her body off the plastic bedpan that was fretting her butt. "What's wrong with the help nowadays that they can't find a decent nurse to work in this death trap? Why, I've had better service from the car wash boys. That bitch put me on this thing and left . . ."

Adele leaned over the woman, close to her face, as she pulled on a pair of exam gloves. "Don't talk about the nurses like that, Mrs. McKinney." Her tone was deadly serious.

The woman's astonishment kept her from saying anything for a few seconds. Adele took her silence as a sign of cooperativeness and got a hold of the edge of the bedpan.

"Lift your hips," she commanded.

"I can't! I'm too . . ."

"Lift your hips and lift them now," Adele said evenly. "I've seen you do it before. I can't lift you by myself."

The patient bit her lower lip, her chin trembling with agitation. She pressed down on the bedpan, trapping Adele's fingers between her buttocks and the rim. "Oh, how can you talk to me like that?" she whimpered. "I'm a sick old woman. You're torturing me."

Before Adele could say a word, Mrs. McKinney pulled her arm back and hit her with her fist in the side of her breast. "You can go to hell!" Raising herself with the spryness of a ballet dancer, she pushed the bedpan out from under her, dumping its contents on Adele's shoes.

Adele was staring in disbelief at her soaked shoes when a handsome man in a beige raincoat stuck his head inside the room. "Oh, you cruel, cruel nurse, Dolores. Are you torturing these poor, sick people *again*?"

Tim Ritmann, detective sergeant for Marin County Sheriff's Department, stood in the doorway. Adele let go with a genuine smile, then checked it immediately with the same warning she'd been chanting since she met the man: *He's still in love with your best friend. He's Cynthia's ex. He's younger than you are. Stay clear.*

Detective Ritmann maintained a stern expression, piercing her with his eyes. "Is there trouble in here, Nurse Dolores? Will we have to punish you again for insubordination?"

Before Adele could answer, Mrs. McKinney jumped at the chance to vindicate herself. "Oh, thank God you're here, doctor," she gasped. "This nurse was trying to harm me!"

Tim watched as Adele threw a couple of towels over the spreading puddle, took off her shoes and headed for the sink.

"Now, now, dear," Tim said, careful to avoid stepping on the towels. "I'm sure Nurse Dolores didn't mean to be cruel. You wouldn't want her to be punished again, now would you, dear?"

"Well, I . . ." began Mrs. McKinney in a doubtful tone, her lips all bunched up under her bulbous nose. She sneaked a peek at Adele, who was busy stuffing paper towels into her shoes. "I wouldn't want her whipped or any—"

Tim burst out laughing, then got himself under control. "Well, we won't whip her, but we might have to slap the back of her hand with a ruler."

"Like the nuns do?" asked Mrs. McKinney, wide-eyed, getting friendly with the idea.

"Uh-huh."

Behind him, Adele snorted.

"But that's only if she was *really* hurting you and not trying to help as best she could."

Adele took the towels away, estimating how much fluid they'd soaked up. Three hundred cc's. The diuretic was working.

"Well, I don't think she *liked* hurting me, but . . ."

"Why don't we give the overworked lady a break then, huh?"

From the corner of his eye, he saw Adele slip out of the room, giving him a little wave as she did so.

"But I think that nurse should be . . ."

"I have to go now," he said, backing quickly away. "I need to make sure that nurse doesn't escape." He was out the door before Mrs. McKinney could finish her sentence about what form of punishment would be best for Nurse Dolores.

The squishiness of Adele's shoes reminded her with every step of her dedication to nursing. She would have to remember to leave the shoes outside when she went home, or else Nelson would want to roll on them, and then she'd have shoes that were not only pee-soaked but all furry as well.

She was toweling her feet dry in her corner by the nurses' station when Tim came up behind her. "Nurse Dolores?" she asked archly.

The detective put out his hands and scrunched up his shoulders—a gesture of half-hearted apology. "What else could I do? It was an escalating situation." He sat down facing the back of the chair, and rolled over to her, trying to avoid staring at her long, long shapely legs—except when he looked elsewhere, he ended up fixed on the smooth, white hollow of her neck. Ripping his eyes from that sight, he got tangled in the luxurious black hair that hung softly about her face.

Everything about her aroused him. Not that he could ever let her know. As far as he was concerned, she wore her feelings about him like a banner: to her he was only a friend and nothing more.

"Now how did I know that you'd be here on your day off and that Jane Doe would be your patient?"

Adele tilted her head and smiled. "Maybe you should get a job as a police psychic. What's up?"

He took hold of his hand and held it down before it could reach out and touch her. If he ever allowed that, God only knew where—or if—he'd stop. "How's Ms. Doe?"

"Stable, but she still doesn't remember anything." Adele took the damp paper towels out of her shoes and replaced them with dry ones. "I have to do a set of checks on her five minutes ago. Do you have any information on her yet?"

He shook his head. "Mostly I've got information on what I don't have. The car was taken to the Mill Valley tow yard. The fire chief thinks the fire started in the engine compartment after the crash, but I'm going to ask the auto arson investigator to go over and check it out. We did manage to come up with the vehicle ID number, so we can check out the name of the purchaser through the DMV. The *Pacific Intelligencer* and the *Chronicle* are running the story in tomorrow's papers. I'm sure somebody is filing a missing persons report as we speak." Detective Ritmann studied her for a moment, keeping his face blank. "I need to get her fingerprints and a photo," he said. "Is that possible?"

Adele thought for a minute then shook her head. "Not a full set. You might be able to get some prints off the right hand, but you're going to have to wait until morning. Her doctor doesn't want the dressings touched tonight."

"Is she able to talk for a minute?"

Adele sucked in a breath and ran her hands through her hair. Momentarily her bangs were pulled away from her smooth forehead, and he was caught again by the look of her. High cheekbones, full lips, and clear olive skin. And always those almond-shaped eyes the color of apple cider.

"Not tonight, buddy. She's being heavily medicated for the pain. I've already asked about the accident. She doesn't remember anything. Give her a day or two. Post-traumatic amnesia often resolves in two or three days—especially if we can find a family member or someone familiar to help reorient her."

"Go do your neuro whatever you call it," he said getting up, making sure his coat was pulled closed over his groin. "I'm going to grab some coffee and biscotti over at Rulli's. Want anything?"

"I want a double espresso with a lemon rind and chocolate biscotti with slivered almonds," said Cynthia, coming up from behind the detective sergeant, a packaged urinary catheter in one gloved hand. The two embraced and gave each other a brief kiss on the mouth. Smiling casually, Adele watched like a hawk for any sign of lingering passion or longing that might exist between the ex-lovers.

Cynthia's assertions—that she terminated the relationship because she was, in California-speak, a commitment-and-intimacy-phobe, and because she didn't want to wake up to the sight of a freckled back covered with fine red hair for the rest of her life—had not rung true to Adele. She thought it had more to do with the investigator's biological alarm going off for kids and the Volvo, coupled with the high-risk nature of his job—not the best combo for a young woman who didn't like children and whose biggest fear was abandonment with a capital A. Cynthia had already lost one fiance to an accidental death; were she to ever commit again, she at least wanted to better her chances.

As the dump*or* of the ten-month relationship, Cynthia had gone back to her usual pattern of bouncing from one man to the next. Initially, Tim took the breakup badly—like most of Cynthia's dumpees. It was Adele's opinion that he had yet to fully recover. He was, she had convinced herself, still in love with her best two-legged friend, and as long as he was, she would never let him know of her interest.

"A half decaf and half Italian roast latte with sesame biscotti for me," Linda called from the doorway of room 802.

"Oooh, are you going for real coffee?" Tina asked, at once showing a rare flash of teeth that might have been interpreted as a snarl of pleasure.

Tim sighed and took out his pen and notebook from his overcoat pocket. "Jack will take your order now," he said in a mechanical voice. He looked at Adele, waiting.

"A large decaf with nutmeg, Equal, and nonfat milk. If they have nonfat biscotti, I'll take one; otherwise, I'll keep my thighs safe from cellulite."

There was an explosion of disgusted snorts. "Oh, right!" said Linda, rolling her eyes. "Your thighs are so skinny and muscular, the fat wouldn't even know where to find them."

"You need a little padding on the insides of those thighs, girl," Cynthia laughed. "You can see landscape through them."

"Yeah," snickered Tina. "Don't you know that guys *like* fatty inner thighs? They act like ear muffs. You know—to muffle the sounds of the woman's screams of ecstasy?"

The group's peals of hard laughter were so sudden and loud that three call bells went off and several more patients craned their necks to see out the windows of their rooms.

Detective Sergeant Ritmann waited while two high school girls gracefully flitted around behind the counter like ballerinas, filling his order. The tall dark-haired one reminded him of Adele—not so much in looks, but in spirit. Light, almost ethereal, yet there was liquid steel for blood.

"That'll be twenty-three thirty-five," said the other girl, holding out a cardboard flat with six large hot cups covered with plastic lids. The white pastry bag filled with a dozen biscotti sat on the top of the high counter.

He gave a low whistle, peeled five fives off a wad of small bills, and put them between her long, spindly fingers. He noted that her fingernails were painted black—the same color as her lipstick. "My father would roll in his grave if he knew that a few cups of coffee and a dozen hard cookies cost what was once two days' salary for him."

The teenager stared at him blankly, without any interest whatsoever, and waited for him to take the flat.

The detective was suddenly and painfully conscious of his tiny creeping crow's feet and the new cropping of ear hair. "I'll bet you think I'm an old fart, don't you?" he asked.

The girl blinked once without answering, although he was sure the corner of her mouth pulled down a bit, denoting boredom. He took the flat from her and picked up the bag. "I'm not that much older than you, you know."

The adolescent continued to stare at him, although she pursed her black lips. "Sure, mister," she said, perfectly deadpan. "Whatever."

He smiled, in a worried sort of way, all the way to his car. As soon as he pulled away from the curb, he felt around the crown of his scalp, searching for any sign of thinning, then he glanced down at the ever-so-slight paunch that had suddenly showed up one morning above his belt and hadn't gone away. Sucking it in quickly enough to give himself a hernia, he wondered—among other things—if a man's sperm aged and made for a less healthy and bright child.

Before he got halfway back to the hospital, he'd fallen into a dark mood, which he forgot the second his car phone rang.

Neuro and vital signs done and charted, meds handed out with a kind word, the anti–pepperoni pizza vs. pro-veggie, rice, and fruit speech given to Mr. Cummings and his family, a stack of comic books pilfered from pediatrics and a disbursed among the stab wound patient and his guards, and a thorough assessment done on each patient, Adele sat down in her charting corner, loaded for bear.

She stared at the clock, punched in the number for the nursing supervisor, and tapped her fingers against the desk surface. Nelson expected her home by now.

Cynthia ran by, her arms loaded down with clean linen: Mrs. McKinney was playing football with her bedpan again. As she passed, she gave her friend a nasty look. "It's only for an easy four hours," she mimicked in a sarcastic, high voice. "This sucks, Monsarrat. You'll never talk me into something like this again. I'd be having a great time with helmet head, getting a great deal on my rent for the next six months . . . but nooooooooo. My best friend Adele sells me into slavery for a lousy day off and . . ."

Adele frowned and turned so as to block Cynthia and her diatribe out of her vision when Mattie Noel came on the line. Without hesitation, she launched into her complaint.

"Mrs. Noel this is Adele . . . Ardel, Ardeen, or Arden to you. You told me—no, you *promised* me Nurse O'Neil and I would only have to work for four hours. Ms. O'Neil and I have been informed that there are no replacements scheduled to come in until three A.M. Obviously the person who told us this was insane, so why don't you set our minds at ease and tell us that our replacements will be coming in at eleven as planned."

"Oh, yes," the supervisor said casually. "Well, Arden, you see we've had a problem finding someone to come in. We thought that you and Candy wouldn't mind working until three. We should be able to get someone in around then. You can hang on that long, can't you, dear?"

"No, dear, Candy and I *can't* hang on. We've both got to come back tomorrow morning. We aren't robots. We need sleep."

There was a pause. The nurse's attitude rankled her. Ingrates, Mrs. Noel thought, they should be glad to have work, let alone be given compensatory time off. But these were Ward 8 nurses—what did she expect? Rabble-rousing radicals with their nurses' rights and code pinks! Mattie Noel sighed. Forty years ago such insubordination would have been severely punished instead of lauded by the professional organizations. Balancing the old ways and the new was not one of her strengths.

"I'll see what I can do," she said reluctantly. "But don't expect much. You may have to work until three." It was probably best to break the news now.

"If we work until three, Mrs. Noel," Adele said between clenched teeth, "we will not be working day shift tomorrow. We refuse to work twenty-four hours with only four hours of sleep. Do I make myself clear?"

"In that case, Arnel, I won't be able to authorize your Christmas Eve or Candy's Saturday. I was more than willing to stick my neck out on your behalf if you would come in and—"

"Ms. O'Neil and myself are going to leave here no later than midnight, Mrs. Noel, and we *will* have the days off you promised us in return for coming in.'

"You'll both be charged with abandonment and fired on the

spot if you leave!" countered Mrs. Noel, wiping at her right eyelid. Her tic was acting up.

Cynthia, aka Candy, tapped Adele on the shoulder. "Use the heavy artillery," she whispered.

"Shall I call my union rep, Mrs. Noel? I'm sure she'll have an opinion on this."

Mattie Noel made a grumbling noise in her throat. Damned unions. Why couldn't these women do as they were told? Who the hell did they think they were—doctors?

She sighed through her beaklike nose. "All right, Ardel. Stay until three, and you can have tomorrow off. But," she added quickly, "you can't have Christmas Eve off, and Candy will have to work the whole weekend. Is that understood?"

"I'll talk it over with Cynthia and Nelson and get back to you."

Nelson? thought Mrs. Noel. Who the hell was Nelson? The new union rep? A man? Oh God, this was going to be trouble.

Adele called her house and waited for the answering machine to kick on. Immediately she pushed the numbers for room monitoring. "Are you there?" she asked.

A long, multitoned whine came in answer. It translated as *Nelson is here and very concerned that She has been gone for so long. Dinner is overdue, it's dark, and I'm lonely.*

"I'm coming home at four," Adele said, and mimicked the chiming noise her mantle clock made four times so the dog would have some idea of when to expect her. "Eat your veggie kibbles and I'll make you a nice breakfast of scrambled eggs and cheese when I get home."

Another whine followed by a series of barks came in answer.

"Yeah, yeah. I know you don't like them, but eat them anyway and deal with it, okay? I've got tomorrow off, so I'll take you with me when I run. Would you like that?"

Silence ensued. She sighed. Nelson was upset. She hoped it wouldn't be enough to send him back to the doggie shrink.

"How about if we sneak up Mount Tam and play dodge the rangers?"

Sounding not unlike Mrs. Noel, Nelson grumbled, picked up his Mickey Mouse rug, and lay down resignedly in front of the answering machine. He kept an eye on the red monitor light.

Hearing the voice but not seeing Her frustrated him no end. The idea/urge to go chew at the front door, or on her good pair of running shoes, came, buzzed around his walnut-sized brain for a fleeting moment, then left before it could be fully processed.

THREE

THE THREE NURSES WERE AT THE DESK CHARTING when Tim came through the double doors. Tina was on him before he could make it to the counter, examining the codes written on the plastic coffee tops. She extracted her cup from the cardboard holder and took the bag of biscotti into the kitchen.

"I got a call on a homicide," he said to Adele, knowing it was as close to a seduction as he could get with her.

Her eyes went bright. "Where? What is it?"

"At the Sweetwater. A guy with a bullet through his heart. I'm heading over now."

"It wasn't drugs," she said simply.

He turned back, amused. "Now what would make you say that?"

"Elementary," she said, pulling out the only cup marked decaf. Their hands kissed. She was amazed no sparks flew.

"The lobby cafe sells the biggest, cheapest, and most excellent pastries and sandwiches in the Bay area. Almost as good as what you get in New York delis."

He craned his neck forward and lifted his eyebrows, waiting for the logic behind the words.

Taking a sip of the hot coffee, Adele closed her eyes with pleasure. "It's a second home for every cop and CHP in Marin, on or off duty. The place is so thick with fuzz, it could be the county peach."

"Well, that didn't stop somebody from pluggin' the guy."

"Had to be a low-profiler then," Adele said. "Someone who wouldn't be noticed. A junkie or a dealer wouldn't go within five miles of the place. Why are you involved anyway? Isn't that Twin Cities jurisdiction?"

"Yeah, it would seem like it, wouldn't it?" Tim said, making a face. "Unfortunately, there's two acres there that are considered the county, and the Sweetwater is right in the middle of it."

He arched an eyebrow and waved his hand around, as if in sudden distaste of his surroundings. "What time do you guys get out of this joint, anyway?"

Cynthia rushed by looking perturbed, an armload of Mrs. McKinney's wet sheets weighing down her arms. "Three in the friggin' morning, thanks to our Ms. Monsarrat." Seeing the coffee, she dropped the sheets in the middle of the hall and made a beeline for the flat. Tina reappeared holding a variety plate of biscotti.

Tim reached for an obviously plain, withered-looking one and handed it to Adele. "Nonfat, no sugar." To Cynthia he handed the largest, most chocolate covered one. "Double deep Dutch chocolate, whole fat, major sugar for the only woman who has ever dumped me. May it sit well within your arteries."

"Estrogen." Cynthia sneered. "The key word to women's health advantage over men."

Adele bit into the biscotti gingerly, as though it might hurt the cookie and watched them, still searching for vestiges of longing in either set of eyes. She thought she saw a flicker of hidden pain and desire in Tim's, but couldn't be sure.

"I've got tomorrow off," she said after a pause. "Exactly where did our Jane Doe go off the highway?"

"Three miles south of Stinson." He smiled. "You planning on spending part of your day looking around? Think my crew might have missed something?"

"Depends who was working," she answered.

The fact was, she was right. The Sheriff's Department had good scene crews and bad ones. Detective Ritmann knew the crew who'd gone out to the scene of the accident wasn't the best he had.

He stuck an entire slivered-almond biscotti into his mouth, and eyed her without letting go of his amused expression. She had a God-given knack for investigative work that was better than most old pros'. "You sure you don't want to come to work for us, Adele?"

She shook her head. "I prefer it as a hobby, but thanks for asking and thanks for the coffee." She held up the cup and tipped it to him in a silent toast.

He tied the raincoat's belt loosely around him. "Gotta run; don't want the patrol sergeant to go postal on me at the scene."

"Yeah." Adele said, casually opening Jane Doe's chart. "You'll want to make sure nobody pulls a Fuhrman."

Parking his white Toyota Camry behind the Twin Cities marked patrol car, Tim got out and headed toward the Sweetwater Hotel, a four-story Tudor-style mansion nestled in a grove of redwoods. The sight brought back memories; specifically, the "hormone storm" days when he was a deputy pup on patrol attempting to fuck anything that moved.

The centrally located, hotel's food was, as Adele had said, fabulous, and the rates reasonable for nicely furnished, clean rooms. Most important was that the clientele was always pleasant and discreet.

The particular memory that stuck with him and would always stick with him, centered around room 245. It had started at the Horizons in Sausalito where he'd been tailing a dealer. While he was on the phone to his lieutenant, an exceptional blonde exited the ladies' room, stumbled over her own three-inch stiletto heels, and fell literally into his arms.

He'd hung up without a goodbye and asked if he could buy the beautiful girl a drink. Fifty-three minutes later they were lip-locked on the overstuffed maroon mohair couch in Sweetwater's room 245, his hand exploring the crotch snaps of her lace teddy.

He found more than snaps.

That was when he realized, despite the low lights and the three bottles of champagne, that the lovely blonde wasn't who she—or he—said she was.

He'd moved faster than a bullet. Never in his life had he treated a human smaller than he with such mindless physical violence. That the transvestite had made it out of the place with his head intact was a miracle.

Tim identified himself to the officer stationed at the elevator and, taking out his pen and notebook, headed down the hotel hall already scribbling first impressions, facts, and questions.

Sweetwater Motel. Third floor. Outside access? Elevator three doors from room toward rear of building.

Outside the room cordoned off with yellow scene tape, Sergeant Harishian was talking to a civilian who, Tim assumed, was the hotel manager. On the hot side of the tape, inside the single occupancy room, the two-person ID team was already at work measuring a station line: the physical point from which all references were to be made. In room 322, it was the uninterrupted wall against which the head of the bed and the nightstand rested.

The police photographer was finishing up shooting the bathroom. The lab man, his hands neatly attired in latex gloves, knelt next to the body to gather samples of dried blood from the white shirt front. A deputy stood at the end of the hall recording the times each person came and went and what their business was.

"He seemed like a regular guy," the balding, middle-aged manager said, rubbing his hands together. Purple and blue veins mapped his face and hands like a Rand McNally atlas of the world. "Checked in on Thursday afternoon. He was from somewhere around L.A. Quiet guy. No trouble at all." He stopped to get his breath, which seemed a difficult task. When he finally managed to suck in some air, it sounded wet and gasping. Both Tim and Sergeant Harishian had a moment of sympathetic suffocation anxiety.

"He paid with a Visa card."

"Did he say when he was checking out?" Tim asked without waiting for the overview.

"At the end of the week," the manager wheezed. "Said he'd let me know what day."

"Would you know what his business was here?"

"Aw shit, I don't know exactly. Had something to do with computer programs. He was pitching some big corporations in Marin and San Francisco."

Inside the room, the finder member of the ID team stopped dusting for fingerprints and drew his partner's attention to an ashtray full of cigarettes on the nightstand. They both laughed, and the recorder wrote something in her notebook. A private joke, Tim guessed. Something about sex and cigarettes or sex and lung cancer.

"Did he have any visitors?" Harishian asked.

The manager shook his head. "Not that I know of. He'd usually leave the hotel around nine in the morning, and come back in the afternoon after three, sometimes as late as seven or eight. Today he left about six and came in early—around noon."

"That's fine for now," said Harishian. "You can go back downstairs. We'll have more questions for you in a while."

The manager turned toward the open door of the room where the body lay at the foot of the bed. Together, he and Tim stared at the victim. The dark-haired, medium-built man looked to be in his mid to late thirties. He was pleasant-looking, despite the grayish white color of his skin—a color Ritmann had seen on countless other corpses on countless other floors.

He stepped over the yellow tape and glanced around. In front of the body was a world of blood. So much of it had leaked out of the center of his white shirt, the solid mass of it looked like a magenta blanket. The hand that wasn't completely under the body was covered with a paper bag. The fingertips of the other hand were purple with pooled blood. There was a wedding band on the left hand, and an expensive watch with a leather band on his wrist. The color or pattern of the man's tie, which was pulled loose at the throat, could barely be seen for the blood that obscured it.

On the luggage rack was a twenty-seven-inch roller-type suitcase, open and neatly packed. Looking around, it struck Ritmann that the whole room—with the exception of the body—was neat and orderly. From his vantage point, he could see that there were no personal toiletries in the bathroom, and that the towels were hung carefully over the racks. A sport jacket lay neatly folded on the bed, alongside a black wool coat.

The hotel manager ran a hand over his sweaty head, then walked away mumbling to himself.

"What happened, Ritmann?" Harishian pretended annoyance. "Take the long way around?"

"Got detained at Ellis on another case," Tim said. "What have we got?"

The sergeant tugged on his earlobe and read from his notebook, which was almost identical to Tim's. "Call came through at twenty forty-five hours, Detectives Berger and Chase arrived at twenty fifty and secured the scene until we got here at twenty-one hundred."

"What the hell were Berger and Chase doing?" Tim asked, obviously rankled. "I thought we were supposed to use phones

with homicides?" It wasn't so much the fact that the two unau-
thorized detectives were in his territory that pissed him off as it
was the idea that calls had gone out over the radio after the initial 911 dispatch was made. With the number of reporters and
other trauma-hounds who listened to the scanners, almost everybody used car and cellular phone communication.

"Keep your shirt on." Harishian sighed, looking up from his
notebook. "We did use the phones. Berger and Chase happened
to be in the cafe having dinner when they heard the hysterical
maid broadcasting to the lobby there was a dead body in room
three twenty-two.

"They helped secure the scene, is all. They thought they'd
check out the other floors and walk the grounds until the lead
dick got here and we sorted out whether it's our case or Twin
Cities."

Harishian went back to reading his notes. "The manager," he
jerked his pen in the direction the bald man had gone, "brought
us up here and said that the evening maid found him when she
came in to do turndown service."

It amused Tim to think of the Sweetwater as having a turndown service, but it was a nice touch—an effort at class he
appreciated.

"The maid goes off screaming all the way down the elevator.
Manager comes up to make sure it wasn't somebody with a
twisted sense of humor playing a joke with the catsup bottle.
He's the one who dialed nine-one-one."

"Does the gentleman on the floor have a name?"

"He's registered as Gerard Deveraux. Listed his business address but no home address. He works for Compucare Computer
Systems, Inc. in L.A. He's got a rental car out in the parking
lot."

"What about the rooms flanking this one?"

"The couple next door . . ." The sergeant glanced at his notes
and snickered. ". . . a Mr. and Mrs. Jones, haven't heard a thing
all afternoon and saw nothing. They said they've been glued to
the TV all day." Harishian lowered his voice, speaking out of
the corner of his mouth. "They got a good selection of dirty
movies here."

Ritmann wondered how Harishian had had time to figure that
out, but decided he probably knew from firsthand experience.

"The guy directly below said he'd been in his room about five minutes before he heard a noise like somebody had dropped a heavy suitcase, or had fallen out of bed. That was around fourteen hundred hours.

"There's nobody checked into the room above this one." He pointed to the two rooms flanking 322. "These two rooms are vacant. They were checked." He turned and pointed to the rooms across the hall—319 and 321. "These two are also vacant. It's a slow time of year, I guess. The stairs were checked, as was the elevator."

Ritmann clicked his pen a couple of times. "Let's get all the vacant rooms in the hotel checked for entry from the outside. Get everybody's—hotel personnel and guests—addresses and phone numbers for follow-up . . . We may need them later. I want to talk to the hotel guests on this floor, so wake them up if you have to. The guy downstairs, too. Find out who checked in or out all day. I'll call the captain and get the rest of the dick bureau down here. I want a clean job on this." He had another thought. "And use the phones. I don't want any reporters showing up. Where's our video guy?"

"He was already up here and in the hall—before it got too crowded. Right now he's outside taping the grounds and the rental car."

Tim walked quickly down the hall through the growing crush of police. Without stopping, he called back to Harishian over his shoulder: "And see what you can do to break up this cluster-fuck of people. There's plenty to do without them hanging out right here."

Outside, Tim called Bill Keats, the department captain, from his car phone to tell him they had a working homicide. He hated to wake the old man, but protocol was protocol. The rest of the dick bureau, Detectives Chernin and Cini, were called next and informed, without any apology whatsoever, that they needed to haul their butts on down to the Sweetwater ASAP.

When he returned to the room, the crime scene team was logging every item within the four walls. He scribbled his own description of the room: *Queen-size bed—made up, neat, oak nightstand, writing desk, wood table and four chairs.*

The house phone and a room service menu lay open on top of

the antique dresser. On the table lay the remains of the man's lunch. It looked as though he had been interrupted: the fork and the knife were placed on the sides of the plate, the fork still holding a carefully cut piece of roast beef.

In his notebook he jotted: *Victim not expecting visit? Meal in progress—no evidence of struggle. Killer known to victim? No sign victim tried to run—surprise attack?*

Outside, the recording patrolman, half laughing, half irritated, yelled out: "Aw, come on, which one of you morons ordered room service?"

"What about room service?" Tim asked the sergeant. "Somebody must've delivered lunch."

Harishian referred to his notes. "A server by the name of Francis Lee. He said he delivered the tray around one-fifteen, and there wasn't anyone in the room except the victim. When he entered the room, he noticed that Deveraux was packing and asked if he was leaving. Deveraux told him an emergency had come up and he'd be leaving right after he had his lunch."

"Is he still here?"

Harishian nodded. "He works the ten A.M. to ten P.M. shift."

Tim watched the lab person take hair and saliva samples. The ID team was still collecting items, bagging them and placing them in the corner on a sheet.

"How far are we from calling the coroner?" he asked, moving closer to the body.

"Another hour," the ID team answered in unison.

"Is somebody working on notification of next of kin?"

"Done," Harishian said without looking up from his notebook.

Tim pulled on a pair of latex gloves, snapping them at the wrists, and stepped over the yellow ribbon to begin his own examination of the room.

He made continuous notations of questions and things for the dick bureau to follow up. *Check friends, family, coworkers. What animosities existed?* It was basic knowledge that over 80 percent of all homicides were committed by one of the victim's family or friends. He added: *Married? Extramarital affairs?*

He checked the pad next to the bed and saw times and numbers had been hastily written. Flight numbers and departure times? He'd have Cini check with the airlines and the car rental agency.

Emergency? Trying to get out early. Problems at home? Threat made? Wife/girlfriend? Work problems? Interview the hotel staff. Check work. Talk to coworkers—bosses.

Pulling his coat tight around him to keep it out of the way, Tim leaned over the body. He breathed through his mouth, to keep the smell of the blood from invading his olfactory glands; all his years of investigations hadn't lessened his aversion to that smell, which had no duplicate on earth.

He was staring closely at the curly light-colored hair on the upper left shoulder. "Hey, did you see this?"

The lab technician, a man in his sixties with heavy dark eyes, looked over the rims of his magnifying glasses.

"Hair on the upper left shoulder? I haven't bagged it yet."

From down the hall, he heard Detective Peter Chernin announce himself to the recording patrolman then ask in his booming Richard Burton voice, "Where the hell is that son of a bitch Ritmann? Bastard got me right in the middle of *Ocean's Eleven*!"

Tim smiled and waved Richard Burton's double down the hall. Almost immediately, Detective Cini, a short, wiry, nervous man, joined them. Styrofoam cups of steaming coffee were attached to their mouths; both deputies looked as though they'd been ousted out of the wrong side of the rack.

Ritmann especially liked working with these two. Each knew how the others' minds worked, giving appreciation to each man's strengths, weaknesses, and idiosyncrasies—and there were certainly a lot of the latter.

Chernin and his bad old movies (his dubious claim to fame was that he'd seen *Ocean's Eleven* over two hundred times), Cini and his short-circuited Little Man Syndrome temper. And then there was him and his—what? His obsession with his job? His *love* of his job? Or his secret passionate obsession with a woman who didn't have a clue how he felt and would run in the opposite direction if she did?

Tim glanced at his watch: 9:32. By the time the coroner was called and was done doing his thing, and he and the dick bureau finished doing the preliminary interviews with the personnel and the guests, and got back to the department and began a storyboard, he figured he'd be getting home about the same time as Adele was getting up for her excursion out to Stinson Beach.

He looked at the growing collection of carefully marked paper bags containing hairs, fibers, cigarette butts, and the like. There was so much to do, sleep didn't seem important now. Once, when they'd been discussing a homicide, Adele had put it perfectly: a crime was like a heart attack; the first twenty-four hours after the fact were the most critical, and nobody could afford to be asleep at the wheel.

At the thought of her, a warm feeling roiled in his chest; it wasn't heartburn—at least not in the physical sense of the word.

Because the relief nurse was late, Adele found herself doing final rounds on her patients at 4:15 A.M. while, six miles away, Tim sat with Cini and Chernin, feet up on the conference table, staring at a poster board covered with time lines and notations of events.

At 3:30, Mrs. Fowler had gone confused and pulled out her nasogastric tube. She whipped her head from side to side as Adele tried for a sixth time to pass it back down. The minute she managed to get it all the way down into her stomach, Mrs. Fowler hooked it with her wrist and gave it a good pull. The tip slid across Adele's face, leaving a trail of Mrs. Fowler's bile, chin to forehead. In a fit of silent frustration, Adele restrained the patient's wild hand with her knee, reinserted the tube, and taped it quickly to the side of Mrs. Fowler's face and behind her ear where she couldn't get at it. Then she eased the woman as gently as she could into a soft restraining jacket and wrist restraints.

"This is to remind you not to try and get out of bed, Mrs. Fowler," she said to the patient, who was in frenzied motion, trying to extricate herself from her new bonds.

Without warning, Mrs. Fowler lifted her head and pecked, like a chicken, at Adele's hands and arms, taking tiny bites. "Hate you. Hate you. Hate you, missy!" she said in a weird little girl's voice.

The whole scene was so *Exorcist*ish, a deep-throated wheeze of uncontrollable Crazy Woman laughter escaped her. Five minutes later, she gathered her wits long enough to wipe her eyes free of laugh tears and move on to the next patient.

Mathilde was finally asleep. The bandaged hands were still. After a few minutes of observing her respirations and carotid pulse, Adele decided to let the neuro checks and the vital signs slide; any nurse worth his or her salt knew the healing power of sleep was more important than waking a patient to record numbers.

At 4:30 Adele was summoned by Cynthia to check out a recent physician progress note on one of her patient's charts.

> 2:45 A.M. *I was awakened after five minutes of sleep to see this 39-year-old patient in ER complaining of itching from Seattle, a pain in ribs, and infrequent bouts of incontinent headaches. During this emission, patient says a rash began in her navel and ended up in an institution in San Francisco. She has been self-treating with external oatmeal, but this has caused her to flake and lump. Biopsy recommended for those.*
>
> *Patient lives with her husband who works as a spermbank. They own four children and no birds, and she is responsible for cleaning their cages several times a week. Will instigate the possibility of getting a pulmonary CAT.*
>
> *Otherwise, the patient is terminal but in good health with many scratches and gouges as birds attack her oatmeal lumps.*
> *Dr. Rymesteade Dhery*

Bleary-eyed, Cynthia snickered then grew serious—as serious as someone could get at 4:30 A.M. after working a long shift on Ward 8. She wasn't familiar with the doctor, but the note intrigued her. Any health professional who decompensated this badly after midnight was someone she'd like to meet.

At the Tam High School stoplight, one mile from his apartment, Tim saw a Mill Valley Carpet Cleaning truck that reminded him, through a complex series of thoughts, to check under the seat for his Walther .380 semiautomatic pistol.

Instead of his gun, he found one of the department's cameras. He slumped over the wheel feeling as much despair as someone who'd found out they had two months to live. He was so tired by the time he left the department, he had forgotten where his car was parked. To the merriment of the rest of the boys, he'd spent fifteen minutes searching for it.

He didn't do well with sleep deprivation. Not that he needed much, but it was well known that after being awake for more than twenty-four hours in a row, he got downright Alzheimer-ish.

He'd forgotten about Jane Doe. Now he'd have to go back to Ellis and go through the rigmarole of getting pictures and fingerprints, then interviewing her and returning the damned camera.

The car behind him honked twice when the signal turned but he continued to stare wide-eyed at the little knob on the rear-view mirror as though it were the head of Rasputin. When several other car horns joined in the fracas, he pulled himself out of his waking sleep state and put the Camry into gear. It jerked forward and stalled. He started the engine, momentarily forgot how to put it into gear, then pulled over to the side of the street.

The homicide was his first priority now. He'd turn the Jane Doe case over to—who? Deputy Rule. Mike Rule was up for something like a Jane Doe.

It didn't matter anyway—Adele would probably resolve the case before Rule even figured out what to do first. But now, before he did anything more, he had to figure out which way to get home.

Because it was a mortal sin to sleep past 9:30, even if one hadn't gone to bed until 5 A.M., Adele forced herself out of bed at 9 and took a cool shower to wake up. Dressed for cold-weather running, she gave Nelson the handle end of his leash to carry in his mouth. It was sort of a joke since no self-respecting dog owner in northern California ever leashed her dogs in parks.

She opened the door to the Beast and slid in behind the wheel, feeling a slight trepidation. "This is not a day for the Going to Sleep trick," she addressed the dash of the car in a warning tone. "We're going on Highway One and that's no place to pull tricks."

She slammed the door and started the car. The Beast was famous for shutting down completely at the most inopportune times—like on steep hills behind police vehicles, or when it was racing at speeds greater than seventy mph on a freeway where the San Andreas fault has opened up a hundred feet away. Without warning, the car would simply go to sleep, thus disabling the power steering and the power brakes, and turn into two tons of uncontrolled steel hurtling blindly forward—the Beast and its devil's soul taking her along as captive human sacrifice.

In the backseat, Nelson drooled and hassled, completely alive with doggie excitement. He was with Her and they were in the car: it was all that mattered in the world. They could have been headed to hell for all he cared.

They ran the length of Stinson Beach for an hour. Adele flew over the wet sand, in which could be seen the reflection of the clouds overhead. When her hands were sufficiently numb and her face burned with the damp cold, she returned to the Beast and changed into a sweatsuit of material said to be made from recycled plastic. She towel-dried her hair, then the dog's, and set out for the site three miles south from where she stood.

It wasn't hard to find. All she had to do was look for the burned-down flares and the darkest skid marks. It was clear that the car had been traveling away from Stinson Beach, south toward Mill Valley.

In one of the sightseeing turnouts, Adele prepared for the climb down. With four or five plastic shopping bags hanging from her fanny pack, she put on leather gloves and followed Nelson down the rocky face of the cliff. She'd thought an animal would instinctively know the easiest way to go. By the time they'd gone a third of the way, she wasn't so sure. She suspected Nelson wasn't really all that bright in doggie terms.

"Well," she said to the imaginary group of Swiss mountain climbers who were appraising her unorthodox progress down the side, "maybe I'll find her driver's license and a personal profile printout."

Nelson barked and whined in answer, pawing at the ground where an unopened package of Certs lay in the crevice of a rock. Adele picked it up and threw it in her fanny pack, while Nelson wagged his tail and barked a demand for his reward. She kissed the top of his head and cooed for him. It wasn't the reward he had in mind, but it sufficed.

Next found was an unused flare, part of a soggy map of

northern California, and the upper of a man's shoe that looked like it had been there since the gold rush days. The shoe she ignored; the flare (no sense letting good go to waste, her mother's voice crooned) and the map she packed.

The rock the car hit first, jutted out from the side of the cliff. Like a fresh wound, one side had been sheared away, leaving exposed a wide, pinkish gray edge. Five yards down was an AA battery, and beyond that, caught in one of the scrub oaks, was a furry stuffed animal of unspecific species.

Inside a thicket of wild mustard she found an ancient Old Milwaukee beer can spotted with rust holes, and an expensive-looking leather boot lined with real sheepskin. Though caked with mud, she could see from the sole that the boot was relatively new. Adele visualized Mathilde's feet, remembering them to be narrow. Sticking her hand inside the boot, she couldn't make a fist. Narrow as a sliver.

Once the boot was secured inside a plastic bag, Adele changed her mode of seeing from "coarse find" to "fine find" as she inched closer to the site where the car had come to rest and burned.

She'd been good at finding things when she was a kid. Her ability was uncanny to the point where her mother thought seriously about renting her out as a lost-and-found expert for small household items. She'd even had cards made up in Adele's name with clever sayings about needles in haystacks and sharp eyes. If someone on the block lost a contact lens on a bathroom floor or a hundred feet of lawn? The golden-eyed girl would be summoned. Everyone thought it had to do with her eyes, the color being what it was and all, but when her mother asked her *how* she seemed to know where things had gone, she'd answered that it was a sort of seeing that didn't have anything to do with her eyes. She would hone in on a bathroom floor or the living room rug and turn up the intensity to find the most invisible of things.

A light rain began to fall. There was something about the lambent light from an overcast sky that magnified things and made them conspicuous in her mind's eye.

For the next hour, she ran her hands over every inch of muddy, rocky ground and inside the crevices of the rocks. She explored each bush and tree. Nelson sniffed and dug alongside her, sometimes wandering off to the bottom of the cliff where he bathed and rolled in yellow mud.

She was working on an elaborate scheme of how to get the dog into the bath when they got home, when another brain compartment shifted from the mud that would be left in her tub to the mud in the vicinity of where she crawled. Two different colors. Dark brown mud from road level to about fifteen feet below her. Below that, the mud changed from brown to beige to cream yellow.

The mud on Mathilde's legs was cream yellow. Had the woman wandered down to the bottom of the cliff then climbed up again? Jellyroll told her they'd found the victim not far from the car.

"Maybe she was thrown to the bottom and climbed up?" Adele asked an imaginary passing hiker.

Don't be ridiculous! he said. *That would be like falling off the Empire State Building and not only surviving, but climbing straight back up afterward.*

"But how did she get the mud on . . . ?"

Her mind answered in the voice of a Mike Hammer character sitting on one of the nearby rocks: *Use your head, pal. The girl had to have been desperate to make a climb like that. She probably thought the kid had been thrown down the cliff.*

"That's it," Adele said, snapping her fingers. "When she didn't see the baby through the flames, she probably thought the kid had been thrown from the car, too. Not seeing her anywhere around the car, she figured the kid had to be down . . . there."

The magnitude of the woman's tragedy suddenly hit her. She sat down and shivered, imagining the horror of not being able to find her child. Five minutes later, while she was fervently digging an object out of the mud next to her, Nelson rushed up the hill, the thing in his mouth clanking noisily against his tags.

They passed each other at the intersection of LaGoma and Miller without knowing it. After a few hours of sleep, Tim Ritmann was on his way back to his department, while Adele, coming from Stinson, was on her way to the wrecking yard to take a look at what was left of Jane Doe's car. In the alleyway outside the wrecker's office, a young guy in faded purple overalls leaned against the fence. He jogged up a cigarette from a pack of Lucky Strikes and pulled it out with two grease-black fingers.

The universal car mechanic look was visited upon him: black fingers and nails, disheveled, greasy hair, and that I've-got-a-whole-trunk-missing-from-the-attic look about the vacant eyes, as though the secrets of automobile repair were indeed a serious burden to bear in life.

Adele approached the man wearing a smile as one might hold out a cross or a garland of garlic when coming upon a vampire. A few feet away, she realized he was handsome in a James Dean sort of way. His eyes were emerald green.

"Hi. Auto investigation from the Sheriff's Department," she said, flipping open the stiff-backed leather case and flashing the deputy sheriff's badge Tim had given her as a joke.

The man stared briefly at her ID photo and then the badge. He lit the cigarette with a blue Bic. His face remained blank.

"Can you point me in the direction of the car that came in here yesterday evening from Stinson? Vehicle ID number . . ." She made a pretense of looking through her oversized purse. ". . . oh, damn, I don't have it, it's the one that burned." She left off the search and watched him curiously. He hadn't moved, even though the smoke was curling into his eyes.

"You know the car I'm talking about? Went off the cliffs out . . . at . . . Stinson?" She craned her neck to look closer at him, wondering when he was going to blink. "Ah, hello?"

The young man shifted on his feet. He took a deep drag on the cigarette and, with eyes narrowed, signed that she was an asshole with weird eyes and he hoped she would go to hell and burn with the rest of the hearing assholes of the world.

There wasn't a moment's hesitation before Adele signed back that he was an asshole too and where was the car that had burned and if he didn't show her immediately, she'd slap him with a big fine for impeding an investigation, thank you very much.

She used an elementary form of American Sign Language, Signing in Exact English, but it got the message across just as well.

He pulled away from the wall. Why, he wanted to know, did she know sign? He glared his disapproval and added, Why didn't she use ASL instead of the inferior SEE?

She signed that she'd learned SEE because it was all that was being taught to hearing people at the time, and she learned how to sign because she loved the way the language of the deaf made her hands dance, and the day might come when she would also go deaf or not be able to speak.

Abashed and pleased at the same time, he smiled and signed that he was sorry for his rudeness and that he was having a bad day because the boss was a big asshole who didn't like him and made him work too hard and long and wouldn't she please follow him to the tow yard.

Halfway across the parking lot, Adele saw the blackened shell of the car and was stunned by the extent of its devastation. "That child had some major bad karma," she said to the back of the deaf man's head.

As if he'd heard, he turned and asked if anyone had died in the wreck.

Yes—she signed, her eyes going unwillingly to where the backseat would have been—a baby. From her purse she removed a pair of yellow rubber gloves, the type used only by American housewives, and put them on. When she looked back at the deaf man, his eyes were filled with tears.

The black gunk was as thick as it was sticky, and the smell that lingered was a sickening mixture of burned plastic and something more animal. She was glad she'd worn clothes she could wrap and throw away.

She went over every inch of the shell, sifting through the goo. When she was finished, she crouched down and surveyed her finds, which were almost as good as Nelson's: three keys and an engraved metal heart with a garnet chip in the center. She turned it over and wiped away the soot. I LUV MAMA—JANUARY 17, 1995.

Through the fence that surrounded the lot, she could see the Mill Valley Plaza shopping center.

A painted sign provided her with a direction.

Tim fought off the tiredness fogging his brain by going over his notes once again, making sure that all the tasks had been delegated and that people were moving on leads, not letting them spoil or get away.

He drummed his fingers and glanced at the wall clock. LAPD hadn't returned his call. It had been hours since they'd been contacted and given the name of the victim and the address of the corporation. He picked up the phone and punched in the number. Within three minutes he was on hold for the detective sergeant in charge in L.A.

The phone clicked twice. "Jack Frazer." The voice was deep and gruff.

"Yo," Tim said. "Tim Ritmann from Marin County Sheriff's Department. I'm calling about our homicide up here on one of your residents?"

There was the rustling of paper. "Deveraux?"

"Gerard Deveraux is the one."

There was more moving of paper and a chair creaking. "Okay," Frazer said on the slide of a sigh. "This is what we've got so far. His employers at Compucare were notified this morning. Everyone displayed appropriate shock. Deveraux was head of his division—worked there for about four years. He was in your area to discuss a product he'd developed for Bechtel Corporation and Autodesk? Something to do with their internal communications. He was up for a promotion to a top executive position in June.

"The coworkers and boss describe him as a hard-working individual. No drugs. No problems at home. No record except a few outstanding parking tickets and one moving violation—all normal for L.A."

Detective Sergeant Frazer coughed and cleared his throat. "His residence is in a nice section of L.A.," he continued, his voice lower than before. "Upper class, but not quite an all-Mercedes neighborhood. Married five years, has two kids. No skirts or fists on the side."

Tim thought it was a strange way to phrase it: "No skirts or fists on the side." LaLa talk for "no extramarital swinging, either way."

"Have you talked to the wife?"

"Not yet. No answer at home and the neighbors say they haven't seen her for a couple of days. She failed to show up for work day before yesterday, and the kids didn't show up at the preschool or the sitter's. We talked to the neighbor lady, who said they were the ideal family. Quiet. Nice people. Not wackos like a lot of them down here, you know?"

Tim did know. Los Angeles was world unto itself. A universe

of loonies and psychopaths, LaLa Land was the single best reason he could think of to divide the state into northern and southern California, and put a very high fence at the border.

His last trip down there was case in point; he stepped off the plane and the first thing he saw was a jumbo billboard that featured a luxury-class blonde driving a new red convertible. The print read:

> HIGH COLONICS IN THE COMFORT OF YOUR OWN CAR!
> DRIVE YOUR COLON CLEAN TODAY!
> DRIVE THROUGH TECHNOLOGY AT ITS BEST!

What got him the most was the deranged, though strangely satisfied, smile on the blonde's face.

"Any other family that wouldn't know at this stage?" Tim asked.

"There's a brother in Chicago, and a sister in San Diego. The brother's shook up. He couldn't think of anybody who would want to hurt his brother."

"No insurance policies or inheritance?"

"Not that we know of."

After a moment of silence, Tim stopped writing. "Can you fax me the interview reports? I need the brother's and neighbor's numbers, and let me know as soon as you find the wife?"

Tim hung up then, peering anxiously outside his window, quickly picked up the phone again and dialed Adele's number. After the short, precise outgoing message, he left a message for Nelson. Being a tree hugger, Adele was a love me/love my dog kind of woman—he could never forget that.

He guessed she was out tracking down the identity of Jane Doe.

The phone rang. As he reached to pick up the line, his gut told him it wasn't going to be Adele, but something much less pleasant.

It wasn't much of a shop, really. Four twenty-foot-high white walls with tall, narrow industrial windows inserted every six feet. The old-fashioned shop bell attached to the inside door jamb jangled throughout the room when she entered.

The big man behind the counter reminded her of Humpty Dumpty: thin at the top and the bottom and very broad around the middle. "Oh my," he said, fluttering his fingers, which were overladen with rings. "Where *did* you come up with this little beauty?"

He held the elaborate brass key to the light and turned it this way and that. Adele's eyes were riveted not on the unusual key but on the large sapphire and diamond ring he wore on his middle finger. The precious gems were cut and set in a yin-yang configuration. He wore earrings to match.

The long glass counter on which he rested his other pudgy, equally bejeweled hand competed for her attention. It was, in fact, the main draw of Mill Valley Lock and Key: tiered mirrored shelves of keys from down through the ages. Every fifteen seconds, the shelves rotated, giving the viewer a brand new selection of keys. The oldest was marked CIRCA 1300 A.D.

"At a garage sale," Adele lied. "It seemed unusual, so I thought I'd bring it here. I figured if anyone knew what it fit, you would."

"And you're probably right," he said immodestly. "I've seen one other one like this that was to the outside door of an old elevator. You aren't old enough to remember the old freight elevators, but I'll bet there are still some left in the Bay area."

She knew the "old freight elevators" much better than she wanted to. When she was young, her aunt Ruth owned a bookstore at 3rd and Minna Streets. In the back of the store, behind a huge sliding door, was a freight elevator that was the parent of the elevator phobia from which she still suffered.

"And the other ones?"

He looked at them with disdain and did not bother to touch them. "The smaller one is a key to a safe or a lock box. That one . . ." He pointed to the key with the broken tip. ". . . is to one of those cheap locks people put on latches—like in storage units." He gave her a sidelong once-over.

"How much did you pay for this one?" He dangled the elevator key out of her reach.

"A buck?" she said, as if bargaining.

"I'll give you two for it," he said hopefully, overshooting the mark on nonchalance. "It's not worth anything to the collectors—they're a dime a dozen—but I don't have one of this vintage for the shelves."

"Oh. What vintage is that?" Adele eyed the key, wondering if it would be rude to reach up and grab it out of his hand.

"The teens maybe. Not older than the twenties."

"It isn't for sale," Adele said in a determined tone.

The locksmith walked over to the windows, still holding the key. The winter sun shone pale lemon yellow through the windows as he examined it again, with such longing that for a second Adele was afraid he was going to tell her he was going to take it anyway. Instead, he handed it back to her and returned to the counter.

She gave him the key to the Beast and asked for a copy. Not that she needed or wanted a duplicate, but she wanted to somehow pay him for the information.

He picked out the appropriate dummy key then fired up the machine. While the high-pitched sound of metal being sheared caused her eardrums to shrink, she made a decision not to tell Tim about the keys. Everything else—the boot excepted—she would turn over as evidence.

There wasn't anything like the elevator key in her own collection of lock picks.

FOUR

DETECTIVE RITMANN HUNG UP THE PHONE, HIS expression solemn. He fixed his eyes on the computer screen until a scratch at the door made him look up.

Adele stood watching him, her head resting against the cheap plastic nameplate DETECTIVE SERGEANT RITMANN. It was one of the easy slide in and out types, designed to keep young cocky investigators on their toes.

"May I come in?" She could see he was disturbed and took a step back uncertainly. "If you're busy, I can give you a call later. It isn't anything super important."

Standing quickly, his chair flew out behind him, bumping hard into one of the three filing cabinets. The plastic model of a 1963 black Corvette fell off its stand and rolled into the bottom compartment of a flat file holder whose levels were marked IN, OUT, and DO IT YESTERDAY!

"Get in here!" he commanded, grinning and coming out from behind the desk, which he'd cluttered in his own masterful way. "I was wondering where you were. I left a message. Have you been home yet?"

She shook her head and plunked down gratefully into one of the two chairs opposite him. "Not since this morning. I've been out at the site of the accident. Nelson and I found a couple of things you might want to check out."

As she spoke, he followed her gaze as she subtly, but meticulously, logged every detail of the twelve-by-twelve cubicle. He was suddenly aware of every effort he'd made to make the sterile cubicle a place he could feel at home. In actuality, it was where he spent most of his time, so the room had a lived-in look, reflecting the carelessness and selective habits of a bachelor workaholic.

She studied his bookcases first, which caused him to consider the books there as though he'd never seen them before in
his life. *The California Penal Code*, *The California Vehicle
Code*, the light blue binder marked *Peace Officer's Source
Book*, *The Art of Interviewing* and *The Zen Way of Interviewing
Criminals*, the myriad drug and chemical books, a dictionary,
and—God knew which of the jokers working in the department
had put it there—a smut novel titled *Sucking Cop* by L. G. Gums.

Her eyes flitted over his degrees and certificates and came to
rest on the group photo of the annual Sheriff's Department river
rafting/camping trip from three years before. In the front row,
resting happily—and, more than likely, drunkenly—in each
other's arms, were Tim and Cynthia. It had been in the beginning of their relationship, when their sexual chemistry was almost palpable to those around them. His hand cupped her
nearly naked breast; hers was conspicuously wrapped around
the tent pole holding up the fly of his pants.

Tim was mortified, blushing as only redheads can. Why
hadn't he discarded the picture a long time ago? Now she'd
think he still had the hots for Cynthia. He wanted to tear it off
the wall, but, somehow, convention held him to his chair.

"Oh right, the amnesia woman," he said, another discomfort
beginning. "Well, the homicide got complicated. The victim's
wife and two kids appear to be missing." He glanced up at her,
then hurried on. "The homicide investigation takes precedence
over anything else so I've given Jane Doe to one of the other
deputies to handle. You know Mike Rule?"

Disappointment rode her face as she turned to him, frowning. "Mike Rule. Mike Rule. Isn't he the attractive man who
was at the chief's retirement dinner last July? Remember? The
party you and Cyn let me tag along to as the fifth wheel? I think
he was the sweet one who kept asking me to dance all the slow
dances."

"Well, personally he's not my type, but I wouldn't—"

She brightened and held up a manicured finger. "Oh, yes,
now I remember Michael. He was stationed at the hospital during the Martin-Gannet murder case. Really a sweetheart. Bright,
too."

"He's okay," Tim said, his gut tugging at the way she'd said
"Michael"—all tenderness and sophistication. For a moment

he couldn't swallow. "I wouldn't go so far as to say he's the brightest I have, but he's . . ."

She stood. "You know I really would like to talk to Michael. Where would I find him?"

He swallowed reflexively. She was so damned eager to toss him off. Rule was a twerp, but he had to admit—Tim bit the inside of his lip—the guy *did* consistently get the best women. Hell, Rule was a magnet for women like Adele: he knew how to play them, using the "sensitive male" tactic.

"Listen," Tim began, "I mean it's not like Jane Doe is out of my hands completely; I'm still lead detective responsible for the investigation. Why don't I take a look at what you've got? Besides . . ." He paused, letting his blue eyes scrutinize her from under bushy auburn eyebrows. ". . . I'm not sure if Rule would understand your unofficial investigations; he's strictly by the book. Arrest his own mother if it came up."

She sat down again. "Are you sure?" she said evenly. "I mean, I wouldn't want you to strain your time budget or anything like that."

He scrutinized her to see if she was being facetious, couldn't read anything beyond the gold eyes, and gave up. "I'm sure. Do you want some coffee?" he asked, lifting his cup.

She shook her head and wordlessly produced a dented Arizona license plate from her duffle bag, laying it out on his desk. The plastic bolts that had once held it to the bumper were snapped off at the level of the plastic frame. "Nelson found it about fifty feet further down the cliff from the crash site. Those are his teeth marks in the plastic frame there," she said sheepishly. "Sorry about that, but he wouldn't give it up easily.

"I figured it had to have come off Jane Doe's car since it isn't rusted." She brought out two plastic bags, one containing the heart-shaped charm and the other holding a mud-caked pager. She placed them in his hand. "The charm was wedged between the floor plate and the crossbar of the front passenger seat rail frame. The pager was under about three inches of mud at the accident site."

He turned the bags around a few times then looked up at her. Her expression was unreadable. He was surprised at himself, that he could not tell what she was thinking.

"What else did you find?" he asked.

"Ingrate." She smiled slyly but evaded his eyes. "Nothing much. A few minor things. A package of Certs, a boot, a flare . . . things like that." She trailed off.

He nodded, knowing that she would withhold something—possibly the most crucial thing—for herself. Typical cop, not wanting to share the best of the goodies. She meant to take the case and run it to the end—with or without his approval.

"Did you get her photos and fingerprints this morning?" she asked.

"Rule did. Her photo and a repeat of the story will run in the afternoon papers. Found person and found body reports will be sent out by teletype by tonight."

"Did Michael say how she reacted?" Adele asked.

Tim picked up a pencil from his desk and tapped it a few times. He wished she'd stop calling Rule "Michael." "She was consistent—doesn't remember anything."

"And . . . ?" She expected him to spill.

"And nothing. If the teletypes don't turn up anything, we'll have the major TV channels air the photo and send the teletypes out to the western states. There haven't been any missing persons reports filed for anyone fitting her description, and the fingerprints turned up zilch at the Department of Justice in Sacramento. It's going to take a couple of days to run them through the other avenues. We're still checking the ID number on the car, but if you can stay for a few minutes, I'll have this plate run."

Adele nodded as he picked up the phone. In five minutes he hung up. "The car belongs to Budget Car Rental in Phoenix. I'll trace it through this afternoon to see if that was the original point of pickup."

He leaned back in his chair, stretched, and yawned. She unconsciously jiggled her leg, waiting for something, but he wasn't a hundred percent sure what.

"Don't you think it's odd that a woman and a child haven't been reported as missing?" she asked finally, her eyes wandering again—looking for something.

"Not if she's from out of state." He pointed to the Arizona plate. "That takes time. You've got to wait to see what shows itself."

She hesitated. "But it seems weird that someone isn't missing them. A husband or a grandmother who wouldn't be going out of their minds?"

He wagged his head. "Oh, come on, Adele. There's lots of women with kids who are alone in the world. All you've got to do is check out a few women's shelters to know that. Also, we aren't sure that the kid is hers. When and if it comes to that, I suppose we could ask her to agree to a pelvic exam, and even then . . ." He suddenly thought of something and jotted it on the pad next to his phone. *1. Distribute Doe photo to local women's shelters. 2. Check w/lab on cigarettes/hair. 3. Call Cini and Chernin for conference @ 5p. 4. Book Adele's finds into evidence. 5. Check pager.*

"So," she said too casually, "what about that case last night?"

So that was it. Inwardly he smiled. She was like an addict— the scent given to the hounds and all that.

She sat there, her hands folded awkwardly over one another, and her legs . . . those long shapely legs, crossed at the ankle as though she were settling in and waiting to hear a story. Which, of course, she was.

For him it brought up the same old dilemma: to share confidential information with a civilian or not, even if the civilian was as fine an investigator as he'd ever known, despite her unconventional methods.

She *was* quick, sometimes seeing an angle to something no rational mind would. The best investigators, he'd been told, rode a fine line between the criminal mind and the law-abiding one. Adele was ever so slightly on the blue side of the line—a blessing in itself.

Kosher or not, he knew as well as she that he would eventually run the case by her, detail by detail. He *needed* to run it by her because he knew he would tell her things that he couldn't— wouldn't—share with Chernin or Cini. Sometimes he let his mind go with her, in a way he couldn't, even when he was alone with himself at night in bed, dancing with the sheets.

He looked at his watch. The department wasn't busy. Some people were on break; most of them were out on investigations.

"Come with me," he said, leading her to the conference room. He closed the door and the blinds and pulled down the storyboard. As he began filling her in with the details of what they had, she nodded and relaxed back into the chair. He watched her as he spoke, her delicate oval face framed in an abundance of thick black hair that was casually pulled back. Her eyes remained fixed on something across the room as she took it all in, fact for fact.

When he was finished, she didn't say anything. He felt her anticipation, waiting for more information, waiting for him to explain things he himself did not know.

Eventually, she uncrossed her legs and cleared her throat. "Okay, so all we know is it wasn't a burglary and he was shot sometime between one fifteen and two thirty P.M. at close range with a twenty-two—probably with a silencer. He was taken completely by surprise either by someone he knew, or someone he wasn't expecting to kill him. There aren't any obvious suspects and no witnesses. And—his wife and kids are missing."

She gazed toward the ceiling, still processing the information. "A professional hit? Mistaken identity?" She sat up straight. "Was there anybody else checked into the motel who might be a big-time player? Maybe this was a mistaken ID? Wrong room?"

He shook his head. "Pete checked. The guest list is benign. A few senior citizens from out of town visiting their sons and daughters, a few young couples on vacation, one poor bastard on a book tour, one adulterous affair, a family with eight kids from Seattle, a few innocuous sales people who don't have lives, and a couple of lesbians on holiday from New Zealand."

He paused again, taking his time to regard her. Doubt and guilt over telling her as much as he had began creeping into his chest. He was a good cop and good cops didn't tell anything to civilians. There was a premise for that, he was well aware. Once you let it out, things had a way of getting spread around and skidding sideways. And if the case ever ended up in court and she was called to testify, his reputation—and his job—went up in smoke.

"You do realize that any information I give you about a working case is completely off the record?" he said. He didn't want to offend her, but he had to make sure she knew. "You can't be talking about any of this to anyone."

She raised an eyebrow in warning. Of course she would eventually share everything with Cynthia, but Cynthia was more close-mouthed about information given her than Nelson; she would die before she'd betray any confidence, whereas Nelson would lead the enemy right to the hiding place at the slightest bribe.

"Once we find the wife and kids, we're going to have a lot of answers," he said, taking a chair close to hers. "I've got my men and LAPD making all the checks: interviews, background, evidence, neighborhood, finances, phone records."

"I don't think finding the wife and kids is going to help," she said, getting up abruptly, as though she'd remembered something. "My guess is you'll end up with a whole lot more questions. When will the lab be done analyzing everything?"

"Most of it should be back by tomorrow." He watched her pick up her purse, feeling acutely disappointed at her leaving. He wanted to plead with her to stay. "In a hurry?" he asked, trying to keep the begging out of his voice.

"Nelson's downstairs tied to the newspaper machines. By this time he'll have gathered a crowd of saps who'll be trying to feed him scraps and wondering why he won't touch them. Then someone will say . . ." She mimicked a whiny voice: " 'Oh dear, maybe we should call the SPCA,' and by the time I show up, it'll be a regular scene with animal rights activists and those bizarre SPCA people, and I'll have to explain about his vegetarianism and that he really is a healthy, spoiled dog."

"Want me to walk downstairs with you?" he asked, uncertain if he really had the time; the clerk had buzzed him at least a dozen times and his pager had vibrated itself halfway around his belt to his sensitive spot.

"No," she sighed. "I've dealt with this situation before, and I can deal with it again. It's the price I pay for owning a dog who's half human and half professional manipulator."

Outside it was raining buckets. Marin County hadn't seen this much rain since the famous flood of '82, which put San Anselmo under water and left many of the county's hillside homes crumbled to nothing at the bottoms of various ravines. Warm and dry in the Civic Center lobby, Nelson sat staring straight ahead, enraptured at being petted and fussed over by five adults and two children. On the floor at his paw were a stainless steel bowl full of water and a napkin with six cubes of medium-rare steak.

Adele headed toward him making exasperation noises, although she *was* grateful for the absence of SPCA personnel. The dog got to his feet, wagging his tail, his eyes bright and smiling for Her and Her alone. Nelson wasn't entirely stupid: he knew on which side his bread, steamed carrots, and rice were buttered.

Adele bent to untie his leash from the *Pacific Sun* box when the woman stepped forward and spoke. Adele steeled herself. The type was easy to pigeonhole—all library marmish and civic-minded behind the inexpensive bifocals.

"You really shouldn't leave your animal tied up unattended," she said, waving a manicured hand around as if she were conducting an orchestra. "You never know about people these days."

"Isn't that the truth," Adele said dryly, kinking one eyebrow.

"He seems to be a sweet-natured dog," the woman continued. "A bit underweight, though." She paused for a beat, waiting for Adele to bite. When she didn't, the woman cast her line again. "I noticed he wouldn't eat any of the steak. I hope it isn't a sign he's sick? I've never seen a dog refuse filet mignon before. Has he been seen by a vet recently? He looks a bit anemic. He *does* have all his shots, doesn't he?"

Adele sighed and commenced untying Nelson's leash. "He's a healthy dog with all his shots and tags," she recited as though reading from a list the millionth time that day. "He doesn't eat meat or any food given to him by strangers, he's not anemic, he's not sick, he's of perfect weight for his breed and age, and . . ." She gave the woman a sharp look as her hand landed on the exit door bar. ". . . he's been trained not to fraternize with carnivorous busybodies who probably own overfed, deballed, declawed, yappy dogs who have as much personality as a stuffed animal."

Nelson barked happily as if in complete agreement.

The woman's wide-eyed do-you-know-me? look told her she'd hit the mark.

"Can you hold out for another thirty minutes?" Adele asked, pulling into the rear parking lot of Ellis.

Nelson whined and slid his head under his Mickey Mouse rug.

"What if I make onion pancakes for dinner?"

He lifted his head and barked twice with enthusiasm. She checked her watch; the doggie shrink said that being consistent was important in dog rearing.

Taking the back stairs to the basement, she entered the morgue office and walked into David Takamoto, chief medical examiner for Marin County.

"Just the man I wanted to see," she said, giving the Japanese man a hug. David and she had been friends ever since he joined the heart-wounded and weary ranks of Cynthia O'Neil's Discarded Men and had gone to Adele seeking solace and advice.

He was an attractive forty-something, although with his muscular build and lack of wrinkles, he could easily pass for thirty. He had the most beautiful even white teeth she'd ever seen. Also known as "Boxer," David Takamoto favored performing his postmortems wearing white T-shirts with the sleeves rolled into cuffs, a pair of boxer shorts, and a plastic apron. In the warmer months, he dropped the T-shirt.

"It was a girl about three years of age," he blurted out before she could say another word. "Since there aren't any dental records on kids that age, that's all I can give you for ID.

"Carboxyhemoglobin was negative for inhaled smoke, so she was dead before the fire started, which would be consistent with the crushed skull; probably from the initial impact. Even though the buckle to the seatbelt was found locked, I doubt the kid was restrained with a head injury like that."

If the date on the charm was the birthday of the deceased child, she thought, he definitely had the right age. "Now, how did you know I came to ask you about that?" she laughed, her mouth open in mock amazement.

Takamoto felt himself flush under her admiration. "I know you, Ms. Monsarrat," he said almost flirtatiously. "Jane Doe is in your ward, so of course you would want to know about the baby. You'll get to asking about the gunshot victim in a minute."

They both smiled, knowing it was true.

"What about the baby's DNA?"

"Sheesh." He stood back from her and gave her a look. "Are you studying this stuff now, or what? The DNA takes six months, and the genetic heritage can't be read from a blind sample. If the woman in Ward Eight is the mother, we'd have at least one parent to compare it with, but at this point we don't know that for certain."

"Okay, now you can tell me about the homicide."

"Two shots through the heart point-blank; one clean through the left ventricle, the other punctured the aorta. The killer paid attention in his human anatomy class. The victim was forty-three. His major organs were consistent with being a heavy smoker, and being shot in the chest twice. No sign of other trauma. The stomach contents were almost completely undigested, so he was eating or had eaten within a very short time of being shot."

Adele checked her watch—she had only a few minutes left before Nelson would start chewing on the piping on the back-seat upholstery.

The coroner paused to study her with dark-eyed curiosity. "Why are you interested in this guy? Did you know him?"

"Not really," she said vaguely, arching her spine and looking around his office. On the wall next to his desk was another group photo taken at the county New Year's party. In it, David and Cynthia were caught in a passionate kiss, their tongues misplaced in each other's mouths. It made her wonder just how many slightly indecent photographs of her friend hung on walls throughout the Bay area.

"It's an intriguing case, is all." *And it's one way to keep tabs on Detective Ritmann.*

David looked down at her, his full lips in a half smile. "Oh, right, Monsarrat. This guy wasn't one of Cynthia's ex men, was he?"

"Did the lab find any pictures of her on his office wall or in his wallet?"

The puzzled look on his face made her laugh. "No, David," she said, patting his arm in a consoling manner. "He was one of a very few lucky ones who got away."

"Hi," she whispered. "Do you remember me?"

"My nurse," Mathilde said, and pulled herself up in the bed using one elbow. "'From last night."

"I'm off duty today, but I had to come in for something else and thought I'd stop by to say hello. How are you feeling?"

Adele gripped the side rails and surveyed the survivor in the dim half light of the room. Her hands were still bandaged, but her eyes were no longer fixed in that lost, spacey trance expression. Her face had some color.

"Sore. My right hand isn't so bad, but my left hand hurts. What bothers me the most is the headache—it's making me nauseous."

"Concussions do that," Adele said. "It'll ease up. You're lucky that hand isn't more painful."

"Yeah, I guess," the woman said listlessly.

"How's the memory coming along?" Adele asked.

A troubled look flitted across her face. She shook her head. "It isn't. The sheriff's deputy who came to take my photos for the paper told me a child died in that car." She stopped and swallowed and began to sob, so that tears rolled out of her eyes and down her cheeks in rivulets. Covering her eyes with the wrist of her free hand, her shoulders shook. "A baby is dead, and I don't even know . . ."

Adele's eyes fixed on her with sober concern as she put her arm around the trembling shoulders. She pulled a wad of tissues out of the box on the side table and put them between Mathilde's exposed fingers.

After a time, Mathilde heaved a sigh, weary of the sadness. "It's not even the pain," she said. "It's not knowing anything. I keep thinking I'll hear a voice, or smell somebody's aftershave or see a face and it'll all come back. But I don't, and this is awful, not knowing. It's like being alive and dead at the same time."

She buried her head in Adele's shoulder, and Adele let her sob for as long as she needed, trying to control her own emotions.

When the crying eased off into an occasional gasp, Mathilde pulled away and wiped her nose, putting energy into gaining control of herself.

"I'm so sorry," she said softly. "What a mess. What a stupid mess I've made."

"No need to be sorry," Adele said. "Do you want anything to drink?"

She nodded and sipped from a cup of water left on her bedside table. When she was done, she lay her head back on the pillow and closed her eyes. In the hall beyond the closed door, Adele heard Skip Muldinardo, the ward's only male staff nurse, call to someone that he'd check the crash cart when he was done with his vital checks, then he commenced whistling the theme to "Twilight Zone."

She waited until the whistling grew fainter and died. "How about if I brush your hair and put it up in a braid?"

Mathilde's hand went to her hair, touching the singed side self-consciously. "I don't have a brush," she said meekly.

"Yes, you do." Adele went into her side table and found the packaged plastic brush the hospital still gave to patients upon admission. Adele pulled the brush gently through the tangles of the woman's fine hair. After a minute, Mathilde's shoulders relaxed like a cat being stroked.

"Does the date January seventeenth, nineteen ninety-five, ring any bells?" Adele asked quietly.

Without opening her eyes, Mathilde took a breath and held it while she appeared to grapple with the locked files of her mind. Then she shook her head. "No. Should it?"

"I don't know," Adele said. "It was on a charm I found near where the car went off. I went out there today and looked around for clues that might have gotten buried."

Mathilde's eyes snapped open. They were still red and swollen. "Did you find anything else?"

Adele began making a high, secure French braid. "A few things. Your other boot, I think. An Arizona license plate. Does Arizona bring up anything?"

"I can't remember ever being there," she said. "It has lots of red rocks and desert, but I know that from pictures."

"It must be scary not knowing who you are," Adele said, using the elasticized tie from her own braid to secure Mathilde's. She stepped in front of Mathilde to check the results of her work, and was astonished at the change. With the hair pulled loosely away from her face, the woman's wide, gray eyes, and full lips were spectacular.

Adele pulled up the mirror in the bedside table and held it up for Mathilde. Instead of finding her reflection pleasing, she looked away in disgust, as if she could not bear to look at herself.

"I'm scared not to know," she said, her lip quavering, "and more scared to find out. I'm afraid I'll never be . . ."

"Listen," Adele said, wanting to stop her before she began to cry again, "when you get out of here I want you to meet my dog, Nelson. He's my . . . doll face." She almost said "baby." "He's waiting in the car, so I have to get going before he begins chewing the plastic upholstery."

She gathered a pen from her purse and wrote a number on the bedside tissue box as she spoke. "I'm on tomorrow, so I'll see you first thing, but if you want to talk before then, here's my home number in Larkspur. Give me a call. I'm less than three miles away."

Mathilde nodded. She looked at Adele for a long moment and asked finally: "Why are you being so kind?"

"It's not kindness," Adele said at the door. "I'm a nurse—we refer to it as codependency."

"Tonight," she said, mimicking Julia Child's asthmatic, exclaiming cadence, while she chopped nine cloves of fresh raw garlic, "we're going to serve a lovely, all-organic lima bean, spinach, and tofu garlic scramble with a delicious side of onion pancakes!"

Nelson, along with her gang of invisible epicurean friends, barked and whooped in culinary excitement.

"And dessert?" she said to the Betty Crocker cooking judge (she also had a Heloise cleaning judge and a whole panel of sleuthing judges—including Sherlock Holmes). "Why, I thought I'd whip up my famous chestnut puree with nonfat whipped cream over Trader Joe's Low Fat Cat cookies—only two grams of fat per serving."

Betty Crocker clapped her hands together in delight then disappeared instantly when the doorbell screamed in that shrill, loud ring that always made her jump halfway out of her skin. She threw the chopped garlic into the pan of hot olive oil, felt a surge of satisfaction at the sound of the sizzle as she jiggled the pan, and went to the door.

It was too late for Jehovah's Witnesses—they went to bed when the sun went down—but it was too early for the magazine sales ruffians, who came only when she already had her jammies and face cream on.

With a stomach-pit dread, she decided it had to be Mrs. Coolidge, the widow who lived across the street with her twenty-four-pound menace of a she-cat named, appropriately, Queen Shredder.

Mrs. Coolidge was a meddling madam of scandal, daily spreading the rich manure of gossip about the neighborhood. She didn't even want to imagine what Mrs. Coolidge said about her and Nelson—probably something having to do with bestiality and satanic rituals.

According to seven-year-old Jessica who lived next door, Mrs. Coolidge had told her parents it was "peculiar" that Adele didn't have a husband or at least a steady boyfriend. "Unnatural" was the word Mrs. Coolidge was currently using to describe Adele's manless lifestyle to all the neighbors—including the kids.

Adele wiped her hands on her jeans and opened the door. In the place where the roundly jowled face of Mrs. Coolidge would have been was the broad chest of Detective Ritmann. Immediately she hoped that he hadn't overheard her talking to herself.

"Jesus, that smells good!" He stepped inside without waiting for an invitation. "Sorry I didn't call first, but I thought I'd stop by real quick to fill you in on a couple of things. What are you cooking?"

"Lima beans, tofu, and onion cakes," she said, still gathering herself at the shock and pleasure of seeing him so unexpectedly at her door. It was the first time he'd ever shown up without a specific invitation. "Nothing a carnivore would find worth chewing."

Through the still open door, Adele saw Mrs. Coolidge across the street pull open a peephole through the middle of her mini-blinds and peer out. The woman's bifocals glinted in the streetlight. Below her peephole, a dark gray paw had created another gap, through which shone the glowing yellow eyes of Queen Shredder.

A sudden, blind urge to erase any thoughts of her unnaturalness from the snoop's mind caused Adele to lean forward and give the unsuspecting man an affectionate hug and a lingering kiss on the cheek. She waited long enough for Mrs. Coolidge to get an eyeful, then kicked the door closed with her foot.

The moment the door clicked, she released the stunned red-head and stepped back, recovering instantly. The less of a fuss made over it, the better. They were friends, after all, and this *was* California, where grocery checkers and store clerks were one's "best friends" and strangers hugged each other at parting if they shared anything more than a simple nod of the head.

"You're welcome to stay for dinner," she said, moving back into the kitchen to tend to her browning garlic. "Although if you start going through flesh-eater's withdrawal, you'll have to leave."

He barely heard her, his mind trying to limp along without the blood supply that was currently engorging his male member.

"I—I don't eat meat anymore," he said, vaguely aware of the meaning of the words as they came from his lips. He had no idea why he would tell such a lie, or even if it was he who had muttered the words. Until this moment, he had never, for one moment in his life, considered not eating meat. Why, he'd actually made *fun* of vegetarians.

But when she turned to him, her face was lit up. He could see real joy in her eyes—as if he'd told her she won the twenty-million-dollar lottery.

"Oh, that's wonderful, Tim! When did you quit?"

"A while ago." Since noon, after he'd downed two Big Macs. He leaned over to stroke Nelson. Nelson wagged his tail happily, glad to welcome him onto the Meatless Family Wagon.

"Are you going vegan or American with dairy?"

He stared blankly at her.

"Are you a strict, no-animal-products type vegetarian, or are you going to include dairy and eggs in your diet?"

"Oh. Well, I thought I'd go into it easy—dairy and eggs included." *And maybe a chicken and some veal?* Those *were* vegetables, weren't they? "I don't want to go into shock or anything."

He relaxed his shoulders and studied the photographs in wood frames on the walls around the stove. Adele and Cynthia standing in front of a chateau in France, Nelson on a rocky precipice overlooking the Golden Gate and most of San Francisco Bay, a stage upon which sat a guitar player and a teenaged Adele, her mouth open wide in song, a black and white of Adele as a young child in the arms of a thin, good-looking man—both of them wearing identical naughty grins. Three laughing young women in nursing uniforms with a ripe tomato balanced on each head; an older man wearing a shoulder holster, leaning back in a swivel chair and laughing; and a hand-colored photo of a serious woman who, if not for the old-fashioned hairstyle and wire-rimmed glasses, could have been Adele's twin.

"That's a good idea," she was saying, adding parsley and cubes of tofu to the garlic. "I did the vegan thing for a few years. It was too extreme. I like yogurt and cheese too much to give them up." She oiled the double skillet she used for onion pancakes and set it over two burners. From the refrigerator she took the onion pancake batter and stirred it gently. The aroma of the raw batter alone was enough to make her mouth water. From the side door of the kitchen, Nelson whined.

"Clear off and set the table, would you?" she asked, and, as he fumbled about, opening drawers and setting used utensils and dishes in the sink, she opened a bottle of her best Napa Valley merlot and poured two glasses. She held one out to him.

"Here's to vegetables," he said, his eyes burrowing into hers.

She watched him bend his head and take a sip, concentrated on the way his lips touched the rim of the glass. His hair was carelessly pushed back in a way that tempted her to touch it. The roller-coaster dip of her stomach caused her to take a sharp intake of breath and turn away. *He's still in love with Cynthia!* her mind shouted through the rush of lust. *Off limits!*

She's not interested in me, Tim thought, watching the shape of her full lips and the way the dark wine entered her mouth. *Put it back in your pants and back off or jeopardize a good friendship. It's better than not being able to see her at all.*

She turned back to the stove so he would not see the fine mist of sweat that covered her face, not to mention the way her nipples had come to attention.

He purposely dropped a spoon, his pelvis doing a little jig as he bent to get it. He was going to have to remember to wear boxer shorts around her.

Nelson whined at the smell of human pheromone, hoping they would put off mating until after the onion pancakes.

He had never tasted anything so good, he thought, as he ladled the last of the mushroom and green onion gravy over his twelfth onion pancake. No one who knew him would believe that he had scarfed down two generous portions of something called tofu scramble and been disappointed there wasn't more. The guys at the department would torture him with it if they ever found out—which they never would, thank God.

"I don't think I've ever seen anybody eat so much so fast," Adele said in awe.

"Oops, sorry," he chuckled, wiping a dribble of gravy from his chin. "I grew up in a family of ten kids. At our house, dinner was not a social occasion—it was a competitive event. Anything tasting this good was inhaled off the serving platters."

"Ten kids?" An only child, Adele was fascinated.

Tim nodded. "Seven boys and three girls—all redheads. It was a hell of an experience."

"I'd like to hear about your family sometime."

"You'd find it boring."

"No. No, I wouldn't. I'd like to hear about how you grew up. Most of what I know about you was filtered through Cynthia, and you know how bent that information must be."

"Make a deal with you," he said, leaning forward on his elbows. "You tell me about yours and I'll tell you about mine."

"Okay," she said, and moved toward the refrigerator. "You got yourself a deal."

There was silence while he drank some of the merlot and savored another bite of onion pancake.

"The car was rented a week ago at a Budget rental place in Escondido," he said out of the blue, watching her as she whipped by hand a white thick liquid in a mixing bowl. "The person who rented it wasn't our Jane Doe."

As he expected, she stopped what she was doing and turned to stare at him.

"It was a man by the name of Jay Fargo. He arranged to drop the car off at San Francisco Airport sometime today. He gave an address in New Hampshire. The Budget agent said she remembered the guy because he paid cash from a wad as big as his head."

Adele spooned a thick white paste into the cream. "Interesting way to keep attention off his face, I suppose."

"I'm having Escondido PD get a sketch artist to her, but in the meantime, we got a loose description and an address. The address the guy gave in Manchester, New Hampshire, doesn't exist," Tim continued, "and neither does Jay Fargo. He gave a false Social Security number."

"What was the description?" She cleared away the dishes from one side of the counter, giving them to Nelson to prep for washing.

"Around five-foot-seven, between forty and fifty. A paunch, but not fat. He had one of those fringe type beards—like the Amish wear. Dark brown hair, but he wore a baseball cap, so she thought he was probably balding. Cowboy boots, and a denim jacket.

"She remembered his glasses because they were so unusual— thick lenses with black wire frames. The lenses were iridescent; she said she couldn't see his eyes through them. He walked with a slight limp or like his shoes were too tight."

"The glasses, the limp, a beard, the wad of money," Adele said, thinking aloud. "Devices to draw her attention away from the more revealing details."

For a minute there was only the sound of dishes being washed and then the sound of whisking.

"Her doctor has scheduled a shrink consult for tomorrow," Adele said. "I'll make sure she's assigned to me." She took a small bite of chestnut puree and hunched her shoulder in a gesture of borderline approval. "I stopped in today to see her. Poor girl is miserable. Scared to death. What do you think this car rental thing is about?" she asked. "You think she knew this guy and borrowed the car?"

Tim had thrown Emily Post out the window and was finishing off what was left of the gravy by licking the bottom of the clear gravy boat. Aware she was staring, he blushed, but didn't stop.

"Maybe," she continued, forcing herself not to gawk at the dexterity and size of his tongue, "he sold her the car."

Tim shrugged. "I don't know. Finding the connection between the two is the hard part. Not that any of it adds up right now, but we don't have all the pieces yet either. The teletype of the found person and found body report hasn't turned up anything."

"And what about the homicide?" Adele placed a dessert bowl in front of him. A small dessert spoon slid magically into his hand.

She was digging now, and he knew it. Right away, there

came a twinge of the old reluctance to share with her—the good cop rearing his dutiful head. He glanced at her waiting, inquisitive eyes, and let down the wall.

"From all appearances, Gerard Deveraux was a normal guy—other than the fact he lived in L.A., that is. Born in Ontario, raised in New Hampshire, went to Harvard, worked for a couple of blue-chip companies in New York, then came out here and worked for a company in San Francisco, got married, and four years ago moved to L.A. when he got the job with an emerging company that works with telecommunication systems. There's a brother in Chicago who says he talks to him by phone about once a month, and a younger stepsister in San Diego who says she barely knew him except through Christmas cards."

She brought the bowl of white creamy stuff to the table and tested it with her finger. It stood in a light, airy peak. The unusual creamy candy scent made his mouth water. The sweet fragrance ignited a memory of letting meringue cookies melt in his mouth in a treehouse somewhere in his childhood.

"Did the hotel people know anything? I mean, did he make any calls or did he have visitors?"

"Um. He made half a dozen calls to his home the day before and another half dozen around noon—none longer than three minutes. There was another call to a neighbor, then an hour later, the hotel operator put through a long-distance call to him which we verified as the neighbor calling back. After that, he ordered lunch from room service and made a call to change his return ticket to L.A. He scheduled himself on the four-thirty flight from SFO to LAX.

"The person who delivered his lunch around twelve forty-five said he was packing when he came in. According to him, Deveraux seemed upset. He said an emergency had come up and asked the room service guy to inform the desk so they could prepare his bill. While the guy was still there, Deveraux took another call. A local call."

She spooned out a large dollop of the thick creamy mixture into his bowl and wedged several thin wafers—shaped like cats—into the side. "And within two hours of the local call, he's dead?"

He nodded. "On a more ominous note, LAPD went to Deveraux's apartment and checked it out. All the lights and the TV were on, and there was food on the stove. The car and the jewelry are untouched, no sign of violence or a struggle. It doesn't look as though they were planning on being anywhere for very long because there was a meat loaf in the oven set to warm."

Adele thought while she gave Nelson the mixing bowl with the remains of the dessert.

Tim took a spoonful and eyed it as it made its way steadily toward his mouth. As long as it wasn't creamed rutabagas, he supposed he could eat anything.

"Women don't leave things in the oven on low for any length of time," Adele said. "She'd know that the meat loaf would dry out and—"

The loud groan of pleasure interrupted her. Tim slid down in his chair grasping his chest. "What *is* this?"

"Chestnut puree and low fat whipped cream, with Trader Joe cat cookies." She beamed. "You like it?"

"Oh my God!" the detective said. "This is . . . unbelievable."

Jesus. On top of everything else, the woman could cook. He sat up and looked at her in wonderment. She was a gift assortment of paradoxical and miraculous traits. Tofu or not, he hadn't had a meal this good since his mother's corned beef and cabbage with real, store-bought white bread.

Adele gingerly took another dainty taste and wagged her head. "It's okay," she said lightly. "I've done better."

"Don't ever let me taste your better effort," he said, "or I'll be here every night for dessert."

She considered the double meaning of his statement and came up with a variety of replies from provocative to unkind. In the end, she restrained herself from saying anything.

"The lab hasn't turned up anything earth shaking from the evidence taken at the scene. The hair found on his shirt didn't match his, and since he's the only player right now, that will go into evidence until we have a suspect."

"The wife wasn't involved with anyone, was she?" she asked.

Having forsaked his spoon, Tim looked at her from over the rim of his bowl. "Jeez," he said grinning, "have you signed on this case, too? Don't you think you've got enough to worry about with Jane Doe?"

Adele stood and pulled the bowl, which had been licked clean, out of his hands. She'd eked as much out of him as she was going to get this night. He was tired and getting irritably coplike.

"Dinner is over," she said, as if she were speaking to a small child—or Nelson. "You need to get some sleep. If you—"

The lights flickered and then there was darkness. At the same time the phone rang. Making her way across the living room, she grabbed the handset off the window seat.

"Hi. It's Cynthia. Has Larkspur lost its power too, or is Mill Valley the only electrical dark horse?"

"It went out when the phone rang," she said. Endowed with better night vision than most, she was acutely aware of Tim groping through the dark, making his way toward her. She remembered that the signs she'd been working on for the nurses' march were on the floor right where he was . . .

The man swore, reached out to the wall to steady himself, and fell with a crash into the door.

"What the hell was that?" Cynthia asked. "Is Nelson acting up?"

"Uh-huh," Adele said, feeling the Crazy Woman laughter well up inside her throat like a piece of expanding dough. "Can I call you back, Cyn? When I've got some candles going? You know how Nelson hates the dark."

"Well, I . . ."

Adele was watching Tim flail at the air like someone mentally challenged. The sight was too much, and she began to laugh in that silent, hard laughter that was almost painful. Immediately, Nelson began to howl, which, of course, made her laugh harder until she couldn't breathe.

"What the fuck is going on over there?" Cynthia asked. "It sounds like the Three Stooges and a dog. Are you—"

Adele hung up the phone and fought to get her breath. But the scene in the dark was too much: the baying dog, the man flailing like an idiot and walking into walls. It was something out of a forties insane asylum movie.

"Adele?" Tim called, not knowing that she was less than three feet from him. "Where are you?"

That did it. Wheezing, she ran for the bathroom at the other end of the house, bent double, trying to beat the release of her bladder from the strain of hard laughter.

After the fit of laughter passed and she was able to walk upright and speak, she lit the candle she kept in the bathroom and made her way out to the living room.

She found Tim sitting in the window seat with Nelson. They both wore the dejected expressions of hurt pride. It was amazing how alike the expressions were in different species.

"I'm really sorry," she said. "I guess your eyes don't accommodate to low light very rapidly, huh?" She was silent for a beat and then burst into a long, wheezy laugh.

"I'm glad you find my weakness amusing," he said in a somber tone, rubbing his shins. "Thank God I'm not deformed or disabled, or we'd really be in trouble."

"Sorry," she said. "Don't feel bad; you have simply proven beyond a shadow of a doubt that the real purpose for shins is to help us find furniture in the dark."

She snorted. Then, when the fit of laughter was almost over, she suddenly came alert and blew out the candle. A shadowy figure moved cautiously up the walk to the house. From the shadow's hand came a dim yellow beam of light.

Nelson jumped down and waited in the middle of the living room for the shrill wail of the doorbell that would not come, because the power was out.

A heavy rapping came instead.

Adele moved to the door. "Yes?" she said through the glass panes, which were covered by miniblinds.

"It's Mrs. Coolidge, Adele."

Of course. The hag couldn't stand not knowing what was going on and who Mystery Man was. Still, Adele did not open the door.

"I'm not dressed, Mrs. Coolidge." That should keep the gossip fires burning for a month. "Do you need something?"

"I want to know if . . . if you have enough candles."

Oh, right. "Yes." Then she added, "We're going to bed now anyway, so I don't need any, thanks." She emphasized the "we."

"My God, it's only nine-thirty," the woman said, prudish delight lacing her voice.

"Good night, Mrs. Coolidge."

"Shall I—"

"Good night, Mrs. Coolidge."

"What the hell was that about?" Tim whispered when she'd returned to the window seat.

"The neighborhood gossip," she whispered in return. "She has me cast in the role of neighborhood pervert because I don't have a parade of men coming in and out of here. And probably because Nelson and I sit in front of the fire talking seriously with our heads together. Or, what really gets her going is when Nels and I turn up the music and slow dance on the front lawn."

One porch over, at Frank and Sue's, Mrs. Coolidge was already knocking at the door in joyful anticipation of being invited in. She could hardly wait to spread the latest news about their wanton, perverted neighbor Adele.

They gave each other a gentle friendly hug, he thinking *stay, stay,* and she thinking, *stay, stay,*—both of them so uncomfortable with their secret emotions that they rushed him out the side door to avoid blowing Mrs. Coolidge's illusions.

When he was gone, she made a fire and placed an army of candles around the room. Then she added the finishing touches to the two banners, one of which read: THE LIFE A NURSE SAVES MAY BE YOUR OWN! The other banner boasted a variety of slogans: R.N. = PATIENT SAFETY, and EVERY PATIENT DESERVES A NURSE, NOT AN IMITATION and, across the top in red, WITHOUT NURSES, AMERICAN HEALTH CARE IS DOA!

While she worked, she replayed her conversation with Tim, mulling over every word and glance. Every so often she would remember the way he groaned over her chestnut puree, or how she caught him with his tongue in the gravy boat, and smile.

She carried one of the candles to bed and tried to work on her speech while Nelson daintily nibbled at his nails, making sure each one was sparkling clean before going onto the next.

After a while she pulled out the boot she'd found and studied it. The way the heel was worn down, indicated that the wearer walked with her weight on the inside of her foot. She checked the inside of the shoe, removing the brand new lining. Underneath were traces of rubber cement. In the days of use and dispose, it was nice to see that someone cared enough about a pair of shoes to replace worn parts. She suspected Mathilde was not type A, but still very careful and logical.

Guilty of the sin the nuns had assured her was mortal, she curled up on the bed fully clothed and her teeth unbrushed. She'd close her eyes for a minute, she told herself, and then she'd get up, floss, and get into her nice blue-and-white-striped flannel jammies—which, coincidentally, had belonged to the late Mr. Coolidge before she bought them at the neighborhood garage sale.

The sleep drool was forming at the corner of her mouth when the bedside phone rang and caused her to jump. Under the bed, Nelson continued to snore, a thread of his Mickey Mouse rug caught on one of his incisors.

She reached up and picked up the receiver.

"Mmunnff?"

"Oh, for Christ's sake," Cynthia snorted. "You're already asleep?"

"Mmff." She wiped the drool off her chin without opening her eyes.

"It's only ten o'clock, Del. You're worse than an old lady in a retirement home in Florida."

"Florida," she repeated.

"I went into work from three to seven today." Cynthia continued. "They paid me double time."

"Time."

"You okay? You sound drugged."

"Drugged," Adele said, rousing a little.

"What kind did you take? Warm milk or root of valerian? Or did you really go overboard and take some Swiss Kriss? I've heard that stuff can knock you for a loop."

"I'm tired," Adele moaned. "Leave me alone."

"I took care of Jane Doe. I think she's lucky she can't remember anything. I mean who'd want to? Pollution? Managed care? Terrorist attacks? Michael Jackson and Lisa Marie Presley?"

"How is she doing? How's her pain?"

"She's okay physically, but her brain is still fried. The burns aren't as bad as I thought they'd be. I don't think they'll have to graft that left hand."

Adele opened her eyes, realizing she'd forgotten to buy an *Intelligencer*. "Did you see the afternoon paper?"

"Yeah. The story was back page of the second section, picture and all. Stupid reporter mentioned that she was in Ellis. Malloy took a bunch of calls from people claiming to know her."

Adele sat up. "What did he tell them?"

"To call the Sheriff's Department. Tim's name and number are at the end of the article, but most people don't read that far."

"Did Mathilde see the paper?"

"I gave her a copy. I thought she should see it. She didn't really have any reaction—she was sort of depressed about it, actually."

There was a long pause. Then, "Did you ever see this new doc—Rymesteade Dhery?"

Adele lay back. "The sleepless doc who wrote the funny progress notes? I don't think so. He's brand new. The senior partners are probably making him take call every night of the week."

"I went through all the charts?" Cynthia started to giggle. "I found another one of his notes written at four this morning. It's on the prisoner's chart. Check it out when you come in tomorrow."

Adele yawned and tried to stand, fell back on the bed, managed a gymnastic contortion and flew back onto her feet again, landing with one foot on Nelson's paw. He yelped and skittered to his feet.

Adele kissed the top of his head as an apology. "Why the interest?" She really didn't need to ask. The mortician-turned-nurse's appetite for sexual conquest and drama, she found reprehensible: too much yang (male) and not enough yin (female).

Cynthia, on the other hand, thought Adele's lack of adventure in the world of men evidence of repression: too much tight ass (prude) and not enough free spirit (nooky).

Neither had seen herself in the larger overview as balancing the other perfectly.

"He sounds . . . I don't know, sort of sexy," Cynthia said dreamily. "I imagine him as helpless and disheveled looking. Someone who might put his tie on backwards or his shirts on inside out."

"And this appeals to you?" Adele asked in her Jewish mother voice as she slipped into the bottom half of the deceased Mr. Coolidge's flannel jammies.

"Yeah. I like the floundering and helpless. Speaking of which—did you go down to Stinson today?"

Adele ran through the events of her day, recounting everything that had taken place . . . right up to the moment Tim Ritmann showed up at her door. She wasn't convinced Cynthia didn't harbor lingering feelings for him.

"Oh, Jesus," Cynthia said finally. "Can you imagine how horrible that was—watching her own kid burn to death? No wonder she can't remember anything."

"We don't know for a fact it's her kid, Cyn."

"Does it really matter though? I mean, watching or—yeuck—hearing a kid burning can't be too much fun."

Cynthia had a point there, she had to admit.

Nelson rested a paw on her thigh—his way of saying, *Don't you think it's past your bedtime, dear?*

After she'd hung up and was crawling into bed, the phone rang again. She looked at her watch. Ten-fifteen. Nobody she knew would call her this late unless it was an emergency. As she reached out to pick up the receiver, she played out several scenarios: her mother had been found dead in the library, overcome by bookbinding paste fumes or shot by a disgruntled library cardholder owing fines; Tim had gone off the Corte Madera–Mill Valley hill, unable to navigate the road because of a delayed allergic reaction to chestnut puree . . .

"Break it to me easy," she said into the mouthpiece. Instead of the coroner telling her her mother or Tim was dead, it was Mathilde's low, husky voice.

"Adele? I'm sorry for calling so late, but I wanted to thank you again before I go to sleep, and to tell you that I remembered something. It's stupid, but you said to call if . . ."

"Don't worry about it. What did you remember?"

There was a hesitation. "I don't know exactly, but tonight they gave me corn for dinner?"

Corn? Adele rolled her eyes. "Okayyyy . . ."

"And I had this memory, a flashback really, of sitting at a table in a farmhouse eating corn on the cob. A man was there. I don't know how, but I know it was on a farm."

"Did you recognize the man?" Adele asked, a stir of excitement beginning.

"No, I . . ." There was a dejected pause, "I told you it was stupid. I'm sorry, I should have waited to tell you, but I was afraid I might not remember by morning."

"Don't be sorry. I think this is a good sign."

There was another, longer pause. "Do you really think so?"

"Yeah, I do. Congratulations. Now get some rest. I'll be there bugging you first thing in the morning."

Adele snapped her tooth guard over her lower teeth and turned out the light. Lying on her back, she did a series of stretches, careful to give her lower back a good workout.

"I suppose the farmhouse kitchen scene could be anything," she said to Nelson, who had jumped up on the bed to give her a kiss goodnight and let her touch his Mickey Mouse rug—his way of pledging his undying devotion.

Nelson looked at her with an expression that said, *Or maybe she saw* Bridges of Madison County *one too many times?*

FIVE

WARD 8 WASN'T TOO BAD FOR ONCE. OF THE FORTY beds only twenty-five were filled, and there were no admissions pending and no patients in the ER. Someone screwed up and scheduled three R.N.'s and one nurse's aide instead of the other way around. That boiled down to her, Skip, and Cynthia. Miroslav Dvorak—Mirek for short—was the nurse's aide. Since he was a first-year R.N. student, they allowed the young Czech immigrant to do more than would have been considered "legal" for a nurse's aide, so it took a little of the pressure off.

The patients were divided up, with Skip losing the coin toss for the added duty of being charge nurse. The minute the night charge nurse gave report and cleared the doors, the four of them scrambled to change their assignments.

Since the beginning of nursing, every nurse has had his or her particular aversions to, and preferences for, certain types of patients. The Ward 8 crew wasn't any different. Skip didn't do well with the denture-dependent, or with middle-aged, menopausal, strong-willed women; Cynthia refused to work with alcoholic and verbally abusive men; and Adele mostly steered clear of spitters and biters.

Mirek was still in his honeymoon phase, when absolutely nothing bothered him and he loved every filthy, rotten nursing task flung at him. The disenchantment wouldn't come for approximately two to three years after graduation from nursing school, depending on how bad healthcare politics got.

Patients appropriately reassigned, Adele hurried through her morning vitals and assessments, putting priorities on each patient on her "just-the-facts-ma'am" list—which was a cousin to the Alive and Breathing report.

807A: 29, M—fresh post-op laminectomy: pain control, flex feet, check for sensation

807B: 58, F—aspiration pneumonia and DTs: the right amount of sedation, keep track of oxygen saturation

815B: 56, F—double mastectomy one day post-op: pain and psych support, check lymphedema

819D: 24, F—thyroidectomy: go over discharge instructions and discharge

803A: 16, F—resolving overdose/suicide: evaluate for turfing to crisis unit, give psychological support

803B: 70, M—fresh transurethral prostatectomy: pain control and keep the irrigation bags flowing till clear

812A: Jane Doe—psych support/evaluation, maintain dressing changes, pain control

819B: 35, M—post-op tonsillectomy: keep supplied in cold iced beverages, check for bleeding, ck. discharge orders

802A: 24, M—MVA—multiple trauma: neuro checks, vital signs, review symptoms, triage needs, give family support

She saved Mathilde for last. She was surprised to find Paramedic Love sitting on the edge of Mathilde's bed, the two holding hands, or rather, Jellyroll guardedly holding her bandaged mitt. The gaze they shared was intense and gentle at the same time. At the sight of her, the paramedic jumped to his feet, although he did not let go of the mitt. Mathilde sat up straight, hooked the bed sheet with her free mitt, and yanked it up to her shoulders.

"Oh! Well, hi there!" Adele did an overkill on the casual cheer, cutting a glance at Jellyroll. "Consorting with the patients, Jellyroll?"

Jelco Love was six feet tall, and while not heavy, he wasn't slender either, although his black Rescue Sixty T-shirt revealed a muscular upper body. He had straight black hair that was thin at the back and almost all gray at the temples.

"I—I was in ER," Jellyroll mumbled. "I wanted to check and see how she was doing. I . . ."

"He stayed with me the whole time I was in the emergency room," Mathilde cut in. "I asked him to please come and see me . . . It's okay, isn't it? I mean, that he comes to see me?"

"I think it's great," Adele said, putting away linens and re-stocking the dressing cabinet. "You need the company, and Jelly-roll should follow through with the people he leaves at our doorsteps from time to time . . . especially if they're as pretty as you are."

They blushed and looked away from each other.

"Well, I better go," the paramedic said. "The guys are proba-bly ready to get back to the station. They'll be leaving rude nu-meric codes on my pager any minute."

Mathilde's eyes didn't leave Jellyroll's face.

"As long as Adele doesn't mind, I'll come back whenever I get a run to Ellis. If I don't get a run, I'll come by when I get off work tomorrow morning?"

Mathilde nodded. "I would really like that."

Adele caught the smile they gave each other and, for one second, felt her own loneliness. She thought of Tim at her kitchen table, how he'd felt inside her hug, and there was a longing that she shut out almost as soon as it surfaced.

"Nice guy," Adele said after Jellyroll left.

Mathilde held out her right arm for the blood pressure cuff. "I feel better with him here." She waited until Adele was finished making notations of her vital signs. "Are you married?"

"Divorced."

"Do you . . ." Mathilde looked at her quickly ". . . have a boyfriend?"

Adele gave the standard excuse she gave to everyone: "I've been too busy to have a relationship these last few years. Someday when I'm . . ." *Atrophied?* ". . . ready."

Ready? She could hear Martha Monsarrat's familiar lament: *Ready for what, Adele? The grave? Until you're too old to give me grandchildren? Ready, my ass.*

For the next few minutes, they were quiet while Adele changed the burn dressings. Even though she wore a mask, talking over open wounds was not a good idea.

There was minimal drainage from the right hand, and as Cynthia had said, the burns on the left definitely looked more like deep second-degree than the serious third-degree they'd originally feared. She spread a thick layer of Silvadene with a tongue depressor, reminded, as always, of frosting a cake. Bulky gauze went over that, then a layer of large-weave gauze strips.

The splint that held the hand in a comfortable position was applied next, followed by winding layers of bulky gauze strip and, finally, encasing the dressing with elastic netting. When she was done, she'd recreated the absorbent, protective mitt.

She checked the morphine pump and was surprised to see that Mathilde had activated the patient-controlled analgesic pump only twice in the last twelve hours. "You haven't needed much morphine. Is the pain not so bad now?"

"Not like when I first got here. As soon as I was allowed to sleep without being awakened every hour or so, that made a big difference."

Adele checked the patient information card. Dr. Murray had written a nighttime "only while awake" order for taking vitals, neuro checks, and giving meds. Underneath that, the NFP notation was now circled and underlined in red.

In report, the night nurse informed her that the newspaper story and televised announcement regarding Jane Doe's misfortune had generated a tremendous amount of public interest. Besides the fact that every crackpot and psychopath from Eureka to San Diego had oozed out of the woodwork, claiming Jane Doe as their own, Ellis's switchboard was jammed with legitimate calls from members of the public concerned for her welfare. Telegrams and special delivery letters were arriving at the reception desk at an alarming rate, and scuttlebutt had it that the producer for "Unsolved Mysteries" was aware of the story.

Because of the attention, Mathilde had been thrust into the realm of hospital politics; Jane Doe was to be Ellis's poster girl for charity work: the unknown soldier with the dead baby, being kept in a private room on a medical-surgical ward—at Ellis's expense—until she was claimed.

"You have a follow-up CAT scan in an hour," Adele said. "Do you feel well enough to go by wheelchair?"

Mathilde nodded eagerly. "Getting out of this room will be a relief."

Adele emptied the urine collection bag and made note of the amount. She washed her hands, watching the woman in the mirror. "Have you had any more memories?" she asked.

Mathilde shook her head.

"Did anyone tell you that Dr. Lavine is coming in to talk with you this afternoon?"

"Is he the psychiatrist?"

"Yes, and he's very good. I went to him myself a few years ago when I had a rough time sorting through something. He's not the kind of doc that automatically hands you a sampler of antidepressants when you walk through the door; he actually listens."

"What did you have to sort through?" Mathilde asked, completely unabashed. At least, Adele thought, the woman's curiosity was alive and healthy.

"Stuff about my dad; he died when I was young. I wanted . . . I needed to deal with the abandonment issues." Adele checked her watch. "I've got to order a transport for you now or you'll never get to the scanner. The hospital's regular scanner broke down, so we had to rent one, and it's out in a trailer in the back parking lot. You set for a while?"

A sad smile turned up the corners of Mathilde's mouth. "Other than a memory, what else could I possibly need?"

Henry Williams was the only patient technician in the house. When his pager went off for the fifty-first time since seven A.M.—only four hours before—he cursed and clenched his jaw.

"Dear JESUS! How they 'spect me to be ten places all at once anyhow?"

He let go of Mr. Bentonni's penis long enough to press the pager's off button with his nonsterile hand. He repositioned the flashlight he held between his chin and his chest and resumed the catheterization procedure. "Call me a patient technician?" the handsome African-American man muttered to himself, threading the small white rubber tube up Mr. Bentonni's urethra. "Ha. I'm a damned orderly is all, doing the scut work, getting treated like a damned slave, and paid like some kinda dishwasher! Don't get no respect."

"What you say, boy?" yelled Mr. Bentonni, cupping his ear with the nonfunctional hearing aid. He continued to stare straight up at the ceiling. "You almost done down there? I got to pee."

Dark concentrated urine flowed out the end of the catheter and into the white plastic insertion tray. Henry hooked the end onto the urine collection bag tubing and secured the catheter to the elderly man's leg.

Taking off the one sterile glove, he pressed another button on his pager. "Crazy Ward Eight," he yelled to Mr. Bentonni. "Gotta go, man."

"Crazy Eights is for children!" Mr. Bentonni cackled. "Draw poker is my game."

Henry cleaned away the debris and washed his hands, checking himself out in the mirror. He took a sheathed toothpick from his scrub top pocket and did a quick round of dental maintenance, straightened the rolled red bandanna that encircled his head, and put his earphones into place. With the sweet sound of Saint Miles Davis filling his auditory canals, he flew up the stairs to the land of the crazies, hoping it didn't involve picking up a 350-pound patient off the bathroom floor or catheterizing another old white man who called him "boy."

At the sight of him, Cynthia's chest tightened, the way her parotid glands did when she ate something tart. She knew it was him by the bags under his eyes and the wrinkles in his shirt—it was Dr. Rymesteade Dhery come to answer his stat page to Ward 8.

The smallish, worn-looking man with the uncombed hair walked onto the ward wearing a tired, stupid smile and looking around as though he were in the hall of scientific wonders. "Someone . . ." He tripped over an invisible hump in the carpet. ". . . page me?"

Cynthia hurried over to him, her hand outstretched. "I did. My name is Cynthia O'Neil." She flashed him one of her sensual smiles as she looked deep into his bloodshot brown eyes.

The moment their hands touched—as she would tell Adele later—their bodies' electrical forces joined and fused.

Dr. Dhery stared at the nurse. It was unclear what he was thinking . . . if anything. Cynthia took this as an unfolding of his mysterious side.

"I've wanted to meet you to tell you how much I enjoy your progress notes." Cynthia clasped his hands together between hers and crushed them with all her Irish farm girl strength. "They're a priceless, brilliant collection of alternative thinking. Playing with the dry, lustless . . ." (Was that the word she wanted, she wondered?) ". . . language of medicine and injecting it with boluses of humor."

With five hours of broken sleep out of the last forty-eight, Rymesteade Dhery tried to make sense of what the nurse was talking about but couldn't quite do it. He wished she would stop squashing his hands; he needed them for when he would finally be able to take off his shoes and lie down to sleep at 7:45 P.M.

Eyes barely focusing, he looked at his watch. Only eight more hours. If he could make it that long without killing someone or himself, he'd be thankful.

He stared at the girl with the fair hair and the green eyes. For a moment, his vision blurred and she appeared hideously eurycephalic. "What do you want from me?" he pleaded like a broken man with a gun to his head. "Are you from the chart reviewers?"

"Oh, no no. Do you think we could have a cup of coffee sometime? Away from here."

He blinked, incredulous. "You're asking me out?"

His expression made her step back. "Well, yeah. I mean, I only want to go have coffee, it's not like I'm committing myself to having your children or anything like that."

Rymesteade Dhery hadn't had a date since he graduated from high school, and even then it had been his cousin who was bribed into going to the prom with him. His whole life had been spent in the pursuit of a career in medicine—girls had simply never been a part of his life. He was myopic, he was poor, he was short, he was a social neanderthal, he wasn't athletic, and he had a face that really only a mother could love—and his mother was deceased.

In his present state, the idea that a woman was asking him out was too much to take in. He squinted at the girl, and focused. To his astonishment, she was gorgeous.

He looked around, suspicion suddenly clouding his face. "Did the group put you up to this? As a test? Do they think I'm gay? I'm not, and you can go right back and tell them that I think they're unethical for . . ."

"Sleep deprivation paranoia," Cynthia said. "What time do you go off call?"

"Seven-thirty."

"I'll meet you in front of the ER lobby," she said, writing down, "ER lobby—7:30—Cynthia" on a yellow Post-it note and sticking it to his belt loop. "Try to remain in a vertical position, and try not to kill any patients until then."

Adele slipped Tina a note and excused herself from Ward 8 by way of the back stairwell. "Back in ten minutes," her note read. "Top secret. Tell no one or die."

Sixteen flights down, she stepped on the black runner and the pneumatic doors with the red warnings of DO NOT ENTER! swung inward with a soft mechanical hiss. Behind the closed doors, life's dramas played out every hour of the day. Birth, death, the final results of love and hate—the Emergency Room in all of its dubious glory.

As she wove her way past rows of gurneys, the variety of smells, sounds, and sights reminded her of an Automat for med students hungry for experiences—exsanguination, screams, parasites in shit, dirty feet, trauma wounds, projectile vomiting, death. It was all there, waiting to be tended, waiting for answers and quick fixes.

Stepping behind an inch-thick partition that separated the personnel from the rows of gurneys, Adele smiled at the three nurses and the two doctors. She thought it best, when entering another camp, to appear friendly. God only knew when someone might go postal and pull out an M16.

Two of the nurses regarded her with tense suspicion. The two doctors acted as though she were invisible. The nurse with an oily complexion and thick granny glasses smiled back. "Hi. Are you the replacement from Registry?"

Adele shook her head. "No, I work on Ward Eight."

Both doctors snapped their necks to look at her again and she squirmed under their scrutiny. She knew the reputation of Ward 8 personnel: they were set apart—oddities to be wary of.

The nurse's smile did not fade or even flicker. "Wow. Upstairs Dementia Hell is what we call Ward Eight," she laughed. "Welcome to Downstairs Dementia Hell of Ellis Hospital. What can I do for you?"

"I'd like to talk to the nurse who took care of Jane Doe when she came in the other evening."

"You're in luck," the woman said and pulled off her headband. It was one of the plastic ones with tiny teeth to hold it in place.

"You?"

The nurse was leaning back in her chair, but she reached forward and grasped Adele's hand. "Glad to meet you. I'm Gladys Page, ER pissant. You're Adele. I've heard about you."

Adele let it pass. She really didn't want to know what she'd heard—it could have been anything. "I'm wondering if you remember . . ." She let her voice trail off and stared at the two nurses who were straining to hear.

Without prompting, Gladys Page got up and led Adele back toward the entrance doors. She pulled herself up onto a gurney. "Do I remember what?" she said, picking up the question.

"Anything. Did she say anything about herself or . . ."

The nurse shook her head wearily. "The detectives already asked. She didn't remember anything. She was out to breakfast, lunch, *and* dinner.

"We were so busy getting labs and X rays that we didn't really have much time to talk to her. She answered questions about things going on in the present—'How's the pain,' 'Do you need to pee,' things like that, but anything else—like 'When was your last period,' 'Are you pregnant,' stuff like that—she said she couldn't remember."

"Any scars or anything that you can remember?"

Gladys shook her head slowly, thinking. "An appendectomy scar. I remember that because her skin and abdomen were so flat. No stretch marks or flab.

"Actually, now that I think about it, she didn't wear any jewelry. I remember now, because I asked if she had any valuables she wanted to put in the safe, and I realized she had nothing of value. Her clothes were ruined."

"What happened to her clothes?" Adele asked.

Gladys screwed up her face, actually putting her fingers to her chin to think. "I was so busy with getting her stabilized, that I didn't . . ." She raised her eyebrows. "Wait. I remember because we had to have a debate over whether or not they should be thrown away or go to Registration. I think in the end the volunteer brought everything to Registration."

"Okay," Adele said. "Thanks a lot."

Gladys waved and rushed toward a gurney on which a man with long, stringy hair and beard was trying to crawl over the side rails.

On her way back to the ward, Adele wondered what would happen to Mathilde if no one could identify her. Would she spend the rest of her life not knowing, having to build a new life completely from scratch? No money, no home, and no one?

At the back door, she stopped and looked out the window at the tops of the trees bending and swaying under the hand of a strong November wind. "Not going to let that happen," she murmured.

As if in answer, a gull swooped by the window, hovered for a few seconds, and then flew on.

Tim passed the mumbling Dr. Dhery in the entranceway of Ward 8, turning briefly to stare.

"Out with the new, in with the old," Cynthia said, rubbing her hands.

Tim cocked his head. "Huh?"

"Forget it. You looking for your partner in crime?"

"Is she around?"

Cynthia jerked a thumb down the north corridor. "Eight-oh-seven."

Tim found Adele suctioning out the back of Mrs. Hyek's throat. Bedpans were one thing, but mucous was where the detective drew the line. He motioned to her from the door.

"Any leads on Jane Doe?" she asked, the second they stepped into the hall.

He rubbed his mouth, exasperated. "Christ. In the last three hours, we've received over a hundred calls. One guy was sounding legitimate right up until he showed us the marriage certificate and some photos of his missing wife. Four hundred pounds and not even the same race."

"Hope is blind," Adele said. "What about the fingerprints?"

"No matches. We've sent out the second teletype reports to the western states. The story is going out on the wire to the national papers. Can I talk to her yet?"

"Sure, but she's not here. Henry took her to the scanner, and when she comes back, Dr. Lavine is coming in for a psych evaluation. She still doesn't remember anything."

Tim checked his watch. "I sent what we have on her down to LAPD for the hell of it. Since I'm kibitzing with them on the Deveraux case, I figured why not?"

"Anything new today on that case?" she asked matter-of-factly.

"Yeah. The lab turned up some white fibers near and on the victim's clothes that weren't consistent with anything existing in the room. They suggested it was like the filling used in parkas or those quilted boots. LAPD initiated a western state teletype on the missing wife and kids."

"Do you have any photos of the wife and kids with you?"

He was going to lie. His mouth was open, the tip of his tongue forming "no" when his hand reached to his inside breast pocket and pulled out the envelope. He was going to show them to the hotel workers and the manager—he might as well show them to her.

"Wow." Adele said enviously, staring at the picture. The woman was about mid thirties, with large, dark brown eyes and high cheekbones. "She's a knockout. No wonder he was in a hurry to get home."

Tim looked at the photos again, shook his head, and snickered. He'd never understood women's tastes when evaluating what made another woman beautiful. Most of the women other women found "gorgeous" no self-respecting man would look at twice. Always there was too much bone, lips, and curls and not enough of what counted—the beauty that shone from the eyes.

"You're a hundred times better looking than this woman any day of the week, Adele."

"Oh sure," she said. *He's just being nice.* "In your dreams."

The three of them were sitting—a mini-miracle in itself—at the nurse's desk. Skip's jaw popped continuously as he chewed a bologna sandwich and finished the patient acuities for the nursing office. Cynthia and Adele ate sliced apples, raisins, and yogurt from plastic containers. Around them, the patients were calmed . . . or dead, thought Adele. No one's call bell was on, and none of the various high-tech equipment that kept the patients alive was sounding any alarm. It was an extremely rare moment in Ward 8 day shift's experience.

"I'm going to take him home, feed him, and put him to bed," Cynthia explained, searching through the San Quentin prisoner's chart.

"Christ on a bike. You just met the guy a few minutes ago,

Cyn. You can't take a virtual stranger and treat him like a stray dog."

"And then I'm going to wash his clothes and iron them. He's so out of it, he won't know the difference, Adele." She found what she was looking for and turned the chart around so Adele could read the latest Dr. Dhery entry. It had been written at 3:30 that morning.

Called by patient that nurse was complaining of having aches and pains of his groined area. Exam reveals a well-developed male of African hermitage lying in bed with his TV control in no distress. Coming out of San Quentin, this man has fathered six children in three months, all seven of which are in good health.

Except for the right leg, exam of groin and genitalia is negative for lumps, hits, runs, and no errors.

Will order 15 mg. of electrolyte panel for morning today.

Thank you for this daily bread.

Below, he had written "amen," but that was crossed out and his signature added.

"He's decompensating," Adele said. "Poor boy needs some serious sleep or he'll end up in Psych with full-blown hallucinations."

"Or the ER," Skip added, "after he kills somebody on the road because he was trying to avoid the elephants."

"And that's why I'm taking him home." Cynthia beamed. "It's not really a date, I'm saving lives. The girls down on Ward Five say that he's really a nice guy when he's awake. They think that what the group is doing to him is criminal. They've lost three junior partners in the last five years because of this same schedule."

Adele scraped the bottom of her yogurt carton. "Where are *you* going to sleep?"

"Right next to him," Cynthia said. "You'll be happy to know I'm taking this one slow; I'm not going to Stage Two until I'm sure he doesn't have any objectionable back hair or hidden tattoos."

For Cynthia, Stage Two meant having sex. This immediately

followed Stage One, which usually meant a hello and verification that the man was heterosexual, relatively clean, free of back hair, carried no weapons but multiple condoms, and had nice teeth. The hidden tattoo item was a new addition.

Adele caught sight of Henry Williams's red bandanna coming off the elevator. As they entered the ward, Mathilde was giggling wildly over something Henry had said out of the corner of his mouth. Her IV bag was two minutes away from running dry.

"Hey, you foxy man," Adele said, giving the orderly a high five. She admired and trusted Henry. He was one of those rare men who had no pretensions whatsoever. What you saw was what you got, and to Adele that meant she always knew exactly where she stood with him. No games. No bullshit.

Mr. Williams wasn't much for following the rules either, which was something else she liked about him. He'd given everybody the proverbial finger by applying to, and being accepted at, San Francisco State. He worked full-time days so that he could be a full-time night student. It hadn't been easy for him, but he was managing to get through without carrying any chips or attitudes.

They gave each other a hug. "How are you, Hen?"

Henry's head bobbed up and down. "I'm gettin' the paper, sister—my life is diddly squat now that I'm stuffin' the 'mones and spendin' all my time with my square-headed girlfriend."

Adele screwed up her eyes and looked at him. "Translate."

"What I'm attempting to communicate ..." Henry had changed his accent to one which might have belonged to a professor at Oxford. "... is that I have very little time due to the fact I'm attempting to learn something in order to graduate and I spend so much of my time with my computer that I'm not surrendering to my body's natural hormonal urges and thus not engaging in any form of sexual endeavor."

Adele looked at Mathilde then back at Henry. "Where the hell you been with my patient? It's been two hours."

"We took ourselves a tour of the famous Ellis Hospital, didn't we, girl?"

Mathilde giggled again. Adele noticed her color was high and her eyes were shining. She wondered if the laundry room crew had given her a toke off a joint. They were famous for that.

"It was great!" Mathilde said, sweeping back her wet hair

like a young girl. "We went all the way around the building, and then Henry showed me all the different floors, the laundry and the library, then we went for . . ."

"Whoa! Whoa, girl, hush your mouth. Don't be telling this here nurse *every*thing we did. We don't want me losing my job now, do we?"

"You took her outside in the rain *and* to the laundry room?" Adele asked, arching an eyebrow. "You didn't leave her with the laundry crew by any chance, did you?"

"Aw, come on, Adele," Henry said, moving his head in that certain way. "I give this girl some of the best times she's had since she got in the accident, ain't that right, Tild?"

"Totally." Mathilde's eyes gleamed.

" 'Sides, I wrapped the girl in a sheet so she didn't get rained on too bad."

Laughing, Adele pointed in the direction of Mathilde's room at the end of the corridor. "Go to your room and sin no more. Dr. Lavine will be here in about five minutes."

Henry hung his head and shuffled behind the wheelchair in mock Uncle Tommery. "Sho 'nuf boss. I'se gawn gets her ready fo' da whippin'."

By the time Adele got to Mathilde's room with a hot cup of tea, Henry had her settled in bed, her left hand properly elevated and the side rails up. She did a quick set of vital signs and ran to catch up with Henry in the hall.

"I need you to do me a favor," she said in a lowered voice.

Henry pulled back to look at her. "What you up to now, girl? You got a look like you're getting ready to stick your nose where it don't belong."

"I need you to go to Admissions and get the clothes Mathilde was wearing when she came into ER."

Henry pulled back to look at her. "Now honey, you *know* they ain't gonna let me have her clothes without a copy of a discharge order or a deceased notice."

Adele gave him a sly look through her long black lashes. "I heard that that girl who works down in Admissions—Millie? I heard she's all worked up over your sweet butt. I'll bet if you go down there with a nice cafe latte, flex a few of those muscles, and tell her that Jane Doe wants to see her clothes, she'll give them to you."

Henry swiveled his head. "Aw shit, Adele, why you want a bunch of smelly old clothes probably covered with blood and everything else nasty? Why can't you never let things alone? The cops—they'll find out who she is by themselves. You don't need to be messin' in this business. Let it be."

"Henry, you know me better than that." Adele straightened. "Will you help or do I have to bribe you?"

He looked down his strong broad nose at her, his expression turned haughty. "What *you* got to bribe me with?"

Adele thought for a minute, her eyes roving the ward. They settled on a doorplate that read GRACE THOMPSON, HEAD NURSE.

"I've got something you can't refuse. Get me the clothes and meet me in the Queen Mother's office at four o'clock."

Dr. Jeffrey Lavine, like most of the psychiatrists she knew, was slightly off beam and as far left as they could get and still belong to Rotary or Kiwanis. She suspected many shrinks started out as fairly normal human beings, but somewhere along the way, their minds slowly but surely got bent, taking on all the neuroses and psychoses of their patients. Surely no one would argue with the fact that spending so much time with the insane would have its effect. Adele was sure most of them used bizarre psychotropic drugs to alter their personalities, as proven by their flamboyant dress and the way they all seemed to take a vow of silence the moment they secured you as a patient.

Dr. Lavine was her favorite. The bearded, attractive man had a sense of humor and a twinkle to his lovely green eyes. He seemed almost normal, though not normal enough to be boring. She'd never held it against him that he understood most of the eighteenth-century poets, or that, eleven years before, they'd had a romance that ended when he asked her to marry him.

It wasn't until a few years later that she realized refusing him had been a mistake. But of course, by then he'd moved on—married some debutante from North Carolina or some such place where they still had debutantes and belles, and proceeded to have two daughters.

They ran into each other right after his second daughter was born and made a pact to stay in touch. Dinner once a year, and an e-mail or a card every few weeks. Once, when she was having profoundly disturbing dreams about her father, he saw her as a patient until she had worked it through.

"Hey you," she said, as they hugged. "You look great." She pinched his waist. "You haven't entered the love handle years yet, I see."

He laughed until his crow's feet dimpled the unbearded part of his cheek and sat down, taking her in. "Thank you. And you still look like you're in your twenties. How the hell do you do it? Is it the rabbit food and the forty-two vitamin supplements you ingest, or do you have a wonderful lover?"

The blush began at her neck and moved upward. "I live like a monk but I have great genes."

"What a waste that you are not being loved." He stared intensely into her eyes, his smile never lessening. "What's wrong with the men who live in this county—are they blind?"

Adele could have gone on a tirade about the majority of California men being developmentally stunted commitment phobes, but she let it go. It was a tired story—one he heard on a daily basis from every one of his female patients.

"You're taking care of the amnesia patient." He scratched his beard. "What's her name again?"

"Jane Doe?" Adele said, handing him the chart. While he skimmed through the medical progress notes, Adele gave him as much detail a she knew about the accident, including the data Tim had provided her about the rental car. Everything she told him was within the realm of patient confidentiality and as sacred as the information shared between priest and parishioner.

"She got back from the scanner about three minutes ago," Adele continued. "Our orderly took her on an extended tour of the hospital grounds. She was practically giddy by the time she got back. I think it was good for her to get out of that room."

Jeffrey took notes, then glanced at her. "Amnesics aren't usually giddy. Has she had any sort of flat effect?"

"Maybe when she first came in, but since then she's been clearly depressed and weepy until this afternoon."

"When she was told here was a baby who died in the crash, how did she take it?"

"Not well," said Adele. "Although my feeling is that it's more about guilt than grief."

The psychiatrist looked over his notes without expression, then stood abruptly. "Which room is she in?"

Adele pointed down the hall. "Eight-twelve—the one under the exit sign. By the way, we're using Mathilde as a temporary name."

"Okay," he said. "I'd appreciate it if you'd make sure we aren't disturbed."

She waved a hand in the air. "Take all the time you need, doc."

She watched him as he walked down the hall, his overcoat slung over his arm. He still wore the navy blue cashmere scarf around his neck—the one she'd given him on their last Christmas together eleven years ago.

Adele found Sunshine Mooney out of bed and standing naked in front of the bathroom mirror. Sunshine was one of those fifty-ish attractive, tanned, and trim blondes one saw on tennis courts and in country club health bars across the nation. The first to volunteer for community outreach projects, and the last to desert a good cause or obnoxious friend, Sunshine was what some called a real trouper.

She was not being a trouper at the moment, as blackened tears ran down her face and onto the bulky gauze dressings that covered her chest, where her breasts had been right up until yesterday morning.

Adele saw, with a kind of horror, that she'd been trying to apply mascara to her eyelashes. It was an attempt to assure herself that she was still an attractive woman.

Leading the pale, weak woman back to her bed, Adele wiped away the smears and sat holding her hand, letting her talk out the fears until she fell asleep.

Adele ran from patient to patient, skimping on care where she could. Like the thyroidectomy and the tonsillectomy who were regarded only as walking wounded: unnecessary overnight stays, practically self-care in any nurse's book these days, as compared to the four- and seven-day stays they might have been fifteen years before.

She couldn't—wouldn't—skimp on Jacob Schmidt, the twenty-four-year-old motor vehicle accident. Of all the patients in the ward, he was the one most likely to slip and circle the drain before someone could scream "Call a code!"

Miroslav Dvorak finished taping down the IV he had just inserted in Jacob's right arm. "How about it?" he asked. "I do a good job?"

"The best." Adele nodded. "You're going to be the best IV nurse we've had since Helen Marval."

"Helen Marval?"

"She was an Army nurse," Adele explained, "who could start any type of IV in any body, anytime. I've never seen any one who could match her."

"She is gone?"

"She's . . ." Adele thought for a minute and decided he didn't need to hear *that* horror story. ". . . not here anymore. Did you check residuals before you started the tube feeding?"

"I do this, yes. He have only ten cc's of the old feeding. His body is hungry?"

She sniffed and wrinkled her nose. "Well, his bowels are working, that's for sure."

Mirek brushed a shock of brown hair back from the patient's unlined forehead. "You must wake up, Jacob," he said tenderly to the unconscious man. "The Forty-niners—they are winning good."

Through the glass, Adele saw Dr. Lavine search for Jane Doe's chart, find it, and sit down. She left Mirek to finish with Jacob and went out.

"Well?"

Jeffrey shrugged, wrote a few more sentences, and handed her the chart. "I'm making an alliance with her, to let her know she's safe and can trust me. Obviously her practical knowledge is intact, and she has a capacity for new memory storage. She told me about the memory she had of the man. That might be a breakthrough experience which would indicate she's closer to letting the reality back in." He went silent, thinking it over.

"And?"

He looked down the hall. "She's not your typical post-traumatic amnesia," he said. "Not unprecedented, but unusual enough."

Adele sat down next to him, smoothing out her scrub pants at the thighs. "Like what do you mean?"

"She's worried and depressed about her memory loss for one thing. Amnesics aren't usually this concerned about that."

Adele thought of Mathilde laughing with Henry, and her obvious interest in Jellyroll. "But she's not that freaked about it. I mean, this morning she was positively radiant, sort of getting off on the attention."

"That's the point, Del. Her affect—it's not the norm. Most dissociative disorders exhibit a flatter affect than this."

"But she did have sort of a flat affect when she first came in—or maybe it was just more depressed." Adele frowned. "But now it's like she's trying to ignore everything and create a new life as fast as she can. I think whatever it is she's blocking out is so frightening or threatening to her, she—"

A series of electronic bleeps from the pager at his waist cut her off. He checked the number. "My wife," he sighed, putting on his coat. "I'm meeting her for an early dinner and then we're off to the city for the ballet."

"Sounds wonderful," she said, making sure her voice was convincingly happy. "When are you going to see Mathilde again?"

"Tomorrow. Are you working?"

"Yes. What time will you be in?"

"Any time after noon," he said. "Why don't you give me a time when you might have a few minutes to spare. I'll take you downstairs for a cup of herbal tea."

"If you come in and see Mathilde at one, and I'll try to make sure I get a lunch break around two."

She didn't watch him leave. She didn't want to kick herself anymore over the foolish choice she'd made all those years ago. What was done was done.

She looked through the glass window at Mirek beckoning her for help in cleaning up Jacob, and tried not to think about the fact that instead of working elbow deep in blue liquid stool, it could have been she who was meeting Jeffrey at some fabulous restaurant and then going to the San Francisco Ballet in a big comfortable Jaguar. Then going home and making love quietly so as not to wake their two well-loved children.

She gave a resigned sigh and wondered what she'd been thinking to turn him away.

* * *

Ward 8's head nurse was a Brit by the name of Grace Thompson. Ms. Thompson was a miserable human being with the personality of a gluepot. Heavyset, white-haired, and jowly, she seemed to dislike anything that wasn't in some policy and procedure book. In short, she lacked joy and spirit, let alone compassion. Grace Thompson was a professional nurse with plenty of initials after her name, but she had never touched a patient—never mind a bedpan—in her life.

The fifty-something nurse was hired on short notice after the previous head nurse was murdered, and had proceeded, within a very short amount of time, to alienate the entire Ward 8 staff—not an easy thing to do. Presently, she was out on an injury; one of the procedure books had fallen onto her foot and broken three bones. The very day she was carried to ER in a wheelchair, there had been a celebration, the likes of which had not been seen by Ward 8 for many years. There was, to put it mildly, dancing in the halls.

Ms. Thompson's normally tidy desk, abandoned for over a month, was piled with all sorts of things that would have sent the anal-retentive, type A Queen Mother into apoplectic fits: boxes of Christmas decorations, a grease-stained pizza box with clumps of cement-hard mozzarella clinging to the inside, a pair of dirty socks, magazines, and paperback novels. On top of the debris was now a large plastic garbage bag to which was taped the name DOE, JANE, and a patient ID number.

Henry didn't let go of the bag entirely. "So what you got for me, Adele?" She loved the way he said her name with the long A sound.

She smiled that sly smile and held out a manila folder.

He looked at it like it might have a snake inside. "What is it?"

"Your complaint file," Adele answered. "See, the Queen Mother was getting ready to turn this over to the staffing office when she got hurt. She's been compiling complaints about you for over a year."

"Complaints?" Henry's voice got high and whiny. "What that old bitch complaining 'bout me for?"

Adele gave him a look. "Oh please, Henry. You aren't exactly Mr. Manners around here."

Henry was all heart and soul when it came to dealing with the patients and a select group of the doctors and nurses, but for the most part, he was surly and peevish with upper management. Regardless of the facts that the patients loved him and he was extremely adept at what he did, he refused to cower at the sight of Grace Thompson. In the head nurse's mind that amounted to treason against the crown.

"She's aiming to get you canned, Henry."

He took the folder and looked through the report sheets, one after the other. "Oh man, that nasty old bitch complaining 'bout my music! She said my box was disconcerting to the patients." He looked up at her. "Hell, most times, the patients want my headphones for themselves. I let them have them, too. The old people love Snoop Doggy Dogg. You know how many white people I've turned on to the Almighty John Coltrane with my box?"

"That's not the point, Hen. I'm sure you've got a good counter-argument for every one of those reports. The fact is, my man, you're alive and spiritually healthy and she's gonna try and squash you. The other fact is," she grinned, "those are the only copies of the reports. If I recall . . ." Adele squinted as if try-ing to recall something from Miss Getty's world history class. ". . . this building has a large incinerator down in the basement, and no one will notice if, for one brief second, that fire burns a bit hotter because of being fed a folder full of horseshit and hate."

He hesitated. That surprised her. "Henry. You've got two more years of pre-med to get through at State and a child sup-port payment every month. You can't afford to lose this job or have a shitty record."

After a minute, Henry tilted his head, grinned, put the folder under his scrub top, slipped his headphones on, and turned up the volume on the Almighty John Coltrane so she could hear the music too. Together, they boogied out into the hall.

In the nurses' lounge Adele opened her locker and reached for the jar with the red plastic top. From a cloth bag she brought out a tablespoon. Settling on the couch, she dipped the spoon into the jar and faced one of her two lifelong addictions head-on.

"Powerless over peanut butter," she sighed, taking a tiny bite from the edge of the spoon. She savored the rich nut flavor, shuddering as she did so. She kept the paste in her mouth as long as she could roll it over her tongue before giving it up to her stomach.

When she had licked every atom of peanut butter from the stainless steel, she found herself in that dilemma of saying no to a second dip. Like any addict, she knew if she gave into the temptation, the game was over. Before she knew what had happened, the jar would be empty, and she'd find herself going to ridiculous lengths to find more. She envisioned telling the kitchen staff she needed an industrial-size jar of peanut butter to spread over some severe burn wounds, and making up a fantastic story about it being a newly discovered miracle cure.

Using the same self-will that pulled her out of bed every morning at 4:30 A.M. to run eight miles in all kinds of weather, she capped the jar and put it away—out of sight. Then she turned her attention to the white plastic bag of partially charred clothes.

The boot inside the bag matched the one she'd found. She put the pair together and took them to the sink to rinse off the mud—yellow clay on the left, dark mud on the right. She dried them and put the pair in her locker.

The once-white blouse was a mess of mud, blood, and soot. There were a pair of cotton panties that were cut, one sock, a bra that had also been cut, and an olive green jacket that stank of mildew and burnt wool. A thin piece of green rayon was all that was left of either a skirt or a loose jumper.

Adele turned the jacket inside out, checking the pockets that remained. At the same time as her fingers landed on a small smooth object in the right pocket, she saw the single letter embroidered on the gold satin lining. Ample curlycues trailed off the ends of the E.

"Elizabeth, Ellen, Eileen, Esther . . . Esmeralda?"

Or it could be the initial for the last name, suggested the couch pillow.

She agreed, and decided that she would go through the phone book that night, writing down the most common surnames beginning with E.

For a minute she thought about taking the coat into Mathilde, to see if it would produce a memory, but its condition stopped her. It was too gruesome.

She could barely bring herself to look at the object in the pocket. The distinctive shape was easily recognizable by touch.

She only needed to look at the color.

Pink. The pacifier was pink.

SIX

THE NEW LOBBY OF ELLIS HOSPITAL WAS DONE IN soft blue and mauve. The practical terrazzo floors had been replaced with impractical thick pile carpet.

Cynthia sank down into one of the plush blue chairs and swung her foot in rhythm with the tune going through her head all afternoon.

"June is bustin' out all over, all over the meadows and the hills . . ."

She'd sung it with Mohawk School's sixth-grade chorus, and could still remember Mrs. Miller's jowls as they jiggled with each downward stroke of her baton. True, they were well into November, but what the hell.

The automatic doors opened and several more nurses, happy to be off duty, smiled their way to their cars. Coatless, she shivered from the blast of damp cold, and glanced at the clock over the information desk. Dr. Dhery was fifteen minutes late. She'd give him five more minutes before she paged again, or went looking for him under the furniture in the various ward lounges.

She was on her way to the information desk when the elevator door opened and he entered the lobby and fell on his face. She ran to help him up.

"Sorry," he mumbled. "Fell asleep against the door on the way up from ER."

The elevator door tried to slide closed, hit his foot, which was stuck in the groove between the elevator and the floor, and bounced back open with an angry *Ping! Ping! Ping!*

One of his fellow passengers loosed the toe of his shoe from the grasp of the crevice and, with Cynthia, helped the worn physician to his feet.

"Come on," she said. "Let's get you fed and bedded."

Minutes later, they were sitting in the A&W stand in San Rafael, giving their order to a waitress dressed in a fifties-style skirt and sweater, complete with a black pillbox hat and roller skates. She yelled their order into a walkie-talkie that hung from her neck by a black string.

"Number twelve! Two double boners in a field, one pig in a cloud, three black jitterbugs with a cow on the side."

They got their black jitterbugs with the cow on the side—regular coffees and milk. He gulped down the first coffee to revive himself so he could work his jaws long enough to get some food down. When the false sense of wakefulness came, he stirred two packages of sugar into his second coffee.

"Sorry I was late but I got called into ER. This couple watched some vampire movie and the boyfriend stabbed her ten times and then drank her blood."

Cynthia shivered, imagining the scene. "My God! Did she die?"

"No," he answered, quietly. "She's still alive. I admitted her to ICU."

She thought for a moment while savoring her coffee. "Jeez, you think they'll get back together?"

He paused, looked over the rim of his cup, saw she was serious and shrugged. "I hope not." He rested against the door, careful not to let himself get too comfortable. "This is a real treat for me," he said. "I haven't been out with a woman in . . ." He didn't think it wise to tell her it had been since high school. ". . . a long time."

Cynthia regarded the dark circles under his close-set eyes and the way his hair was beginning to grow over his collar. Maternal juices flowing, she reached under the flaps of his parka and felt his ribs. It was as she expected: he was all skin and bones.

Sensing her thoughts, he ducked his head, embarrassed. "I'm a little out of shape right now . . . I look like hell, but I'm okay when I'm awake."

He yawned, a huge, cavernous yawn that shook his frame with its power. "It's only that I haven't had time to do anything while I've been on night call, and I only get one day and night off a week. I keep meaning to do all these things like getting a hair cut . . ." He tugged the long ends self-consciously. ". . . and doing laundry, but there's so much to do, that I end up not doing anything at all."

"Why is that?" she asked, yawning herself.

"I get distracted."

"What do you mean?"

"Distracted." He took in a deep breath and looked out at the rain running in rivers down the windshield. "Like I'll start walking from the living room into the kitchen thinking that I'm going to do a load of laundry, but then I'll see an open door, or maybe one of my photo albums." He got a strange light in his eyes. "Then it's all over. I'm gone."

She smiled nicely at him as she slowly but surely became more and more infatuated. "Once a long time ago," she began, after a pause, "I was visiting a friend who lived in a small backwoods town in Mississippi? Well, one day I was hanging around the local garage, getting my tires rotated, and a Down's syndrome boy went by driving a pickup truck. So I said to the old man fixing the tires, 'I didn't know they gave Down's syndrome people licenses to drive.' And the old guy turns to me with this stricken, totally surprised look on his face and says, 'Hell, lady, that weren't no Down's syndrome person. That was the mayor!' "

Rymesteade Dhery stared at her without blinking, wondering what parallel she had been trying to make, when their waitress tapped on the driver-side window with her elbow.

"Two double boners in a field . . ." She handed them two jumbo hot dogs on a bed of french fries. ". . . and a pig in a cloud." She handed over a large platter of pork ribs with a side of mashed potatoes.

Cynthia paid the bill, not wanting him to have to strain his mind trying to figure out how to put the currency together to add up to the right amount—let alone figuring out the tip.

He ate as though he hadn't yet been introduced to chewing. By the time they were done, he'd missed his mouth enough times that his shirt and tie looked like a tablecloth off the children's party table at Chuck E. Cheese's.

She pulled out into the downpour and popped a New Age

tape into the cassette player. His hunger satiated, his head began to nod, and his eyes kept sliding back into his head. "So," he began, unsuccessfully stifling a yawn, "why did you ask me out?"

"Well, you have an unusual charting style which I appreciate. It suggests a man who is a true individual in his thinking. A man who isn't afraid of the pressures of convention and can turn the most mundane of tasks into an art form." Bashfully, she added, "I understand completely about being distracted by an open door, and . . ."

There was a noise, distantly reminiscent of night shift. Glancing over, she saw his profile: head flung back, mouth open. He'd begun to snore.

Francis Lee was nervous. He kept swallowing the way a man does when there's nothing left to swallow—not even his own saliva.

Police had that affect on some people, Detective Ritmann thought. There was something about the authority that made some people nervous and fearful, and some people—even the nicest of people—turn instantly defensive and even vicious. He believed it all depended on how they were raised.

The power the police had over others boiled down to two things: death or loss of freedom. There were rare occasions when wielding that power could give him an advantage, but mostly he treated others, including criminals, as his peers. No mind games, no threats, no surprises, unless he had been given a reason.

"May I buy you a cup of coffee, Mr. Lee?" Tim asked, wishing the guy would relax.

"No, sir. I'm fine." Sitting bolt upright in a crisp black uniform, Mr. Lee looked around the busy cafe like a man who thought the walls contained hit men with guns trained at his head.

"I know what you told the other investigators about what Mr. Deveraux said and how he looked, so I won't go over that again, but I'd like to know what you think—subjectively."

Mr. Lee's eyebrows knit in a frown. "Subjectively, sir?"

"I mean, what were you thinking when you were in his room? What ran around . . ." Tim tapped the side of his head twice. ". . . up here? You know, like your personal thoughts."

The young man bobbed his head, looked down at the table's bright daisy yellow Formica top and then back at Tim.

"Like what was my own opinion?"

"Exactly."

Anxiety showed through the thin line of his mouth as he stopped to think. "I don't know. Maybe he was freaking out because he . . ."

"No. I want to know what *you* were thinking at the time," Tim pushed. "Close your eyes and try to remember walking into the room and tell me what you were feeling."

Hesitantly at first, Francis closed his eyes and bowed his head. After a few minutes, he broke into a silly smile. "I'm thinking the tray is damned heavy." The man opened his eyes and looked at Tim expectantly.

"Exactly what I want," Tim said. "Keep going."

Francis closed his eyes again and the smile disappeared. He frowned. "The man is packing, and I think he's upset—no, not that, more sad. That's it. I thought he was upset and sad, but that he had it under control, because he wasn't rushing around, but he was very del—delib . . ." Frances grappled, and finally threw up his hands. "I can't think of the word."

"Deliberate?" Tim said.

"Yeah, that's it. He was deliberate about putting in the shirts just so, and rolling up his socks. I didn't say nothing and put down the tray, which is when he said there was an emergency at home and he had to leave right away, and he asked me to tell the desk to prepare his final bill. I remember he called me Francis, and I liked it that he remembered my name from the other times I delivered his lunch. He tipped good, too. Always cash—you know, like from him to me, like a real tip. I liked him." Francis's eyes remained closed in concentration. "He was a nice guy, not like some we get in here. I told him I hoped his emergency wasn't bad and I really meant it, too. And he said he hoped it wasn't bad either, and I thought that maybe his old lady left him or something."

"Why did you think that?"

Francis opened his eyes and blinked until he grew used to the light. He was more at ease now. "I don't know. He looked like a man whose old lady run off somewhere she shouldn't. You know the look I mean?"

Tim nodded. He'd seen the man in the mirror wearing a similar expression once or twice. "What happened then?"

"I asked if he wanted me to set up the lunch on the table, you know, take off the covers and put out the silverware, and the phone rang. He said, 'Thank you, Francis,' and answered the phone. From what he was saying, I could tell it was the airlines calling him back with his flight information and stuff. He wrote some stuff down, and hung up. One second didn't pass, and the phone rang again and he picked it up and says hello—like he's surprised there's another call."

"Then what?"

He lifted his shoulders and hands and let them fall. "I finished putting up the table. He wasn't saying nothing; just standing there listening real intent. I told him to have a good trip and left."

Tim thumbed a few pages back in his notebook to his notes from talking to the hotel operator. The call Francis Lee had heard was the local call that came in at 1:25 while Deveraux was on the line talking to the airlines. The caller—the operator couldn't tell for sure if it was a man or a woman—had insisted on waiting until the line was clear.

"I thought he would call me back to give me a tip, but he didn't. That wasn't his usual way, so I kinda looked at him when I got to the door, and he was real still . . . real serious, like he was getting some bad news or something. His eyes was closed, and I heard him say, 'I have it with me' and 'Yes, I understand.'

"I felt bad for him. I thought about asking if there wasn't something I could do for him, but it wasn't my place to be eavesdropping or sticking my nose into the man's business neither."

Francis shook his head, and Tim could see the shining brown scalp through the closely shaved hairs.

"He wasn't a happy man."

"Did he say anything more?" Tim asked.

Francis shrugged again. "Don't know. I didn't wait around to hear. I was kind of hoping he wouldn't let the lunch get cold, so I wouldn't get blamed for taking it up to him cold or nothing."

"Did you go back to the room again?"

"No, sir." Francis shook his head. "Not to his room. But there was a couple in the room next to his that kept ordering from room service all day." He rolled his eyes. "They ran me ragged, I'll tell you. Must have ordered up twenty times. I delivered champagne and sandwiches to them thirty or forty minutes after I dropped off Mr. Deveraux's tray, and then again about two hours after that, I delivered some desserts to the same couple. Mr. Deveraux's tray wasn't out in the hall either time."

"You didn't hear or see anything unusual?"

"No, sir."

Tim searched in his jacket pocket for his card and handed it to the man. "Thank you, Francis," Tim said sincerely. "You did real good. If you think of anything else, please call me."

"That all you need from me?" Francis was visibly relieved.

Timothy stood and smiled. "Yes, sir. Thanks for taking the time to talk to me."

They shook hands. "No problem, man." Francis Lee smiled, the relief still clinging to him. "If I think of anything, I'll call you right away." The man ambled away whistling, happy as Larry.

Tim drank the rest of his coffee and got ready to leave when his stomach growled in protest. He hadn't eaten since the small bowl of Special K adorned with a banana and skim milk.

This was the best place in town for a four-inch-high Reuben or a grilled hamburger smothered in onions. He raised his hand for the waitress.

"Oh, so now you want to order, huh?" The waitress primly showed a bit of tooth and readied her pen and paper.

"Give me a Reuben on rye with extra swiss and pickle."

"You want that now, or to go?"

Something must have been at work in his unconscious, because he was sure she'd said, "You want that cow, or no?"

He stared at her, amazed that she could have known he had promised to break the dead cow habit.

"Pardon me?"

"I said, do you want the Reuben to eat here, or do you want it to go? There's an extra charge for a take-out order."

Tim didn't hear her. He was seeing Adele's face light up at the news he'd stopped eating meat.

"Cancel the Reuben," he said, his soul full of regret. "Make it a veggie burger with sprouts."

*   *   *

Dr. Otis wasn't really a doctor. He was her optician, but Adele called him doctor anyway because he had all the arrogance and bad manners of a physician. She was really glad he liked her as much as he did; she'd seen the way he treated his other customers and likened it to seeing snails being crushed under the drum of a steamroller.

Even though he claimed to be her eyes' Number One Fan, the guy gave her the creeps. He liked to remind her that if she died before he did, he wanted to enucleate her eyes and have them preserved in a jar in his room. She didn't know exactly what room he considered "his" room, but she envisioned it to be loaded with mounted cataracts and lamps with shades made from human eyelids.

"What can I do for you today, Goldie?" The gaunt replica of Bela Lugosi smiled.

Tombstone-shaped teeth, she thought.

"Well . . ." She took in a breath and let it out, trying not to look at the poster on the wall behind him. It was a blowup of her own eyes. In exchange, he'd supplied her with several pairs of expensive sunglasses. "I was wondering if you've ever seen a pair of glasses where the lens are iridescent?"

Otis rubbed his hands, one over the other and nodded almost imperceptibly—like Boris Karloff. She couldn't help but wonder what the man did for Halloween. She hoped he put this natural talent to some use and rented himself out.

Without a word, he disappeared into his postage-stamp-size office. When he reappeared, he held a black case, the kind that is made of metal and covered with pigskin. "I got them in this week." He grinned, and she spontaneously thought of Lon Chaney in *The Hunchback of Notre Dame*. "They are the latest rage in L.A. and the Big Apple."

Her short burst of nervous laughter had a hysterical ring to it.

He snapped open the case. Inside lay a pair of black wire-rim glasses with iridescent lenses. In astonishment, she sucked in a breath and cautiously removed them. The kaleidoscope of colors—blue, indigo, purple, lavender, yellow, red—undulated and shimmered with each tiny movement.

"Exquisite, aren't they?" Dr. Otis asked, sounding like Vincent Price.

"They're different," Adele said. "How much are they?"

"As expensive as they are exquisite. They run upwards of three hundred dollars a pair—and that's without corrective lenses."

She swallowed. "Okay, so how much to rent them for a day?"

Adele lay staring at her bedroom walls. On the wall at the foot of the bed hung a simple bamboo backscratcher—the ultimate symbol of her singleness. She thought about Jeffrey and his wife, and then about Tim. When she was good and sorry for herself, she turned on the light, pulled a notebook from the drawer of her bedside table, and began to write below where she'd registered her last dream about the monkey and the midget.

Mathilde

1. Accident approx. 4 p.—3-year-old child in car—traveling southbound.
2. Rental car—Escondido—man w/iridescent glasses, beard, limp—fake ID Jay Fargo, NH. Sketch pending.
3. Car finds: Keys (elevator, security lock, safe?)—charm w/birthdate 1-17-95. Coat with monogram E, L. side of all clothes charred—L. boot and Arizona license plate found at bottom of cliff.
4. Concussion, PTS amnesia, new memory intact, non-personal memory okay. Left side injuries prominent over right—(Right-handed—right door of car jammed. Facing backseat/child with left side to fire?)
6. Jane Doe—Fingerprint—0 return. Found person teletypes—0 return. IDs from local newspapers—0 return. Not local.

Adele rubbed her eyes and set the notebook against the foot of her bed. Then she sat back against the pillows and squinted, using her intuition more than her mind.

The department was practically deserted; only the night clerk worked at her desk, fielding the calls. Tim leaned back in his swivel chair and surveyed the storyboard, picking off the "flesh" he and his deputies were in the painstaking process of putting on.

Pull back, squint, and look at the skeleton, he told himself. Sometimes it worked to strip away all the extraneous information—the extra stuff could cover up the answer.

He had a dead business man—shot point-blank in a hotel room seven hundred miles away from home in the middle of the day. No apparent motives. Happy personal life, good job. Well liked. Family vanished into thin air, plucked out of their home without notice. As far as anyone knew, there wasn't any extramarital nooky going on.

Deveraux has called home a dozen times and gotten no answer. Calls neighbor. Neighbor checks apartment and finds family has vanished. Deveraux panics, makes arrangements to go home even though he has two important meetings the following morning. Why did he have cause to panic? Fearful for their safety? Had someone threatened to hurt them—and/or him? When lunch is delivered at 1:25, he's on phone with airlines, but receives a local call and tells the person on the line, "I have it with me." He's got something someone else wants, or maybe he's going to sell something. Was someone blackmailing him? Deveraux wasn't poor, but he wasn't any millionaire either.

He takes a few bites of lunch; someone comes to the door—to do business? To give them whatever he had? He expected them; that much was obvious. And surely, he wasn't expecting to be dead.

Power? Revenge? No apparent power struggles at work—not enough to kill the man, not like he was ready to knock off the top dog. He hadn't stepped on any toes.

Money? He was doing okay, heading up. He wouldn't jeopardize his position. Unless he were getting greedy. Was he blackmailing someone else?

Jealousy? Sex? Lust? Reports from those who knew him said the guy was Mr. Straight Arrow. Tim stopped there. Straight arrow or not, there was a chance he could have had a dalliance no one knew about. A Fatal Attraction number? Maybe the wife had a jealous lover. Maybe he was experimenting with other kinds of thrills and got in with a rough crowd.

Tim bit into a Snickers bar and paced in front of the board, his eyes focusing over and over again on the time frames and the lack of "flesh" on the bones. He was going to have to dig deeper on this one.

His preconceived mental picture of Mrs. Joylyn Dove as a normal, upstanding citizen was not what he got. He'd forgotten to factor in the fact that the fifty-seven-year-old had lived in Los Angeles her entire life. The pollution and the effects of the alien ambience had had their effect on her personality.

"I understand you're good friends with the Deverauxs," he said after explaining why he'd called.

She laughed the laugh of a heavy smoker—or, in L.A., someone who breathed a lot. "As good as friends get in Los Angeles, I guess." Her words grew disjointed, the way they did when someone was trying to talk and light a cigarette at the same time. "We share—top floor—the building."

"How long have you lived there?" he asked.

"Let's see . . ." He imagined her picking a piece of tobacco off her tongue with three-inch-long fingernails painted black. ". . . Milky and I bought this place about the same time as Gerry and Sandie bought theirs, so I'd say about four years or so."

"Milky is your . . . ?" He'd let her fill in the blanks. Husband, child, pet canary.

"Milky is my business partner," she said casually. "Milky is a major boa constrictor."

He had to think about this for a minute. Was she calling some person named Milky a snake, or did she mean . . . ?

"You mean a snake?"

"Exactamundo. We work in the industry together. I'm Milky's trainer and agent."

She said "the industry" as though the words were capitalized and crowned with gold.

"You're a snake charmer?"

"Oh, puleeeez!" she said indignantly. "How vulgar. Milky is a professional animal. You know we were on the Johnny Carson show twice? Milky is the snake you see in all the jungle movies. He's in high demand. Hell, Milky bought this apartment with his own money. We've done three films this year alone. Big films starring major players. We've worked with Demi, Arnold, Harrison, Sean, Brad. Big-league talent."

Tim was stuck on the idea that a boa constrictor had his own bank account. He wondered if the bank knew, and what Milky's last name was. A professional animal, she'd said.

"Okay, well. Can you tell me about your call from Mr. Deveraux?"

"Look, sweetheart, I went over this already with the cops down here," she said, irritated, blowing out smoke. "Can't you get it from them?"

"I want to hear it from you, Mrs. Dove."

"Call me Joy," she said and blew out another lungful. There was a pause. "Gerry called me around noon thirty and said he was really worried about Sandie and the kids because he'd called and left ten messages the night before and no one was home. He asked me if I knew what was going on, and could I go over and check on them."

"You have a key?"

"Exactamundo, baby. After that incident last year, we exchanged keys in case something went wrong."

He debated asking, and couldn't help himself. "You had an incident?"

She blew out again. "Yeah. My apartment got broken into, and the assholes left the door open, so Milky got out. The gay guy downstairs had one of those nasty little dogs? The white fluffy ones? Her name was Baby Babbette. Stupid name."

Tim nodded, seeing the scene unfold in colorful detail.

"This dog was extremely aggressive. Believe me, you can't trust those little dogs—they'll bite your face off in a second. Anyway, Milky ate her. I mean, what do you expect?" Her voice had turned suddenly angry. "Milky's an animal of the jungle—a predator. He's worth six of those hairy yappy things."

The detective wanted to ask about whether or not the thieves had actually gotten away with anything, or if they'd been scared off by the snake. After thinking about it for a second, he decided that Los Angeles robbers were probably used to all sorts of eccentricities in their victims.

"Earlier in the day I'd let Milky out on the patio for a little exercise and I'd thought that it was weird that I hadn't seen the kids or Sandie for two days. I usually see them every day. So I let myself into their apartment and right away I knew something was twisted. It was too quiet. No kids crying. Nothing human happening except the TV, right?"

Someone who worked the industry *would* think the TV was human, Tim thought.

"Then I see the stove, and all the vegetables out and everything is wilted and getting old. The oven was on, and the meat loaf looked like a hundred-year-old cow chip. Sandie would never do that—waste food like that, I mean. Then I looked down in their garage and the minivan is there and everything. I called a couple of Sandie's and my friends and nobody's seen her or the kids, and Gerry said he'd already called her sister and the sitter.

"I called Gerry back and told him. He said he was coming home right away, and that he'd call the cops when he got here."

"Do you remember seeing or hearing anything unusual around the building at all? Like strange cars pulling in the driveway, or people you didn't recognize?"

"No," she said, lighting another cigarette. He imagined her lighting it off the old one. "There's four of us in the building. Nobody saw or heard anything. Nobody next door either."

"Were you and Mrs. Deveraux good friends?"

"Yeah. We talked a lot. Sandie's a nice lady—neurotic at times, but hey . . ." Mrs. Dove laughed. "This is Los Angeles; she couldn't live here if she weren't. It's a requirement."

He couldn't have said it better himself.

"Would she have told you if she were—"

"Fooling around?" she finished for him.

"Yes, or even if she was getting involved with someone, or if there was an entanglement or—?"

"Sandie didn't fuck around," she said, inhaling sharply on her cigarette. "Not that she couldn't; men were constantly after her. But she was a hundred percent true blue to Gerry. They were going to have another kid if he got a promotion at work. She loved the kids more than anything. She wouldn't do it. And believe me, if she was screwing around, I'd a been the first to know."

"What about him? Do you know whether or not Mr. Deveraux—"

"Honey," she said in the tired voice of an old madam, "that man wouldn't so much as get a hard-on in his dreams unless he was dreaming of Sandie. I know, 'cause I've got a friend who works in his office. A couple of fast-lane girls tried him and got turned down flat. And they aren't the types who ever get turned down if you know what I mean.

"No," she puffed again, "not Gerry. No, Gerry was a real . . ." They said it in unison: ". . . straight arrow."

"Listen, Mrs. Dove, I have to ask one more question."

She sucked in another lungful of smoke. "Shoot."

"About Milky . . ."

"Uhn?"

"Does he get to have his own dressing room with a star on the door?"

She ignored the explicit warning on the neck of her rubber hot water bottle and poured in boiling water directly from the kettle. The phone rang. Screwing in the plug, she carried it to her bed. On the fourth and last ring, she picked up the receiver one fifteenth of a second before the answering machine activated.

"I've found my soulmate," Cynthia whispered into the phone.

Next to her, Dr. Dhery slept with mouth hanging open like a roadkill. She gazed at him, still unsure about how she managed to carry him up the three flights of stairs, prop him up in a chair, give him a decent haircut, undress him, get him into the shower, and then drag him into her bed—all without him ever having fully awakened.

"Sure you did," Adele said sarcastically. She'd heard this same thing from Cynthia a thousand times with a thousand different men. "The real question is, does he know it yet?" Adele snapped the hot water bottle into a terry-cloth cover.

Cynthia sighed. "I'm serious, Del. Rymesteade Dhery is the man I've been looking for my whole life. I've never felt so close to a guy without knowing him. I don't even want to screw him, I'm so sure this is the one for me."

"That's a perverse reverse of the way things are usually done, you know." Adele lay down, positioning the hot water bottle under her. For her, the warmth seeping into the small of her back was the equivalent of downing a hundred sleeping pills.

"He told me he noticed me the first day he ever came to work at Ellis," Cynthia continued excitedly.

Adele was sure Dr. Dhery wouldn't notice if there was a live armadillo attached to his collar. He was oblivious and blind—a combo sure to help one glide over the minor divots in life.

"Well?" Cynthia asked. "What do you think? He's really nice, Adele."

There was a pause. "Yeah?" Adele said finally, roused from where she'd dropped off consciousness.

"He hasn't had a date in fifteen years!" Cynthia squealed. "Can you believe it? He's weird—like me."

The pause wasn't interrupted this time. Adele, lost in the middle of the Amazon with a midget named Nancy and a monkey named Wayne, began to snore into the receiver.

In an ongoing effort at behavior modification, Nelson crawled out from under the bed and nipped at Her toes until the terrible noise stopped.

The loud, dreadful noise tore Tim away from his dream of multicolored boa constrictors devouring giant carrots. Instinctively, he made a grab for the Walther next to the bed and lay still, his heart beating for all it was worth. Had someone broken in? An accident in front of the house? Maybe the old lady upstairs had fallen out of bed . . . all 235 pounds of her.

He tried to remember what the sound was which pulled him from unconsciousness. Loud. Grating. He chuckled. It was his own snoring—a condition that grew worse as he grew older and his ear hair grew longer. He'd been meatless for a while, too. Maybe his body really was in some kind of cow-hormone withdrawal that caused him to have nightmares and snore louder than usual.

Flinging himself onto his side, he had a fleeting thought about whether or not Adele would mind a habitual snorer and was almost out for the count when the phone rang.

The digital alarm next to the bed read 4:32 A.M.

Reaching around the lamp, he let his hand rest on the phone

through two more rings. The extra five seconds gave him the waking edge he needed to deal with the disaster waiting at the other end of the line.

SEVEN

SHE COULD HEAR THE PHONE RINGING AS SHE rounded the side of the church next to her house and checked the time: 5:36 A.M. Picking up her pace to a sprint, she bounded up the steps and through the front door. She experienced a rush of positive thinking as she picked up the receiver with a buoyant, "Why yes, I'd love the day off, Mrs. Noel."

"Are you dreaming?" came the amused male voice.

"No, just got back from my run and hoping against hope they were calling me off. What's up?" She suddenly brightened. "You got an ID on Jane Doe?"

"Nothing so nice," Tim said. "I think you might want to come into work early and share in the hubbub going on in ER."

"What is it?" She was already tearing off her running clothes and heading for the shower.

"A woman was murdered in Kentfield. Looks like the same person who did Deveraux."

She changed the shower nozzle to "hard pelt" and turned the water on to extreme hot. Waiting for the water to inch toward lukewarm, she ran to the closet and pulled out a fresh set of scrubs.

"Who's the victim?"

"Bernice Barry. Director of Autodesk in Terra Linda."

"When?"

"Three this morning. The sound of the body hitting the floor woke the gardener who lives in a mother-in-law unit downstairs."

"I'll be there in twenty minutes. Can you hang out that long?"

"For you, I'll wait as long as I have to," he said, and hung up.

119

The seriousness of his tone caused her to falter for a split second until the ice-cold water hit her full blast.

Fifteen minutes later she kissed Nelson goodbye, opened the door, and stepped into Mrs. Coolidge, who was on her tip toes, peering into the high, horizontal window of her living room.

The woman's mouth flapped, making a *blop blop blop* sound.

In a moment of PMS indecision, Adele wavered between breaking into the Crazy Woman laughter or giving the woman a verbal lashing.

"A little early for peeping, isn't it, Mrs. Coolidge?" she said evenly.

"I—I—I was wondering if your young man is around?"

Adele cocked her head. She'd never heard Nelson referred to as her "young man" before by anyone other than herself and her mother. "You want Nelson?"

Mrs. Coolidge clucked, exasperated. "For heaven's sake, not the dog! The young man who was here the other night? The red-haired boy? I—I need someone with muscles. He looked like such a healthy lad. I was wondering . . ." She craned her neck and looked past Adele, into the house, ". . . if he could move the branch that fell across my driveway during the storm ."

Adele pulled the door shut hard enough to make the blinds hit the glass of the door. "My young man left early." *Very early—like, last night.* "And I'm on my way to work. Call the city—they'll send out a nice young policeman or a nice young city worker to help you." She herded her neighbor gently, but firmly, off the porch.

"He certainly looked like a nice young man." Mrs. Coolidge wagged her eyebrows at Adele as best she could while being shoved off the porch. "Have you known him long?"

"Do you mean that in the biblical sense, or the friendly sense?" Adele opened the door (arm) of the Beast and slid into its overstuffed plastic seat (lap).

"Well, I—I . . ." Mrs. Coolidge licked her lips nervously. "For goodness' sake, Adele, that's an awful thing to—to—to . . ."

Adele turned the key in the ignition (pacemaker) and was thankful that the Beast was awake and raring to go the three miles to Ellis. "Mrs. Coolidge," Adele said patiently with a straight face, "have you ever heard of the Big Brothers organization?"

"The one where men volunteer to spend time with fatherless boys?"

Adele nodded, and activated the wipers (eyelids) to clear away the ginkgo leaves that covered the windshield (lenses). She turned on the headlights (eyes).

"Right. Well, the fact of the matter is, the nice young man isn't a hundred percent mine; he's actually Nelson's male role model. I signed up for him through Alpha Dogs R Us? He takes Nelson out, they sniff around, lift legs together, swap mating techniques. You know, cross-species bonding."

Mrs. Coolidge grasped the side of the car and leaned against it, settling in for a good, long talk. She was already relishing the expressions of shock her neighbors would wear after she got done bending their ears with this piece of news. "Oh, you kidder," she cackled a little uncertainly. "My, what a sense of humor."

"I have to go now, Mrs. Coolidge," Adele said, eyeing the squarish body using the side of the Beast as a lounger.

"I know, but you can take a second to tell me about this new man. He's so handsome! Does he get that red hair from his mother or his—?"

Adele faced forward, making her eyes go blank. In a nasal, monotone robot's voice, she suddenly began to chant: "Move away from the car! Move away from the car!"

Astonished, Mrs. Coolidge moved away from the car, watching the Beast's tailgate (buttocks) disappear down Baltimore Avenue through the fallen palm fronds.

The cars were so thick that even the South Forty—the furthermost parking lot from the hospital, normally reserved for the nurses—was full. Across the main road, she spied the tired figure of a night nurse coming toward the lot. Tracking her, she pulled up into position behind a weathered Honda hatchback. Patiently she and the Beast waited while the nurse juggled her lunch bag, purse, morning paper, coffee cup, umbrella, and keys, unlocked the car door, got in, started the car, let it warm up, fought with the gears trying to get it into reverse, checked her hair and lipstick, and painstakingly backed out.

The Honda had cleared the space by approximately one foot when a red Spyder skidded around the corner and pulled in in front of her.

The tree-hugging, laid-back principles of love, peace, spirituality, and joy that were her cushions against the nasties of the world vanished into the fog. In a word, Adele snapped. It was parking-lot rage at its homicidal best.

Before one could say chill out, she ejected from the Beast like a termagant in the throes of a menopausal storm and ripped open the door of the sports car.

Joe Rickey, reporter for the *Pacific Intelligencer*, looked out at her and smiled, unashamed of the wide gap between his front teeth. "Hey! I know you. You're the nurse up on Ward—"

"I've been waiting for that spot for ten minutes," she growled, containing the shrieks waiting at the back of her throat. "Get your car out of there and wait for your own space."

The Jimmy Olson look-alike jumped out of the vehicle, chuckling like a moron with a crew cut. "I've *got* my own space. You snooze, you lose, sweetheart." He glanced at the Beast with undisguised disdain. "That old buffalo couldn't fit in here anyway," he snorted. "See ya."

Not one to waste time, Adele scrutinized the lake of mud that bordered the lot. A sudden calm came over her. His off-key whistling faded as he and his checkered jacket disappeared over the top of the hill. It didn't take her long to park the old buffalo. It would, however, take some time getting the Spyder out of the mud.

The ER was caught up in an abnormally high level of early morning turmoil. There were only two or three drunks sleeping it off in the gurney garage, but the ER lobby was alive with paramedics, investigators, reporters, and television cameras.

She saw Tim before he saw her—standing off to the side of the throng, talking to Paramedic Love. The redhead's right elbow was cupped by his left hand, his chin resting in his right. His hair was disheveled, and his white shirt looked more exhausted than he.

She made herself part of the group without greeting, lightly touching Tim's back. Jellyroll nodded, his face pinched around the eyes from too little sleep.

"Essentially she was dead when we got there," Jelco Love continued. "We didn't even take time to stabilize her, just hooked her up, loaded, and went within three minutes."

"What do you mean 'essentially she was dead'?" Adele asked.

"She was in an agonal rhythm, and was taking maybe four respirations a minute. There was enough blood coming out of her chest to fill a pool. Doing CPR was gross." Prompted by the recollection, Jellyroll checked the sleeves of his jacket for gore. "The lady downstairs says the woman was talking when she found her."

"Did she mention what she was saying?" asked Tim.

The paramedic tossed the question off. "Nothing. You know how trauma victims are. Cerebral anoxia. Death talk. It made no sense."

Adele opened her mouth to press, but Tim beat her to it: "In a homicide, any and every thing could be a lead."

Jellyroll waved a hand, nettled at being pushed over a point he felt was useless. "I don't know. She said something about the lady repeating, 'tell . . . tell . . .' Like tell so and so I love him, or tell my husband the diamonds are hidden under the geranium pot."

"That was all?" Adele asked.

"Yeah." Jellyroll coughed and waved to his partner, who was coming out of the ER with the ambulance stretcher freshly made up and loaded down with the monitor and defibrillator. "But that's hearsay. She wasn't saying dickshit by the time we got there." He made his way quickly toward his partner, who was already at the back of the rig.

"Hey, I gotta run." Jellyroll glanced back over his shoulder. "Tell Mathilde I'll try to stop by sometime this morning."

Adele lifted her chin in answer. "Who was assigned as lead on this one?" she asked before Jellyroll was out of sight.

Tim continued to scan the ER lobby. "Bill Krenshaw. He called from the scene; thought it might be related to the Sweetwater murder." The detective's mein abruptly changed to one of the professional-cop-on-business as he greeted an approaching man of striking appearance. "Hey, Bill. How's it going?"

Bill Krenshaw was in his thirties; his confident swagger broadcasted an attitude. He wore his black hair slicked back into a short ponytail and was dressed in a fashionable baggy black suit and white collarless shirt. Detective Krenshaw nodded to Adele, turning an investigative eye on her. Seemingly satisfied that she wasn't in any way a threat or of use to him, he herded Tim off to another part of the lobby.

As the two detectives went into a huddle, their heads close together, Adele made herself as inconspicuous as possible. If the nursing office spotted her, they'd insist she head up to Ward 8 to help night shift get ready for report—without paying for her time. They would contend it was her duty to the hospital.

Finding a place to sit in the lobby was like trying to find a place to park. Finally, she picked up a day-old *San Francisco Chronicle* and sat down next to a man with a bulbous red nose and an instant ice pack strapped to his ankle with an elastic bandage that had lost its stretch. She opened to the personals and browsed through the various categories of what gender was seeking what gender and noted with some amusement that the category that had collected the most advertisements was Unconventional Arrangements. She'd begun reading a pitch for those interested in combining karaoke and kink when the elderly man tapped her on the arm.

"You're welcome to read my paper," he said, turning his rheumy blue eyes on her, and chewing what she recognized from the smell as Juicy Fruit gum. "I've been waiting since last night to see the doctor."

"Oh, I'm so sorry, I didn't know the paper was yours . . . I . . ." She stopped. "You've been here since last *night*?"

The man nodded, all movements painful except his jaw. "I slipped on the wet steps in front of the house. Hurt my ankle. I think it's broke."

Adele sighed. It was another example of managed care—lots of managed, not much care. "How's that ice pack? Still cold?"

"The hell it is," the man said, chomping angrily. "I'm heating it up for my coffee water."

Adele set her purse down and without a word went behind the closed doors of the ER. Taking a large exam glove from the box near the ice maker, she filled it with crushed ice and tied it off. On her way back through the department, she passed a trauma room that was littered with post-resuscitation rubbish. She looked past the tubes, blood, and IV poles, and studied the victim lying naked on the gurney. Dyed black hair was disheveled and matted, but the style was still recognizable as one frequently sported by middle-aged female executives. Her manicured nails, caked with blood, were purple. Adele quietly studied the bloodless face. Wrinkled, puffy—probably a heavy smoker. In the corner was what had once been a pink silk nightdress. It was torn apart and stiff with dark blood.

Behind her someone approached, rubber soles screeching. "May I help you?" came the terse voice.

Adele turned. The sallow face of the nurse was exhausted, the eyes lackluster. A pair of skinny graying braids were fastened over the top of her head. Strands had escaped and stuck out wildly.

"You've got a patient who's been waiting outside in the lobby for about seven hours with a broken ankle." She held up the makeshift ice bag. "I'm bringing him an ice bag."

The nurse didn't react in any way to her answer, but went inside the room and deliberately removed the doorstop. The door slammed in Adele's face.

The nurse did not look up from her task of readying the body for the coroner when Adele pushed the door back open.

"Who would I speak to about getting this man in to be seen sometime before his next birthday? He's in pain and he's older than—"

"I don't know." The ER nurse unclamped the connecting tubing from the endotracheal tube to the ventilator. "Just don't talk to me about it," she said. "It's been hell. I haven't sat down once since I got here. Right now I wouldn't care if my daughter was out there bleeding to death."

Adele knew how the nurse felt at that moment—a well gone dry.

"There were only two of us scheduled and we've had every psycho in the state in here," the nurse said in a less bitter tone.

She clamped the urinary drainage bag and set it in the dirty utility sink. "Tell the inside clerk about the ankle," she said wearily. "His chart probably got lost in the shuffle."

"Thank you." Adele reached for the door. At the last minute, she turned around. "You are appreciated, you know. What you do here does make a difference. Hang on."

"Oh, sure," she sneered. "Hang on to what? They keep cutting back the staff and heaping on more work. We can't have an opinion on what goddamned IV catheter to use, let alone how to practice. Everytime you turn around, some nurse is getting fired for some minor infraction. I'm waiting until my son gets out of school. Then it's goodbye to this crap."

"Come to the nurses' march in San Francisco. It's—"

"Jesus!" The woman looked around at the two doors on opposite sides of the room. "Shut up about that around here, will you? Are you trying to get me fired?"

"Not trying to get you fired, only trying to save the profession. Come if you can."

The nurse waved her away. "I've got a kid to feed. No thanks."

Adele told the clerk in the main room about the forgotten patient with the broken ankle and hurried back to the lobby, where Tim was sitting talking to the old man. Both of them were smiling, as though they shared a joke only the two of them could understand. The man's injured foot had been elevated on an empty computer paper box. Tim watched as she placed the ice pack on the old man's ankle. He took her purse and held it out to her. "Walk me to my car."

They wished the old man luck, turned down his offerings of a couple of bright yellow sticks of Juicy Fruit, and headed out the front entrance of Ellis. To her relief he was not parked near the South Forty mud flats. At the Camry they turned to face each other.

"So?" she said.

Ill at ease, Tim shifted his eyes to the entrance of the hospital, where Detective Krenshaw was smoking a cigarette, talking to several other detectives. Krenshaw had a reputation for being a hardass department man. He'd go off the deep end if he knew he was sharing sensitive developments with an outsider, let alone how adept she could be at putting things together.

"So, nothing much. A break-in and homicide."

"Oh come on," Adele scoffed gently, deliberately seeking his eyes. "You didn't call me over here to tell me that."

In one fluid movement, Tim reached out and took her hand, smiling like a schoolboy. "Play along," he said in a voice that did not match the smile. "I can't afford to have anyone think I'm passing out information. Krenshaw has eyes in that ponytail." His smile transformed into a genuine one. "Flirt with me."

She blushed, smiled coyly, and arranged his tie knot. "Okay, so bring me up to speed."

"It's a mirror of the Deveraux murder. Same caliber gun, same style of killing. Our lab guys are pretty sure the fibers found near this body are the same as those found on Deveraux's body."

"What time did it happen?"

"The tenant downstairs said a crash woke her up a few minutes before three." He laughed. She followed suit.

"I don't need any more convincing this is a professional," Tim said. "Most street criminals are stupid. They always screw up somewhere."

"What about witnesses?" She touched his shirt and then lifted up her hair and let it drop. She licked her lips; he licked his. Acting out the mating dance, she marveled at how truly strange the varied behaviors were.

"That's a maybe." He stood up and stretched, flexing his muscles for good measure. "A neighbor across the street was working on his computer when he heard a car start. He saw a dark colored Jeep traveling without its lights. He wasn't sure where it had been parked, but he's sure it was driven by a man wearing a cop uniform. Krenshaw's crew are checking with the other residents in the area."

"So the murderer dressed as a policeman, wakes the victim, and tells her some story about how he has to come in and check the premises for whatever reason." Adele giggled and poked him in the chest. "Scared that someone might be in or around her house, she lets him in, and bang. Sounds damned smart to me."

He squeezed the tip of her nose, smiled, and got into the

Camry. "I'm cutting you off now, Monsarrat. You're getting too attached to my, I emphasize the pronoun *my*, case. Your turn. Anything new on Jane Doe?"

She leaned down and rested her arms against the car. "The shrink saw her yesterday. It's too soon to expect anything from that. I went through what was left of her clothes." She shifted on her feet. "There was a monogrammed E on the inside of her jacket. I'm going to try and jolt her memory a little today. I'll let you know what happens." She laughed and rested a finger on his lips. They were cool and soft. Her face started forward to kiss them when she yanked herself back. That was going too far.

"Jellyroll—the paramedic you were just talking to in the lobby? He and Jane Doe have a sort of thing for each other. It's kinda cute, actually." She punched him lightly on the arm. "You're going to let me know if you find any information waiting for you when you get back to the office, right?"

"Why, of course," he dripped sarcasm. "I always tell you everything I know, unlike you, who gives out details like they're gold ingots."

Cynthia wore the limerance glow like a woman with wings and no worries.

Adele was cynical. She'd seen the same glow on her friend too many times before. Dealing with Cynthia's romantic exploits, she decided, was rather like going through Liz Taylor's wedding albums.

They sat at the nurses' charting desk, Adele going over her patient information cards while Cynthia chattered on about Rymesteade who, through familiarity, had been bastardized to simply "Rhyme."

803A: 63 F—Post-stoma revision with secondary ileus: Nasogastric tube, antibiotics, watch fever.

"He's wonderful, Del."

"Uh-huh." *815B: Unknown age—Female suffering from Too Damned Much Money Syndrome: Pamper, keep door closed, make sure phone, tissues, Jenny Craig diet snacks and full makeup case are within reach.*

"I woke up at four o'clock this morning and he was lying there, watching me sleep and taking my pulse."

"Oh?" *812A: Jane Doe approx. 36—pain control if needed, give her her boots, ask about keys, talk to Jeff after he talks to her, dressing changes, check labs.*

"When I asked him what he was doing, do you know what he said?"

"No." *819A: 40 M—Hepatitis C with bleeding after biopsy of liver: watch abdomen for distention and change in pain. Watch hematocrit and take to CT scanner. Check urine output—none since midnight.*

"He said that I have a pronounced sinus arrhythmia." Cynthia sighed.

"Oh, uh-huh." *819B: 52 F—Abdominal pain: status post ileocecal resection: Watch bowel tones, fever, abd. distention, check for bleeding.*

"He said I needed to have the mole on my left shoulder removed and biopsied."

"That's nice." *819C: 39 M—Gunshot Wound to R. leg—Twin Cities Cop: Deal with Loyalty to the Blue Brothers problem first thing. Keep the visitors to a dull roar! Keep them from meandering the halls! Threaten if necessary. Patient: watch fever, antibiotics, pain meds, dressing changes, bowel care—offer milk of magnesia or Dulcolax suppositories.*

"And that I need to have my sugar checked, because my sweat smells like I might be borderline diabetic."

"Hmmm." *819D: 31 M—MVA/broken right fibula, bruise on sternum: observe for symps/signs cardiac tamponade, check cardiac labs, pain control.*

"And you know that fungus I have on my nails? Well, he said he could give me a cream that would take it away completely."

"Oh, uh-huh. That's nice." *802A: 24 M—MVA from yesterday/sl. more stable!!—more of the same except better.*

"He also told me that I should have this cyst under my chin taken out and—"

Adele looked up, exasperated. "Christ on a bike, Cynthia, what is this—a romance or a goddamned house call?"

Cynthia was unruffled. She gazed at the notes on her report sheet, not seeing them. "Then we sort of made up our own stress test."

Adele sighed, motioning her to go on.

"It was his first time, you know."

Her mouth dropped open. "You deflowered the poor bastard?"

Cynthia nodded, lustily pleased about the whole damned thing. "For two hours."

Adele hit her forehead with the palm of her hand and got up. "Whatever sanity he had is really going to go to hell in a handbasket now."

The room was neat and clean, everything in its place. No messy cellophane shucks from graham cracker packages strewn about the bed and floor, no crumbs or spilled juices on the linen. Adele regarded Mathilde in silence. She was a woman who had a need to be exact and orderly. Her hair was immaculate and pulled into a tidy ponytail; her hospital gown and white sheets were crisp and smelled of fresh laundry instead of perspiration and sickness.

Setting down the large glass of orange juice on the side table, Adele pulled the pair of boots out of a plastic bag and held them up for Mathilde to see. For a nanosecond, Adele would swear she saw recognition in the steady gray eyes, but it passed before she could be sure. The moment lodged at the back of her mind the way a stone sometimes got stuck in her shoe while she was running. She wished she had a videotape of the moment, to play over.

"I believe these are yours," she said. "Do they bring up any memories for you?"

"Was I wearing them at the accident?" Mathilde asked, as though the accident were an event she had attended long ago.

"I think so. You came in wearing one, and the other I found at the scene. Want to try them on?"

Mathilde stared at them uncertainly and shrugged. "Why not?"

She unhooked her left hand from the sling and reluctantly slid her legs off the side of the bed. Adele brought out a pair of white cotton socks that she'd thought to bring with her. When the socks and shoes were in place, Mathilde walked around the room with the light step of a ballet dancer. "Strange to be walking around in shoes that I walked in when I was still whoever I was."

"If only shoe tongues could talk, huh?"

"Maybe," Mathilde said slowly. "I've been thinking a lot. Maybe I'm better off not knowing who I was. Maybe I wasn't such a good person."

It was an interesting thought, Adele had to admit. "Well, I doubt you were a murderer or anything like that," she said with a slight hesitation. She was thinking of the man who'd rented the car Mathilde was driving. "You don't have the feel of a murderer."

Mathilde stared at her, surprised. "How can you say that? Have you known any murderers?"

"A few," she said, digging in her pocket for the keys she'd found in the car. "What about these? Do you recognize them?"

A curious expression came over Mathilde's face. When she finally looked at Adele, it was clear that the keys were familiar to her, but not entirely. She fingered the elevator key, weighing it in her hand.

Adele watched her neck while Mathilde examined the key, concentrating. The carotid pulse and the rate of her respirations doubled.

"I'm not sure," she said faintly. "I don't know."

Adele was aware she was treading on ground she wasn't sure of. She wished she'd thought to ask Jeff how much to tell and what to keep back. She tested the ice. "It's to a freight elevator."

"How do you know that?"

"I took it to a key expert. It wasn't difficult."

The steel gray eyes narrowed. "Why would you do that?" Mathilde asked, her voice rising and shaky. "Why are you going to all this trouble? Do you think you know me or something?"

"Mathilde," Adele said softly, "all I'm doing is trying to help find out who you are."

Mathilde forced a smile. "Like I said, I don't know if that's a good thing."

"Can you stand one more test?"

Mathilde became guarded, unsure. "What?"

Heart jackhammering in her chest, Adele pulled out the black glasses case and snapped it open. In a single movement, she put the iridescent glasses on and faced the woman.

If she thought she'd needed a video before, she had no need

of one now. The change in the woman was immediate and dramatic. Adele had seen patients in full cardiac arrest look better.

Reaching back for the bed, Mathilde made a noise in her throat and sunk down onto her haunches, her eyes still riveted on the glasses.

Scared that she had upset the woman enough to cause some sort of setback, Adele took off the glasses and kneeled down in front of her. "What's going through your mind?" she asked. "What did you remember?"

Mathilde covered her face and began to rock. Her voice, when it came, came in gulps. "Those . . . I remember there was a man. I don't know why, but I'm afraid of him."

"What's his name?"

Mathilde shook her head. "I don't know . . . I can't . . ." Her face crumbled and she began to cry. "I'm frightened."

The nurse took her patient into her arms and rocked with her, stroking her hair. "Shhh. It's okay. I'm so sorry, Mathilde. I shouldn't have done that."

"How did you . . . ? Did you find those glasses in the car?"

Adele shook her head. "They're similar to the ones worn by the man who rented the car you were driving."

"Who is he?"

"I don't know. The IDs he gave the car rental agency were phony." Adele helped her patient to her feet. "Come on, you need to drink your orange juice. Your potassium is on the low side this morning."

Stricken anew with concern, Mathilde searched Adele's eyes. "Is that bad, the low potassium, I mean? Will it hurt my memory? Is it why I feel so tired? Can it be taken care of?"

Adele laughed. "I said it was a little low, I didn't say we needed to call a code. It's not anything that can't be corrected with some OJ and a banana, or, if you're a junk food person, a bag of potato chips and a candy bar will do. It won't hurt your memory unless you have way too much or way too little, and if it were that bad, you'd be too worried about your heart stopping to worry about your memory."

She prepared for the dressing changes, placing packages of sterile gauze, tongue depressors, sterile gloves and Silvadene on the bedside table. Once the dressings were removed, Adele marveled at how well the burns were healing. The drainage was minimal on the right, and pink, healed flesh could be seen. She scraped off the pseudo eschar—the tan-colored cottage cheese that represented dead tissue—from the deeper burns on the left hand, noting with great satisfaction there was some pink tissue underneath.

The knock at the door was followed by Tina's voice and then her head coming around the opening. "Supervisor is at the desk," the clerk said in her churlish tone. "She wants to talk to you." When Adele didn't respond appropriately—that is to say, go white with fear and run out the door—she added: "Stat!"

"Tell her I'm busy tending lives," Adele said casually. "You can remind her that's what the hospital pays me for."

"Remind her yourself, babe," Tina said. "I'm not getting caught in any frontline crossfire."

Adele finished her assessment and, fully irritated, went to the desk to face the day supervisor.

Mattie Noel was a true administrative nurse: she'd graduated from nursing school and immediately gone on to receive her master's in administration, and then her FAAN (Fellows of American Academy of Nurses—or, in Adele's interpretation, Furthest Away from Actual Nursing). The last time the woman had direct physical contact with a sick person was about fifteen years before when a drunk in the ER mistook her for a pay phone and tried to dial her breast.

It was Adele's observation that a nurse with lots of theory and academic degrees but no practical, hands-on bedside experience, was indeed a dangerous person in health care.

Clipboard perpetually clamped to her bosom like a breastplate of armor or a nursing child, Mrs. Noel stood at the nurses' station brooding over a chart. Her salt-and-pepper hair was shaved on the back and sides, but the top she kept long and curly.

From ten feet away, Adele could read the name on the chart: JANE DOE. Her heart sank. The chart reviewers had been there—sneaked in while she was gone.

"Hello, Ardel. I need to talk to you about our Jane Doe problem. I understand she's your patient?"

"That she is, Ms. Noel." Adele rubbed her hand over her face. "Care to tell me what the Jane Doe problem is exactly?"

"We need to get the doctors geared toward moving Ms. Doe toward discharge as quickly as possible. I see that her second

CAT scan came back negative. We've kept her far beyond the limits of what any insurance company will cover—*if* she even has insurance."

"First of all, the woman isn't ready for discharge." Adele counted off the points on her fingers. "Second of all, I don't think her doctors would agree with your or the chart reviewer's opinion, and third, what, pray tell, happened to Ellis's promise to the public that she'd be taken care of until her family could be located?"

"Ellis has stood by that promise for four days, and we have subsequently taken a financial loss on this woman's recovery, but everything must have its limit, Ardel. After all, we're not running a flophouse here."

Mrs. Noel fingered the chart. The tic in her eyelid was fluttering madly. "The charge reviewers feel she should be medically cleared for discharge."

"Chart reviewers don't know medicine from a hole in the ground." Adele could feel her neck veins begin to fill and distend. She tried to remember the adage that her mother had taught her: 'Don't wrestle with a pig; all that happens is you get dirty and the pig loves it.'

"Chart reviewers are bean counters," she continued. "They aren't medical people. All they know is dollar amounts. They look at the diagnosis, half the time don't even know what the hell it means—let alone give a shit—and look it up on a list that tells them how long an insurance company will pay and how much. They could care less about the patient and what the intricacies of the individual and his family are. All they care about is money. It makes me want to puke . . ."

Adele stopped. She'd lost control of her temper and knew she should walk away. She turned and started blindly down a hall.

"Come back here right now!" demanded Mrs. Noel. "We aren't done."

Five yards down the hall, Adele slowed. She was a patient advocate first and foremost, not a politician. Counting to ten, she turned on her heel and went back to Mrs. Noel.

"Mrs. Noel," she began in a reasonably calm voice, "the patient has been here three days. She is still amnesic, she still has some significant burns to both hands which require attention and some pain control. Psychiatric Services have evaluated her merely once. Can't we give her a break? The poor woman is a wreck; it's bad enough she doesn't have any idea who she is, but she may have lost a child."

Adele sighed. "Please. Can't we let her go for a day or two more and then transfer her to Crisis?"

The supervisor continued to look determined, but there was a sort of softening of her jowls and the hard lines around her mouth. "It isn't my decision," she said finally. "Of course we wouldn't move her out before tomorrow, but I think two more days is pushing our luck."

"Will you put in a word for her?" Adele asked, reaching for a mug of coffee that she'd left on the nurses' desk. "Keeping her is the best kind of publicity. It shows the public their community hospital still has some modicum of human compassion."

Mattie looked at Adele. Rumors about this particular Ward 8 employee had flowed fast, filthy, and furious over the years. Everything from fornication with deviates to witchery. Not much of a stretch, it was true. But, she was a good nurse and there was a certain truth to her words about the publicity. As of late, there had been an exodus of patients out of the private sector and into the HMOs.

Mrs. Noel sighed a consenting sigh and threw up her hands. "Okay, okay. I'll see what they say, but you'd better prepare her. She's got about nineteen hundred dollars in cash waiting for her downstairs, so it's not like she'll be homeless."

"Nineteen hundred dollars? Where did that come from?"

"Donations. They've been pouring in since the night the story came out." The supervisor pushed up her glasses, her demeanor changing from dragon to doe. "Ardel?"

"It's Adele."

"Sorry. Adele, do you think you might be able to work a double tonight? We're desperate. I've called everyone on the staff list and—"

"No."

"How about until three A.M.?"

"With the day off tomorrow?"

"No. We're short-staffed tomorrow, too. I couldn't—"

"Have you lost your mind?" Adele asked, astonished by the woman's brass. "I can't work twenty hours, get three hours' sleep, and turn around and work another twelve. I'd kill somebody or myself." She cocked her head to the side. "Isn't that against labor laws?"

"It's against the law only if you complain about it." The supervisor studied her fingernails. "I'd make sure you got double time for the last four hours of night shift, and time and a half for your regular seven A to seven P shift tomorrow. That's good money, dear."

Adele chewed her lip thoughtfully. She'd done a suicide shift only once before when she was younger and didn't know it was called a suicide shift because toward the last few hours of it you wished you were dead.

"I won't do it," she said, finally going with her better judgment. "But I'll tell you who will and be glad for the hours."

Supervisor Noel, bloodhound on the scent: "Who?"

"Does Jane Doe get a guaranteed forty-eight hours?"

Mrs Noel winced. "Well, I don't know . . ."

"Guarantee her forty-eight hours and no backtracking—on your word of honor."

"Okay. Who's this willing party?"

"O'Neil."

Cynthia came around the corner, ambulating a post-op bypass patient at the rate of about two feet a minute. "Is my name being taken in vain?" she asked, eyeing the two women.

"Is your new friend still on the suicide schedule?" Adele asked.

Cynthia nodded.

"Well, Mrs. Noel here is going to give you an opportunity of a lifetime. She's offered to let you work the same hours for all sorts of wonderful monetary compensation."

"Really?" Cynthia said, her eyes gleaming.

"Think of the possibilities, Cyn," Adele said. "The supply room? Nobody ever goes into the supply room at night. You'll be working thirty-two hours and only get four hours of sleep. Think of all the fun you can have creating new and unusual charting styles—together. You might even be able to collaborate on a book together: *Effects of Sleep Deprivation on Charting: Humor in Health Care*—you'd have a runaway bestseller."

"What are you talking about?" Mattie Noel asked, growing suspicious. She'd began to wonder if Cynthia would be a good substitute, although it didn't really matter—a body was a body—psychotic, deviant baby-sitters or not, who cared?

"We're discussing benefits," answered Cynthia. "Now tell me about these horrible hours and great pay."

EIGHT

MALLOY TOOK OVER FOR TINA AT 3, AND THE mood at the charge desk changed from darkly depressive to buoyant in the time it took the shrewish clerk to put on her raincoat and leave. Smiling in that Right Path sort of way, Malloy turned off the rock station and put on his *Tibetan Bells* tape, then turned down the bright fluorescent lights to a level that made the place feel downright Zen-like.

Jeffrey Lavine came up behind Adele while she sat in the computer corner charting, her forehead resting against the top of the monitor.

"So you changed from working eight-hour shifts to twelve?" he asked, glancing at his watch—something gold and expensive.

Startled, she pulled away from the monitor and rubbed her forehead where she knew there would be an ugly red mark. "For now. I'm saving up money for Nelson's college education. How was the ballet?" She couldn't help herself.

"Fabulous," he said, taking off his Burberry. "Why do you work so much? What are you trying to avoid?"

"Shrinks." She rolled her eyes. "Never satisfied to take people at face value." She went to the chart rack, and handed him Jane Doe's. "For your information, Doc, my dog and I have to eat. My landlord lives next door so I can't skip the rent—not to mention car expenses."

The psychiatrist nodded in the understanding manner shrinks learn in Comforting Gestures 101. "So what's expensive?" he said in a burlesque Yiddish accent. "Your rent isn't exorbitant, you and your dog eat rabbit food, your clothes come from shmatte city, and you drive a self-maintaining junk heap."

"Okay, then how about this: I'm saving up for a trip around

the world. As soon as I have enough money, I'll take off and catch up on the life I'm missing now."

His mouth only twitched at her jest. "Why do you make a joke of it, Adele? You're a vital, intelligent, and beautiful woman. Go find an Italian prince or an English lord. Share yourself with someone; complete yourself. Make the effort to love."

"I *am* happy," she protested vehemently. "I'm content with my life as it is. I don't need another person in order to feel complete." For a second, she thought of Tim and wondered if the longing she felt for him could be interpreted as need. "I constantly make the effort to love." She waved her hand around to indicate the ward. "What do you call what I do for a living?"

All at once, she remembered why she'd said no to him. It was because he had needed her to complete himself. She'd felt his need as a sailor feels an anchor dragging on the bottom of the sea. Underlying his love would be the need, strangling her, cutting off her ability to love him as a free spirit.

He opened the chart, sighing in resignation. "I give up, but methinks the lady doth protest too much. How's our patient?"

"Improving physically. Administration is going to eighty-six her in a couple of days."

"I thought—"

"So did I, but apparently Ellis Hospital goodwill has a time limit."

Jeff raised his head in understanding. "Ah, I see. Well, I'll see what I can do—maybe I'll talk to her primary doctor and get her transferred to Psych. I admit people to Psych for a lot less than what she's suffering from." He stroked his beard with his fingers. "It's an extreme measure, but I'm toying with the idea of doing an interview under Amytal—if she'd permit it."

"What if she doesn't?"

He shrugged. "I doubt I'll be able to get her admitted without insurance. If that happens, I'll continue to see her on an outpatient basis."

Adele hesitated. "There was an incident this morning. I'm not sure whether I did more harm than good, but I think you should know what her responses were."

He pinched his lips between his fingers and leaned back while she explained Mathilde's reactions to the iridescent glasses. When she was finished, Jeffrey wore a mildly astonished expression. He sat studying her, blinking repeatedly.

"Del, I think you take your investigative skills too seriously."

That, she recalled, was the other reason she'd refused him. He had never understood her deep love of investigation—analyzing how the pieces fit together. "Come on, Jeff. Don't you think this gives you something to work with—these memories about a farmhouse and a man she's afraid of?"

Jeffrey shook his head. "Psychiatry isn't like being a detective . . . It's more like working in an information booth at a psychological Disneyland or a house of horrors."

"So what does that mean?"

"It means that understanding and fifty cents won't buy you a cup of coffee."

After she stopped laughing, he said, "Really, modern psychiatry is a mix of so many things. It's reparenting, it's loving the person, it's being unconditional, it's having understanding, it's providing stress reduction and giving positive sense of self-esteem, it's giving practical advice, it's providing ways to reduce anxiety and offering insight into destructive patterns, it's a consistent process of refining behaviors so it produces the desired state of mind. The real essence of it is really outside the realm of understanding."

He wagged a thoughtful finger at her. "See, Adele—you're the type of woman who, from time to time, separates herself from her surrounding reality and enjoys a moment of appreciating the bizarre nature of things. You delight in the twisted, despite putting on a decent show of being normal and responsible. You get away with it because you're so goddamned bright and charming and beautiful."

He grinned. "When you do these wild things in the name of sleuthing, it's akin to watching a frog respond when one inserts a pin in its spinal cord. It is precisely with a similar combination of indifference and spellbound fascination that you do things like you did with my patient this morning. And I'm totally powerless to chastise you for any breach in professionalism because I'm influenced by my admiration of your ability to go into your own personal world of entertainment while still managing to attend to the mundane medical care without skipping a beat."

Adele crossed her arms and continued to stare at him without blinking. "Well," she said, "I'm ready for a cigarette. How about you?"

They both laughed, until Malloy shushed them into silence.

"Thank you for the wonderful profile analysis." Adele smiled at him after they'd gotten themselves under control. "I take that as a compliment."

"As well you should." He leaned very close. She stiffened, terrified that he would kiss her, or that she might kiss him. At the last nanosecond, they both moved their heads away, the end result being an embarrassingly klutzy hug.

Locked inside the gray metal walls of the nurses' locker-room toilet, Adele dialed Tim's pager and entered the number of the toilet phone, adding the numeric code for CALL NOW! Two minutes and fifty-two seconds later, the phone rang.

"How about business connections?" she said upon picking it up. "Did Deveraux ever work for this woman or vice versa?"

"Way ahead of you," said Tim, who'd received the information from Detective Cini only an hour before. "They both worked for a San Francisco corporation called Citadel. Ever hear of it?"

Her mind rapidly sorted through the files and came up with a fat one marked "Cynthia's Heartkill." She pictured a wimpy-looking character who smoked a pipe and had warts all over his fingers.

"Yeah. Our mutual girlfriend used to date a computer nerd who worked there. He traveled to lots of foreign countries hawking satellite dishes or something. Their logo is 'Uniting the world through better communications.' I think it's telecommunications on a big scale."

"I'm headed over there to talk to the CEO right now," Tim said. "You want to have dinner tonight?"

She ran a fingernail over a patch of graffiti: THERE'S MORE THAN MEMORY, BUT I DON'T REMEMBER WHAT IT WAS. "Thanks, but I'm on till seven then I'm off to a march meeting."

"Tell me you don't mean the nurses' march in San Francisco in December."

"You know about the nurses' march on City Hall?"

"All the agencies in the area got notices about it. Are you actually going to be a part of that?"

"I'm one of the speakers. Why would they send notices about it to the law enforcement agencies?"

"Lower the hackles, Adele. Any time there's a major demonstration, for good cause or not, notices are sent out."

"That doesn't answer the question," she said bluntly. Her fingers went to the graffiti she liked the best: NURSES ARE BATTERED WOMEN IN UNIFORM. She thought she might use it as a banner slogan.

"*Why* are the law enforcement agencies notified?"

He sensed a sudden tension in her, one he'd run into before with true-blue-fighting-for-the-good-cause people. In a way he admired those souls who fought so wholeheartedly for what they believed, but he also knew it was a way to get oneself killed.

"Sympathetic insurrections," he said, trying desperately to sound casual and informative, like a talking head in a training video. "Outbreaks of violence or public demonstrations in surrounding areas. Nurses make up ten percent of the workforce. That's a significant group."

Sulky defiance flared in her as she unfolded her long bones and stood straight. "Why is it that if a woman feels strongly about something in this culture, she's automatically made part of the lunatic fringe? If she gets emotional, she's probably having PMS or menopause, and if she gets angry—she's a bitch or a psycho? Instead of trying to quell the nurses, the police ought to listen to what they have to say. They might find themselves wearing the same shoes some day when the departments fall under the wheels of redesign."

"Adele, for Christ's sake, be reasonable. No one said anything about trying to quell them. There'll be officers there to make sure things stay peaceful."

Something irrelevant whisked into Timothy's mind. LAPD called. Detective Frazer. A body—no, bodies had been found.

"Listen, I have to go. I've got to call LAPD before I go to the city. I don't want to get caught in traffic."

They both laughed, breaking the tension. In recent years traffic in the Bay area had grown into a nightmare of congestion, right up there with the freeways of Los Angeles. Going into or out of San Francisco was a bumper-to-bumper proposition twenty hours a day.

"Call me when you get some information on Jane Doe, will you? Ellis is going to axe her in two days."

"I've got Rule working on it. When he gives me something, I'll call you right away." Through the window of his door, he could see the department secretary wave her arms. She mouthed "L-A-P-D" holding her hand with splayed-out little finger and thumb to her ear in the universal sign for "phone."

He took the blue plastic bottle of antacid from his top drawer and drank freely. Then he picked up line two to hear the full baritone voice of Detective Jack Frazer.

"Howdy. You guys must be busy up there."

"A whole lot busier than I want to be," Tim answered, wiping the mustache of white antacid off his upper lip. "What's up, Jack?"

"We found our missings. A hunter discovered the bodies of the Deveraux woman and one of the kids in the woods east of Paso Robles. They were both shot at close range in the chest with a twenty-two. Coroner thinks they've been dead about three, maybe four days. San Luis Obispo set up Paso with a couple of search-and-rescue dogs to look for the other kid."

Tim sucked in his breath. "Holy shit," he mumbled, and sat down hard. The involvement of murdered children gave everything an evil hue. "How did you ID them?"

"They left her purse with her. Nothing was touched; had her license, money, and everything still in it. The coroner cleaned her up and took Polaroids before he did the postmortem. I just got back from running them by the neighbor. She confirmed the ID as Sandie Deveraux and her older daughter."

"Did you confirm with family?"

"Better than that," Jack Frazer said. "One of our boys found dental bills at the apartment and double-checked with the dental records. No doubt it's them."

"What about the other child?"

"Not a sign. Paso Robles has run those dogs all over that hill and the two miles surrounding it."

Tim swallowed. It was a long shot, but what the fuck? "Do you have both of the Deveraux kids' birthdates there?"

There was the rustling of paper as Jack Frazer sorted through the six-inch-high pile of correspondence and files that covered his desk like a thick wall-to-wall carpet. "If you're thinking of ordering birthday cakes, Tim, you're a little late," the man said, holding the phone between his shoulder and his chin.

Tim didn't acknowledge the remark with so much as a smile. Any insensitivity around the death of children was sacrilegious at best.

"Okay," said Detective Frazer. "The one we have is confirmed as Anna Marie, born April fourth, nineteen ninety-three, and the missing girl is Bettina Claudette, born January seventeenth, nineteen ninety-five. Why are you asking? You think you got a lead?"

Tim held the plastic Baggie containing the charm up to the light and stared at the date inscribed. He took another swig of Mylanta before answering. "What would you think the odds are that the cremains of a child we pulled from a burned vehicle up here would have the same birthdate as the missing Deveraux girl?"

"About one in a gazillion, I'd guess."

"I think they can call off the dogs, sergeant," Tim said in a weary, cheerless voice. "I don't think they're going to find the other missing; I think we've got her right here."

"What are you talking about?"

Tim leaned back and related the details of the accident. "See if you can locate any dental or medical records down there on Bettina Claudette so we can confirm the ID."

"Sure. I'll have one of my guys check with Budget Rental agency again, too. See if we can turn up something." Then, in a dejected voice, Frazer said, "You realize this makes us both co-agencies with the yokels at Paso Robles."

The city slickers groaned in unison.

Detective Frazer studied photos taken from a family album of Sandie Deveraux and her two little girls. One of the children—the one found in Paso Robles with her mother—resembled his granddaughter. "I'm going to encourage Paso Robles PD to check the local motels, gas stations, and quick stops. Maybe you can push them from that end."

One of them made reference to the Barney Fife Brigade and they guffawed, only a little ashamed of themselves.

"We've got another problem up here that you might find interesting," Tim said, flicking at a loose corner of the Mylanta label. "We had another one-eighty-seven victim last night with a lot of similarities to the Deveraux homicide. Same kind of weapon, same type of wound. I'm pretty sure it's the same shooter."

"You got a connection between the victims?"

"Both victims worked for a San Francisco telecommunications company called Citadel. I was headed over there when you called."

Tim sucked in his cheeks. "Do me a favor and check with Paso Robles' lab. See if they found anything like Hollofil or kapok fibers on or around the bodies. Both our one-eighty-sevens had fibers near or on them."

"Will do," said Frazer. "Anything else?"

"Not now." Tim fished his car keys out of his pocket and grabbed his jacket. "Keep working at your end, I'll keep working on mine. We're bound to meet in the middle somewhere."

She read his expressions under the beard and mustache by how the hairs moved: he was mystified, in deep thought. His eyes went bright as soon as he saw her.

"Ready for herbal tea?"

She nodded, leading the way to the nurses' lounge. Her ducks were all in a row: Mirek was watching her patients, Malloy and Linda knew where she would be in case they needed her. Cynthia was floating from patient to patient on Cloud Nine, giving in to every demand no matter how unreasonable. She had the happiest patients in the place.

The Mrs. Tea teamaker brewed up a pot of chamomile tea while he perused the profusion of cartoons, short clips, and printed slogans that were pasted or taped to the outsides of the nurses' locker doors and the walls. He stopped at the magnet that read THE MORE I KNOW ABOUT MEN, THE MORE I LOVE MY DOG.

"This must be yours," he said, accepting a mug of tea.

"No, actually it isn't." She added skim milk to her tea and sat down on the couch. "I don't have anything against men. I'm just very picky."

They sipped, burned their lips, blew on the surface of the clear yellow tea, then looked at each other.

"How's Mathilde?" she asked.

"Damn!" he said with a smile. "I thought we were going to talk about us."

"Is that your shrinky way of saying you need to talk about us? I didn't think you were the romantic reminiscent type."

He sighed. "I'm not, but every time I'm around you, I'm reminded of how much I like you. You own a permanent nook in my heart."

Adele lowered her eyes, pondering the permanent nook.

"Too Hallmarkian?" he asked after a minute.

"No," she said. "I was wondering how much rent to charge for that nook."

When they regained themselves, he shook his head. "Mathilde's a challenge, all right."

Adele waited, sipped her tea, and checked the time on the wall clock. The crew in 819 had meds and vitals due in fifteen minutes.

"I'm attempting to build up a therapeutic partnership as a starting point to go deeper, but she's having a hell of a time taking what she remembers of the accident beyond what she's already told us. She has no remote recall at all, although her intermediate memory of the last few days is intact, and her immediate recall is better than mine."

"Like I told you before, she's far more concerned about her memory loss than most amnesics." Jeff paused and took a sip of tea. "She doesn't seem fully dissociated even though she's amnesic. Actually it feels like she's more in shock than anything. She's been psychologically shaken to her knees, but she could get up at any time."

"Are you seeing her again tomorrow?"

He nodded. "Of course." Then, as if in warning, added: "You're getting attached. I was under the impression nurses didn't have time to get attached to their patients anymore."

Adele shrugged. "Her life has been irrevocably changed, Jeffrey. She's . . . needy. I think about if I were in her shoes. In a strange place where nobody knows me . . ."

". . . including yourself," Jeffrey added.

Unashamedly irreverent, they broke up, each spilling tea onto their laps.

Detective Sergeant Ritmann stood in the plush waiting room outside the executive office of Phillip Yates III, looking out the picture window. Fifty-seven stories above San Francisco, the breathtaking panoramic view of the Bay, Marin, and most of the north side of the city lay before him. Because the sun, window, and desk were in the right places at the moment, he also had a perfect view of Mr. Yates's private secretary in the reflection of the window glass.

Laurel Saches was probably forty, but she was one of those plain, nervous women who went gray and lined early. He wouldn't have paid her much attention except that when he'd gone to the window, he felt her staring at him. He heard her shuffling papers, and even clicking the keys of her computer, but he could see in the reflection that she never took her eyes off him unless she thought he was going to turn around and catch her at it.

"How do you get any work done?" Tim asked, turning to her. She averted her eyes instantly.

"Pardon me?" she said, pretending to have been engrossed by the monitor screen. She stood and walked around the desk. Her dark eyes were round and small, although she had done a decent job of making them up to look larger. He noticed also that she was nicely—almost elegantly—dressed in a simple black jacket, a gold silk camisole underneath, and a black skirt. Her legs were well shaped and she was trim, having managed somehow to avoid the "secretary's spread" of hips, thighs, and buttocks.

He pointed at the view. "I'd be staring out the window all day instead of working."

She laughed pleasantly. "Please notice that my desk is on the other side of the room. It was placed over here for exactly that reason. I'm sorry Mr. Yates has been delayed longer than

I originally thought. His meetings with the marketing department heads sometimes go over quite a bit. May I get you a cup of coffee or tea? We have a variety of fruit juices, soft drinks, or . . ."

His stomach growled and made a low yowling noise—as though he'd swallowed a cat whole and it was still alive. Ever since he'd gone meatless, he was hungry all the time. Tim held up a hand: *How about a couple of buckets of fried, dead fowl covered with grease-soaked bread and a three-pounder Mc-Hoof?* "No, nothing for me, thank you."

He sat down on the leather couch and sank into it. It was the most comfortable couch he'd ever sat on. "That is, unless of course you supply pillows and blankets to go along with this couch."

Her laughter was genuine this time.

"How long have you worked here?" he asked, using the show of lightheartedness as permission to probe.

The laughter died, and she again took on the sober tone of executive secretary. "Fifteen years in June."

"Did you start with Mr. Yates?"

She returned to her desk and sat down behind the monitor. "No. I was in the secretarial pool for the first three years, but I was frequently assigned to Mr. Yates when he worked in the research department. We discovered that we had similar linear thought and work patterns and our organizational skills complemented each other. When he advanced to CEO status, he requested me as his office-manager-slash-private-secretary."

Tim nodded, making what he could out of the comment about linear thought and work patterns and complementary organizational skills. "What, if you don't mind me asking, does a job like this pay?"

She named a figure that was almost double his yearly salary from the county. His reaction was plainly written in his expression.

"It sounds like a lot," she said archly, "but I assure you I earn it, Mr. Ritmann." She averted her eyes again. "I believe even Mr. Yates would agree that there are times when it seems I'm the one running the corporation."

The large oak door opened and several men emerged, carrying notebooks and artist's portfolios. Without a word, they nodded at the secretary and disappeared through the outer door.

Laurel Saches excused herself and entered the inner office, closing the door behind her. Five minutes later, she opened the door and invited him inside. Her smile was artificial, strained. Even her voice had changed to a tighter, less friendly timbre.

He entered the immense office, which the floor-to-ceiling windows made seem even larger and more open. It had a futuristic, unreal feeling to it, like something out of a black-and-white sci fi film about advanced societies on other planets.

Phillip Yates greeted him from behind a simple ebony desk. Judging from the smooth skin of his forehead and the strength of his grip, the detective guessed the man to be in his early fifties, maybe late forties.

"Ms. Saches tells me you're with the Marin sheriff's office, Mr. Ritmann," he said, gesturing to a chair at the opposite side of his desk.

"Yes." Tim sat in a chair decidedly less comfortable than the couch in the waiting room. He regretted it instantly—standing would have given him a psychological advantage. "I'm a detective sergeant with the homicide division." He was going to add, "Please, call me Tim," but everything about the man told him it would be a breach of corporate etiquette. He wondered if his wife called him Mr. Yates. If the guy had children, he was *sure* they did.

Ms. Saches was silently headed for her office when Tim turned and asked that she stay. There was a moment of awkward uncertainty while looks passed between the two linear thinkers. Mr. Yates nodded and Ms. Saches silently took a seat in the far corner by the door. An observer rather than a participant.

Phillip Yates folded his hands on the desk and inspected him with placid blue eyes that were more suited to a clergyman than a multimillion-dollar CEO. Two of the fingers on his right hand were bandaged completely in gauze.

Within a few seconds, he tapped his forefinger once. The small movement by the manicured digit screamed at him: *Get on with it, pal, you're boring me. My time is money!*

"I need some information about two of your former fingers."

Puzzled, Mr. Yates cocked his head and said, "I beg your pardon?"

Ms. Saches leaned forward, as if she had not understood what he'd said.

Instantly, Tim heard his own words and stumbled over his lips to correct himself. "I mean former employees. I need to ask some questions about two of your former employees."

Mr. Yates's well-defined eyebrows rose. The forefinger tapped again.

Tim stood, starting over as he paced. "I'm sure you've seen the afternoon papers," he said with a certain amount of disgust.

The murder of Bernice Barry had blown the covers off and changed everything about the investigations. The media were swarming over the story like flies around rotting meat. As Tim knew they would, the reporters immediately connected the two murders. To increase interest and thrills, they'd erroneously used the words "serial killer." This was not someone killing randomly selected victims; this was someone carefully eliminating connected people.

Initially it pissed him off, but he'd let it go after a while. To his way of thinking, the media were the media: just doing their jobs the same as the SS during the Third Reich.

"We have two homicide victims and the only connection we can find between them is that they both used to work for Citadel," Tim continued. "I'm hoping you can provide me with some information about them and if there's any reason you can think of that someone would want them dead."

Phillip Yates's hands unfolded and gripped the arms of his chair. The color drained from his face. "Who?" he stammered, rising to his feet. "Who are you talking about?"

"I'm sorry—you haven't read the *Chronicle* or the *Intelligencer*?"

Mr. Yates shook his head. "I only read *The Wall Street Journal* and *The New York Times*."

He should have seen that one coming. "The victims are Gerard Deveraux and Bernice Barry. They . . ."

Yates leaned forward in slow motion and covered his face with his hands. Ms. Saches looked thunderstruck, frozen to her chair. Her skin turned the color of eggshells.

The thought that the man was going to have a coronary crossed Tim's mind. Desperately, he tried to remember his CPR: was it two breaths to every fifteen compressions, or four breaths to every ten?

Ms. Saches stood and took a few steps toward her boss's desk. "Are you all right, Mr. Yates? Do you want me to call the nurse from the employee health center?"

Phillip Yates waved his hand, took out his handkerchief and dabbed his face. "No. No, I'm okay . . . It's . . . I can't believe this. When did this happen and how? Were they—are you sure they were murdered? Were they—together? Was it . . ."

He pointed to an ebony and oak cabinet on the other side of the room. "Please. Get me a bottle of water out of the refrigerator."

Tim and Ms. Saches both started for the cabinet, but Tim reached it first. Inside was a full-size refrigerator stocked with every sort of beverage one could think of. He found a dozen chilled bottles of Calistoga water and handed one to the CEO and one to Ms. Saches.

Tim waited until Yates had taken a few sips. "They were shot. We think both murders were committed by the same person. Mr. Deveraux was shot in a hotel room in Corte Madera, and Mrs. Barry was killed at her home in Kentfield early this morning."

Yates had his head bowed, staring at the top of his desk. Ms. Saches had retreated to her chair in the corner and was still holding on to the unopened bottle. She looked ill.

"I'm sorry to be the bearer of bad news, but I thought you'd have read about it by now or heard . . ."

The man pulled himself together and answered slowly, "I was out of the country until yesterday. I've been too busy to read the news. Have you heard anything about this, Ms. Saches?"

Ms. Saches shook her head slowly.

Tim waited a moment. "I understand how you must feel, but I do need to ask you some questions. Do you think you're able to answer them now, or would you rather I come back tomorrow?"

"Of course," Yates said, without lifting his eyes. "I'll give you whatever information I can."

"When did Mr. Deveraux and Mrs. Barry work for Citadel and in what capacity were they employed?" Tim pulled his notebook and pen from the pocket of his sport jacket.

The CEO took a deep breath and pushed it out with puffed cheeks. "Let's see. Deveraux was head of computer telecommunications research. I can't remember when he was hired, but I think Bernice was hired on as the head of foreign markets about a year after Gerard."

"When did they leave?"

While he thought, Yates's forefinger sneaked out for a tap. "They both left in the same year. About four or five years ago?" He looked to Ms. Saches for help, but the woman had a faraway look in her eyes. "I don't know, I'd have to check on that."

Tap. Tap.

Tim ignored the finger. "Were there any problems with them while they were here? Were they fired, or—"

"None at all. No. They were excellent employees. They both resigned with excellent recommendations."

"Do you remember the reasons they gave for resigning?"

Tap. Mr. Yates let his head rest against the back of his chair, and Tim noted that the bandaging job on his fingers looked homemade. "I believe Mrs. Barry's husband was quite ill and she wanted to devote more time to him. I told her that her position would be held for her for a year, but she declined the offer. Mr. Deveraux was offered more money at another company, in Los Angeles, I believe."

"So, in your opinion they left Citadel happy?"

Mr. Yates nodded. "Yes, I'd say they did."

Tim stopped pacing and turned his back to the CEO to stare out one of the wall windows. He found himself having a clear reflection of Mr. Yates. The finger silently pumped up and down. Tap. Tap. Tap.

"What do you know of their personal lives? Were there any friends or enemies within the company?"

Here, Yates seemed at a loss. He opened his mouth to answer then closed it again and shook his head. "I doubt either of them made enemies here. They were well respected, if I recall, but I can't remember whether or not there were any close ties made."

"Would you mind providing us with a copy of their personnel files?"

In answer, Mr. Yates got up and walked over to his secretary. He bent slightly to look into her face. "Ms. Saches?" he said almost in a whisper. His tone was gentle. "Can you pull yourself together to get copies of those files?"

Wordlessly, she nodded and walked out of the office. Mr. Yates followed her out. Beyond the door, they had a hushed exchange that Tim could not hear.

"I'm sorry," Mr. Yates said when he came back in and sat down. "Ms. Saches will get those files for you shortly."

"I know next to nothing about what it is your company does, Mr. Yates. I was wondering—could you explain to me exactly what it was that Mr. Deveraux and Mrs. Barry did for Citadel?"

Tap. Tap. Mr. Yates sucked in his cheeks and tapped some more. He leaned back in his chair and then bolted forward again. "It's rather complicated, really, but simply put, Mr. Deveraux researched various companies and organizations and what they might need in the way of computer telecommunications systems. He would turn that information over to marketing, who would contact the heads of those concerns. He also helped design the programs themselves. Mrs. Barry dealt with foreign companies—mostly the European markets."

"I'd like to talk to some of their coworkers if that's all right with you?"

Tap. "Of course. I think there might be one or two people left from when they were here. The turnover in the specialty departments is high. Employees move on with greater frequency now than they did even ten years ago. I'll have Ms. Saches call you with the names and departments."

Tim put on his coat. "I'm sorry for springing this on you, Mr. Yates. I realize it's been a shock." He fished his wallet out of his back pocket and handed the man his card. "Please call or page me anytime day or night if you think of anything that might help find out who or what is behind these homicides."

Phillip Yates examined the card. "Of course."

Laurel Saches came in carrying a large brown envelope. "Personnel files on Barry and Deveraux," she said, handing them to Tim. She did not look at him. Her hands were trembling.

"Ms. Saches, I'll also need you to provide Detective Ritmann with a list of present employees who worked with Mr. Deveraux and Mrs. Barry."

"Certainly," she said, and looked down at the floor some more.

"If either of you can think of anything," Tim said, "any details about their employment or any other aspects of their lives, I'd appreciate a call."

Tim thanked them both and shook hands with Mr. Yates.

Halfway down the hall to Mr. Yates's private elevator, he remembered he had not given Ms. Saches his business card. Pulling one from his wallet, he wrote his home number and a brief note on the back and returned to the outer office.

Ms. Saches was not at her desk, and the door to Mr. Yates's office was closed. He warded off all the boss-secretary dictation jokes that immediately crowded into his head and stood the card up on her keyboard. That was when he saw part of a hastily written word—"personne—"—on the top sheet of a yellow memo pad. The rest of the message was obscured by a folder. Glancing around, he pushed the folder off the pad.

'1 co. personnel f. − pp cd. 99 = DEVERAUX/BARRY.'

He pulled his notebook from his pocket and copied the message exactly as it appeared on the memo.

Jane Doe was eating dinner when Detective Ritmann reached Ellis. He was glad he'd missed Adele; he disliked her pet patient on sight. The woman's timidity did not soften him, but rather grated on him so that he had to constantly remind himself to be civil.

"You are aware that there was a child in the car you were driving?"

Jane Doe pushed away the side table holding her lunch tray and nodded.

The detective made a note. "Did you know the child?"

"No." The woman flushed under his hard scrutiny. "I don't know if I did or not. I can't remember anything."

He fished in his jacket pocket then laid the photograph of Mrs. Deveraux and her two children on her lap.

She dropped her gaze to the photo. She didn't move.

"Does the name Bettina Deveraux mean anything to you?"

The corners of her mouth dropped, but her eyes didn't move from the photograph.

"No. I—I don't remember," she answered slowly as if in a dream.

"What about Jay Fargo?"

"No."

Tim stuck his hands in the pockets of his raincoat. "The younger child, who burned to death in the back of the car you were driving, was named Bettina Deveraux. She was three years old. Her mother and five-year-old sister were shot to death the day before. Her father was murdered only a few hours before your accident. Do you know anything about that?"

Reluctantly, Mathilde raised her eyes and regarded him defiantly. "I told you: I don't remember anything."

"The man who rented the car you were driving gave his name as Jay Fargo. Two days after he rented it, you were behind the wheel of that same car with the only surviving member of the Deveraux family in the backseat." Without wavering, he stared at her. "I find that rather remarkable, don't you?"

"I said," Mathilde's eyes flashed, "I don't remember anything."

The woman's anger didn't faze him, but he saw no point in continuing to question her. He would have to wait until after she was discharged and saw the sketches of Fargo and photos of the Deverauxs.

"One more thing," he said. "When you're discharged, I need you to stay put. You're no longer the victim of a tragic accident, Ms. Doe. You're a suspect in a murder. I suggest you get a lawyer first thing. We'll want to talk to you again."

"Fine," she said evenly, glad that the interview had come to a close.

On his way out, Tim saw Cynthia, but she was busy mooning over some goofy-looking dork of a guy. He waited until he got to his car to call Adele and leave a teaser of a message.

The fact that he was sure Jane Doe was about as amnesic as he was, he kept to himself.

* * *

It was late when she left the nurses' rally meeting in San Anselmo and headed toward Larkspur. As she entered Kentfield the urge overtook her and drove her to the pay phone behind College of Marin. Luck was with her; the phone book was actually there and in fairly good condition at that—only the P's and part of the G's had been ripped out.

Double fortune shined on her when, to her jaw-unhinging awe, she found a listed address for B. Barry in Kentfield. In the county that boasted being the third wealthiest in the nation, to have a listed phone—let alone an address—was considered *mauvais goût*.

She drove up the winding hill that was Woodland Avenue, past modest homes with manicured lawns and one- or two-car garages. Within a quarter mile, the modest dwellings grew farther apart as the quarter-acre lots grew to one-acre redwood-studded parcels and the two-bedroom homes expanded to four- and five-bedroom, four-car-garage mansions. On the corner of Woodland Avenue and a narrow unmarked lane, the Barry home was a beautiful three-story house with a wraparound porch. The windows were dark, and there was yellow scene tape across the driveway.

The Beast came to a stop behind an old VW Rabbit convertible. She got out and took in the surroundings. The residence across the street was a three-story masterpiece of windows and vaulted ceilings. In one of the middle-story windows, a futuristic desk holding a computer monitor was clearly visible. Face aglow with the soft fluctuating light, a man with mouse in one hand, keyboard under the other, stared at the screen with total concentration.

The house directly next door was separated from the Barry property by a deep ravine, while the lane and a grove of redwoods created the divide from the other adjacent property.

She walked up the street a short way, out of the view of the man in the window, and searched for a less obvious path to the back of the Barry house. The best way, she decided, was simply to walk up the driveway.

She ducked under the scene tape, giving the gray Mercedes in the driveway a quick once-over. The footpath to the downstairs apartment was clearly marked with regularly placed outdoor lights.

Ten feet from the French door, she'd caught sight of a young woman in a pink robe when the back of the house and the yard went ablaze with light. Adele clenched her back teeth. Motion sensor lights were the bane of her amateur sleuth's life. Outwardly she kept a straight face, bit the bullet, and knocked.

Fearless and dumb were the two words that crossed Adele's mind when the girl didn't so much as flinch at her sudden appearance, but rather looked up and smiled.

"Hi," she said, flinging open the door, which had not been locked. She was not a cautious girl considering there had been a murder committed a few yards away less than twenty-four hours ago.

Adele returned her friendly smile. "Hi. I'm Adele Monsarrat," she said truthfully, then sailed right from there cleanly into a bold-face lie: "I'm a reserve deputy with Marin Sheriff's Department?" she said in an engaging, confident way. "I know the detectives have been at you all day, but I was wondering if I could ask you a few more questions."

"Sure." The girl opened the door wider and walked back to the stove. "I'm making some hot cocoa. Want some?"

"Sure," Adele said and regretted it immediately. Hot cocoa upset her stomach.

The woman was perhaps twenty-five. Her oval face held lovely dark blue eyes. Her hair was waist-length, thick and blond, tied back by a black scrunchie.

"I won't keep you long," Adele began after her first sip of the cocoa. In immediate response, her stomach groaned. *Why are you doing this? You know what chocolate does to me!*

" 'S okay." She flipped her hair back away from the creamy skin of her face and sat down.

That was when Adele realized she didn't know the young woman's name. Instantly, her eyes searched the counter at which she sat for something with a name. There was a magazine lying at her fingertips. Pretending not to be paying attention to what she was doing, she flipped it over.

"I'd like you to go over the events of last night one more time . . ." She glanced down at the addressograph. ". . . Terry."

"Oh, call me by my first name. It's Lesa."

To cover her embarrassment, Adele made a production of taking out her notebook and pen. "Can you run through it again?"

Lesa nodded. "Well, first of all, I'm a landscaper and work outside all day, so I sleep hard. My boyfriend says nothing short of a bomb could wake me up."

Adele smiled. She could relate.

"I remember for sure the motion sensors were on earlier when I went to bed because the raccoons tripped them a few times." She looked into her cocoa. "Mrs. Barry would never have turned them off. She was really paranoid about people breaking in and stuff like that. *Really* paranoid. She liked reading true crime books even though they freaked her out. When I heard the noise and ran upstairs, the first thing I noticed was that the sensor lights weren't on."

"What time did you go to bed?" Adele asked.

Lesa kneaded her hands. "Let's see. I fed Ricky and Fred around nine." She looked up. "I've got a family of coons who come to the door every night for their dinner. I feed them eggs and veggies that Safeway throws out. After I fed them, I did a facial, so it was probably about ten by the time I actually fell asleep."

"Then what happened?"

"A loud noise woke me up. The house shook. At first I thought we were having an earthquake, but when I woke up more, I thought maybe Mrs. Barry had fallen down her stairs." Lesa pointed at the ceiling over her bed, which was in the middle of the long rectangular room. "The bottom of her stairs are right over my bed. Mrs. Barry usually went to bed even earlier than I did, so I knew something was wrong."

They both stopped to listen to a jet going overhead. Adele wondered where it was going and who was on it.

"Okay," said Adele. "So you heard this noise and then what did you do next?"

"Got up, put on my robe, and ran upstairs to the back door, but it was locked. I knocked a few times and tried to see inside, but it was too dark so I went around to the front of the house. The front door was open. I—"

"Do you mean actually standing open or was it unlocked?"

"It was open," said Lesa. "About four inches. The foyer light and the lights from upstairs were all on. I knocked and called her name and went in. She was lying on the floor between the foyer and the living room at the base of the stairs."

The girl took a long drink of her cocoa. She shivered and looked up at Adele. "It was awful with all that blood. I called nine-one-one immediately. While I was waiting for them, I didn't know what else to do, so I held her hand and told her it was going to be okay—that the ambulance was coming."

"Was she alive?"

Lesa drank again until the cocoa was gone. Adele took another small sip to be polite.

"Well, she was *trying* to talk. I think she wanted me to tell someone something. She'd say, 'Tell . . . Tell . . .' but she never finished what she was saying before . . ." Lesa trailed off and studied the bottom of her cocoa cup. ". . . the cops got there and the rest you know."

"Did Mrs. Barry have a boyfriend or—"

Lesa snorted, as if the mere suggestion of it were absurd. "No way. I asked her once why she didn't date or anything, and she said as far as she was concerned, one husband had been more than enough. I think I said something about how having a man friend or a companion would be nice, and she said it wasn't any of my business." The woman blushed. Adele noticed a scar over her left eyebrow.

"You knew Mrs. Barry for how long?"

The girl counted on long slender fingers. "I started working for her about five years ago?" She gazed across the cozy apartment, still calculating. "Yeah, five years this December, but I didn't move into this apartment until two years ago. I really didn't know Mrs. Barry very well. I mean, we weren't close or anything. She liked to keep business separate from her personal life."

"Would you know if she had friends—any one friend in particular who she was close to?"

"Mrs. Barry wasn't . . ." Lesa started again, uncomfortable with saying something negative about the newly departed. "She wasn't a very warm person, you know? I don't think she had a close friend. I mean, once in a while she would have people over for dinner, but I think they were business associates.

"I felt sorry for her that way. Her husband died right after I came to work here. I always wondered what she was like with him. I mean, I couldn't imagine her being very affectionate or anything like that."

Adele looked up from her notebook and bit the end of her pen. "What about enemies?"

"You know, I know this sounds dumb, but I really doubt she had any. She was too fastidious or—no, that's not the word . . ." Lesa bowed her head while she thought. "She was unemotional. No highs or lows—not even anger or hate. She wouldn't have engaged in struggles or arguments with anyone."

There was a knock at the door, which caused Adele to jump.

"Be right there," Lesa yelled, picked up a bowl off the counter, and opened the door.

Standing on hind legs, hands outstretched, Ricky and Fred, two medium-size raccoons, silently demanded dinner like kids on Halloween. Lesa handed each a hardboiled egg and waved as they rolled their treats across the lawn and disappeared behind a thick hedge of rosemary.

Adele got up to leave. "Do you know the man across the street who saw the car driving away?"

"All I know is that his name is Jason Humbold." Lesa laughed. "I've never actually met him. He's like a computer robot. He sits at that computer for *hours*. In four years I've never seen him leave the house, and I've never gone by the house that he isn't in front of that screen. I don't think he even leaves it long enough to go to the bathroom." She giggled. "I think he must have tubes hooked up to his dick or something. I don't think Mrs. Barry ever met him either. She wasn't friendly with any of her neighbors. I doubt she even knew their names."

"What are you going to do now?" Adele indicated the apartment.

The girl made a face indicating a major dilemma. "I don't know. I guess I'll start looking for rentals, but I hope I can stay on for a few months at least until I can find another neighbor who'll cook eggs for the coons."

Detective Sergeant Timothy Ritmann leaned back in his desk chair, lacing his fingers behind his head. He stared at the thermostat on the wall opposite him, as if it might have some answers. The dead-end streets were piling up. Four murders, and no witnesses. A bearded man wearing weird glasses, a woman with no memory, the cremains of an unidentifiable child, and Citadel.

He looked at the pile of reports and the odd bits of paper on his desk, and his thoughts again returned to Laurel Saches and Phillip Yates. Taking out his pocket notebook, he got up and moved quickly to the marker board by the door. He duplicated what had been written on the memo on Ms. Saches's desk. He sat down to stare at the message.

1 co. personnel f.s. − pp cd. 99 = DEVERAUX/BARRY

"One copy personnel files," he read aloud. "Dash pp cd period ninety-nine equals Deveraux slash Barry."

While he thought, he picked up one of the Chinese takeout containers and shoveled the last few clumps of green beans with garlic sauce into his mouth. In his freshman year at college, he'd been on the staff of the college paper and had to do a lot of the proofreading. A double p meant plural pages . . . or pages.

Opening the dictionary on his desk, he turned to the abbreviations list. Cd. was the abbreviation for cord or cords, which made no sense. He doubted it meant "compact disc." Then it dawned on him that "cd." was followed by a number. Code. Code ninety-nine.

"One copy personnel files," he began again. "Dash. Pages code ninety-nine." The equal sign was an indication of whose files were needed. Linear patterns. She'd said she thought in linear patterns. It was mathematical thinking. She wrote her to-do lists like an equation.

An equation.

He yelled loud enough that the cleaning woman at the other end of the department dropped the wastebasket she was emptying and ducked.

"One copy personnel files for Deveraux and Barry minus the code ninety-nine pages."

After the elation came the letdown and then the obvious question: what the hell was on the code ninety-nine pages that Yates didn't want him to see? He looked at his watch and was disappointed that it was so late. He was desperately in the mood to sit around a seedy out-of-the-way bar and run it all by the boys over a couple of brewskis.

But Cini was a family man with five kids, and Chernin was a pussy about bars and late-night brainstorming. He could, he thought for a total of one second, stop by Adele's, but she had her rabble-rouser meeting—she also had to work the next morning.

The cleaning lady, a cheerful Mexican woman named Inez, knocked on his door and entered. "It's okay I empty your waste-baskets, Mr. Tim?"

"Sure."

He watched her as she emptied the two full baskets, sprayed them both with antiseptic, and wiped them out. Every so often, she would push back the flyaway strands of hair that had escaped the bun at the nape of her neck.

"Hey, Inez?"

She stopped wiping down the door jamb and around the light switch, turned, and smiled at him. "Yes?"

"Do you like detective novels?"

"My son, he read the novels—I like the detectives on TV. It is exciting to see how they find out who did all the murders and robberies. Just like you do."

He practically stumbled over his feet to pull out a chair. He took her gently by the arm and sat her down. Confused by this, Inez giggled and covered her mouth with her hand.

"Okay," he said excitedly, half sitting on the corner of the desk. "I'm going to tell you a detective murder story like on TV, and you tell me what you think."

She hadn't meant to talk to Jason Humbold—not really. The hour was later than what was considered socially acceptable to go calling on people. Plus she didn't really have any business interviewing these people, but, well—when she waved, he nodded and smiled back. It really *was* an invitation to her way of thinking. And then, when she held up her deputy badge and ID photo, he nodded and smiled again, then motioned with his head for her to come up. It would have been rude to turn the invitation down.

When she reached the front door, there was a framed plaque giving instructions to those coming to the door to walk right in and go up the stairs to the right. At the second floor, an electric eye sensed her and the ornate steel gate rolled back to admit her.

Jason Humbold yelled for her to come in.

The man possessed a truly forgettable face. His hair was thinning on top, and his gray sideburns had been brushed back to blend with the rest of the darker fringe that ended in a fuzzy swirl at the back of his head above the neck brace. He had a beard, and round, smallish eyes of an undetermined color.

The focal point was the wheelchair. Fully automated, with a keypad built into one of the arms that more than likely did all sorts of incredible things: open or lock doors, signal for medical, police, and fire help, change seat pressures, and—as Lesa Terry imagined—probably it really did regulate the waste tube attached to his dick.

"I'm Jason Humbold," he said, still in front of the computer monitor.

She introduced herself and, on automatic response, held out her hand. At once she pulled it back and sort of shook the back of his wrist instead. He lifted his forearm, and took her fingers in his. "I have partial use of my right arm and fingers," he said. "I'm a lucky quad, especially now with cyberspace. A mouse and a keyboard require no wheelchair access. How about a cup of tea or cocoa? I was getting ready to make myself a cup."

"I'd love some," she said, forcing a smile. By the time she got to the Beast, her eye teeth would be floating and her bowels would be in utter revolt.

"I'd like to ask you a few questions about the person you saw behind the wheel of the Jeep this morning."

"A San Rafael cop," he said calmly, motoring toward what she now saw was a specially constructed kitchen. Everything was built low and wide for easy access. He had the kettle on and the cups, spoons, milk, and sugar out before she could pull out a chair and sit down.

"Why are you so sure it was a cop?"

His eyes met hers and stayed level. "It was a San Rafael cop, Miss Monsarrat. I wore the same uniform for ten years. I'd recognize it if it were on a mongoose two hundred yards away."

Adele's mind cranked. Jason Humbold. Humbold. Of course. He'd been one of the infamous Brat Pack—ten San Rafael policemen who had a reputation for being tough, sometimes too tough.

In the late 1970s Humbold, his attorney, two judges, and three other Brat Pack members were shot when an unhappy victim of the Brat Pack's justice system opened fire in the county courthouse with a semiautomatic .38-caliber Llama. Humbold was one of two to survive. The other survivor—the attorney—was being kept alive as a broccoli at Napa State Hospital, compliments of California taxpayers.

He filled the cups and brought them to the table with several varieties of tea bags and a box of instant cocoa. She grabbed for the box of Sleepytime tea bags.

"When you sit in front of the same window every day for fifteen hours or more, and you're seeing the same neighborhood, you get to know the sight and sound of every car, license number, and face by heart. Hell," he laughed, dropping two sugar cubes into his cocoa, "without ever having met any of them, I could probably tell you most of the neighbors' schedules, what kind of car they drive and what mechanical problems they have, what's in most of their wardrobes and a little bit about their personal relationships."

Adele stopped dipping her tea bag and took out her notebook. "Did you get the license plate number?"

"Wasn't any front or back. I looked. We don't get much traffic at that time of the morning."

Adele checked her notes. "I know you got a visit from the sketch artist, but was there anything unusual that you might have remembered about the guy?"

Humbold's right leg made a spastic jerk. Neither of them paid any attention to it—it might have been another person there at the table with them who had just committed some small social indiscretion.

"Glasses, big nose." Humbold snickered. "The geek wore his cap. Cops don't wear their freakin' caps unless there's a formal event."

"What did the glasses look like?" Adele asked.

"Silver wire-rims. Couldn't see the eyes too well, though. The sketch man did a good job."

"And you didn't see anyone go into Mrs. Barry's house?"

He shook his head, pursing his lips. "He must have come in from the other end of Woodland Avenue, because I didn't see anybody, and the last car to go by was two-fifteen and that was Al Clovis from six houses up on the left at four-nineteen. He owns the German bakery in Corte Madera.

"The Barrys' motion detector lights came on about four times from ten o'clock until the time I saw the car. It might have been less, but I don't usually pay much attention to them anymore because it's almost always the damned raccoons. I think I would have seen a body walking down the driveway, though."

"Approximately when was the last time you saw the lights go on?" Adele asked.

"About twenty minutes before I saw the Jeep, but like I said, I didn't notice anybody walking around."

Adele stood and looked out the huge window that was the wall where he worked. The Barry residence was angled so that the front door and a large portion of the porch could not be seen. The main walkway, however, would have been clearly visible had he been at his desk.

"He must have gone through the neighbor's yard and down the ravine," she said, thinking aloud, "tripped the lights when he got up on the porch the first time and then disconnected the motion sensors and climbed back up over the porch railing to the front door."

"Had to or I would have seen him."

"How'd you see the glasses and the uniform patch in the dark from that distance?" she asked.

He let his hand down into a canvas pocket off the side of his chair and brought out a pair of binoculars. "Never go anywhere without them," he chuckled, looking her over now, paying attention. "How long did you say you've been with the Sheriff's Department?"

Her heart did a backflip. Not exactly what she needed—to be caught misrepresenting herself to an ex–San Rafael Brat Packer whom she was grilling. With all her might, she willed the phone to ring or an earthquake to rumble so to distract him.

None of these things happened.

"Three years, sir," she lied, saying it proudly, exactly the way a rookie might.

"Oh, hell, you're just a baby," he wailed, then: "Those guys treat you okay down there?"

"Oh, you know how that goes," she said. "There's a few who've got to prove they're too macho to accept a woman into the ranks. Well." She cleared her throat and stood to go before he asked to see her badge again. "Thanks for the tea. I'm going back over to check out the railing and the motion sensors."

He started to ask about whether or not Bob somebody-or-other was still working Task Force when she turned back suddenly.

"Say, listen, how would you like to take over boiling eggs for a couple of needy neighbors named Ricky and Fred?"

Putting herself in the mindset of one who did not want to be seen going to the front door, Adele found an easy path through the neighbor's side yard and down the ravine. She climbed up the side of the Barry porch. Even with her strong legs, it took a major effort to haul her body over the railing. Her first step onto the porch tripped the motion detection lights.

She set her stopwatch and raced back down off the porch, making a frantic search for the switch box. It took five minutes to find it cleverly hidden behind a panel that blended in with the exterior of the house.

The lock had obviously been broken. She opened the small door and flicked the switch marked "sensors." Immediately the yard went dark.

She climbed back up the porch, ran around the back side of the wraparound porch to the front door, and mentally reenacted ringing the doorbell, waiting for Mrs. Barry to get out of bed, put on a robe, walk down the stairs, check through the security peephole, see it was a policeman, open the door.

She had to imagine the scene of the killer walking in, saying a few words, putting the gun to the woman's chest, and bang bang. Then she ran back around the porch, jumped over the railing at the same place she'd jumped on, ran to a logical place where the car would have been parked, mentally got in, started the engine, and drove away slowly.

She clicked the stop button on her watch. Seventeen minutes had elapsed. Except for driving down the street, at no point had she been able to see Humbold's window, or, for that matter, any of the other neighbors'.

It was, she thought, entirely possible that was the way things had actually taken place.

NINE

ADELE COULD HEAR NELSON OVER THE PURR OF the Beast's engine when she pulled up in front of the house. Hauling her purse over her shoulder, she dragged herself to the front door and let herself in. The Westminster chimes of the mantel clock finished playing their half-past-the-hour ditty: 11:30.

Nelson, delighted and furious at the same time, whined and barked, then in doggie confusion, reverted to playing his favorite game: he laid his Mickey rug on top of Her feet. This was Adele's cue to flop down on the couch and remain still until he couldn't stand it anymore and barked wildly. Following this, She'd give him a veggie biscuit, kisses, dinner, fresh water, a walk, and another biscuit.

Tonight, however, Adele was utterly still, not because she was playing a game, but because she fell into the sleep of the exhausted. When She began to snore, Nelson was incensed. She hadn't played by the rules.

Placing his muzzle very close to Her upturned ear, he barked in pure indignation.

She gave him his biscuit, kissed him between the ears, cooked him a batch of leftover green onion pancakes, served it with chickpeas covered with yogurt, gave him fresh water, and let him out in the backyard. While he sniffed and lifted his leg around the fig trees, she undressed and brushed her teeth standing in front of the answering machine.

Cynthia's message at 8:07: "Why aren't you home yet? Did you stop to buy a lettuce for Nelson's dinner and fall in love with the produce man? I just finished admitting one of

Rhyme's patients—a twenty-eight-year-old asthmatic who can't breathe worth a shit." She covered the mouthpiece and said, " 'Tell him to put another nitro under his tongue and I'll be right there.'

"The night supervisor brought me a complimentary dinner— half a stale tuna sandwich and an apple with brown spots. I swear I can smell the ptomaine.

"By the way, you miserable rat, I saw the new schedule— you've been switched over to eight-hour shifts for the next month starting tomorrow. Why did you decide to do that and whose soul did you sell in order to swing it with the Queen Mother?

"Oops. Jane Doe is ringing her call bell. Gotta go."

Tim at 8:42: "Hey Nelson, when your mom gets home, would you tell her that I've had a very interesting, informative, and horror-filled day and that the birthdate on the charm she found matches the birthdate of one of the Deveraux children . . ."

Adele choked on the toothpaste suds and hit replay, her pulse racing. The third time around, she let the message play to the end.

". . . tell her if she wants more information, she's going to have to have dinner with me tomorrow after work."

Her mother at 9:17: "Hello, darling. I have the new audio books catalog, and thought you'd like to help me pick out a few for the library one evening this week. Oh, and you need to let me know about whether or not you'll be having Thanksgiving with me and the old ladies. I've invited your aunts Ruthie, Eleanor, and Florence. I'll need to know soon so I can buy the ingredients for a meatless meat loaf. And you're welcome to bring Cynthia and/or a special friend."

Adele rolled her eyes. Her mother was still hoping that one of these days "a special friend" would turn out to be a viable, matrimonially eligible man instead of Nelson.

". . . I love you . . . Give my granddog a scratch behind the ears."

Mathilde at 10:12: "Hi, Adele. It's me—whoever that is." Mathilde laughed, yawned. "Cynthia said the hospital gave you a hard time today about keeping me here. I hope you didn't get into trouble because of me.

"Dr. Murray came in tonight and said my burns are healing

fine and I can be cleared for discharge in a day or two, but Dr. Lavine said he might try to have me transferred to another unit.

"The detective . . ."

Adele could hear the change in her voice.

". . . Mr. Ritmann came in to ask me questions. I didn't like him very much. He was rude and he practically accused me of lying." There was a pause, then, "Well, I'll see you tomorrow."

Sometimes, she thought, it was probably best if she didn't listen to her messages late at night. It was way too frustrating not to be able to call people back and follow up.

She opened the side door off the kitchen, took out her tooth guard, and whistled for Nelson. When he didn't come within the minute, she swore and whistled again. The last time he'd failed to respond to her call, he'd wandered down to the Silver Peso, Marin's oldest and roughest biker bar. By the time the bartender called to tell her where her wandering boy was, the patrons—most of whom wore their beards tucked into the fronts of their extra-large kidney belts—had hoisted the black Lab onto the pool table and gotten him blitzed on Coors. In his drunken state, he'd eaten twenty dollars' worth of Corn Nuts, then heaved them all up on the way home.

She whistled a last time, waited, and headed for the phone. She was dialing the Silver Peso when Nelson pushed open the door and, head lowered to the floor, made a mad dash for her bedroom.

He'd done something bad. Very bad.

Alarmed, Adele ran after him wondering exactly how very bad bad was. Perhaps he'd ripped up the landlord's rose bushes, or maybe he'd found something dead and rotting and was going to hide it under her bed. Maybe he'd stolen something from Mrs. Coolidge's front yard . . . like maybe her mailbox or one of her plastic cat-shaped planter boxes.

Adele found him on the bed half under the covers, his snout buried under her pillow.

"Nelson," she said, drawing out his name in a warning. "What have you got? Show Mommy."

Nelson burrowed his head deeper; a series of sounds like baby lamb bleats came from the pillow.

Adele stopped in her tracks. Christ on a bike in creature Hell.

What *had* he brought to her bed *this* time? "Please," she pleaded with the powers that be, "please let it be anything but a rat."

"Nelson off!" Adele commanded in her "Do-It-NOW!" voice.

The dog immediately jumped off the bed, but stood ready to leap back on. His eyes darted back and forth between her face and the pillow.

The pillow moved like an inanimate object possessed. Finally, as her nerves were about to give out, a brown rabbit, no more than two or three months old, crawled out and looked around.

Nelson made a quiet yelping noise and nudged Adele's hand with his nose. He was the type of dog who brought strays home. *Please, Mom, please can we keep it?*

"No," she said. "You can't keep it. Take it back to its mother, Nelson. Its mommy will be worried."

He barked his refusal, then whined at her.

With anxious yelps and doggie mutterings, Nelson fussed around her as she took a shallow storage box from her closet and scooped the rabbit into it. Before she took the animal out to the backyard, she cleaned and cut up several carrots, a bunch of romaine lettuce, and an apple, which she put into the box.

To her distress, the rabbit, suddenly unconcerned with its strange surroundings, began devouring the lettuce as fast as it could chew and swallow. She added a second bunch of romaine, a dish of water, and an old cotton sweatshirt which she made into a nest in one corner. Then, she placed the box against the water heaters in a shed at the back of the house.

By the time she lay down, Nelson had crawled under the bed with his rug and refused to look at Her, let alone complain about Her cold-hearted ways.

While she waited for her mind to settle down, Adele tuned in the night rerun of *Forum* on KQED. The topic was one of those scraping-the-bottom-of-the-barrel types: "The Psychological Effects of Roadkill on Drivers." The host, Michael Krasny, had taken a call from a man in Berkeley who was describing in a broken voice how badly he felt when bugs hit his windshield and died. While he painfully described the broken wings of various insects, she imagined she heard Krasny off mike, muffling snorts of laughter.

The sound of it set her off laughing until Nelson crawled out from under the bed and impatiently slapped a paw across her mouth.

Nurses tend to have nightmares. As soon as she got past the twitch and hypnic jerk stage, Adele spiraled down toward the circus of midgets, insects with monster antennae, unanswered call bells, and Nelson trapped in a burning house.

At 4 A.M., the sounds of the nearby sirens woke her from a dream where aliens from space had instilled in her (by way of a capsule stuffed into her nasal passages) the power to levitate. The moment she opened her eyes and realized—with some disappointment—she was *not* on the ceiling, she knew with absolute certainty that the fire was at Ellis and Ward 8 was the source of the blaze.

She slipped into her scrubs and padded quietly around Nelson who was lying half under the bed curled around his Mickey Mouse rug. In a dead sleep, his paws pumped in the air, keeping up with the rabbit.

At 4:21 she awakened the Beast, put the car into gear, flicked on the headlights, and screamed like bloody hell.

Standing on the median strip between two palm trees, caught in the headlights' glare, Mrs. Coolidge stood wide-eyed frozen, like a deer. She was wrapped in a fuzzy imitation Navajo rug, her terry-cloth slippers sticking out underneath. There were two pink rollers in the front of her hair.

Adele tapped the horn once—enough to wake the woman out of her trance. Instantly, Mrs. Coolidge smiled and waved. "Trying to see where the fire is," she yelled, pointing in the direction of Ellis. "I hope it's not the hospital. Do you think it's the hospital? Is that where you're going? Did they call you? Oh dear, how many patients have burned? Was it someone smoking in bed? What do you—"

"Go back to your house and hide under the bed until you get the all-clear signal, Mrs. Coolidge," she said in a stern official voice.

"My God," the woman breathed, fear gripping her eyelids, "What is it? What's happened?"

"We've been invaded, and they're bombing hospitals, nursing homes, and military bases all over the county. They're trying to disable us where it'll hurt the most."

"Who? Who's doing this?"

"The Idahoan Terrorist and HMO Executive Coalition troops," Adele said matter-of-factly.

Mrs. Coolidge's brown-spotted arthritic hand flew to her mouth.

"The authorities are cautioning everyone to stay indoors and not turn on their radios or TVs."

"Don't turn . . . ?"

"They've taken over the stations and are sending deadly sterilization waves through the tubes. They might even come door to door." Adele let the Beast roll forward.

"What do they look like?" Mrs. Coolidge asked, taking a few steps backward, toward her porch, where Queen Shredder glowered at her from the window, both huge paws pressed against the glass.

"They're cunning. They look like us. You know, like your garden variety nice young man."

Mrs. Coolidge sprinted for her porch while Adele followed the sirens directly to Ellis Hospital.

She avoided the crowds by sneaking around to the back utility entrance, a substandard-size metal door that was cleverly hidden inside a concrete alcove cluttered with garbage bins. Unless one walked behind the bins to the back of the alcove and looked out, the door would never be seen. She had discovered the door some years before, once she decided that after working in the same building for as many years as she had, and considering the earthquakes and flooding disasters their area was prone to, she wanted to know all its secrets in case of emergencies. The hidden hobbit door was one of many.

She pulled the door open with some difficulty and entered the dark stairwell. Running up and down a maze of stairs and passageways, she finally entered Ward 8 from the back stairwell.

The familiar-smelling smoke hung in the air. There was silent chaos as yellow-slickered firemen wandered aimlessly through the halls while nurses ran around them answering call lights. As was the custom in hospital fires, all the doors to the patients' rooms were tightly closed.

She had never understood the reasoning behind the policy of shutting the patients in during a fire, except maybe as a way to keep the bodies organized when someone came through in the aftermath to pick them up. The nurses' evacuation plan, as stated in *The Ellis Hospital Nurses' Handbook*, indicated that all nurses were expected to go willingly and bravely up in flames with their patients—as part of their duty. In the general hospital policy and procedure book, however, the evacuation plans for physicians and administrative personnel present in the building at the time of a fire or other natural disaster were six pages long and minutely detailed. The rambling epistle stated that Doctors and Administration were to be the first to evacuate either under their own power or using whatever means necessary. Air-flow filtration masks were available to "specified individuals" only.

Adele wondered if nurses—since they had already been deemed disposable—might be used as body shields for the docs.

Sitting at the charting desk, Cynthia sat surrounded by firemen—some on their knees at her feet. She was weeping, although Adele could tell by her friend's body language that the tears were not genuine.

Adele rolled her eyes in a sort of disgusted yet envious wonder, and headed toward the desk. She hadn't taken ten steps before her olfactory glands found the right file in her brain. Popcorn. Burned popcorn. That was the smell that went with the smoke.

Without a pause in the flow of tears or words, Cynthia held out her arms to Adele. "I forgot," she was saying. Adele noted that her friend had developed a southern twang.

"You don't know how busy it gets here. I'm in charge of ten patients and I've been on duty for over twenty hours straight."

She blinked rapidly, as if to stave off a new flashflood of tears. "You men can relate to that, I guess, with your own exhausting schedules."

There was a round of commiserating murmurs. One fireman reached out to hold her hand.

It occurred to Adele that Cynthia might go on forever like this. It needed nipping in the bud. She took a fistful of the back of Cynthia's scrub dress and yanked her to her feet. "I need to attend to Ms. O'Neil now," she addressed the audience of men through clenched teeth and hauled the nurse down the hall to the nurses' lounge.

"What," she asked, once they were inside, "happened?"

Cynthia hung her head and sniffled in unashamed embarrassment.

"Stop the Pitiful Pearl nonsense!" Adele stamped her foot.

Cynthia giggled. "Nothing. It's so dumb. I was getting ready to give report and I put a bag of popcorn in the microwave so I could have something to munch on on the way home to keep me awake?"

Adele screwed up her mouth on one side and nodded.

"Well, Rhyme happened to come up to see one of his patients, and one thing led to another, and we went into the supply room for just a second, I swear, and . . ."

". . . and the bag caught on fire, and someone took it out of the microwave and flapped it around real good, and it set off all the alarms." Adele plopped down on the couch, letting her hands dangle between her knees. "Christ on a bike in hell."

"Joe Dane is missing," Cynthia said after a minute.

Adele cocked her head. "Who the hell is Joe Dane?"

Cynthia shook her head and giggled. "Sorry, I mean Jane Doe. When I closed her door during the fire alarms, she wasn't in her room and she's not on the ward and—"

Adele bolted to her feet. "What!?"

Cynthia patted her hand consolingly. "Don't worry, Del, I called the nursing supervisor—she'll find her."

Following blind instinct, Adele was out of the lounge and heading toward the back stairwell before Cynthia could ask where she was going. Seven minutes later, Adele found Mathilde crouched in the furthest corner of the landing between the basement and the first floor. The woman was rocking on her haunches, her head resting on her knees. Her eyes were closed and she was perspiring heavily.

Adele knelt next to her and put an arm around her shoulders. Her body was hot to the touch. "It's okay. The fire is out. There's no reason to be afraid now."

The woman turned frightened eyes on her. "I tried to get inside," she whispered. "Tried to reach in and pull her out, but the fire . . . It was so . . . I couldn't . . ."

Mathilde clamped her bandaged hands over her face and shuddered. "I smelled the smoke and heard the alarms. Someone yelled that there was fire. I saw the baby . . . all flames. Her face . . ."

Adele rocked her, wondering if it wasn't for the comfort she herself took from it. "That's over, Mathilde. There was nothing you or anyone could do."

The woman began to tremble. "That poor child . . . that poor baby . . ."

"Let me take you back to your room," Adele whispered into the ash-colored hair. "Come on, now. It's late. You need to sleep."

As they stood, Adele saw that the woman had brought her boots. She pointed to them. "You were prepared, at least."

"I was afraid I'd have to run," Mathilde answered. "I got as far as the exit door and didn't know where to go. Then I thought it would be better if I died in the fire. It would be . . . equal justice."

Adele picked up the shoes and guided the woman up the stairs, taking each step slowly. "There isn't any fire; only a bag of burnt, smoky popcorn."

"Popcorn?" Mathilde asked doubtfully, "But it smelled so much like the fire in the car. Like chemicals."

"You were asleep. People become disoriented when they're asleep—even their sense of smell. I once woke up on a beach in Greece thinking I smelled fresh brewed coffee and toast, only to find out it was the rotting fish next to my head."

Mathilde stopped to stare at her, and without another word, let herself be led to her room.

By the time she persuaded Cynthia to sleep the two hours she had left of her "break" at her house rather than risk driving the six miles to Mill Valley, there was only enough time to tuck

Cynthia in, run a few miles, shower, half carry Cynthia into the cold shower, cook hot oatmeal for the three of them, spoon-feed Cynthia, help her put her shoes on the right feet, and return to work.

Normally she might have been a bit short of temper, but today her good mood was bolstered by the surges of pleasure she got from imagining Mrs. Coolidge huddled in her closet with a twenty-four-pound, bad-tempered cat and reading the latest John Grisham novel with a flashlight.

If Mr. Ghazi could have screamed, Adele was sure he would have been waking the dead. His mouth, opened in pain as she moved his body—all ninety-nine pounds of it—to the side of the bed. She plucked at the large bolster of sheets and pads under his body, pulling them out toward her with a crisp snap. With one hand still holding the skeletal body up on its side, she tucked the sheets under the mattress with the other.

"There you go now," she said, moving around the bed, tending to a dozen small tasks at once. "All clean and nice. I'm sorry if I hurt you, but I couldn't let you lie in that mess."

Mr. Ghazi mouthed something, his eyes ablaze with orneriness.

"Yes, I know your new hip hurts," she said as if in answer. "But you must begin to use it, so I'm going to stand you at the bedside and you're going to take a few steps in place. In a few days, you'll be walking with a walker."

The scowl disappeared and was replaced by an expression of wonder. The eyebrows shot up and his lips moved again.

"Honest," she said.

The craggy mouth, crosshatched with deep lines, mouthed more words. Reading lips was a necessary skill in nursing.

"No, it's not too soon and I promise it won't be too painful. You'll feel more of an ache than a sharp pain. And don't worry about hurting that new joint. It's made out of material tougher than your bones."

There was another round of unrestricted, wordless mouthings.

"How do I know?" She pulled back the covers, folding them accordion-style at the end of the bed. His nonskid slippers were on his feet before he knew she had them in her hands. "Because I've helped about five hundred new hips take their first steps.

Since I'll probably be a candidate for one myself someday, I've done my research."

There was a thud at the door, as though a large bird had flown into it. Another thud followed and then another, yet the door remained closed. She knew by the quality of the thud and the steadiness of the television screen that it wasn't the floor cleaner. Adele pulled the door open just as Cynthia was about to bang her head into it again.

"I can't do this," Cynthia slurred and stumbled into the room toward bed 803B, which stood empty. Adele redirected her to the lounger. The nurse bumped into the side, pivoted, and fell into the Naugahyde chair.

Mr. Ghazi stared at her, mouthing questions.

"She's working too hard," Adele said in answer to his question. "If you don't mind, perhaps we could ignore her for a while."

She helped the older man manipulate his body so that he was able to sit and then slide off the bed onto his feet. With Adele holding him steady by a special belt, he marched the march of the newly hipped until he was tired.

After he was safely tucked back into bed, Adele slid the trainer belt around Cynthia and helped her out of the room. It was more work than Mr. Ghazi, because the nurse kept slipping toward the floor—perchance to sleep.

"Just because you like this guy doesn't mean you have to follow him into sleep deprivation hell, Cyn," Adele said, pouring a cup of Mr. Coffee's rich black spewings. "You have your patients' welfare to think about, not to mention your own sanity and safety or the fact that you can barely walk, let alone chart creatively. Then there's your patients' medications that you can't be trusted to give out, so Linda and I have had to take those over. Then there's patient treatments. You'll never be able—"

Cynthia nodded. "I know, I know. I figured that out when I fell sound asleep while listening to Mrs. Harrington's lungs. Thank God I landed on the call bell. Henry had to pull me out from behind her or I might have suffocated."

Adele checked the time. "You've got to buck up—you have eight more hours left to go."

Cynthia looked at her the color draining from her face. "I can't, Adele. I can't do it."

"What? What happened to the girl who could stay out partying all night, get three hours' sleep, and work for twelve hours without a problem?"

"She got old," Cynthia said wearily. "She danced too hard."

Adele thought for a minute. "I know how you can get through the next eight hours."

"You're going to inject me with methamphetamine?"

"Make believe you're making love with the new boy."

Cynthia stared at her through the slit between the drooping eyelids on top and the puffy bags underneath. "I'm too tired to figure it out," she said after a minute.

"Have you ever been too tired to make love?"

"Never."

"For fifteen years you've been telling me that making love recharges your battery. Think about making love with the new boy toy while you're taking care of the patients. For example, when you pump up the blood pressure cuff, think of the rhythm. When you listen to someone's lungs, make believe it's his heavy breathing as he's getting excited. When you brush someone's dentures, think of his teeth nibbling at your ear lobes."

"That's the dumbest thing I ever heard," Cynthia said, staring at her. "What am I supposed to think about when I'm measuring urine and cleaning up blood, diarrhea, and vomit?"

Adele had to stretch. "Make believe that you and the doc are on your honeymoon in the far reaches of the Amazon and he's contracted a rare tropical disease where, between bouts of bleeding, diarrhea, and vomiting, he is compelled to have madly passionate, wild, and kinky sex."

As the light dawned, Cynthia smiled a little. "Hmmm. Well, it wouldn't hurt to try it, I suppose." She stood without assistance, and her eyes took on a new brightness.

Adele watched Cynthia walk down the hall with a spring in her step, compliments of the power of sex and love.

"What's wrong with me?" Mathilde asked. Worry lines etched themselves between her eyes.

Adele compared the morning lab results with the ones done the night before. "How's the appetite lately?"

"I eat like a pig," Mathilde said.

"You're not a closet bulimic or anything, are you?"

Mathilde shook her head. "No. Why?"

"You're down two kilograms in weight and your potassium is down again."

"Is that all?" Mathilde was visibly relieved. "That's not bad, that's great. I'm too fat. I thought you were going to tell me you found a brain tumor or something."

"You aren't fat," Adele said, eyeing the taut, muscular body. "I'm sure you must be an athlete of some sort. Women around your age don't naturally have builds like yours—those are muscles acquired through extended daily exercise."

Mathilde cocked her head and shrugged. "Maybe," she said, looking away.

Jellyroll Love came through the door bearing a mixed bouquet of orange and white lilies. In Dockers and a cotton long-sleeved shirt, the man took on a completely different appearance than when he was in his uniform; he was a man at ease in the world, not one who dealt with death and danger every moment of his working day.

Mathilde's eyes locked into his with such intensity that Adele left the room without another word, making sure to close the door tightly behind her.

Passion and desire were all around her like a virus during flu season.

Every time she picked up the phone to page Tim, something happened to prevent her from completing the call. This time, it was because her new admit was rolled through the door at top speed by the ER crew. Dropping the phone back into its base, she ran ahead of the gurney into 801A and stood on the far side of the prepared bed.

Barbara Greiner-Dell was a thirty-seven-year-old who had been knocked unconscious when the boom of the boat she and her husband were sailing reportedly crushed the back of her head. While unconscious, she had aspirated her own vomitus and choked. From the old and new bruises—especially the

"fingerprint" bruises around her upper arms, neck, and face—
Adele doubted anything had been accidental. Her injuries
looked hours old, as if he'd sailed around for quite a while before bringing her in to shore.

Still dressed in expensive sailing clothes, the husband hovered over his wife, angrily demanding this or that of the staff.

Her initial assessment of the patient left no shadow of a doubt
that the woman would not survive. She notified the Sausalito
police, only to discover the ER nurses had already called. An
hour later, two plainclothesmen appeared and took the husband
for a walk from which he did not return.

Adele picked up the phone out at the nurses' desk for another
try at calling Tim when Tina grunted in her direction and held
up two fingers.

"What is that?" Adele asked testily. "Victory? Charades?
Two syllables? Two words? Sounds like?"

"Line two," Tina hissed and answered another line as though
the person on the other end were her bitterest enemy.

"Your clerk having a bad day?" Tim asked when she said
hello. "Whenever she answers the phone, she has a way of
making me feel I should apologize for calling. I came close to
offering monetary amends."

"That's how she finances a new car every year," Adele said.
"I was actually calling you on the other line to tell you I think
you're a scum for leaving me that message without any explanation. I barely slept at all."

"Then why didn't you call me when you got home?"

"It was late, and I didn't want to wake you."

"Christ," he moaned, "I'm a detective, Adele. I don't sleep. I
was at the office until two. I wish I'd known," he sighed. "I
needed someone to bounce a few things off of last night."

"Lost opportunities make me nuts," she said, then, "So, you
think the cremains belong to one of the Deveraux girls?"

"Well, it sure would be a hell of a coincidence, don't you
think?"

"Yeah," Adele said, feeling afraid for Mathilde, and not
wanting to believe she was connected to the murder at the
Sweetwater—or with the Barry woman. "Jane Doe said you were
rough on her. You obviously suspect she's involved."

"I sure do—like up to her fucking armpits. I think the amnesia bit is bullshit. I think she's as phony as they—"

"Oh, come on, Tim!" she said, her temper flaring. "I've been—"

"How about we save this conversation for later?" he asked. He'd tell her about the found bodies of the Deveraux woman and her other child later. "Like over dinner and a game of Scrabble?"

The detective was the undisputed Scrabble master. Adele thought he cheated, although she couldn't figure out how he did it. She, on the other hand, ruled at backgammon—he'd yet to win more than once per session.

"How about over dinner and backgammon?" she countered.

"How about over dinner and one game of each, so that we both get to cancel out feeling like a moron after we each lose?"

"Okay, but what if one person loses both games?"

"Then they deserve to feel like a moron."

"I get out of here at three-thirty, but I have to take Nelson to his doggie shrink appointment and then I want to run a few miles. I should be ready by six."

He knew better than actually to verbalize the several million snide doggie shrink jokes that came to mind.

"Where do you want to eat?" he asked, managing through an act of sheer will to keep a straight voice.

"Have you returned to eating barnyard flesh?" Her voice was subdued yet judgmental.

"Not yet," he answered, ecstatic that he had said no to the pepper steak and onion sandwich Detective Chernin had offered at lunch. "But it's getting harder. I'm hungry all the time. I've been eyeing four-legged domestic animals, imagining how they'd taste, and last night I had a food dream about working at McDonald's and trying to take bites out of all the customer's burgers—right through the tissue paper."

"Protein," she said resolutely. "You aren't getting enough protein. Have you been mixing your grains and legumes?"

"I would never do that," he said indignantly.

"Numbskull. You're *supposed* to mix them for a complete protein. What about tofu, yogurt, hummus, soy butter? There's a thousand tasty meatless proteins out there."

"Where are they?" he asked. "I'll eat them even if they taste like kindergarten paste."

She sighed. "I'll bring a list of foods you need to incorporate into your diet and where to get them. I've got to make sure you're in top shape—we've got a lot to talk about."

"Jellyroll suggested a residence hotel not far from here that isn't too expensive," Mathilde said later, drinking the third glass of orange juice Adele had pushed on her. "I might stay there. He said I could stay at his house, but I don't think that would be a good idea. Do you?"

"Maybe not right away," Adele said, riding the fence. "You've got a lot on your plate right now."

"Did they say anything more about my having to leave?"

"No, but don't worry. Dr. Lavine is going to try and have you transferred to the psych unit for a day or two. And . . ." She did a one shouldered Italian shrug. ". . . if he can't get you transferred, it might do you good to be out of here. I live three miles down the road, so I could do your dressings once a day, that's no problem. I know Jef—Dr. Lavine will be glad to see you either free of charge or for a nominal fee until you figure out what you're going to do."

Adele finished assembling the materials for the dressing changes; they'd grown skimpier as the amount of drainage from the wounds decreased. The right hand had healed well except for the pinky. Pulling the light close, she studied the finger carefully. There were two rows of puncture type wounds on either side of the finger that she had not noticed before. They looked suspiciously like teeth marks. The marks were consistent with someone . . . or something with a small mouth—like . . . a child?

The right hand she left uncovered while she soaked off the bandages from the left in a bowl of irrigation saline. Later, she made note in the chart about the puncture wounds and that the pain had dramatically abated, allowing Mathilde to use her hands with increasing dexterity.

"Is Dr. Lavine late today?"

Holding the ball of sterile gauze, Adele paused in one of her loops around the third and fourth fingers. She looked at the clock permanently displayed in the corner of the TV.

"He'll be here," Adele said. "He was probably caught in traffic. It's really bad this time of day." She studied her patient for a moment. "You think you're ready to be out on your own?"

Mathilde shrugged. "I think so," she said, plainly making the effort to sound at ease. "I can't hide forever."

Adele studied her a moment longer. The gray eyes did not have the hardness of someone who could deliberately hurt another person . . . let alone a child. She'd looked into the eyes of enough murderers to recognize the tinge of violence that dwelled inside them always.

In one monumental round, Adele gave skilled nursing care to all of her patients. Final assessments, administering IV and oral medications, straightening rooms and supplies, giving comfort measures, suctioning, doing procedures, checking labs and treatments—all done with adroit expertise.

The last patient she tended was Barbara Greiner-Dell, who was, she figured out quickly enough, in dire trouble. Her intercranial pressure had suddenly shot up and she'd stopped having even the most basic of reflexes. While Cynthia notified the neurologist and the primary physician, she readied the woman for an emergency craniotomy.

When none of the docs responded immediately with a course of action, she called the primary and asked for the skinny. He threw a lot of medical jargon into the pot, stirred it around with some pregnant pauses, spiced it with a few significant hems and haws, then finally kneaded in some insurance coverage quotes. What came out of the oven was the lumpy, half-baked reality of modern health care for the individual patient: they weren't going to bother trying to save her because according to records she was an unrehabilitatable alcoholic with a load of DUIs to her credit, had several arrests for various and minor civil disturbances, been a victim of domestic violence, and basically was not a very productive member of the community.

Adele did what nurses whose hands are tied by the system do: provided comfort measures only for the unsavable—those lost through the cracks of the system.

* * *

To document findings and facts so as to get around the medical-legal issues in a way that would stand up to the malpractice lawyers was something that had to be done with careful precision. With the added complication of a possible murder or manslaughter issue, Adele had to be especially judicious when charting on Mrs. Greiner-Dell.

Cynthia half sat, half lay next to her, trying to chart. For the first five minutes, she repeatedly checked the end of her pen and gave it a shake until Linda came by and turned it around—writing point down.

The pen wasn't the only problem. Keeping her writing confined to the page was proving tricky. Instead of moving her pen to the next line, Cynthia continued with the line she was on until she was writing on the desk. Adele built a barrier of books at the right-hand side of the chart.

Then there was the drooling. Cynthia was charting with her chin resting on the bottom of the page. Her level of exhaustion had reached a degree where controlling certain muscles was virtually impossible. Linda and Adele intervened again: Adele lifted Cynthia's head while Linda placed an absorbent pad under her chin.

When the devitalized nurse finally staggered off to answer a call light, Adele glanced over at the page of Cynthia's nurse's notes.

Neuro: Patient was alert and unreasonable to pain. Reflexes present when struck and bitten.
Vital Signs: Yep. Has them for sure.
Cardiac/Respiratory: Lub dub with a sort of swish on the lub. Respirations in and out, in and out.
Genitourinary: Bladder and kidneys present and leaking.
Gastrointestinal: Food goes in one end—comes out other. What happens in between is apparently working.
Musculoskeletal: Yes. Skin moist and dry. Elbows present.
Psychosocial: Patient here for high strung hamstrings, however, family uninformed of both decisions.
Labs and Treatments: Both. Tests indicate abnormal culture growths despite absence of orgasms.

From over Adele's shoulder, Linda read the notes and groaned.

"Oh, Lord," she said, her voice wavering, "The chart reviewers are going to go absolutely insane."

She filled her lungs six times over and entered the morgue with a smile. David "Boxer" Takamoto waved at her from the steel table at the end of the long, narrow room. Under the surgical lamp his blue-black hair gleamed. Even from the door, she could see his boxer shorts through the clear plastic apron. There were turkeys printed on them.

"Hi, David," she called, still holding her breath. She wondered how low her blood oxygen level could go before she'd pass out.

"As if I didn't know why you're here," he said, holding his scalpel away from her as they bent over the body between them and kissed.

When she could bear it, Adele looked down at the body, which lay open neck to pubis. She took several steps back. Even though she breathed through her mouth, her olfactory glands still managed to catch the edge of the greasy sweet rotting-flesh smell. It felt as though an invisible hand had reached into her gut and grabbed a handful of intestines. Nausea crawled up her throat.

"Still can't deal with the smell, huh?" he asked with an odd sort of kindness in his voice.

She shook her head. "Guess not."

He paused. "Well, just don't pass out in the body, that's all I ask."

The thought made her want to throw up. "So what's the story on the Barry woman?"

David pointed his scalpel at the body on the table. "Adele, meet Mrs. Barry."

Adele looked closer at the face. It was the same woman she'd seen in the ER the day before.

"Mrs. Barry is a victim of the same bad guy. Same type of gun. Same angle. Same bullets. Forensics say the white fibers found near Deveraux's body match the fibers found under one of Mrs. Barry's fingernails and stuck to the palm of her right hand."

"What are they?"

"Kapok—the kind sold in bulk at every craft and fabric shop in the country."

"So what did she do? Grab at the killer?"

He screwed up one side of his mouth. "I'm not sure I'd make the assumption she grabbed at him because the fibers were on her hand—maybe because I'm not familiar with people dressing up in sleeping bags or life jackets."

Adele ignored his snicker. "So where do *you* think the fibers came from?"

"From a forensics point of view, it'd be more likely that she was wrapped in something that contained kapok for transporting her somewhere, although the body wasn't moved after she was shot."

He assessed her doubtful expression and shrugged. "Or, she could have reached out for him and grabbed his sleeping bag."

She still refused to laugh. "The woman who found her said she was alive for approximately four minutes after the shooting. Is it possible that the victim would have been mentally intact at that point?"

"Sure," he said, and from the counter behind him, he selected a labeled plastic jar containing a human heart in formalin solution. Once on the cutting board, the dark brownish organ glistened like a liver coated in egg whites. He pointed at a darkened area with his scalpel. Adele held her breath and peered down at it through the huge magnifying glass.

"As you can see here, unlike the first victim, the murderer missed Mrs. Barry's aorta altogether, but nicked the pericardium and the atrial wall, which could have put the loss of consciousness off for a few minutes—long enough that the victim would have known what she was saying, or trying to say."

Again she backed away from the table and noiselessly let out a breath. Blue and white spots rolled softly around her peripheral vision. Leaning over, presumably to retie her shoes, she breathed slow, even breaths until the spots disappeared and she was able to feel her lips when she bit them. She concentrated on the medical examiner's Thanksgiving shorts and his white hairy legs. She didn't dare look at his sock garters for too long or she'd never stop laughing.

When she straightened, David was trying to conceal his amusement by examining the inside of the body's chest wall.

"There really isn't much else to report," he said. "I've gone over both victims inside and out with a fine-toothed comb and a magnifying glass. Both entry wounds had burned margins with muzzle marks, which meant that he had the barrel of the gun right up against them when he pulled the trigger. It was quick and fairly unexpected, I think—especially with Barry.

"Neither of them showed any signs of restraint, no tape residue, no scratches, no bites, no missing hairs, or unusual bruises. Tissue, fluids, and blood toxicology were all negative, and nothing ingested or inhaled. Nothing unusual about the organs except, of course, the bullet wounds."

Takamoto shifted positions and carefully returned the heart to the jar. "Oh—there was the hair found on the first victim's shirt."

She momentarily forgot the smell that was making her nauseated. "What about it?"

"Like a child's hair: fine and curly, six inches long, light brown, completely undamaged or chemically altered."

"So what do you think? You've worked with murder victims for enough years to have an opinion of your own."

Takamoto pursed his lips and cut his eyes to the corpse's toe. "Come on, Adele, you know I don't like giving opinions off record."

"So who's recording?" she said, her hands outstretched. "Your opinion won't fall from these lips outside this room." She wanted him to hurry so she could get out into the cold November afternoon and breathe normal, polluted air. "What's your profile analysis on this guy?"

"Both of these murders were done by a practiced killer. They're precise and clean. This is a shrewd, businesslike individual who has a job to do and doesn't waste bullets or movement doing it. There aren't any remorse signs or the various psychological or psychosexual oddities that often show up— you know, bites from one portion of the body, missing patches of flesh, carving symbols or words into the body, no sexual marks or leavings or arrangement of limbs or clothes.

"From the postmortem reports on the two Paso Robles victims, it sounds like the killer has no regard for age or gender and will exterminate anyone who threatens the security of his anonymity."

Adele opened her mouth and the question "What Paso Robles victims?" was leaving her tongue when her mind did a back flip and realized she was talking not only to a friend, but also to a public official who was rather tightly wrapped—about his job, anyway.

Adele lowered her chin and pulled her jacket collar over her throat so he would not see her carotid artery pumping at race car rate. She had to remember to remain *indifferent*, as if this was all old hat. Ho-hum. She said the first, most basic thing that popped into her mind.

"What *were* the ages of the Paso Robles victims, anyway?" she asked casually. "I can't remember."

"The mother was thirty-eight. The child was seven."

"And Paso Robles didn't find any evidence on them either?" She had gone fishing with her father only once before he died, but he had taught her about the game of patience when trying to hook the fish.

"San Luis Obispo county coroner didn't find anything remarkably different other than Mrs. Deveraux was four weeks pregnant. I sent down one of our deputies to assist. They were copies of our two victims."

Was this the information that Tim had wanted to share, she wondered, or was there more? Is this why he'd been so hard on Mathilde—because he thought she might have been involved in the murder of the woman and the child?

"Tim Ritmann called today," David said, as if reading her mind. "He's interested in having us check the cremains on the child who died in the car fire over at Stinson."

"Yeah, I guess he's thinking she's related to the case?"

"It's going to be a bitch trying to prove that," the coroner said. "The Department of Justice in Berkeley is doing DNA testing. I've sent over what tissue I had left. If the specimens are good enough, they could get a definite match with tissue from the parents and sister, but the fire is going to make that tough. Your color is back."

"Huh?"

"I said your color is normal now. You were looking gray

when you came in. You must be getting used to it." He waved
his scalpel in the air and grinned. "We need a new diener down
here. If you ever want to change fields, let me know."

"Ah, that's okay, David. I think I'll continue on in the land of
the living for a while—even if it is Ward Eight."

TEN

MS. SACHES MISSED HER CALLING AS A VOICEOVER person. Her voice was one of those universally soothing and sensual voices. He waited for the end of the outgoing message.

"Hello, Ms. Saches. This is Detective Ritmann. I wanted to make sure you got my card and to say that any information you might uncover about either Mr. Deveraux or Mrs. Barry would be appreciated."

He recited his numbers again and replaced the receiver, thinking about Phillip Yates's eyes. Close set, narrow, hazel. He found it curious that the guy couldn't look him in the eye when talking about either victim—not to mention that damned tapping finger.

Turning to his computer, he entered the CEO's name again, hit the search option, sat back, and waited.

Nelson watched Her dress, commenting with his eyes and lips how he felt about the outfits She would pull out of the closet, jerk about in front of the glass, then throw on the bed in disgust.

When she put on the short black dress, he bit his upper lip and cocked his head to the side. Adele agreed: she thought it showed off more leg than was proper for having dinner with a male pal.

And don't forget that's all Tim is, Adele—a friend who desires nothing more of you than a talking head, said her most critical of invisible friends, a snobbish-looking woman Adele had named Melinda.

Next, Adele tried on a pair of full-leg rayon pants with a pink silk overblouse that matched the pink flower design of the pants.

Nelson snorted. She thought she looked like a moose wearing

an Easter basket. Tim might be only a buddy, but she still took some pride in appearing attractive.

It doesn't really matter, does it, Adele. Melinda nagged in her imaginary snob's voice. *He won't notice what you're wearing. He's still in love with Cynthia—your best friend. Why don't you wear a burlap sack?*

"Oh, shut up," Adele said, and picked out a pair of black leggings and an extra-baggy forest green turtleneck sweater that reached to mid thigh. Under the floppy collar, she pulled a narrow silk scarf and let it hang loose. A little eye makeup, a pair of simple gold earrings, and a spray of Aliage perfume, and she took stock of herself in the mirror. The end result was not bad. Even Melinda couldn't find fault.

To show his approval, Nelson smiled and lay Mickey rug on Her Italian leather boxer's shoes for exactly five seconds— which for him was a long, long time.

Invisible Melinda was replaced by Invisible Randolph the Brit who told her she looked good enough to eat and that Tim would not be able to resist falling madly in love with her—even though he probably really was in love with Cynthia.

The moment the doorbell rang, she did an immediate attitude adjustment. She reminded herself there was no romance between them and that they were simply friends going out to refuel their bodies and exchange a little information.

When she opened the door, she had a clear view of his nicely shaped buttocks. He was bent over, his backside to her, and cooing to the dark in a strange falsetto voice she'd never heard him use before. She said nothing, wondering if the stresses of his job had proved too much for him.

"You've got a bunny rabbit under your porch," he said with a child's delight. "I think he's tame. He came right up and sniffed my hand."

"That's Nelson's lagomorph," she said dryly. "He brought it home last night and I made the mistake of feeding it."

"Aren't you going to let it stay in the house? It's cold and wet out here."

For a moment, Adele clearly saw Timmy Ritmann pleading with his mommy to let him keep the snake he caught in the garden. Exasperated, she put her hand on her hip. "Christ on a bike, you're as bad as Nelson. No."

"Oh," he said, disappointed. "Well, is it okay if *I* come in?"

She opened the door. Before Tim could get all the way through the door, the rabbit hopped between his feet and went for the kitchen, where Nelson welcomed his pet by sharing dinner—an onion pancake and a Waldorf salad.

At the restaurant, Adele insisted on being seated in the "Monkey Room"—that out-of-the-way place set aside by every restaurant for the undesirables and unruly children. At the Larkspur Landing Good Earth, the Monkey Room was a spacious, mirrored room at the back of the restaurant.

The natural, earth-mother waitress showed them a table in the far corner. Facing the rest of the room, Adele could see that three other tables were occupied: a mother and father and three children ranging in ages from one to three sat farthest from them; directly opposite the family was an older couple and an ancient, wrinkled woman who was finding it impossible to remain upright. She had been rescued from her salad—which was several times larger than her head.

The other table, diagonal to their booth, was apparently a retirement party made up of eight nuns: a Last Supper of sorts.

"Do you think we should put in a call to the writers of *Saturday Night Live*?" she whispered, wondering if it had been a good idea to be seated among such distractions.

"I think they've already been here," he said, watching the room in the mirror behind Adele's head.

Adele ordered the Planet Burger and a spinach salad with spicy Thai dressing. For Tim she suggested the sesame tofu salad with spinach, hold the artichokes and heap on the hardboiled egg whites, sunflower seeds, fresh raw peas, jicama, carrots, and avocado. When their meals came, he ended up eating his salad, part of her Planet Burger, and then a second Planet Burger—which they shared. Three tapioca puddings later, he topped off his meal with a frozen yogurt protein shake.

"So," she said, truly in awe at the amount of food he'd consumed, and the abandon with which he'd eaten it, "was it good for you?"

Sated, he sat back in his chair and sighed. "I was so hungry I could have eaten Nevada."

Adele laughed, and let her attention wander back to the antics of their fellow Monkey Room patrons. The couple with the three hyperactive, under-Ritalinized children had left right after the amazing corncob incident, when the middle child began to scream at an impossibly high pitch and throw his food at the table of nuns.

Over carrot cake bearing the inscription BLESSED WONDER YEARS, SISTER MARY JOHN and tea, the retiring nun was opening her presents and was showing off an obviously homemade rosary made from aluminum can tabs when a corncob missile hit her square in the head and knocked off her veil.

The nun resembled a drunken penguin as she teetered backward into the table where the ancient crone had been allowed to fall asleep, head next to her soup. Exclamations of "Thar she goes!" and "Hosts of heaven!" followed while the sister rescued her headgear from the corn chowder of the somnolent antique.

The nuns were still dawdling over their tea and cake—growing louder and more giddy, it seemed to Adele, as the peals of giggling escalated.

That was around the time earth-mother waitress brought in three tough-looking biker types, all with multiple earrings, long beards, and handlebar mustaches, and all wearing studded leather wrist belts. Dumb or diabolic, the waitress seated the trio next to the Holy Sisters.

The older couple, barely enduring the company of the breathing antediluvian relic, were trying, without attracting attention, to wake her up in order to exit the place. Sleeping Beauty wasn't having any of it. Deep snores vibrated the silverware.

"They found Deveraux's wife and one of the kids in Paso Robles," Tim said without any fanfare.

"Oh?" she said, her concentration instantly back on him.

From her lack of reaction, he could tell she already knew. He started to ask how, but stopped. He didn't really want to know how she'd found out; it would only serve to complicate things, and right now all he wanted to do was uncomplicate things.

He grappled with the usual mild uncertainty as to the wisdom of spilling to her, and then told her about his interview with

Yates, and his conversation with Jack Frazer, sparing only the
uninteresting details.

She wrote furiously while he spoke, filling page after page
with wild handwriting, punctuated with arrows, underlined
words, circled words, and asterisks. To his immense surprise,
she reciprocated, admitting with the appropriate amount of cha-
grin that she had passed herself off as a deputy and interrogated
witnesses in a case that wasn't his.

"Jesus, Adele." He shook his head, studying his own notebook. "You've got to stop trying to be the FBI. You pay taxes
that pay my salary . . . so why don't you let me do my job,
huh?"

She refused to let his Big Dick on Campus insecurity affect
her. Ignoring him completely, she launched immediately into
what was uppermost in her mind.

"Okay," she began, using her pen as a pointer. "Lesa Terry
said she thought Mrs. Barry was saying 'tell.' " She paused.
"Maybe it was only part of a word that Lesa heard. Maybe Mrs.
Barry was trying to say 'Citadel.' "

A thought crossed his mind. "Before we get into that, why
don't we start with Jane Doe and the car crash."

She flashed a smile of utter delight. "Sure," she said. She
didn't know what she'd expected, but it wasn't Detective Ritmann wanting to engage in official brainstorming with her. Somewhere in the Melinda part of her thinking, she also thought it
incredibly pathetic that she was as excited about engaging in investigations as a normal woman would be about engaging in
sexual relations.

"Fact," began Tim. "We've sent teletyped found person photos
and prints to all western state law enforcement agencies and to
all the western state newspaper agencies and we've yet to get a
positive ID on her. That's surprising."

"What about Canada?" Adele asked. "Maybe she lives in
Canada."

"Good idea." In his notebook, Tim wrote: *1. Send notice to
Royal Canadian Mounted Police.*

"In a day or two we'll send the photo and prints to the rest of
the states, including Alaska, the U.S. Virgin Islands, and
Hawaii." He folded his arms over his chest.

Adele leaned back, picking at a stray shred of carrot. "What I want to know is, if the child who burned in the car was in fact the other Deveraux daughter, what was she doing with Jane Doe? Who is Jane Doe to the Deveraux family?"

In his notebook, Tim entered: *2. Ask LAPD to show Jane Doe photo to Deveraux friends and relatives—baby-sitter? Relative? Visiting friend?*

"Okay," Tim began. "Mrs. Deveraux and the two children were kidnapped—"

"*If* they were kidnapped," Adele reminded him. "Remember LAPD said there was no sign of force, only that she didn't plan on being gone long."

Behind him there was a commotion, and Adele let her eyes wander back to the narcoleptic relic. The three bikers and three of the nuns were helping to carry the wizened old lady out the back door—pallbearers sans coffin.

As they passed, Sister Mary John tittered, "You boys remind me of the apostles Peter, Paul, and Luke." She gave a flirtatious wagging of her one continuous eyebrow. "They're my favorites."

"Okay," Tim said. "Mrs. D and the two kids were abducted the evening before Mr. D's murder—probably between five and six P.M. According to the San Luis Obispo medical examiner, Mrs. D and her oldest daughter were probably shot between ten P.M. and midnight that night, which would be about how long it took to drive from Los Angeles to Paso Robles.

"From Paso Robles to Marin County is a three- or four-hour drive, which puts the murderer here in the early morning hours. That leaves the murderer and possibly the child hanging low until Gerald Deveraux was shot between one and two P.M. that afternoon. Approximately two or three hours later, Jane Doe and the kid go off the road out at Stinson."

Tim sat back, his eyes still on his notes, his jaw muscles working.

"What about the pager?"

"There were four pages, all of which were to the same number." He shifted his position and rubbed the back of his neck. "We traced them to a cell phone that's registered to a Leslie Normac. I've got one of the guys working on it."

Adele watched his jaw for a moment and went back to her own notes. "Can we get a police sketch of the man who rented the car from the Budget agent and send it to Paso Robles, and L.A.?"

Tim nodded. "It's on its way to both agencies. They'll post it along with the photos of Mrs. D and the children—gas stations, rest stops, bulletin boards, motels, show it to all the witnesses."

He rested his chin on his thumbs. "Why didn't the killer get rid of both kids in Paso Robles?"

Adele shook her head, recalling a week she'd spent in Paso Robles. She found the town beyond bizarre: a place Clive Barker might want to use as a setting for one of his novels. For the most part, the people were a strange mixture of Vietnam vets, Camp Roberts military people, immigrant Mexican farmworkers, horse people, farmers, grape growers, and supposedly rehabilitated patients from Atascadero State Mental Hospital.

"Maybe both kids weren't with him," Adele said. "Maybe Jane Doe already had the other child. Or . . ." Adele raked her fingernails through her hair. "Paso Robles is as rural as they get. The town closes down when the cows come home. One of the flashbacks Jane Doe had was of sitting in a farmhouse at a table with a man. When I surprised her with the glasses the man who rented the vehicle supposedly wore, it brought up a memory of a man she feared was going to hurt her. A bad person, as she put it."

"Maybe whoever kidnapped and killed the Deverauxs kidnapped Jane Doe as well. Maybe she was visiting Mrs. Deveraux or maybe she was a baby-sitter."

"Or," Tim said, "she could have witnessed the killings by mistake and been forced to go with the killer, escaping with the child and the car when they got to Marin. Or . . ." He looked directly at her. ". . . Jane Doe could be an accomplice to the kidnappings and the murders."

"No." Adele shook her head. "Absolutely not."

"You don't know that, Adele. She could be faking this whole—"

"Not possible," Adele said. "Next."

Tim sighed, and commenced writing in his book. She wouldn't even entertain the possibility. Stubborn as a mule. It was the one weak area in her otherwise flawless profile as an investigator. *4. Photo of Jane Doe to Paso Robles for community posting. 5. Budget agent composite—show Jane Doe.*

"My guess is she's an innocent bystander who got pulled into the fray," Adele persisted. "Somewhere along the way, the killer realized he couldn't handle the kid by himself and needed a baby-sitter."

"That's iffy," Tim said tilting his head. "I think we would have had a positive ID on her by now. If she was kidnapped off the street, someone would have reported her."

"What if Jane Doe knew the killer and was bribed or black-mailed into going along?" Adele asked.

"Except this guy is a professional," Tim said. "He's going to have minimal outside involvement if any at all. One thing I know for sure is that I want to avoid risking a media frenzy by publicly connecting Jane Doe with the Deveraux cases. The media love Northern–Southern California cases. They'll put the whole state into a mass panic with serial killer or conspiracy stories. The *Pacific Intelligencer* is already playing up the serial killer aspect."

They both sat back, studying their notes.

"The child could have been used as a bait to get to Deveraux or to get something from him before he was killed," Adele volunteered.

"Okay, but what did Deveraux have that someone wanted that bad?"

"Information?"

Tim rapped out a tune with his pen and stopped. "Maybe, or maybe he was being silenced—removed from the playing field."

"Or maybe both," Adele said. "Which brings us back to Citadel. Why would Yates clean the personnel files?"

"I'm going to assume it's something personal." Tim shifted, "Maybe Yates was sleeping with Mrs. Barry and they were caught by Deveraux, or Deveraux and Yates were having sex and Mrs. . . ."

She raised her head and gave him a weary look. "Oh please. That's totally outrageous. Please, Ritmann, please tell me you're kidding." She took a roll from the bread basket, ripped off a piece, and chewed like he'd seen baseball pitchers chew to-bacco. "First of all, that stuff wouldn't be in a personnel file," she continued. "Secondly, this is San Francisco—nobody cares about anybody else's sexual proclivities."

She tapped out a rhythm on the rim of her teacup. "I think Yates had to have been involved up to his balls with them in something shady. Why else would he hold back parts of their files?"

Tim opened his mouth to answer, but Adele held up a hand.

"Yates would withhold information if he thought it was going to reflect badly on him or the company. Both Deveraux and Barry quit at the same time. Maybe they were involved in a scam of some sort where they got in over their heads. Can you get ahold of what was in the original files?"

Tim pulled back his lips and cocked his head. "Doubt it. If Yates doesn't want us to see it, you can bet it's history. I want to see what we can do outside the company—talk to the families, check bank accounts. Deveraux and Barry might have had something on Yates.

"Chernin found someone at Citadel who remembers both Barry and Deveraux. She said one day they were there, and the next they were gone. Neither of them even came in for their personal effects. Their secretaries sent everything to them."

The three bikers strode back in with the nuns twittering at their sides. The rough-looking gentlemen held out the nuns' chairs for them. The whole crew looked as pleased as schoolchildren after playing their first game of spin the bottle.

Tim looked over his to-do list, resting it against the empty tapioca dish. "What about Jane Doe?" he asked finally.

Adele chewed another piece of the nine-grain roll, shook her head and sighed. "I don't know. I went over the psychiatrist's progress notes this afternoon. He was thinking of asking her permission to do an Amytal interview. If she refuses and Jeffrey can't get her transferred to Psych, she'll be eighty-sixed tomorrow or—"

"*Jeffrey?*"

She looked away. The blush began at the base of her neck and moved upward. "Dr. Lavine. The psychiatrist assigned to—"

"*Jeffrey?*" he repeated with a sickly smile. His stomach was going into a jealousy death knot somewhere up around his throat.

She gave him a look that would have fried the lice off a kindergartner's head. "What *is* the problem, Timothy? I happen to work with the man professionally."

"No problem," he said defensively. "It's just that I've never heard you call a doc by a first name before."

"Jeff and I were . . ." She searched his face, looking for the true cause of his accusatory tone. It couldn't be jealousy; it had to be a case of pity: in his eyes she was the desperate divorcee trying to imply that she had some sort of intimacy with a man— even if he was a shrink.

Her blush went to scarlet. She hoped to God he wouldn't add insult to injury and try to set her up on another mercy date. His last attempt to fob her off on Peter Chernin was almost more than she could take.

Fighting off his masculine insecurity demon, Tim suddenly felt his guts tighten around a ball of broken glass. What if she and this Jeffrey guy were involved? A shrink? A shrink might be clever and adjusted enough to interest a woman like Adele.

Adele found herself stuttering. "A—a long time ago, we were, ah . . ."

Tim grabbed for his cell phone, which was vibrating on his belt. "Hello?"

"Tim?"

Tim had an auditory memory like some people had photographic memories. Once he heard a voice or a sound, it was imprinted forever. "Here's to you, Mr. Robinson, Jesus loves you more than he can say. What's happening, brother?"

"How the hell did you know it was me?" Hermonicus Robinson asked, pausing in his hopping from foot to foot.

"I'm psychic. What's up?"

The San Anselmo homicide investigator pulled his collar closer around his neck and shook his head. "Listen, I hate to bother you, man, but we've got a one eighty-seven working off Redwood Road. The widow of our victim says he used to work for a company called Citadel. I heard you and Twin Cities are working a couple of cases with victims who were employees there."

Tim turned around in his chair frowning, uncertain whether or not Adele should overhear any of this. "Yeah, well, you heard right on that."

"I don't know if there's any connection," the detective continued, "but I thought I'd run it by you before we get too far into it. You might want to get on over here and take a look."

"Who's your victim?"

"Alan Hightower. Sixty-eight. Retired. No record. Mr. Model Citizen."

Tim reached up and pressed his thumb into the tense muscles of his shoulder. "How'd he die?"

"A centerpunch gunshot. Maybe a twenty-two or a twenty-five. It looks old, like maybe he was shot last night or early this morning. The—" Robinson covered the mouthpiece and shouted to someone that the entrance was over there to the left—no, to the left! He came back on the line muttering, "Christ Almighty, peckerhead doesn't know his left from his right. The coroner's investigator has arrived."

Tim paused, reached back and raised his coffee mug. "It sure does sound similar to our other two victims. Both of them were done with a single round to the heart." He took a sip. "I can't imagine the odds against three people from the same company all dying the same way within a few days of each other *not* being tied in, but I sure would love to bet those odds."

"Hey, even I'd put something down on that one, and I ain't no gambling man." Robinson blew into his hand to warm his fingers as he watched the widow being led down the front porch steps in the freezing rain. She was the whitest white person he'd ever seen, except the ones he'd seen pulled out of the bay after a few days.

"Does it look like the wife knows much?" Tim asked.

"Naw, man. She was visiting her sister down in San Jose for the last two days. She's the one who found him. She says the last time she talked to him on the phone was last night about ten. That woman was so shook up, I thought she was going to be joining the old man."

"Who else is working with you on this?"

"The best," Robinson said, feeling in his coat pocket for his gloves. He'd started to shiver. "Sandberg and Yuen are here."

"How long have your ID guys been there?"

"About an hour." He hopped from foot to foot again—he hated these goddamned northern California winters.

"Shit. Well, I guess I ought to come over and have me a little look-see. Appreciate you letting me know right away on this. What's the address again?"

As he wrote it in his notebook, Adele leaned forward and

pointed to herself, smiling a wide, questioning grin. He waved her away.

"Okay. I'll be there in fifteen, plus ten minutes to convince my date that this is important enough to interrupt a near-perfect evening."

Adele shook her head and glared at him.

"Why don't you have your dispatch try to reach Krenshaw and let him know what's up? He might want to get a look—that is, if you can find him this time of night."

Both men chuckled. Detective William Krenshaw, a recent divorcé, had an active social and sexual life.

"You think we might have something bigger than we want to know about here, boss?" Robinson asked.

"No doubt, my man. At the least I think we'll all need to put the three cases in parallel and see what's up. I'll bring the coffee. See you in a few."

Adele had already come to her feet and was gathering her things, firing questions one after the other, before he could even put his cell phone back into his pocket. She wore an enraptured expression until he shook his head.

"You absolutely cannot go to the scene with me. I couldn't even allow you to wait in the car."

She did not throw a fit or get pouty—that would have been easy to walk away from. Instead her exhilaration faded into a sadness that made him want to fall on his knees and kiss her feet, begging for forgiveness. It was like taking milk away from a starving baby.

"Oh. Okay," she said quietly, playing out the role of the brave little soldier. "I guess you'd better get over there. I'll take a taxi home. Don't worry about me."

Her hair was pulled back in a French braid though much of it had worked its way loose and hung in strands around her thin face. The look of those loose strands somehow made him feel lower than a snake. He wished there was a way to make it up to her. "Don't be foolish. Your house is on the way."

She marched past him toward the front of the restaurant. Halfway to the cashier, right next to a table occupied by a lone diner, she turned, her face glowing with new hope. "Want to come over afterwards for coffee? We can discuss this some more?"

Tim hesitated, then, as his guts went into revolt, shook his head. "Can't. It's going to be a late night. It's already eight."

"If he doesn't want to," said the man by whose table they'd stopped, "I'd love to come over for coffee."

Adele laughed and hurried on to the cashier, disappointment burning in her temples. "How can you turn me down after what we've shared just now?" she asked, trying to keep the pleading out of her voice.

The older couple in front of them turned to glance at Tim. The woman looked him over head to foot, one eyebrow arched. She smiled at Adele.

"It's not me, Adele," he whispered. "I can't show up at a scene with a civilian, and I honestly don't know how long it's going to take. We could end up in a bull session that could last until tomorrow morning."

"But if it doesn't—will you? Please say yes."

The woman in front of them suddenly turned and jabbed him in the arm with her car keys. "You treat this girl nice!" insisted the woman, in an accent like Mirek's. She glared at him with a ferocious look similar to the police attack dogs he'd seen. "She want yes, you tell her yes!"

Tim rubbed his arm where the key had gouged him. "Okay, okay," he laughed, holding up his hands. "Yes. I promise yes, I'll stop by."

"Good." The elderly woman stuck out her chin in stubborn righteousness. "Life—it is too short for no."

"That's right," Adele said. "No is not an option."

ELEVEN

ADELE CHECKED HER MESSAGES. THERE WAS HER mother pushing the institution of Thanksgiving again, and then a barely coherent message from Cynthia about how Officer Sullivan had been *so* kind to have followed her home and did she know that in Florida women were frequently arrested for indulging in the male-dominated sport of running? There was a hang-up, then Mrs. Coolidge asking, in a nettled tone, where she *ever* got the idea of Idahoan terrorists bombing the city, and didn't she think she should have come to tell her as a *common* courtesy, because she and Queen Shredder had almost *starved* to death in that tiny closet.

Last was a message from Jeffrey wanting to know if they could do dinner sometime and please page him whenever she got home.

"An adulterous germ of trouble waiting for an accepting Petri dish in which to philander," she said to Nelson as she exchanged her dinner clothes for her night-time sleuthing clothes—leggings, turtleneck, socks, gloves, and watchcap—all black as night. Even her running shoes had been blackened with shoe polish.

According to the white pages, Alan Hightower's address was an easy two- or three-mile run from the hospital. It'd be like taking a stroll.

She crouched against the back wall of the garage having flashbacks to when she was ten years old and spying on the neighborhood boys by pressing her ear against the back wall of their fort—a refrigerator box that had been painted camouflage green and brown and had window flaps cut into the sides.

Instead of farting and belching contests, baseball trivia, and absurd boastings about who had the fastest bicycle, these grown boys had gathered around the massive pool table that stood in the middle of the Hightower garage to discuss the particulars of murder. But her hearing wasn't as acute as it had been when she was ten, the wall of the garage wasn't cardboard, and the windows were shut, all of which made it extremely difficult to hear the particulars.

She'd managed to steal a peek at the scene going on inside: Tim was standing to the left of the pool table, Detective Krenshaw sat on an old bar stool at the opposite end of the garage. Leaning against the other side of the table from Tim was a fortyish black man of average height and weight. His hair was prematurely thinning in front so that his forehead looked abnormally large, thus giving him a scholarly look. He wore a fifties style of glasses, where the top of the frame was black plastic, and the bottoms were metal. This, she guessed, was Hermonicus Robinson.

Pieces of sentences in three different voices made their way through the wall to her waiting ear.

". . . neighbor said she saw . . ." Mumbling and then an exclamation in Tim's voice: ". . . at two in the morning!?" General laughter. ". . . like a Catholic priest . . . last rites!" Burst of loud, prolonged laughter. Long period of mumbling and then a few four-letter epithets. "Could . . . disguise?" "Costume shop . . . cop uniform as easy as a chicken suit . . ." Laughter. A pause. ". . . check . . . wife doing okay?" Mumbling while a door opened and closed. ". . . heart problems . . ." A loud yawn. Another yawn. "Don't *do* that!" "What . . . Citadel CEO?" "Christ, the guy . . . file . . . he wouldn't look . . . finger . . ." Mumbling. "Cini checked . . . clean record as far as . . ." Silence. "Need . . . talk with Yates . . ." Mumble. ". . . Jane Doe at . . . Budget . . . car." "Connection . . . Deveraux?" "Fuck, man, that's . . ."

A wave of pins and needles went down her shoulders and arms as her attention shifted from the voices in the garage to the rustling of the leaves behind her. Matching the rhythm of the steps in the leaves, she moved backward, then broke for the cover of a hedge five feet away, parallel to the side of the garage.

Judging from the wheezing respirations, whoever had taken

her place at the back wall either had asthma or severe chronic obstructive pulmonary disease. Lying flat on the ground, she crept the length of the hedge and peered through the thick branches.

An elderly man stood with his ear in approximately the same spot where her ear had been seconds before. On the end of a leash at his feet sat a sorry excuse for a dog. It was the dog who was wheezing.

She stood. "Pssst."

Engrossed in straining to hear the conversation going on inside the garage, the old man didn't hear her. Adele had to move directly in his line of view and jump up and down before he noticed and made his way over to her.

"Hello," she whispered in a conspiratorial way—as though skulking around other people's yards and listening through walls was normal. "What's going on over there?"

"I think . . ." The man pulled back to look at her. "Who are you?"

"I'm a new neighbor. I recently moved in down the street and I saw—"

"What number?" The old man was eyeing her suspiciously, forgetting that he'd been the one caught eavesdropping.

Adele tried to recall the street map of the area. "The third house from the end down there." She waved her hand in the general direction of where the road wound around for another half mile. "The cute Cape Cod? With the green bird bath in the side yard, and the sundial in the front?"

At her feet, the boxer busily sniffed her legs and shoes, getting a snoutful of Nelson.

The man grunted and pulled on the leash. The collar was red leather, on which someone had painted "MAX" in white.

"What's going on?" Adele asked, pointing at the Hightower house.

"I don't know," the man said slowly, depressed. "Somebody broke in and murdered Alan Hightower. Irene Graham . . ." The man jerked a gnarled thumb at the house across the street. ". . . says she saw a priest walking out in the middle of the night."

"Did you know Mr. Hightower?"

He tilted his head tentatively and shrugged one shoulder. "Oh, you know. We were neighbors twenty-five years. I'd borrow tools, he'd borrow tools . . ." The man looked away and wiped his nose with his thumb. "Al and I shot the breeze. He was a good bridge player. He—"

He stopped, hunched his shoulders. "This is a crazy world you young people live in. People breaking into your house in the middle of the goddamn . . ." His eyes filled again. A choking sound came from his throat.

She looked away, her throat tightening. "Is Mrs. Hightower okay?" she asked after a minute.

"They took her off to Ellis." He wiped his eyes. "Jeannette's heart isn't so good. She's the one who found him when she got back from visiting her sister. Come home and found him on the living room floor. A hole as big as a plate right in the middle of his chest."

He looked up at her, his eyes wide and wet with his question. "Why would somebody want to do that? God knows he didn't have any money or anything of value around the house. He didn't have anything . . . nothing worth *killing* the man over."

Adele reached out to him. The tears rolled down his face and landed on the back of her hand.

"I don't know," she said softly. "It isn't fair."

He shook his head and took in a breath. "It sure isn't. It's a downright shame. Makes a man think he's lived too long."

They were silent for a minute, then he stretched out his hand. "I'm Bud Winters. I live at number four-twelve." He pulled on the leash. "This old guy here is Max."

Adele shook his hand and introduced herself. She made a fuss over Max, who reciprocated by lifting his leg and trying to relieve himself on hers. She was too quick for the canine and jumped up and away before he could activate the stream.

They bid each other goodnight and walked in opposite directions. Ten feet away, they looked over their shoulders, checking on one another. Adele wondered how long it would be before Bud Winters's ear would again be glued to the back wall of the Hightower garage.

She couldn't pass by Ellis without stopping in. It was a sickness of nurses, the need to verify that the patients were able to survive without their personal help. At the same time, going into a hospital when she was off duty gave her a sense of freedom, of being safe from Administration's rules, regulations, and reprimands.

Ward 8 felt like Customs in a foreign country. The 7 P.M. to 7 A.M. crew was mostly made up of unfriendly and unhappy registry nurses, most of whom she'd never seen before. Only Malloy was joyful in his baldheaded Zen way, doing what ward/monitor clerks did best: keeping the cogs rolling forward, under control and within normal limits.

When he saw her, he waved and nodded. His large blue eyes lent even more of an air of calm to his demeanor. "Good to see your lovely face this evening, Ms. Monsarrat."

Adele returned his greeting, picked up Jane Doe's chart, and sat down in the computer corner. She opened to the physician's progress notes and found the discharge orders form filled in and signed by Dr. Murray. Mathilde was to be discharged in the morning with orders that she see him in his office for follow-up burn care the following day.

A transfer request to the psych ward appeared nowhere in the chart. The last line of Jeffrey's notes read, "Pt. refused Amytal interview. Will follow as outpatient in office 3 × wk. Pt. agreeable to this contract."

For a moment Adele was baffled; Jeffrey had been so adamant about keeping her within reach. Dodging the inquiring stares of the nurses, she strode boldly down the hall to Mathilde's room, knocked, and entered. The room was different. Gone were the IV poles and the cache of burn dressings that the nurses had stockpiled. Absent, too, was the "goodies box" on the windowsill—that stash of graham crackers, cans of juice, wrapped sandwiches, and fresh fruit that most of the patients kept as emergency rations for either midnight snacks or when the regular meals were more unpalatable than usual.

All were signs that Ellis was weaning her, getting ready to kick her from the nest.

Mathilde sat in a chair next to her bed reading the evening edition of the *Pacific Intelligencer*.

"Sorry for barging in," Adele began. "I came by to check on something, and saw you're being discharged in the morning. Are you okay with that?"

Mathilde folded the newspaper. No longer pale and hollow eyed, she seemed almost happy.

"It's fine with me," Mathilde said. "Mrs. Noel came in right after you'd gone home and told me the hospital was letting me go. I decided it was the best thing. I've rented a room at that residence hotel Jellyroll told me about and . . ."

Adele counted to ten and tried to listen at the same time. It wasn't so much that Mathilde was being discharged, but that Mattie Noel had deliberately waited until she'd left work to tell Mathilde she had to go. Sneaky. Backhanded. It was so nursing-administration-ish.

". . . I gave a list to Jellyroll of some basic things I'd need. Comb, toothbrush . . . a pair of jeans or a simple dress, a blouse, jacket and gloves. I remembered all my sizes. I was making the list and they came out automatically. I didn't even have to think about them."

"Does Dr. Lavine know that you've been discharged?"

"He was here when Mrs. Noel told me. He tried to sell me on going with the drug-induced trance."

"And you refused?"

Mathilde didn't answer right away, but there was an immediate change in her demeanor. She glanced out the window then back at Adele, her eyes motionless and deep. "I don't want to do that. It scares me to death."

"Why is that?"

"I don't have much control over my life, and that's giving up the trivial control I do have. I'm not ready. I'm afraid I'd go crazy, or end up a blank." Her voice still had that odd melodious huskiness that was so soothing, but it suddenly went higher. Mathilde grabbed her hand. "They can't force me to do that, can they? They can't get a court order to make me have the drug?"

Adele almost laughed until she saw the panic in the woman's eyes. "Of course they can't," she said gently. "It's your choice."

Mathilde visibly relaxed and sat back. "I'm going to see Dr. Lavine three times a week in his office to start. I'll pay him as much as I can. I hate the idea of being a charity case.

"There's over two thousand dollars in donation money. That will last until I get a job. I can work as a receptionist or a grocery clerk. I'll make up a Social Security number and a name if I have to. Until I'm able to buy a junker or lease a car, I can take buses and taxis."

Adele saw nothing in the woman's face that indicated she was apprehensive about leaving and being on her own. Knowing Mathilde felt safe eased her mind. "I'm off tomorrow. How about if I give you a ride to the hotel? We can swing by my house and then you can meet Nelson. If you want, I've got a lot of clothes you can go through."

"Thanks for the offer, but I can't let you do that. You've helped so much already. I've already arranged for a taxi to—"

"Taxi shmaxi." Adele sighed. "Forget it, Jane Doe. I'll be here at ten." Adele got up to leave. "Besides, Nelson is dying to meet you."

At the nurses' desk she paged Jeffrey and, while she waited, watched the nurses flounder around the unit looking for supplies, trying desperately to fall into the routine of a ward most of them had never worked before. Every few minutes one of them would ask her if she worked there and did she know where this or that was kept. Adele wondered if they were R.N.'s or L.V.N.'s, or nurse's aides, and decided she didn't want to know.

When Jeffrey hadn't called by the end of twenty minutes, she first imagined him at a formal dinner, surrounded by San Francisco politicians and celebrities. Then she exchanged that image for the idea that he was probably in the middle of making love with his wife. She ended with the vision of him and an architect, pipes lit and hanging from their mouths, fastidiously going over plans for his new, six-thousand-square-foot house on Mount Tam.

She was on her way out of the unit, having convinced herself that he was in Paris renewing his wedding vows, when Malloy announced with the right amount of Zen calm that Dr. Lavine was on line three.

"Did I interrupt anything important?" she asked, sounding much too hopeful.

"Yes, you did," he said. "I was crawling under the house with the butt end of a flashlight stuck in my mouth, sliding around in the mud, scorpions, black widows, and mice turds, looking for a leaky pipe."

"How repulsive."

"My sentiments exactly. I'll bet you're calling about Mathilde?"

"Ayuhn. What happened to the transfer to Psych?"

He took in a long breath and let it out slowly. "I changed my mind. She was adamant about not having the Amytal, which was fine—she doesn't need to be hanging out with a bunch of crazies down in Psych. Unfortunately there isn't a pill I could give her. Despite all our pharmacological breakthroughs, we have yet to come up with a really good reliable drug treatment for dissociative disorders. But I think therapy will be enough, especially as she continues to develop trust in me and in her own ability to handle the bits of the puzzle as they emerge from the darker, terror-infested places of her memory."

"It sounds like under your house."

Jeffery burst out laughing. "God, I miss you sometimes, Adele," he said, warmth in his voice.

She wondered if she ever missed him, and decided that what she really missed was the companionship of someone secure and normal; it really wasn't so much *him*. Was it?

"I'm going to see her three times a week," he continued. "She'll need it. I'll keep pressing on the edge where comfort meets discomfort, moving back and forth just below the level of her correct test strength. I'll ride out the fee, though I probably shouldn't."

"Then why are you?"

He hesitated. "Impure motives," he said hesitantly. "This is definitely a once-in-a-lifetime case to publish. Either an article in the Green Journal—"

"The what?"

"The *American Journal of Psychiatry*, with a case presentation. Actually better than that would be a psychiatric thriller—maybe something along the lines of the movie *Awakenings*?"

"You'd never get Mathilde to agree to that," Adele said.

"I know, but I could probably get away with writing directly about the case without a release. I mean, after all, exactly who is there to sign it?"

Both of them laughed. Yuppie or not, it was part of his twisty side that she loved. Warding off the old feelings, she listened hard, reaching for solid reasons not to fall under the allure of him. In the background, she heard a child babbling and a female voice cooing.

"You aren't mixed up with any of Ellis's political b.s. in this situation, are you?" she asked. "I mean, you didn't give in to their bullshit about not wanting to carry a charity case?"

"Definitely not. Mrs. Noel came in during our session and told Mathilde she had to go. The rest is exactly as I told you. Are you questioning my integrity as a professional?" He sounded amused.

"No. I want to make sure you weren't pressured into releasing her, that's all."

Two call bells went off simultaneously.

"By the way, why *are* you at the hospital, Miss I-Have-a-Personal-Life?"

Her defense hackles rose. "I stopped in on my way home from a date to check on Mathilde."

"A date?" he mocked. "A serious date? With whom?"

"My date is your business? You don't find me asking you about your wife, do you?"

"No, but you want to."

"Pffft! Shut up." Suddenly an idea hit her like a softball to the forehead. "Hey! What would you think of Mathilde applying for a job at Ellis?"

"Depends on the job. I don't think she could handle anything too strenuous—mentally, physically, or emotionally. I mean, you don't want to start her out in the morgue or anything like that."

"I was thinking along the lines of a clerk in the administrative offices or maybe the medical library."

"That might be okay, as long as she doesn't have to deal with a lot of stress. Did you get the message I left for you earlier tonight at home? I was wondering if you wanted to have dinner some time this week?"

"Ah. The Petri dish."

"Huh?"

"I'd love to have dinner with you and your wife. It'll give me a chance to check out the winner."

"Hey, that's great! Rita has wanted to meet you for a long time. How about Thursday night? Do you like Japanese food?"

Adele swallowed. "Thursday?" Her voice had risen in pitch. She sounded like a Barbie doll might if it had a voice. "I'll check on that and get back to you."

"Sure." He laughed. "Get back to me, you yellow-bellied coward."

After she hung up, she ignored the momentary stirring in her stomach, thinking about how she would feel sitting across a plate of rice and raw dead fish staring at Mrs. Lavine. She had picked up the phone again to call the personnel office to see if there was an open position suitable for Mathilde when she looked at the clock. It was late; the office was closed.

Retracing her steps down the hall to Mathilde's room, she ran through how she should present the idea of a job at Ellis, though the back of her mind was still working on what it would be like having dinner with Jeff and Mrs. Lavine. The thought alone made her squirm with discomfort—she'd never put much stock by women who ended up making friends out of their ex's wives or new girlfriends.

She was running through a list of excuses a psychiatrist might buy when she pushed open the door to Mathilde's room.

The three detectives sat in the private back room of the Twin Cities station studying the artists' sketches of the Hightower shooter, the Barry shooter, and the car rental man, with the concentration people give to a card trick.

To Tim's eye, there wasn't much similarity, except they all wore glasses. The Barry suspect appeared to have a larger nose and thinner face than the others; the Hightower suspect, a higher forehead. The car rental suspect had a beard, bushy eyebrows, hooked nose, and chipmunk cheeks.

The rest of the physical descriptions conflicted as well. The car rental man was about five-nine with a limp and a paunch. Humbold thought the "cop" driving the Jeep in Kentfield was taller and had broad shoulders, no extra fat. The priest was shorter, maybe five-seven, and thin.

When his cell phone buzzed, all of them automatically pulled out their sets and answered in unison.

"Mr. Ritmann?"

"Yes, Mr. Lee?" said Tim, getting up from the conference table and walking out into the hall.

There was a pause. "How'd you know it was me?"

Tim reminded himself to stop surprising people that way. "Oh, I've got an ear for voices. What's going on, Francis?"

"I was thinking about that day the man got shot? You said to tell you anything I could think of that was different?"

"Did you come up with something?"

"It might be nothing, but I thought . . ." He swallowed nervously. "I . . . I thought you could, you know, see if it means something."

"I'll do my best. I want to know anything that seemed out of the ordinary."

"Okay. 'Member I told you that I kept going back to the room next door to Mr. Deveraux's? And the time I delivered the champagne . . . about forty minutes after I dropped off Mr. Deveraux's lunch? Remember me saying that?"

"Sure. I remember. What about it?"

"The time I delivered the champagne, there was this dude got on the elevator with his kid when I was going back to the kitchen. The little girl was holding a stuffed animal. She was— oh, I don't know, maybe 'bout three or four years old?

"I didn't think nothing of it before, 'cause we had this family in the hotel that had eight or nine kids. But then I was thinking about it, and I remembered that the family with the kids was one floor above Mr. Deveraux. The man I saw with the kid that afternoon got in the car one floor below Mr. Deveraux's floor. There weren't no kids on that floor, and no candy machines or anything like that, either.

"I remember I thought the man with the kid had got off at the wrong floor and was getting back on the elevator to go up to his own floor, but he got out at the lobby and went out.

"Then, about nine o'clock that night I brought up a bunch of cereal and milk to the family with the kids, and saw that it wasn't the dude that got on the elevator. There weren't no other kids checked in the hotel that night unless maybe the man and the kid came to visit somebody."

"What did the guy look like that got on the elevator?" Tim asked.

"Not big. Maybe he was about five feet, eight inches. He had one of them fringe beards and a beer belly. Big nose that was kinda red."

"What about the eyes?"

"I couldn't see the eyes, man. He was wearing these glasses, made his eyes look all psychedelic."

"Psychedelic?"

"You know, they was all different colors. What's that word you call it when they shine all colors? Fluorescent? No, that ain't it . . . I mean . . ."

"Iridescent?"

"Yeah, that's it. My old lady, she's got earrings look like that."

"Would you recognize the child from a photograph?"

Francis thought for a second. "I think so. She was fussing and crying, but I think I can remember what she looked like."

"You say she was fussing?" Tim asked.

"Yeah. I remember now it was kinda strange because she was hollering for her daddy."

"When they went through the lobby, did you see where they went?"

"No, I sure didn't. I stayed on the car down to the kitchen."

"Okay, Francis. You at the hotel now?"

"Yes, sir."

"I'll be over before you get off work. Maybe you can take a look at this photo. I want you to look at a police sketch too. See if you recognize the man."

"That's fine. I'm working for my friend José tonight, so I'll be here until six in the morning."

Tim hung up and was halfway through the conference room door when his ears picked up the word "Ellis." He backed out, following the sound of voices until he found himself outside the dispatcher's office.

"What's up? Something going on at Ellis?" he asked the very pregnant woman behind the console.

The dispatcher pulled the microphone part of her headset to her mouth, and waved at him. After a second, she clicked a couple of buttons and looked up. She was ten words into her answer when Tim hurried back to the conference room, excused himself, then ran for his car.

The only light was from the street lamp. "Mathilde?" Adele whispered to the lump under the covers. "Are you awake?" The horizontal blinds stirred from the cold breeze that came in through the open window. Other than the "do not disturb at night" order, Mathilde's second request when she first came in was that the window be kept open at night. She claimed she needed fresh air; Adele guessed it had more to do with feeling trapped.

"Mathilde?" She took a step closer to the bed and froze. It suddenly occurred to her that Mathilde was not there, and that she had left—climbed out the window and escaped by the fire escape. She wouldn't be the first patient of Ward 8 to depart using that route.

Or, Mathilde could be dead—killed herself, or died from an undetected injury.

"Mathilde!" she raised her voice in a sharp command. Her hand came in contact with the bed—which was empty. Her eyes focused on the rumpled, haphazard sheets and blanket. Behind her was a scraping sound and a breath. The hair on the back of her neck stood up as she crouched and swung around at the same time.

In the shadow of the bathroom, Mathilde's body was dangling, feet off the floor, her neck wedged at an odd angle in the crook of a muscular arm. The man's hand was so tightly pushed against her mouth and nose that her eyes were forced almost shut.

Seeing Adele, Mathilde kicked backward, slamming her bare foot into his knee joint. There was a sound—*kunk*—and then a stifled cry. The man flung Mathilde aside as if she were a rag doll and sprang forward, head-butting Adele in the center of her chest.

The force of his hit knocked the wind out of her and paralyzed her throat. Falling back against the side table, she grabbed at the call light, pulling it out of the wall. Alarms went off loud enough to wake the dead.

In a graceful Baryshnikovian leap, the man seemed to sail over her, making his way to the window. All her mind could process was that she had to see his face. On pure reflex her leg shot up and caught him squarely in the groin. She felt the soft sac of his testicles shmush up into his body. He grunted loudly as the two-inch-wide shaft of light from the street caught his face. She saw a length of forehead, one eye, a cheekbone, a scar, nose, and the corner of his mouth.

For a moment, the man seemed to crumple inward, but the momentum of his body carried him to the window, where he rolled—lying sideways—outside. Adele managed to get to her feet. Ignoring the searing pain in her chest, she managed to stumble to the window and look down. The top of their attacker's head shone in the streetlight as he slid down the fire escape. When he hit the bottom, he didn't run out into the parking lot as she had hoped, but rather disappeared around the corner of the building.

Instead of the hordes of medical personnel she expected to respond to the emergency alarm, two registry nurses walked at a garden stroll pace into the room, bitching about their hourly pay rates. One of them switched on the lights. The sight of Adele slumped against the wall trying to breathe and Jane Doe's legs sticking out of the bathroom made for an instant attitude adjustment.

"Call security and get an ER doc up here stat," Adele gasped. "Then call the cops."

One made a dash for the door; the other knelt next to Mathilde, who was on her knees, rubbing her throat. The nurse helped her to the bed. Mathilde opened her eyes slowly, like one waking from sleep, and blinked in the light. Her face was damp with perspiration; she attempted to push back the hair sticking to her forehead, then let her arm fall to her side.

After taking Mathilde's pulse and blood pressure, the nurse turned her attention to Adele. "Are you okay?" she asked, helping her to her feet and over to the bed to sit next to Mathilde.

Adele nodded. "Don't worry about me. I'm fine. I—"

"I was almost asleep." Mathilde clutched Adele's hand. "He pulled me out of bed and I think he was getting ready to snap my neck. I couldn't breathe."

"Do you know who it was?"

"I ..." Mathilde stopped, seeming to struggle with her thoughts for a minute. "I think it was the man with the glasses," she said, staring at Adele. "I remembered the fear, and then I remembered him. He was going to kill me and the girl. We were in a cabin, and I waited until he was asleep, took the girl, and ran away."

A security guard, gun drawn, ran into the room.

"Radio downstairs!" Adele barked. "Tell them to look for a man with a crew cut and a scar on his right cheek. He's wearing a black leather jacket and black pants and he might be hunched over and limping. He went down the fire escape and around the west side of the building right below us."

Dr. Briscoe, the house doc, hurried into the room, looked from Adele to Mathilde. "What's going on?"

Adele pointed to Mathilde. "A man broke in and grabbed her. He had her in a neck hold when I came in. Head-butted me in the chest."

"Any loss of consciousness for either of you?" the physician asked, examining Mathilde's neck. Adele shook her head, suddenly too tired to speak. Her limbs felt leaden.

"Call the primary MD on this patient," the physician addressed one of the registry nurses. "Explain what happened, then put him through to me. What BP and pulse did you get?"

The nurse recited Mathilde's vital signs while Dr. Briscoe continued his exam. "No hoarseness, stridor, dyspnea, swelling, or tenderness," the physician said into his minicorder. He checked the foot that Mathilde had used to kick her assailant, then ordered a limited c-spine X-ray.

Confusion escalated as the room filled with medical personnel. Dixie, the night nursing supervisor, was making out an incident report, talking to the head of security. The charge nurse was reviewing the chart aloud for Dr. Briscoe, who in turn was talking into his minicorder. Abruptly he left off and turned his attention to Adele. "Can you breathe and do you have a pulse?" he asked.

"Victim number two" winced when he palpated her sternum. Shaking his head, the physician ordered Adele be taken to ER for rib films and an EKG in case of cardiac contusion.

A Twin Cities policeman entered the room, then Malloy, then the X-ray tech to gather Mathilde, and, finally, the most beautiful blue eyes she'd ever seen.

At Twin Cities PD's insistence, Jane Doe was moved to a different room closer to the nurses' station and interviewed by the same officer who interviewed Adele an hour later. The thousands of questions he asked ran the same course for both: Did you recognize him, did he say anything, why would someone want to do this, did you recognize his voice, was he strong, did he have an odor, an accent, a speech impediment, anything that might help you remember him if you heard or saw him again, describe his hands, was he taller than you, weaker, heavier, more slight, did you feel a watch, a ring, or other jewelry, what about his clothes, tattoos, shoes, his genitals, hair, scars . . .

Their answers were similar, with the exception that Jane Doe recognized him and knew what he had come to do, but only within the limits of her memory, such as it was.

By the time Adele was released from ER to the attentions of Officer Ramirez, Mathilde was in session with Dr. Lavine, who had been called in on an emergency basis.

They were sitting on the couch in front of the fire he'd built. Adele rested her chin on her knees as Timothy pushed invisible itch balls around her back. Under his touch, her muscles shed the day's unrelenting tension, and she felt sleepy . . . almost stoned.

It didn't hit her until after she was discharged from ER that she'd narrowly escaped a disaster. The man could have had a gun or a knife and killed them both, or she could have been one second later and found Mathilde with a snapped neck.

The warmth from the fire put her into deep thought—eyes closed—until Tim called her back. Even as she swam up to the surface of conscious thought, she was aware that she had not changed out of her sleuthing outfit, her hair stuck out at all angles, and there was no question that her mascara had smudged.

"Are you okay, Adele?" Tim asked, his voice tight with emotion. "I can spend the night on the couch here if you want." He had to make a conscious effort not to try and kiss her. It may have been that he was overwhelmingly grateful she was alive, but he'd never seen her look so beautiful. Despite the ordeal at Ellis, she had the look of a woman fresh from sleep—or love.

Truth was, Adele felt needy. It was an effort to keep her hands from wandering to his body. Leaving him on the couch where Nelson and the rabbit still slept at one end, she went to the kitchen to brew tea. Her mind was only half on the task, but it was necessary; she needed to put physical distance between them, or end up making a fool of herself. Shaking out her braid, she tried to block out the image of Tim when he'd brought her home: the way the moonlight crossed his face and shoulders as he stood on her porch wrestling with her oversized purse while he unlocked her front door. It had taken her breath away.

"Well, one thing good was that you kept your promise and showed up," she laughed, trying to break the heat that was almost tangible between them.

"I'd rather it were under different circumstances," he said, shoving his hands into his pockets as a safety measure. "Are you sure you don't want me to stay? I could run to the office to pick up a few things and be back here in—"

"No. Really, I'm fine, but thanks anyway." She handed him a cup of steaming tea, then sat down on the hearth rug facing him. "Now that my big excitement is over, it's your turn to tell me what's going on."

It was then that he noticed she was dressed in unrelieved black, head to foot. The clingy leggings and the turtleneck showed her pliable body to its best advantage. Tim stretched his long legs, so that one accidentally touched her thigh. Electric shocks went up his leg to his groin.

"More than I can even begin to tell you." He sipped his tea, hoping it contained special Chinese herbs to make him momentarily indifferent.

"Encapsulate," she said firmly, and leaned back against the leather hassock, careful of the constant ache of her sternum.

"Another murder exactly like the other two—or four if you want to include the Deveraux woman and child."

"When was the time of death?"

He put his mug on the side table. "Takamoto's initial guess was between two and three this morning, which coincides with a witness who said she was in her kitchen when she saw a priest walk out the front door at two-thirty and get into a Jeep parked in front of her house."

"Did she get a license plate number?"

Tim shook his head. "It was too dark, and the outside lights weren't on—same as with the Barry murder. The woman thinks she got a fairly good look at the face. The sketch artist spent two hours with her. Tomorrow we'll compare the sketches with yours and Jane Doe's. I think Jane Doe should see them all." He looked at her with his amused smile. "Do you think Jeffrey . . ." He put a slight, sarcastic spin on the name. ". . . would approve?"

"I doubt Dr. Lavine would mind," Adele said, straight-faced. "Mathilde is being discharged at ten. After I'm done with the sketch artist, I'm picking her up and then we'll head over to

Twin Cities. She can hang out with the sketch artist while I look over the mug books. Then I'll take her to my place for lunch and then drop her off at the San Anselmo Hotel."

He made a sour face. "Why the San Anselmo Hotel? It's a fire-trap. It hasn't been renovated since it was built by the cavemen."

Adele screwed up one side of her mouth and shook her head. "I don't know—Jellyroll recommended the place. When she finds a job, she'll move."

The detective snorted. It seemed darkly humorous that a fireman would suggest such a place to someone he liked.

Adele got to her knees and leaned against the couch. Tim turned to study her. He saluted her with his teacup and drank, never taking his eyes off her.

She felt herself blush under his gaze, wondering what it would be like to reach over and touch his face, his lips.

Smelling rutting pheromones, Nelson's head popped up. Looking from one to the other of the humans, he took stock of the situation and got to his paws. The rabbit, who was sleeping curled into Nelson's belly, was accidentally stepped on and went hopping to the dark shelter under the couch.

Nelson paced nervously for a second, then jumped up on the couch between them, passing the most noxious of wind.

It put more than a damper on the pheromones—it drove Tim out into the night, gagging. At the door, Adele wiped away the tears of hard laughter and apologized for Nelson's bad manners. Finally able to breathe, he waved it away with the excuse it was time to go.

"What's on for you tomorrow?" she asked.

"Going back to Citadel to find out what the hell is going on. After you and Jane Doe finish with the sketch artist and the mug books, I'll want to talk to both of you. You do realize that who-ever tried to kill her tonight will probably try again," he said with prophetic confidence.

She flinched and nodded. "Yes."

"Do you still have that peashooter—that Colt?"

"It isn't a peashooter. It's a thirty-two-caliber Colt."

"Might be a good idea to keep it handy."

"Can you guys do anything to protect her?" Adele asked.

"She needs a twenty-four-hour watch." He gave her a look.

"And you *know* nobody around here is going to provide that for anybody except maybe the President."

"Doesn't the county have some sort of witness protection program?"

He laughed. "That's Hollywood, darlin'. Unless the FBI is involved, all we can do is suggest she get out of Dodge and let us know her forwarding address."

She set her jaw and stared at his shoes. Her body, if not her mind, was momentarily at a standstill.

"Adele? I hope you aren't thinking what I think you're thinking."

"Oh, probably not," Adele said innocently, looking up. She lied as fluidly as mercury sliding across a marble floor.

"Once Jane Doe is discharged from Ellis, she's no longer your concern." Tim heard himself say this, knowing it was not the thing to say to Adele Monsarrat. Maybe it was because of the close call, maybe it sprung from his guilt over spilling his guts to her about the cases, but somehow, he couldn't stop his mouth.

"Stay out of this, Adele, or you're going to get hurt. Leave it to the big boys to solve."

In the deadly silence that followed, there was a barely perceivable widening of her gold eyes, then the terrible narrowing followed by the flare of her nostrils. He was chilled by the change in her demeanor.

"Sure, Tim," she said in an even, icy monotone. "Maybe you ought to cut back on your testosterone intake. I hear my mother calling so I've got to go now. Goodnight."

"Adele, let me ex—"

"Goodnight." She pushed against him with the screen door.

"Talk to me, Adele. Don't—"

"Believe me, Timothy, the last thing you want right now is for me to talk to you. I have important things to do, you know, like check the calendar to make sure we aren't living in the Stone Age, because I was certain I just heard one of the primates in blue try to tell me to join the women and children at the back of the cave."

"I didn't mean it that way, Adele. You're making more . . ."

She didn't hear the rest of his sentence, because the door,

which was quite thick, made a lot of noise when it slammed shut in his face.

Marin County had once been mentioned in a national magazine and once on David Letterman for having one of the largest collections of doctors who truly lived up to their names. Dr. Hand specialized in surgical reconstruction of hands, Dr. Bebe was an obstetrician, Dr. Kidd a pediatrician, Dr. Mohl a dermatologist, Dr. Cutter a surgeon, and Dr. Foote was a podiatrist. It was the same for Nelson's doggie shrink, Dr. Nutt—with whom Nelson had a standing quarterly appointment.

Adele thought of it the same way she thought of bringing in the Beast every few thousand miles for an oil change: minor modifications made along the way to steer clear of the big problems. After all, animals went postal too: one day little Rex is a sweet, cuddly doggie, and the next—boom!—he's bringing home somebody's face between his teeth.

There was no explanation of Dr. Nutt's methods. He had a room full of doggie toys, a sandbox, several blow-up dolls—human male and female, a female doggie with teats, and a kitty—a hot tub, a massage table, and lots of animal videos.

The video Nelson favored was the one of cats running away. The one that got him nervous and whining was the one of other dogs frolicking in a dog park.

This visit, Dr. Nutt probed Nelson's "unhealthy" attachment to his Mickey Mouse rug. For the first fifteen minutes they played in the sandbox with the rug, then they took a hot tub (together—with rug) and then, still dripping, Dr. Nutt gave Nelson a massage, moving the rug, inch by inch, out from under him.

Nelson was no fool. He let the man massage and knead right up to the last quarter inch of rug, when he growled and showed his teeth as a warning.

No fool himself, Dr. Nutt backed off and left Mickey rug alone.

The advice was the same as always: Prozac. Meat. Twenty-four-hour-a-day companionship. They were, Nutt swore, the only cures for Nelson's various personality idiosyncrasies.

While Adele sat on her bed cleaning her gun, she and Nelson discussed his Mickey rug dependency and his visit to Dr. Nutt.

The rabbit, a neutral on the subject, slept through most of the discussion.

In the end, Adele and Nelson agreed there was nothing to be done until the damned thing was down to its last measly thread.

"That's close to the man I seen in the elevator," Francis Lee said, moving his finger over the sketch of the Budget car rental man. " 'Cept his beard was more out this way." He pointed toward the angle of the jaw.

"And you're sure this is the child you saw?" He held up the picture of Bettina Deveraux.

"Yessir."

"Would you swear to this under oath in a court of law, Francis?" Tim held his breath, looking for a sign of doubt.

"Yessir, I would."

There wasn't an instant of hesitation in the man's answer.

When the telephone on his bedside table rang at 2:30 A.M., he stared at it, mouth agape. His stomach tightened into an excruciating knot. The thought that it was another murder waiting at the other end of the line was paralyzing. He let it ring five times before he brought himself to the point where he could pick up the receiver.

"Hello?"

"Tim?"

It was Cini speaking in a low, muffled voice. Automatically his mind reeled through an index of reasons why Cini would be calling at this time in the morning.

"Yeah."

"I couldn't sleep. I kept thinking about the Citadel financial records."

"I can barely hear you, speak up."

"Can't. The wife's asleep right here and the kids broke the other phone. But, listen, I've got a feeling."

Tim sat up and turned on the light. He knew that whenever one of his men got a feeling about something—enough of a feeling to wake him up at 2:30—he should listen carefully. He took up his pen and notebook, and walked into the kitchen. "I'm all ears."

Enrico Cini looked around to make sure Stella, his wife, was still asleep. She was out cold—like most women with five kids.

"Citadel Inc. owns a half-dozen companies, small businesses that deal in satellite parts, computer components, things like that. Some are offshore—one in Japan, a few overseas, and a couple here in the States. So I check around and I find out that for the most part they're legit."

"But?" Tim asked, hearing the opening.

"But the ones based in Switzerland and Germany don't really exist. They're shell companies—all on paper."

Tim picked up a cup off the cluttered counter, the last half-way clean one, and rinsed it out. "So are we looking at laundering vehicles?"

"I'm not sure yet, but there's major money flowing through them."

"Have you traced where the money's going?" Tim poured the last of his bottled water into the food-spattered object shaped like a tea kettle and turned on the burner under it.

"Can't. It's going into untraceable accounts in Switzerland. In the last two months, there's been some heavy outgo of funds."

"No names?" Grease from the last (and he realized it really was The Last) turkey burger he'd cooked smoked on the coils.

"No names."

"Do we even know who owns the companies?" Tim peered down into the instant-coffee jar. There were a few clumps of the dark brown powder stuck to the sides.

"There's an attorney. I'm trying to get ahold of him, but you know what bastards they can be."

"I've heard the jokes," Tim laughed. "So where are you going from here?"

"I'm going to try Paul Bergman."

"You're kidding. Paul Bergman, the California financier who ended up in a Swiss prison?"

"Can you think of anybody better? The guy has written six books about this sort of thing; he's an expert on how to do it. Maybe he'll have some ideas."

"Where is he?"

"Bergman? He's living in Sonoma. Writing another book,

from what I understand. There's something else, too, that is really weird. I can't find any records of payment for the victims."

"What do you mean?" Tim poured the hot water into the coffee jar, swished it around, then poured the results into the cup. He took a tentative sip, made a face, and poured it out into the sink full of dishes—it might kill some bacteria.

"I've gone over the tax records for all the departments— employee salaries right down to each paycheck. Every employee is in the records except our victims. If they were paid, they sure weren't getting their money through weekly paychecks."

Tim thought about that for a minute and decided it fit into Yates's pattern. "You want something else to think about?" he asked.

"Sure," Enrico whispered, laying his head on the pillow. "I need something more to keep me awake."

"There was another hit over on Redwood Road in San Anselmo tonight. Same sort of shooter. The victim worked for Citadel. He retired . . ."

". . . four years ago, right?" Cini finished for him.

"You got it."

"You going back to talk with Yates?"

"Brother, I'm gonna be waiting at the door when they open."

TWELVE

SLEEPING IN WASN'T AN OPTION. BY 5 A.M. SHE AND
Nelson were out the door and running through Larkspur over
the Corte Madera–Mill Valley hill to Seven Curves Trail. They
returned to the house as it was getting light. By 7:15, she was in
the Beast and headed to Ellis.

The traffic light at Magnolia Avenue and Ward Street was
one of those that helped provoke road rage: it stayed red for five
minutes and green for five seconds. Not willing to run the blink
of a yellow light, Adele stopped.

On the corner, a figure bent in front of a *Pacific Intelligencer*
box trying to read the paper through the clouded yellow plastic
window. The general outline of the body—low to the ground
and wide—left her with no question as to whom that figure belonged to.

Under her seat Adele kept the defunct remnants of a car
phone that she'd found at Goodwill. It had come in handy in the
past when she'd wanted to talk to herself aloud, but didn't want
other people to think she was talking to herself. She took it out
and began to talk, cursing the traffic light.

When the mittened hand knocked at her passenger window,
she pretended not to hear, speaking louder to an imaginary
friend she named Bubba. But when Mrs. Coolidge began to
bang with her fist, Adele gritted her teeth and rolled down the
window.

"Off to work?" the woman asked. In her arms she held a
garish Thanksgiving wreath made from plastic holly and pil-
grim corn husk dolls. In the center was a plastic turkey with a
neon orange wattle.

"Sort of," Adele said. She looked at the turkey and frowned.
"Listen, I'm sorry about the other day, Mrs. Coolidge, but I

was assured by my friend that we were being attacked. She told me—"

"Oh, that's okay. Listen, dear, I was wondering if you might have an idea whose dog is doing his doodie on my front lawn?"

Duty? Since she was a nurse, the normal person's understanding of the word escaped her. "What kind of duty?" She was thinking in terms of military duty, or being on duty.

Mrs. Coolidge searched her face to make sure she wasn't joking. "A dog is making his business in my yard," she repeated in a whisper.

Grasping the woman's meaning, Adele at once had an image of a sinister-looking dog poring over a map of the neighborhood, and marking off Mrs. Coolidge's yard with a big brown X. It was enough to send her into a sudden, high-pitched peal of Crazy Woman laughter. By the time the light changed, she was wheezing and slapping the dashboard, barely able to drive.

Ward 3, the Coronary Care Unit, was so orderly and calm, that it bordered on the brink of hospital picturesque. For fifteen seconds, Adele entertained the idea of transferring from Ward 8 to the wonderfully sterile and proper environment of the heart unit before she realized she'd go insane with the efficiency of it; chaos was in her blood. Nursing without the bombs and mortar shells whizzing by wouldn't be the same.

She knocked on the door of 318 and entered. On the bed, a woman of about seventy-five stared out the window at the rain.

"Mrs. Hightower?"

Slowly, the older woman took her eyes from the rain and looked at Adele with a penetrating gaze. Her eyes were red-rimmed, and tears glistened in the deep wrinkles of her face.

"Mrs. Hightower, I'm Adele Monsarrat, I am sorry to disturb you but I . . ."

At once, Adele couldn't do it; she couldn't ask cold, hard questions about finding her husband of fifty-something years dead in their living room. She felt lower than a *paparazzo*'s nuts.

". . . I just wanted to tell you how sorry I am about your husband. I'm so—sorry."

In response, the woman reached out and took her hand, folding it inside her cool dry ones. "Thank you," she said in a quavering voice, similar to Katharine Hepburn's. "He was a good man and had a fine life. We had many wonderful years together."

Adele felt her throat close off, the way it did just before she cried.

"Are you with the police or the hospital?" Mrs. Hightower asked, lowering her head to see Adele's face.

"Both, actually. Listen, I'm sorry. I shouldn't have disturbed you. I'll come back and see you some other time."

"No," Mrs. Hightower said. "It's fine; it takes my mind off myself. Tell me what you need." She moved over and patted the side of the bed, indicating Adele should sit there.

"I—I don't think this is the time for questions, Mrs. Hightower, I—"

"Don't be a ninny," she said, pushing back the pure white hair that framed her face like a cloud. "You came here to ask me something. Go ahead."

Adele hesitated, then sat on the woman's bed. "I wanted to know about Mr. Hightower's job," she said.

"He was a retired communications expert," the woman answered without hesitation. "He was very good at what he did."

"Mr. Hightower worked for Citadel Incorporated?"

"And General Electric, and Microsoft. He took an early retirement from Citadel four years ago."

"Was he happy with Citadel?"

Mrs. Hightower paused, pursing her lips. "For the first few years it seemed to fit him all right, but toward the end . . ." Her voice trailed off. She shook her head. "Alan didn't like to talk about Citadel—not even to me. One day he came home and told me he wouldn't be going back."

"Did something happen? Some specific event that made him feel that way?"

"Yes, I think so," the woman said, nodding. "But I never knew what it was. He said it wasn't worth talking about, and when Alan said that, you knew the subject was closed. I didn't *want* to know."

Adele stood. "Thank you," she said. "Is there anything I can do for you? Anything I can get for you?"

"That's all you wanted to know?" the woman asked, surprised.

Adele nodded.

"Well, my goodness, that wasn't very much."

"It's enough."

Adele left the Beast sleeping in the Ellis parking lot and, taking the paved trail through the estuary, ran the mile and a half to Twin Cities Police Department, where the sketch artist was waiting for her.

The composite drawing created between the two of them in under two hours was close enough to the real thing to make the hair on the back of her arms stand up.

"Ready for the real world?" Adele asked, walking through the door to Mathilde's room. She stopped short and whistled.

Dressed in a soft green jumper, Mathilde had brushed her hair back into a loose French braid, away from her face. The steel gray eyes were even more outstanding with a light application of eye makeup. Other than the hint of lip color, Mathilde needed no other cosmetic: her skin was flawless.

"Wow, you look great!" Adele said, awed by the woman's appearance.

"I don't feel that way." Mathilde bent at the knees to fix her scarf in the small bedside mirror. "How long do I have before I have to meet the sketch artist at the police station?"

"About fifteen minutes. We can be a few minutes late. I'm going to go over mug books while you're with the artist. When you're done, we'll have lunch. I have something I want to talk to you about."

"What?" Mathilde asked tentatively, and sat down on the arm of the lounger.

"Well, I thought since you need a job, that you might consider working here at—"

The door opened and Cynthia came in with discharge papers and a small pharmacy bag containing a bottle of pain pills. She looked ten years younger than the last time Adele had seen her.

"Hey Cyn," Adele laughed. "How'd you sleep?"

"I don't remember," Cynthia said. "I was unconscious until the alarm went off this morning. I do remember a highway patrolman carrying me up the stairs, however. He kept saying something about how I didn't *look* that heavy."

"You don't remember leaving a message for me about women runners in Florida?"

Cynthia gave her a skeptical look and shook her head.

"And I suppose you're going to tell me you don't remember calling in on the Michael Krasny show to talk about roadkill?"

Looking from Adele to Mathilde then back to Adele, the nurse's eyes widened. "Oh, my God, I really did that?"

The public address system crackled with static and then paused. Both nurses froze in place as their adrenaline surged.

"ATTENTION ALL PERSONNEL. CODE PINK. CODE PINK. WARD FOUR, WEST CORRIDOR."

Both nurses excused themselves and ran through the wheel-chair littered corridors toward Ward 4.

"You goddamned imbecile! Why wasn't I called?" The physician's white mane shook with the force of his words. In contrast, his reddened face appeared dark and menacing as his features twisted in fury. "I wrote a specific order that I be called each morning about the glucose level! Are you illiterate?"

"I didn't call this morning," the nurse answered in a mea-sured tone, "because yesterday morning when I called in with the blood glucose on this patient, you verbally abused me." The worn-looking nurse of forty-something cradled the chart as though she were cradling a baby. "You threatened to have me fired. When I tried to explain that you'd written the order to be called regardless of time of night, and whether or not the level was normal, you called me a . . ." The nurse paused. ". . . a couple of names and hung up."

The physician roughly wrestled the chart away from her, scraping the delicate skin on the insides of her arms. His lips drew back from his teeth and he took a step nearer. "Are you trying to blame me for your inability to do your job?" He gave her a push with the sharp edge of the chart cover. "Answer me! Are you saying *I'm* at fault here?"

"No! I'm trying to explain why you weren't called at five A.M. with this glucose. You put me in a no-win position. If I follow your orders and call you when the results come back, you ver-bally abuse and threaten me, and if I don't, you verbally abuse and threaten me."

His neck had turned purple. "You get what you deserve.

From now on, follow my orders no matter what. If you don't, I'll make sure . . ." Out of the corner of his eye, the physician noticed the sudden materialization of bodies converging on them.

Twelve nurses, from six different units, circled around the nucleus of trouble and linked arms. They stood silently focused on him.

"What the hell is this?" the doctor asked, swiveling around.

A male nurse from ICU spoke up. "Shouting was heard, and one of the nurses felt there should be an intervention."

"This is none of your concern," the doctor said.

"Doctor, we aren't going to interfere with whatever you have to say to this nurse," interrupted one of the nurses from Ward 3. "We are here only to offer nonbiased support of our nursing colleague and to provide physical protection should that be necessary. You may feel free to continue with whatever discussion you were having with this nurse as long as it remains professional and nonphysical."

"This is outrageous," the physician said, his voice regaining its impatience. "Are you insinuating that I'm not professional? You're only nurses. My God, you're trying to tell *me* how to practice . . ."

The Ward 3 nurse spoke again: "And as nurses we are professional colleagues of the physicians and the auxiliary staff. As for your professionalism . . ." She stepped forward and held up the nurse's scraped arms—one of her wrists was bleeding. ". . . you could use some work on your attitude toward your colleagues."

"Colleagues?" he sneered. "That'll be the day. Nurses are subordinates of the physicians. Don't forget it. Colleagues my ass. When you get your medical degree, then we can talk."

Annie Braden, the nurse from Ward 2, smiled. "Really, doctor? Well, I suggest you look at who actually treats and helps the patients to heal—or better yet, ask the patients themselves."

"Christ! This is outrageous!" He wiped his forehead with his fingers. "Larry Milbank is going to hear about this!"

"Actually, doctor," said the male nurse, "we encourage you to take this to the administrator. It speeds the process."

"What process?"

"The Code Pink review," said Annie Braden. "It's an emergency intervention for when verbal or physical abuse is being committed on a nurse by another healthcare professional. All Code Pinks are reported and a formal hearing takes place with a board of both nurses and physicians. You'll be served a summons at your office. If we can't—"

"Bullshit!" the doctor interrupted, furious. Spit flew with his words. "No physician would ever lower himself to . . ." He gaped at the faces surrounding him, threw the chart to the floor, and pushed through the circle.

"I didn't expect to hear from you so soon, Mr. Ritmann. You've caught me at a bad time." Phillip Yates nervously looked at his watch then snapped his jacket down over his cuff. "I've got a meeting in about fifteen minutes . . ."

"I think we've had a breakdown in communication, Mr. Yates," Tim said staring hard into the man's eyes. "Another former Citadel employee has been murdered."

The CEO stopped, then walked around his desk and sat down heavily. "Who this time?"

"With all due respect, sir, don't you ever read the newspapers?"

"Who was it?" Yates repeated.

"Alan Hightower."

Yates groaned and let his head fall into his hands. He sat very still.

"What was Mr. Hightower's area of employment?" Tim asked, taking his notebook from his coat pocket.

"He was our head man in cybernetic communications."

Tim walked to the window. "Let me be blunt. I think you have more of an idea about what's going on than what you're telling us."

Yates shook his head. "I don't know why this is happening."

Ritmann turned to stare at him, his jaw working. "Listen, we've got three murder victims, all of whom worked for you. All of them left the company at the same time, and all of them received a very generous sum of money when they left—much more generous than what would be considered standard."

Mr. Yates crossed his legs and cleared his throat. "I don't know anything about that, Mr. Ritmann. That would be our personnel department." The finger, now unbandaged, began to tap.

The red marks looked like burns one might get from an oven or a grill.

"How did you injure yourself?" Tim asked, nodding at his finger.

The man looked down at his finger self-consciously. "I was trying to keep a fire going; I grabbed a log in the fireplace that wasn't as cold as it looked."

Tim walked around the desk. The green light on the intercom box was on. That was good; he wanted Ms. Saches to hear this. He was thinking of the credo detectives and cops lived by when investigating a case: Information is power; hold on to what you know until the right moment.

"Would it be at all possible that there were some pages missing from the personnel files that you gave me? They felt a little light."

"I don't know what you're talking—"

"Yes, you do." Tim opened the door to the outer office. Laurel Saches sat at her desk, staring out the panorama window, an earpiece in one ear. Instantly, she pulled the earpiece out and leaned back in her chair, looking embarrassed.

"Ms. Saches, would you come in here, please?"

She nodded without looking at him and walked, head down, into the office. She looked pale and visibly troubled.

Yates tilted his head toward the detective, his finger tapping like mad. "Mr. Ritmann thinks we've given him incomplete personnel files, Ms. Saches. Did you give him the complete files?"

"I gave him the files I received from personnel," the secretary said, looking anywhere but at either man.

"What about the files on these people that you keep here in this office?" Tim asked. "The ones with the code ninety-nine descriptions?"

The air went electric. Laurel Saches and her employer exchanged glances. "I don't know about any code ninety-nine descriptions," she stammered.

"There is no code ninety-nine." Yates stood and straightened out his cuffs, again. "Excuse me, Mr. Ritmann, I don't mean to be rude, but I must attend a meeting which began five minutes ago." He headed toward the door. Ms. Saches will provide you with Mr. Hightower's personnel record, if you'd like."

"I can have all your files subpoenaed," the detective said. "Why don't you save us the trouble?"

Yates looked deliberately at him, then reached for the door. "There really isn't any need to subpoena the files. You're welcome to look through any of them. Tell Ms. Saches which files you want to see and she'll be happy to help you."

Five minutes after the CEO had left his office, Tim put the steaming mug of coffee to his lips. If he'd hoped to read something from Ms. Saches's expressions, he could forget it: Ms. Saches didn't give anything away.

"I'm very sorry about Mr. Yates's behavior," she said after a minute. "He's under a great deal of stress right now."

Tim nodded, swallowed his mouthful of coffee, watching her over the rim of his cup. "Have you thought of anything you might want to add?"

"No." She looked away—a gesture of avoidance. "No."

He let the silence settle for a minute then slapped his knee. "Well, I've got to head back to the office. Things are busy."

She nodded.

"Detective Cini will be here later this morning. He'll want to go over more of the financial statements."

"Yes."

He stood and took his coat from the ornate coat rack. "By the way, did you know that Mr. Deveraux's wife and one of her two young children were murdered? Shot point-blank and left to rot in shallow graves."

One corner of her mouth twitched, and her fingers went to the buttons on her blouse, where they fidgeted. He didn't wait for a response. "The kid wasn't even five years old yet. Can you imagine?"

Ms. Saches twisted the buttons.

He walked to the door and pushed it open. "I hope you think of something, Ms. Saches," he said, trying hard to keep the threatening edge out of his voice. "Real soon."

Mathilde's sweet face was caught in a moment of indecision anxiety.

"It's a generous offer, but I can't," she said finally. "I couldn't intrude on your privacy like that."

"You also can't take the chance of being attacked again."

Mathilde looked out the Beast's passenger window, watching the passing landscape of Larkspur. "I won't put you at risk, Adele. You've done enough for me already. Has it occurred to you that being roommates doesn't mean that this—this person won't kill you, too?"

"I'll be prepared next time," Adele said. "I have a gun. I'm very good with it. Load to shoot under two seconds with ninety-five percent accuracy."

Mathilde stared at her. Adele thought she saw something akin to pain come to the surface behind the woman's eyes, and then it was gone.

"It's hard to imagine you with a gun." she said.

"My ex was a Green Beret," Adele said. "We used to do surprise combat drills and go to the firing range for fun."

There was a silence, and then Mathilde turned to the window. "Have you ever killed anyone?"

It was not the first time she'd been asked. "As a nurse or a civilian?"

"Either. Both."

"Yes," Adele said turning into the Twin Cities police station parking lot. She avoided looking at Mathilde. She did not want to see her expression. A minute passed while she parked.

"About staying with you?" Mathilde looked at her. "I'm sorry, but I wouldn't feel right."

Adele rubbed her hands over her face. "Okay," she said, "but don't rule it out completely. Come to my house for lunch, meet Nelson and the Bugs, and then make up your mind."

"You have bugs?"

"Yeah. A new addition to the family."

While Mathilde was with the sketch artist, Adele went through a couple of mug books until she couldn't stand it. The policeman in charge of feeding her the books, listened patiently while she complained that she didn't want to have any more nightmares than she did already, and these faces were giving her plenty.

He said he understood then, crunching all over her delicate emotional balance, told her she could take a break and then go over a few more.

She agreed to a break, and went to the pay phone outside the building to call Tim. "Hi, it's me," Adele said after the beep had shaken her eardrum. "I'm still pissed off at you, but I need information, and if you can get over your Big Dick on Campus testosterone rush, you'd realize you need what I have to offer."

She heard her words and faltered. ". . . In the way of information I mean." She cringed inwardly over the awkward silence. "Yes, I know I don't have a PI license, and I know my methods aren't kosher, but remember this, Timothy—my intuition is intact.

"Why don't you come by for dinner? I'm cooking vegetarian shepherd's pie with tomato coulis, and roasted garlic soup. I invited Jane Doe to stay at my place, but no go. I'm treating her to lunch to see if Nelson can work his charm on her.

"Oh. And if and when you come to dinner, bring the collection of sketches. I'd like to see them all at once. Mathilde is finishing up with the composite artist now, then we're heading to my house. Afterwards, I'll . . ."

Mathilde and an officer pushed through the door and walked into the hall close to the pay phone.

"I have to go. Leave me a message at home about dinner."

Adele replaced the receiver and hoistered her twenty-pound purse up to her shoulder. In a quick, almost imperceivable movement, she checked the .32 Colt tucked neatly into the outside zippered compartment. She wondered just how hinky the cop would get if he knew she was packing a heater in their own backyard.

The serious-looking officer helped Mathilde on with her jacket. "We'd like you to come back tomorrow morning to take a look at some mug shots if you would, Miss . . ." Caught, the officer stammered awkwardly. "Er . . . Doe."

Mathilde wasn't the gushing type of woman, but had she been, she would have gushed over Nelson. Adele read it in her eyes and the way her bandaged hands lingered over his coat, stroking gently and more firmly in the right places. It surprised her that Nelson, like Timothy, gave Mathilde a somewhat cool reception. She wondered if it was the smell of her bandages— or her depression?—that put him off.

"I take it you like dogs?" Adele asked, preparing quinoa to go with the baby leeks and tomatoes soaked in olive oil.

"I love animals—especially dogs. They don't play games."

Adele lifted her eyebrows. "Maybe you have a dog?"

Mathilde shrugged. "I don't know. I don't think so, but I couldn't even remember if I had a baby, so that doesn't mean much." She fell into silence.

Adele searched out the rabbit and put it in Mathilde's lap. Mathilde sucked in her breath and a smile rearranged her face into something extraordinarily soft and wonderful. She cooed like a new mother.

During lunch Mathilde's spirits lifted, and she began talking freely about her few days on Ward 8 as though she were reminiscing about college days. She discussed the different nurses who had been assigned to her, recounting with exceptional accuracy their full names, what they looked like, how they sounded, and their identifying personal details. Linda was newly divorced, had three children, she liked to cook, Christmas was her favorite time of year, and she had a habit of falling in love with "bad boys."

Skip lived alone in an apartment in San Rafael, loved his mother, was still in love with a nurse who was killed, was afraid of women, couldn't decide whether or not he was gay, and didn't like nursing. Cynthia, Mathilde said laughing, had the energy of an overactive thyroid.

"I take it Cynthia is your best friend?" Mathilde asked when they were almost done eating.

Adele spooned out the last of the quinoa onto her own plate. "She's a pain in the ass."

Mathilde wagged her head. "Yeah, but who cares if she's your friend and you trust her?"

"Do you remember loving or trusting anyone?" Adele peered at her.

Holding her cup with both hands, Mathilde blew on her tea, staring at the surface of the hot water. "No," she said, her voice carrying a distant sadness. "No, I don't."

Later, while Adele did the dishes, Mathilde put a New Age music tape into the player and, as the relaxing strains of the etherial music filled the house, wandered room to room, inspecting Adele's collection of artwork and family photographs.

She lingered over the photographs, studying the faces of the children, then laughed at the photo of five-year-old Adele kissing a goat on the lips, her eyes crossed.

"Sure you won't change your mind and stay?" Adele asked coming up behind her in the hallway wiping her hands on a hand towel. "At least until you get a job? The sofa bed is comfortable, and I'm at work most of the time. Save your money for the deposit on an apartment."

The woman pursed her lips, and patted Nelson who ducked because she came too close to his Mickey rug. "I appreciate your offer, and it is tempting, but I need to do this on my own. If I get stuck and run out of money before I can get a job, I'll take you up on the offer—if it's still available."

"Just give me enough notice to make sure the sheets and towels are clean."

The phone rang. Adele reached around to the kitchen wall phone.

"Hi," Tim said. His voice sounded as if it were coming through a long tube. "I'm parked right outside. Can I bring in the sketches?"

Adele craned her neck to look out the living room bay window. She could see the nose of the Camry against the Beast's back bumper. "Oh. Okay. Give me a few minutes to prepare her."

When Adele replaced the receiver, Mathilde looked at her, questioningly.

"That was Detective Ritmann," Adele explained. "He wants to come by and show you a couple of composite sketches?"

Mathilde tensed. "Now?"

"I know he was rough on you, but it's not him, really. He takes his job a little too seriously sometimes. "Is it okay for him to come in?"

Mathilde lifted the rabbit to her chin. "Might as well," she said, stroking the animal's fur. "Anything to jump-start the memory."

The faces of five men stared up at them from the floor: the Budget rental man, the cop, the priest, and Adele's and Jane Doe's composites of their attacker. Each face was distinctly different from the others except the two of the man with the scar—those two were strikingly similar.

"You're sure?" Tim asked.

Mathilde nodded. "This is the man." She tapped first hers and then Adele's composite sketches. "Put those crazy glasses on him, and that's the man I remember from the farmhouse and the car. These other faces are all wrong. I don't recognize any of them."

"And you're sure you don't remember anything other than you were in a car with him and a little girl?" Tim asked. His tone was kinder than when he'd spoken to her before, but he maintained his professional edge.

Mathilde thought for a minute. She didn't seem inclined to go on. Avoiding Adele's eyes, she put the rabbit on the floor, got up from the couch, and walked to the mantel. She picked up an antique mortar and pestle set and smelled the inside of the bowl. Tim thought it an odd gesture—something an investigator might do.

"Last night, after the attack," she began slowly, staring at the mortar, "I remembered being in a cabin with this man and the little girl. It was out in the woods, I think, because the man with the glasses drove down a dirt road to get there.

"He fell asleep and I took the girl and ran away."

"Tell us about the cabin," Adele said.

"It was cold." She squinted as though she were trying to see the scene in her mind. "There wasn't any heat. It had a wood stove, but the man wouldn't build a fire because it would have attracted attention. There was a bed and a shower, maybe a couple of chairs. It was very sparse, I remember. It was too dark and foggy to see outside, but I think we were on a bluff of some kind."

"Was there a gate at the beginning of the dirt road?" Adele asked.

"Yes." She looked at Adele, startled that she would have guessed. "It was a metal bar, but he had a key that he used to open it."

"A dirt road and a cabin," Adele repeated. A distant memory of adolescent group experimentation with beer, marijuana, and cigarettes flitted through her mind. She walked to the bay window and looked out. Across the street, Queen Shredder sat in Mrs. Coolidge's front window, glaring out at the world. Mrs. Coolidge was scooping "doodie" from her lawn into the gutter.

"I'll bet I know where you were," Adele said. "It sounds like it's south of Stinson Beach at Steep Ravine. There are five or six cabins that used to be privately held by San Francisco's politically favored families until the National Park Service took them back in the mid or late seventies. They're always rented out in spring and summer, but they're too cold for people during winter.

"In high school we used to go up there for weekends during Christmas break. The rangers never checked on us, and the lock could be sprung with a paperclip."

Tim took out his notebook and made a note to himself. "This is through the park service?" he asked.

Adele nodded. "Yeah. They used to have a caretaker out there all year, but I don't think that's the case anymore." She glanced at Mathilde. "Would you be up for going out there tomorrow? Take a look around to see if you can remember more?"

Mathilde frowned and pushed herself off the couch. Apprehension pervaded the room. "I don't know. I have to go back and look at mug books tomorrow, and then I have to find a job. I'm—I'm tired. Can we go to the hotel now?"

Tim and Adele looked at each other. The woman's sudden change left both of them uncomfortable.

"Of course," said Adele. "I don't blame you. You've had a hard day."

Without further comment, Tim gathered the sketches into a large portfolio. At the door, he told Adele to check her messages, and squeezed her arm. She smiled in return. The two gestures, though brief, were a complete set of apologies and acceptances.

The rain hadn't let up for longer than a half hour at a time in six days. And the longer it rained, the less tolerance Adele had for it. As was the norm for rainy days, there wasn't a parking space available anywhere near the residence hotel, which was situated between a popular Italian restaurant and a chic clothing store. Even the bank parking lot that was kitty-corner to the hotel had a waiting line of cars.

Before she could object, Mathilde grabbed her duffle bag and jumped out of the Beast, insisting on checking in on her own. From the determined look on her face, it was useless to battle with her.

Released from the car, Mathilde squared her shoulders, hesitated for a beat, and headed through the iron gate to the patio and down the brick walkway. Adele watched until the plethora of ferns and juniper trees swallowed her.

The smell of mothballs, frying garlic, and onions filled the small lobby of the hotel. Erin set her duffle bag down at the bottom of the narrow carpeted stairs, and hung her purse over an ornate wooden banister. She let her shoulders relax, kneading the back of her neck, and let her eyes wander.

At the top of the stairs, a door to one of the rooms stood open. The corner of a green bedspread and an old pine dresser were visible. A leg mapped with purple and blue varicose veins came into view. The shoes were black with thick rubber soles—the type worn by hotel maids all over the world. A sweeper followed the shoes.

Wearily, Erin gathered her purse and headed up the stairs. At the fourth stair, someone gently—almost lovingly—grasped her by the arm.

Tim pushed in the unfamiliar phone number that appeared on his pager. It barely rang before it was snatched up and a muffled female voice said hello. It was a pay phone; he could tell from the hissing sound of tires dividing rain puddles and the dull humming noise of a heavily populated street.

"Ms. Saches?"

There was a long whisper of a sigh as unseen hands scrunched and squeaked on the receiver. He could hear her breathing—fast and regular. Nervous fear.

"I take the five-thirty Sausalito ferry every night," she said in a low voice. "I have a vodka tonic outside on the second aft deck. Rain or shine."

The phone clicked. His heart beating rapidly, he snapped his fingers and whispered with enthusiasm: "Yes!"

Her answering machine yielded a particularly rich group of messages, beginning with Cynthia who had agreed to work an extra four hours, and then Jeffrey who wanted her to page him when she got a free minute, and another from her mother who left a message for Nelson asking him if he wanted to come for Thanksgiving with or without his mother. The last was from Tim.

"I know you have a beeper hidden away in a drawer some-place, Adele," Tim said. "Do yourself a favor and carry it, or better yet, invest in a cell phone. If you're going to play with the primate testosterone team, you have to have the basic equip-ment, and I don't mean testicles—have gun and cell phone, will travel.

"Dinner sounds so healthy I'm afraid it might kill me, but since you're a nurse, I'm willing to go for it."

There was a pause. In the background were the sounds of his office: twenty phones ringing at once, people talking and yelling to one another. "Listen. About last night, I didn't mean it the way it came out. It was the close call and seeing you in the Emergency Room. I wouldn't like it much if anything were to happen to you, you know?

"And yes, Adele, I do value your input on these cases, civilian or not. If I don't hear back, I'll see you between six-thirty and seven."

She relaxed. A smile crossed her lips. She glanced at the mantel clock, considered how bad traffic would be, grabbed her purse, and ran to the Beast.

Halfway to Circuit City, on one of the only two hills between her house and San Rafael, the Beast—at least a month overdue—pulled its Sleep Trick. Today, the Beast had chosen the ideal conditions for its performance: Highway 101 during heavy commuter traffic, in torrential rain, on a long, seven-percent-grade hill, behind a California Highway Patrol car and next to a school bus loaded with young children.

She jumped up and down on the brake pedal while using the weight of her upper body to wrestle with the steering wheel. Cars behind her and in the lane next to her honked and made other road-rage gestures as the Beast barged a half inch at a time into their spaces.

Maybe it was her terrified expression or perhaps it was the blinding white of her face and knuckles that finally persuaded the drivers to her right to let her veer off the road. This time she was lucky: she'd missed the exit sign, the stop sign, the no-parking sign, and came to rest one-sixteenth of an inch from the edge of an eight-foot ravine filled with water.

For several minutes, she cursed and beat the dash/chest of the Beast until it woke up from its sleep, completely refreshed and death-wish free.

The Sausalito ferry rose to do battle with the waves, shear through them, and fall back into the watery arms of San Francisco Bay. A wannabe race-car driver, but not a sailor, Tim fought back the headache and growing nausea by slowly sipping his Diet Sprite and chewing on a saltine. He wished Ms. Saches took the bus.

He also wished she'd show. He was getting soaked from the spray and the rain. There was also the looming menace of the gulls hovering over him, waiting for crackers—waiting, too, to leave white deposits on his raincoat.

As they approached Alcatraz, he'd begun to fear she wasn't on board when she appeared at the top of the stairs holding her drink.

Without giving any sign of recognition, Laurel Saches sat on the opposite side of the bench, so they were back to back. Her perfume wafted over him—a light scent of musk. After a few minutes, he heard her unzip something—a purse? An attaché? There was the click and hiss of a lighter and then the smell of her cigarette.

"Don't turn around and don't talk," she said finally. "No one must see me speaking to you. It's dangerous."

There was another long silence, then he heard her—felt her—shift in her seat. "The missing pages of the personnel files documented a project titled Code Ninety-nine. It was highly confidential—only five people were involved and they were sworn to complete secrecy."

"Who were they?" Tim asked, covering his mouth as he rubbed his nose.

"Yates, Deveraux, Hightower, Barry, and Hoffman. Yates was the head of the project. It was such a secret that they actually hand-carried their billings to Yates and gave them to him personally. Yates paid them out of a separate account.

"A year after the project was begun, the four suddenly quit and Yates paid them off. I don't mean the money Detective Cini found in the records. It was five times that amount. All but Deveraux refused to accept it.

"Six months ago Deveraux came to the office and threatened Phillip with going to the authorities and exposing the Code Ninety-nine project. He said he'd been in touch with Barry and Hightower." Ms. Saches hesitated, "He said he had enough proof to put Phillip in prison for the rest of his life."

"What about the other one . . . Hoffman?"

"Conveniently dead. He committed suicide in San Diego a few months after he left Citadel."

"And the proof? What was it?"

"Pfff. I've no idea. It could have been anything from a computer program or a computer chip or a document—I don't know."

Tim lowered his head and rubbed his forehead. "What was the project?"

She didn't answer, but instead got up and walked to the rail where she finished her drink. He sipped his Sprite and let his eyes follow her.

Laurel Saches dawdled by the waste can, threw away the empty tonic cup, and opened a fresh pack of cigarettes. That she smoked unflitered Lucky Strikes surprised him; he would have guessed she smoked one of the skinny "girl's" brand of cancer sticks. She lit one and casually returned to her seat.

"You're not going to believe this, detective, but I don't exactly know."

Tim closed his eyes and let his head fall back.

"Phillip warned me right at the beginning to stay out of it. What I know, I picked up by listening through doors and prying. I can only guess what this is about—I can't prove anything. You must understand that what I'm telling you is purely hypothetical."

"Okay," Tim said. "I understand."

"It had something to do with illegally retrieving classified information from top investment bankers' computer files and then trading on that information in a manner that wouldn't arouse suspicion. The files disclosed inside information from people who were on the cusp of mergers and acquisitions."

She inhaled, blowing out the smoke in a stream. "Code Ninety-nine itself had to do with the development of a computer program that could break the secret codes on those top security files without being detected.

"Some of these people were the best in the world when it came to knowing who the movers and shakers were in investment banking. The others were geniuses when it came to computer codes and programs.

"The one thing I know for certain is that Phillip made a lot of money. Millions. I've tried to find it—to verify how much, but I can't. Wherever it went, it's untraceable."

"Were the others—Barry, Deveraux, Hightower—did they know what Yates was doing with this information?" he asked, his mouth on the lip of his cup.

"Not right away, but when they figured it out, they quit. By that time Yates had them nailed down so tight so they couldn't turn him in without implicating themselves. He'd made deals in their names, traded stocks, and then funneled the gains somewhere else. I don't know how or where, but I do know how Phillip thinks."

"Linear," Tim said, getting up and going to the rail. After a while, she came and stood near to him, throwing bits of cracker up to the gulls.

He turned his back to the passenger cabin, looking directly at her now. She was somber; the circles under her eyes made her look older than she was. "What do you know about the creation of shell companies?"

"Only that they were created. I was kept out of that, too. When Phillip wants to keep things from me, he does it for a reason. I never question his judgment."

She turned her back on him. "There's an attorney. A despicable man by the name of DeMello who sets up the other companies, including the ones offshore."

The sound of the motors lowered in pitch as the ferry moved closer to the Sausalito dock. Passengers began descending the stairs toward the lower deck. There was a beaten look on many of their faces: people wanting to go home to eat and sleep so they could get up and do it all over again the following day.

"Where is the Code Ninety-nine description?"

"Oh, I'm sure Phillip shredded them before you were even out of the building." She paused. "It doesn't matter. They didn't explain anything about the project—it was more a confidentiality oath."

The boat slowed to a crawl. "I want to talk to you some more," Tim said. "Where do you live?"

"Don't," she said, panic in her voice. "I don't know what's secure and what isn't. I'm sure my phone is bugged. Maybe the house is being watched, too, I don't know. Why do you think I had you meet me here?"

"I want you to look at some sketches. How can we do that?"

She headed for the stairway. He followed. They were going downstairs when her purse slipped partway down her arm, spilling several things onto the deck. He gathered the items that rolled near him: a lipstick tube, a credit card case, a packet of Kleenex. She thanked him, stuffing the contents back into the black bag.

"Tomorrow—the six-oh-five A.M. ferry. Put them in an envelope and drop it in the women's room waste canister before we leave the dock."

He wanted to asked her more, but the passengers were thick around them, pushing en masse to the disembarkation ramp. By the time he was on the dock, she was twenty yards ahead, walking with her head down.

Pulling a handful of antacids from his pocket, he chewed them one at a time until they were gone.

The salesman doing the hard sell number was one of the slick, too sexy for his shirt breed. Which is why Adele, who had actually already decided on the cell phone she wanted, let him think he was working sales pitch magic, while she returned all her calls using the store's demo cell phones.

She spent five minutes on one demo phone with her mother explaining that Nelson would love to have Thanksgiving with her and the aunties, and could he also bring a new friend?

Claiming that the quality of tone was not acceptable, Adele was given another demo, on which she called Jeffrey directly at his office.

"What's up?" she said when he came on the line.

"Did you bring Mathilde to her hotel today?" he asked. As much as he tried to sound composed, the concern crept into his voice.

"Ayuhn." She turned away from the salesman, who was hanging over her, eyebrows perpetually raised.

"How did she seem to you?"

"Edgy, but okay. Why?"

He let out a breath. "I'm a bit concerned. I sort of expected her to call after she was released. If her defenses are about to break, I don't think it's a good time for her to be alone. A breakthrough now might cause her tremendous suffering and a maybe even stronger dissociation."

Adele moved a few feet away from the salesman, who moved with her. They were heading out of electronics into household appliances. She put a finger in her free ear to block out the noise of the store.

"Well, I tried talking her into staying with me, but she wouldn't budge. She said she needed time alone. Do we need to worry about suicide here, by any chance?"

"I don't think so. Yes, she's depressed, but I don't see any of the risk factors: no signs of self-destructiveness or poor impulse control. Physically there isn't any indication of alcohol or drug abuse. Actually, our alliance was fairly good. She contracted with me at the beginning to discuss any suicidal or destructive ideation if it emerged."

The persistent salesman was inching with her past household appliances toward the televisions, where forty-three different sets were playing clips from "Captain Kangaroo." On the screens, the Banana Man pulled strings and strings of bananas out of his pockets and sleeves, singing his weird little ditty in falsetto, punctuating it with an occasional "ooooooooooohhhhhhhhhhh!"

She turned away from the salesman again, and headed for the speaker room. "Listen, I've been wondering about why she nixed the drug interview? I know why *she* didn't want it, but can you run through the shrink's side of it again?"

"You want the long or short version?" Jeff asked.

"Short," she said, looking over her shoulder at the oncoming salesman.

"Besides the obvious fears—some of which she expressed to you—I sensed she might be feeling ashamed, like she was afraid she might have done something. Initially I was concerned about the shame and her suffering, but later I realized that if she was really dissociated, she would have blotted out those feelings."

She heard him blow out a long breath that ended in a groan.

"I don't know, Adele. I think I missed the twenty-foot billboard."

"When did you decide all this?"

"The other day. I was talking to her about the Amytal interview and I got the distinct feeling she was trying to act ashamed, and then she wound up sounding angry." He sighed again. "Oh, hell, I don't know."

Hands on hips, the salesman was talking at her, asking her what she thought. Adele could tell he was running out of salesman patience as quickly as she was running out of salesman tolerance.

"Listen, Jeff, you keep thinking about it and call me later," Adele said. "Right now I've got to buy a phone."

"When I was a kid," Adele explained, "the other girls used to play with paper dolls—cardboard cutouts of little girls and boys. Then you could buy books which featured pages of clothes that you could cut out and attach to the doll's form by bending paper tabs.

"I thought they were pretty stupid, although I admit to being fascinated by the way the doll's whole appearance would change just by going from one outfit to the next. That's what I want to do with these. I want to rearrange the hair, the glasses— except instead of tabs, we're going to use rubber cement."

Tim nodded, and together they spread the sketches over the floor. The faces stared up at them again. They studied them from different angles, including upside down. Then she blocked out the glasses on all the faces and stood back. Together they squinted, tilted their heads, moved further away and close up. None of it made sense.

When they were done, the sketches sat, propped up in a line against the wall.

"Sort of like a lineup down at the precinct," Adele said.

Tim nodded, though he hadn't heard what she said. He'd grown tired of the sketches. He was thinking about Phillip Yates. He pulled out his notebook, flipping through the pages.

"Anything from the Canadian Mounties about Mathilde?" Adele asked.

"No," he sighed. "I think that's a dead end. The next-door

neighbor and Deveraux's brother didn't recognize her—neither did any of Mrs. Deveraux's family.

"We've got multiple postings of the Jane Doe photo and the Budget man sketch all over L.A., Escondido, Paso Robles, and Marin. So far there's been no bites."

Adele got up and moved Bugs out of the way of the Budget sketch. "Are you going to tell me what you've been chewing on all evening? You barely tasted the shepherd's pie, let alone the garlic soup."

"Not true," he smiled. "I'm *still* tasting the garlic soup." He stretched his feet toward the fireplace and, hugging one of the throw pillows to his chest, spilled a wealth of information about what had transpired at Citadel and with Laurel Saches.

Hastily gathering her notebook, Adele took notes.

"There's your reason why the one Deveraux girl was left alive," Adele said when he was done.

He let his eyes drift to the crackling fire, letting himself be hypnotized by the yellow and orange tongues of flames. "Share."

"From what Ms. Saches said, we can deduce that Deveraux was blackmailing Yates—maybe he was holding an essential piece of damaging evidence and that's what he was threatening to turn over to the authorities." Adele ran a finger around the rim of her cup. "Yates wanted that evidence, and either he or the killer used the child to get it."

"Sounds right."

"I think this is the big time." She bit her bottom lip. "My guess is that Yates has the means and the connections to hire himself a professional killer."

Tim didn't answer right away, considering how he would frame his reply. "But remember what I've said: criminals always do something stupid; they always screw up somewhere. There's got to be a weak link or an oversight. Yates is bright. He might not fuck up now—but he will."

"Damn it!" Adele said, bobbing her head. "I wish Mathilde would come around."

"Have you spoken with the shrink?"

Adele stared into the fire. "This afternoon. He's concerned about her, but he doesn't think she's a suicide candidate. She's supposed to see him tomorrow." She turned to him. "Do you think she's going to be okay?"

"As long as she stays put and out of range of whoever it is that's gun-happy."

"You know," Adele tilted her head, drew up her legs and hugged them, "I was thinking about that last night. This guy who attacked us? I don't think he had a gun."

"You can't say that for sure," Tim said, trying not to look at the neat tuck of her buttocks.

"No, I can't, but he didn't have one in his hand, and it would seem to me that if he were the same guy who killed these other people, he would have had the gun out and ready to use by the time he got inside the room."

"He didn't want to attract attention with the noise," Tim countered.

She shook her head. "I don't think so. There wouldn't have been much noise using a silencer or a pillow with a twenty-two or some other little gun. Not at that range."

Adele got up and threw another log onto the fire. Her movements were fluid and graceful. Tim didn't want to take his eyes off her.

"What are you thinking?" he asked after she'd sat down again.

She shrugged. "That either he was going to kill Mathilde by snapping her neck, or he wasn't going to kill her at all. She says he hadn't said anything to her before I came into the room. Maybe he was bringing her into the bathroom to talk to her. Maybe he thought she had information." Adele brought the cup to her lips, sipped the cold tea, and set it down.

"I mean if he was going to snap her neck, how long could that have taken? A half a second? Less? When I went in there, he'd dragged her five feet into the bathroom. He wouldn't do that if all he wanted was to kill her."

She ran one of her long fingers up and down her throat while she thought. "Let's say he wanted information from her, or to give her information," Adele said. "Maybe Jane Doe has a tie-in with Yates? Or maybe they know each other?"

Tim shook his head. "Did you ever think he might have been planning on kidnapping her? Hell, there are three dozen possibilities."

Still staring into the fire, she began to untwine her braid. He had to look away. For him, to see a woman—especially *this* woman—play with her hair was as erotically stimulating as kissing.

"When you drop those sketches tomorrow, make sure there's a photo of Jane Doe in there," she said.

"Already thought of that," he said.

"What about the other witnesses? What reactions did they have to the sketches?"

"Krenshaw ran them by Jason Humbold this afternoon. He didn't recognize your attacker, nor could he make the connection between the other sketches."

"Did you contact Hoffman's family?" Adele asked, shaking out her hair.

Tim grimaced. "Yeah. Mrs. Hoffman said her husband had been depressed for a month or two before he left Citadel. He hated Yates with a passion. She says her husband used to talk about wanting to turn him into the authorities for illegal business practices, but wouldn't give details."

Adele yawned, and carried their cups to the kitchen. "Time for bed, sweetie," she called back over her shoulder to Nelson.

Tim closed his eyes, imagining she'd meant the comment for him. When she turned around, she found him grinning like a fool.

Adele entered the room in her old house, where her father sat working at his bench, making a book. Going closer, she noticed the front cover had been fashioned with a set of binoculars sticking out of it. When she looked through the eyepieces she saw herself in the old Mill Valley bus depot, doing a spot of soft shoe to the guitar accompaniment of an older black gentleman.

Seated on the benches around them were five people all dressed in light gray polyester suits. As she danced, her eyes slid from one face to the other—the Budget man, the scar man, Mathilde's scar man, the priest, the cop—and then back again. The cop, the priest, Mathilde's scar man, her scar man, the Budget man.

She screamed when it came to her and jumped seven or eight feet into the air, hovered, and fell. When she hit the ground, she awoke drenched with sweat.

She sat up. Nelson was at the side of the bed, looking into her face, waiting for the verdict or orders. Searching back through her dream, she wrote two short sentences in the notebook. Underlined one.

Nelson whined.

"Buddha on a bike," she said miserably, staring at what she'd written.

She leaned back against the headboard, glanced at her watch, and weighed her courses of action. It was too late—or early, depending on how one looked at it—to do much of anything except sleep.

Turning off the lamp, Adele invited Nelson to lie down next to her. Arm and foreleg entwined, they fell asleep, each twitching at her and his own pace.

THIRTEEN

ADELE STUDIED THE THIN WHITE FACE OF VIVIAN Vanderlise, trying desperately to mold it into the face of Edith Hatter on "Moon Alley"—a show that had been playing reruns for generations.

Vivian Vanderlise wasn't the first Hollywood star she had taken care of, but she was the only one Adele worshiped. Edith Hatter was as much a part of her childhood as her own mother. All the hours she'd sat and watched in fascination as Edith and Molly got themselves into fantastic and hysterically funny situations episode after episode. Vivian wasn't like the other stars— self-involved ego-Nazis. Vivian was *real*.

Adele wondered if that was because she was dying, or if it was because she'd never been corrupted by fame or Hollywood hype.

"Vivian?"

Eyes the color of brown velvet turned to her. The woman looked startled, as if to say, "Who? Me?"

"I need to turn you on your side so you don't get pressure sores on your back. I'll give you a back rub while I'm there."

"Oh, you doll," Vivian said in that husky brass horn of a voice that had been mimicked by thousands. Adele had a flashback to being five, ten, twenty-five years old and hearing Edith say, "Oh, you doll!" to Molly for the zillionth time. Who would have thought that Edith Hatter would someday be saying "Oh, you doll" to her?

With impeccable care, Adele turned the woman onto her side and began to massage the white, translucent skin, every stroke a thank-you.

* * *

The first buzz of the cell phone was drowned out by the two obnoxiously loud and pushy seagulls who routinely hung out at Sausalito ferry dock. Known to the regular commuters as Stan and Ollie, the two had been working the dock for three years, entertaining commuters and tourists alike. Theirs was the world of fresh sourdough rolls, sticky buns, and chunks of deboned bass and halibut thrown to them by a cook who worked at one of the local seafood restaurants.

Tim laughed as Ollie hopped around on one leg to elicit sympathy from the unknowing tourists, while Stan picked food from their hands. The second buzz of the phone reached him.

He clicked open the device, doubting it could be Ms. Saches—the ferry wouldn't have reached the San Francisco pier yet.

He was wrong.

"Detective Ritmann?" Her voice was drowned out by a passing bus on her end. She was at an outside phone on the Embarcadero, probably outside the ferry terminal.

"Yes, Ms. Saches." He was surprised at the animation of her voice. She was excited, her breath coming in quick, nervous gulps.

"I recognize two of these people," she said, her words rushed together. Her voice was shaking.

"Which ones?"

"The man with the scar. He works for Citadel as one of . . ."

The roar of another bus blanked out her words.

". . . name is Ed or Ted, maybe. He drives for Mr. Yates when people come in from out of town and also at private affairs." There was a loud, prolonged honk and then a car backfiring. "The weirdest thing about—the—other one . . ." Her voice faltered and stopped.

"What is it, Laurel? Do you see someone you know?" His blood pressure shot up, and he felt in his pocket for an antacid.

"Oh my God," she said from far away. "Something . . . I think . . . they shot me. They shot . . ."

The phone clanked against something hard and Tim began running to his car and yelling into the phone at the same time. "Talk to me! For Christ's sake . . ."

In the background he heard a woman say, "What's wrong

with her?" and then he heard someone scream and say, "Jesus! She's bleeding." A man yelled that he was calling 911.

Tim shouted again, trying to get someone's attention. Time crawled by while he continued to yell and tried to listen at the same time. After the unmistakable sounds of confusion and a crowd gathering—he'd worked the beat too long not to know that sound by heart—a young man, probably a teen, picked up the phone and said, "Hello?" He was breathing hard, like he'd been running or was hyped on adrenaline.

"I'm a cop," Tim said. "What's happening there?"

"Oh man, the lady? I think she's shot, man. Blood coming outta her neck. It's bad, man. They got an ambulance coming."

"Is she breathing?" Tim asked, letting go of the wheel long enough to put his blue flasher on top of the car. "Is somebody doing CPR?"

"Yeah, somebody . . ."

"Is there a cop there?"

"Yeah. Two cops here now."

"I need to talk to one of the cops right now!"

Without ceremony, the phone was dropped, clanked six or so times, and was picked up again a minute later.

"Who the hell is this?" said the gruff voice that answered.

"Timothy Ritmann with Marin Sheriff's Department. I was just talking to a woman who's a C.I. She was naming names then she said she was shot. Is she shot? Is she alive?"

"This woman is a confidential informant?"

"Christ! Yes. Who is this?"

"Denning. SFPD. We were driving by and . . ."

"Is she . . ."

"I think she's alive, but she isn't conscious. Looks like somebody got her in the neck and the chest."

"Where are they going to take her?"

"SF General probably. It's closest."

"Could you ride with her? Maybe see if she can talk, if you can get a name from her—ask her for the name of the other person she recognized in the file."

"I'll see what I can do. The medics don't like anybody in the rig."

"Okay, Denning, I'm halfway over the bridge right now. Meet me outside the General's ER with good news."

* * *

Adele almost never went to the cafeteria except for every third Tuesday of the month, when instead of being the place where questionable food was served to indiscriminate diners, the cafeteria turned into a salesroom for remaindered books donated by local book distributors. The proceeds went to help feed and house Marin's lodging-impaired.

Cynthia went to look for a book about sleep deprivation and sexual techniques, while Adele browsed through true crime books. She was thumbing through a book on the history of serial killers when she noticed Jellyroll across the cafeteria, looking through the gardening books.

She waved and headed toward him. He met her in the middle of the room carrying a book—obviously new—with the sales slip closed between the pages. She took it out of his hands and turned it over.

Post-Trauma Stress: Psychological Studies and Evaluations.

"Exciting reading?" she asked, lifting her eyebrows.

Jellyroll shrugged and gazed around the room. Like a lot of big men she knew, he had a hard time looking anyone in the eyes—especially women.

"Have you talked to Mathilde today?" she asked.

"Nope. I called over at the Firetrap Hotel a couple of times. The manager said she wasn't there."

"Yeah," Adele laughed uncertainly. "I wondered why you recommended the place. I thought you were kind of sweet on the girl. I figured you saved her from a fire once, and wouldn't want to have to do it again."

Jellyroll stared at her. "She tell you that? That I recommended that place?"

"Didn't you?"

He shook his head emphatically. "Not me. I wouldn't put a rat in that fucking hole unless I was thinking of trying to roast it. That place is a fire looking for a hot thought to start it. The department has tried to condemn the building five times in the last few years.

"I told Tild not to stay there, but she wasn't going to listen to me, by God. If she wants to stay in a firetrap, I'm not going to twist her arm. It's none of my business. When she first told me she was going there, I figured she wanted to keep her expenses down, but one of the guys at the station said the place was expensive as hell—like two-fifty a week for a room without a bathroom and more for a room with a toilet—real bullshit prices for a death trap."

Adele's mind was doing a sort of flip-flop in time with her stomach. "You're kidding."

"Nope. I'm going to call again after I get off work. See if I can't talk her into grabbing some grub . . . maybe a movie, too."

"If you do get ahold of her," Adele said, writing down her new cell phone number on the back of his sales slip, "call me and let me know she's okay."

"If I remember," he said, moving off toward the door.

The response irritated her. She grabbed his arm and placed herself right in front of him, forcing him to look at her. "Make sure you remember, Jellyroll. This isn't playtime. She's got more than a few people worried about her, including the police. If you find her before we do, call me."

He studied her long enough to know she was serious about what she'd said. "Okay," he said, less flippant this time. "I'll call you as soon as I connect."

"Tim called," Cynthia said, sticking her head in the door of Mrs. Vanderlise's room. "He wants you to call him on his cell phone as soon as you can."

Adele concentrated on sliding the intracath needle at a forty-five-degree angle into Vivian's vein. The vein rolled away. Adele chased it.

"Jeffrey called, too," continued Cynthia. "Said to call him as soon as you can."

Adele bit her lip and put more traction on the skin, pulling until the vein remained motionless while she tried to pierce the side. It was tough—like trying to stab a piece of rubber tubing.

"Anybody else?" Adele asked, and felt the tiny pop of the wall of the vessel as the needle went through. She smiled and pulled back on the plunger. The sight of blood was her reward.

Not jiggling the hollow catheter, she pulled out the needle and hooked the IV tubing into the hub of the catheter.

"Sounds like you've got a lot of boyfriends," said Vivian.

"They line up outside the hospital just to see her walk to her car," Cynthia said in a droll little voice. "She's very popular."

Adele rolled her eyes and threaded the IV tubing through the pump, setting it at a slow rate. "My popularity is limited to psychiatrists, cops, and dogs," she said dryly.

Mirek came to the door. "Adele? The phone it is on for you. Tina says to come now or she will not be kind to any more peoples who call you here and disturb her work."

Adele couldn't imagine what Tina might consider "not kind" since she was a nasty piece of work to begin with.

"Mirek, would you finish taping this down and give Mrs. Vanderlise her two P.M. Keflex?"

Mirek was already studying the new IV, measuring out pieces of tape. "Yes, I do this now for you. Please. Go to the phone before Tina goes off her stack."

"Blows her stack," Cynthia corrected.

Adele hooked her arm through Cynthia's and went for the unrelenting phones.

"What!?"

"She was in a booth on the phone with me, telling me she recognized two of the sketches when somebody shot her," Tim said, moving back against the wall out of the way of a speeding gurney.

"Who did she know?"

"The man with the scar for one. She was shot before she got to the other one."

"Where *are* you? It sounds like—"

"A hospital? You're right; I'm at SF General waiting for her to get out of surgery."

"Were there any witnesses?" Adele asked.

"A couple of high school kids said they saw a guy in a black leather jacket running from the scene. One described him as having a scar on his cheek."

"So now what? Are you going to Citadel to look for the guy with the scar?"

"First I need to find out from my medical consultant what kind of a chance she has for coming out of this."

"I don't know," Adele said. "I'd have to know where she was shot and what the damage is. Was she conscious?"

Tim moved out of the way of a gurney holding a young man with a bloody leg. As the gurney passed, Tim looked at the open wound and felt queasy. "No, but she was breathing. They brought her right to surgery."

"How long ago?"

"Three hours."

Adele wrote something down on the palm of her hand. "You want me to call the surgical office and see what I can find out?"

"I'll be completely indebted to you for fifty-four days."

"Make it sixty-seven and I'll call."

"You've got it."

Betsy, the nurse-secretary in the Operating Room office at SF General, had to have been a close relative of Tina's. When Adele—aka Thelma from SICU—asked for details, the woman reluctantly divulged that Ms. Saches was still in surgery and she was hypotensive, but expected to live. Dr. Wong was having a tough time repairing her shoulder so that she would have future use of her arm. A bullet had collapsed a lung, but no, she hadn't caught a bullet to the neck. The nurse-secretary narrowed down the time left in surgery to between one and seven hours, a time span that Adele thought unnecessarily wide.

"Have somebody from Recovery call you as soon as she comes back from surgery," she said when she finished passing the information on to Tim. "Wave your badge around. Nurses love cops—especially handsome ones. They'll trip over themselves if you smile nice at them."

He was momentarily stunned into silence by the plethora of straight lines she'd handed him on a platter. By the time he got his mouth to moving to mumble something about "if I come to your door some midnight and smile and wave my badge around, will you trip over yourself," she was gone.

"What?" she asked for a second time. Adele couldn't believe the amount of bad news she was getting in one day.

"Mathilde never showed up for her appointment," Jeffrey repeated. "Do you know where she might be?"

"No, I don't. Did you check at the hotel?"

"The manager said she hadn't seen her. I made them go to her room and check to make sure she wasn't there. I'm not sure what, but something isn't right, Adele. For her not to show up is a serious breach of our contract."

Adele checked her watch. "I've got twenty more minutes before I can get out. I'm going over there to look around. I'll page you."

Her charting was done almost entirely in abbreviations: *Pt. ok alive & breath. All systems go.*

"Hey, you doll."

Vivian opened her eyes and nodded. Adele took her hand.

"I'm going off duty. See you tomorrow?"

"God willing," the star said, then moved her head on the pillow to look more closely at Adele. "You're flushed, darling. Where are you going? Are you meeting a lover?"

Adele blushed deeper shades of red. "No, I'm going to do a little private investigation work."

The actress raised her eyebrows—or what was left of them. Chemotherapy had not been kind.

"I used to do that, too, before I got into the Industry."

"Really?"

"Really. Early forties. I worked for a private eye in Los Angeles. Mostly it was trailing unfaithful wives. Sometimes it was more dangerous. But fun. It beat walking the streets."

Adele cocked her head. "You walked the streets?"

"I was a . . ." She lifted her hand and struck a pose of glamour. ". . . professional escort. Sounds sweet, doesn't it? Two bucks for a blow job, and five for around the world. Twenty bucks for two days and nights, anything goes. If the guy had money, the price went up to a hundred. In those days a man couldn't make that kind of pay in a week." Vivian chuckled and closed her eyes. "Don't look so shocked, doll. That was how I got my first big break into the movies."

Eyes sparkling, Adele smiled and sat down on the bed. "How's that?"

"One of the top executives of MGM picked me up one night for a blow job, but he couldn't get it up. He was down in the dumps, so I started cutting up, trying to get a laugh out of the old stiff. He thought I was hilarious, so he got me a bit part in *Oh*

Suzannah Girl—a three-liner, but I got the biggest laugh in the show. The rest is history. Who are you trailing?"

"Not trailing," Adele said. "Searching for a lady."

Vivian lifted her eyebrows again. "Ah, a woman. Women are easier than men. Women hide close to home. Men travel. Remember you have to look in all the corners close to home."

The Beast was having a temper tantrum. In a moment of tightwadism, Adele filled up with the 87 octane instead of the 97, and it had upset the Beast's gas tank. Now the mechanical nightmare was on strike.

"Can't you do this in the driveway at home?" she asked, turning the key again. "Why do you wait for the times I need you most to do this?"

The Beast did not budge.

She swore, got out of the car, lifted the hood (mouth), and looked around. The Engine—that demonic tangle of metal and wire innards that was the soul of the Beast—mocked her. She kicked the tire, cursing herself for not finishing the automotive mechanics course at College of Marin.

The simple checks—distributor, spark plugs, battery cables and connections, oil, water, carburetor—gave no sign of anything wrong. She was screwing the nut down on the air filter when a 1989 Citroën Deux Chevaux pulled up next to her and parked.

Mirek got out and came to stand next to her. He stared at the large engine. They didn't say anything for a few minutes.

"It is big," he said finally.

"Big and evil," Adele replied.

He looked at her oddly. "The car is evil?"

She nodded. "This, Mirek, is Christine's brother Le Beaste."

"I do not know this Christine," Mirek said. "She is bad?"

"Christine is a mechanical version of the Veřejná Bezpečnost."

"Ah."

Again there was silence. Presently, Adele sighed. "Are you going back to school for your postclinicals?"

Mirek nodded. "Yes. We discuss our patients and what actions we made."

She remembered her own tedious postclinical sessions and

shuddered at the memory. "Can I get a lift from you to the college? I need to get to San Anselmo."

He snapped his white nursing shoes together at the heels and bowed. "I am honored to lift you to San Anselmo."

"You don't need to do that, Mirek, I can—"

"You take my car. I am done at six. I trust you drive good."

Adele was about to refuse his generous offer, but then looked at the Beast. It would serve it right.

"I'd love to drive your beautiful car, Mirek," she said, louder than necessary, hoping that if the Beast really was possessed, it would hear and its little coils and cables would burn with jealousy. "It will be nice to see how a *normal* car responds."

As they drove away, Adele glanced back at the Beast. She swore it had taken on a forlorn look. Alone and aging, the shandrydan had never looked so sad. To rub it in, she beeped the Citroën's cheery-sounding horn twice and waved.

The spunky little Citroën wasn't half as nice to drive as the Beast. Whereas the Beast was solid and impenetrable, rather like driving a big overstuffed couch, the Citroën felt like she was riding inside a Pepsi can over a bumpy road.

It was, however, easier to park, especially when parking in Marin was at a premium. She pulled into the small lot behind the hotel, ignoring the three red-and-white signs that stated SAN ANSELMO HOTEL PARKING ONLY.

Across the alley was the side of an antique store, and at the back of the alley was a wrought-iron fence, the kind with the sharp spikes on the top. The back of the hotel reminded her of old tenement houses she'd seen back east; the stairs were partially enclosed. Under the stairs was a wide double door and what looked like a wooden receiving dock. She guessed the place had at one time housed some sort of retail store, or maybe it had been a small factory of sorts.

Hoisting her purse onto her shoulder, she walked around the corner to the front of the building and missed the entrance to the hotel twice due to the numerous ferns that hid the brick patio and iron gate from view.

By the time she finally found the entrance, she was soaked to the skin. She surveyed the postage-stamp-size lobby, wiped the rain off her neck, and went to the glass window under the hand-written REGISTER HERE! sign. Past the round hole cut into the window was an office—of sorts. A desk with a marker board on it leaned against the wall. In one corner was a cot made up with an army blanket and several pink and red throw pillows and, in the opposite corner, a sun lamp. It had the feel of a prison cell, or a room in a 1930s mental sanitarium.

She stepped quietly around the corner, following the sound of an afternoon talk show. On the wall was another handmade sign and a black, uneven arrow: NO ONE IN OFFICE? GO TO END OF HALL.

Ten feet down the narrow hall to her left was a wide doorway, which led to the main kitchen of the ritzy Italian restaurant next door. Two of the cooks smiled at her. One shouted something in Italian and beckoned her inside.

Adele laughed and moved on to the end of the hall, where the smell of frying onions in butter battled with the smell of garlic frying in olive oil, and won.

Through the open top half of the Dutch door was a very dark and cluttered apartment. With the exception of the wall-mounted television, it resembled an apartment from the turn of the century: velvet drapes, silk-tasseled lamp covers, and busy Oriental carpets.

A lump in the middle of the living room floor moved and stood. It was, she realized in amazement, a Saint Bernard of the same vintage as the decor. The animal shuffled down the hall and stopped, dumbly staring up at her.

"Hello?"

Somewhere from inside, a refrigerator door closed and there was shuffling of slippers on linoleum. A muffled voice said, "Hrummmft."

"Hello?"

"Rummfed mmmfter."

"I'm sorry, I can't hear you. I want to inquire about . . ."

The hallway filled with pink-and-red-checkered material, and then an arm, the size of a side of beef, showed itself. The object kept moving into the hall, angling itself sideways in order to fit. There were breasts—more than likely weighing thirty or fifty pounds apiece—and a set of chins—four? five?—stacked like so many powdered jelly doughnuts one upon the other.

The face, plain as an uncarved pumpkin, was hidden inside a block of flesh and topped with a red curly wig. One meaty hand held a triple layer ham sandwich on white bread. In the other was a Coke Classic.

"Hi." Adele managed a small wave.

The gargantuan chewed, and then wheezed, as if breathing was a full-time job. Adele wondered why she'd never seen this woman before as a patient. She also wondered why the woman wasn't dead yet. She looked to be about fifty. To have lived that long with that much weight had to be a world record.

The woman swallowed her mouthful. "What can I do for you?" she asked in a high, breathless voice.

"Are you the manager?"

"I am," the woman wheezed. "I'm the sergeant in charge of this outfit."

"I'm looking for a woman who checked in here yesterday?" Adele said, "She's about five feet, six inches tall and—"

The woman eyed her scrubs and took a major chunk out of the sandwich. "Are you a nurse?" A slice of onion slid down her front, smearing a streak of yellow mustard over the red and pink checks.

Adele smiled, resolving immediately not to give advice about weight loss medications or hypertension. "Ayuhn."

"Me too."

"Oh. Uhn-huh. Well, that's . . ." What? Enough to commit suicide over? ". . . nice."

"Retired from service right after Nam."

"You were a nurse in Nam?"

The woman nodded and daintily drank off half the can of soda. "Yep. Had fifteen corpsmen and six R.N.'s under me."

Adele wanted in the worst way to ask if perhaps they weren't all still under there, but bit the inside of her cheek hard enough to make her eyes water. It was the only way to keep the Crazy Woman laughter at bay.

"You must be looking for . . ." She looked down at the floor as if the name was written there. "Ah . . . Mathilda? She's in room twenty-six. Go right at the top of the stairs. It's halfway down the hall, one beyond the latrine."

Adele thanked her and began to back down the hall. She'd

reached the other end when the manager called out, "She's not there."

Adele walked partway back so she wouldn't have to shout. "Do you know where she went?"

"I don't baby-sit, I just manage the place," the manager said, reaching into a baggy side pocket of the tent. She pulled out a breath spray, uncapped it, and sprayed. "I'm out in the front office most of the time except once in a while I have a kid come in to cover for me for a few hours in the evenings. We get a lot of people in and out of here all day. The nighttime is easier."

"You stay out there all night, too?" Adele asked in disbelief.

The woman nodded which caused her chins to jiggle like Jell-O. "It doesn't bother me. I don't sleep too good, anyway, so I might as well."

"How do you know Mathilde isn't here?"

The manager swung the top half of the door closed. There was a clinking of metal, and when she opened it again, she was holding a chain with an old-fashioned key dangling from it. "I require the renters to drop off and pick up their keys every time they go in or out. There's somebody minding the front desk twenty-four hours a day, seven days a week, including Christmas. Security-wise, the system works great. Sometimes the patients . . ." The woman realized her slip and giggled. "I mean the tenants grumble about it, but they turn in those keys. Once in a while I'll find out somebody is sneaking out the back stairs, but not very often."

"Sort of like running a mental ward, is it?" Adele joked straight-faced.

The woman laughed a rich, deep belly laugh with a hint of wheeze. It was a fat woman laugh, a sound Adele found charming.

"Exactly. You wouldn't believe some of the people we get in here."

"Oh, yes, I would," Adele said, thinking of the Marin transients she'd seen come in and out of Ward 8. She was willing to bet most of the hotel's guests had been in Ward 8 at one time or another.

"Do you know when she dropped off her keys this morning?"

The woman sipped her Coke and thought for a minute.

"Early," she answered. "I went to the latrine. When I came back, it was on the desk out front."

"What time was that?"

The woman squinted with one eye, her gaze growing more keen. "You related to her or something?"

"Her sister."

The woman shrugged, which set waves of motion off in the entirety of her body. "I dunno, maybe four-thirty, or somewhere around there. I was in the can for about thirty minutes."

Adele could easily believe it would take the woman thirty, possibly even fifty minutes to go to the bathroom.

"Well, thanks. I think I'll run up and leave a note for her under the door."

The mountain of shoulders shrugged. "Sure. Be careful of the stairs, though. Somebody spilled something sticky on the runner."

"Will do."

Adele took the steps two at a time, sticking briefly only once on the bottom step. At the top of the stairs, she took a right as directed, listening carefully. The place was more silent than a tomb.

She rapped on number 26, and put her ear to the door. There was nothing but the muffled sounds of the kitchen below. Looking both ways before crossing into the illegal territory of breaking and entering, Adele searched her bag. At the bottom she found a set of standard keys along with her lock picks. She slipped a standard skeleton key into the lock. It turned with the slightest of clicks.

For good measure, Adele knocked once more, waited, and entered.

"Mathilde?" she whispered, closing the door behind her. The room was dark except for the light coming from the streetlamp a few buildings away. Slowly her eyes adjusted, and she could make out the outline of the furniture well enough to negotiate her way across the room to the window. She found her penlight and lashed the thin beam around the room.

Moving up a couple of decades from the downstairs decor, room 26 had been decorated 1950s style: chintz curtains, chintz bedspread in the famous fifties color combo of black and pink.

The furniture was Danish modern, the cushions of which were covered in fabric of pink cubes and boomerang shapes on black. Everything was extremely neat and orderly, exactly as Adele figured it would be.

Laid out on the bed was the jumper Mathilde had worn the day before. On the chair was her duffle bag, mostly still packed. In the bathroom, the toiletries were arranged around the sink and shower—unused. The bristles of the toothbrush were dry as a bone. Boxes of emergency gauze and a jar of Silvadene were neatly arranged in the medicine cabinet.

Adele picked up the blank pad of paper off the top of the dresser and held the penlight to the side of the page, checking for impressions. It was there, faint as a down feather: "American 6:05."

The trash can yielded a cellophane wrapper without marking and a piece of crumpled notepaper. On it were her own name, address, and phone number.

She made her way to the closet, careful not to touch anything or knock so much as a wrinkle out of place. Hanging in the middle of an odd assortment of plastic and wire hangers were a sweater and a pair of slacks. On the floor were a new pair of Rockports and a regulation motel/hotel in-room safe, which was locked.

Adele went down on her hands and knees on the black wool rug, searching under the furniture, feeling for taped-up places in the flimsy covering of the box springs.

Standing, she brushed herself off and started to sit down, thought better of it, and checked the closet once more. As a nurse who was trained to use all her senses, she sniffed. There was a faint odor of something that was familiar to her—something that triggered unpleasant memories.

Searching out the source of the smell, she put her nose to each of the articles hanging. When she got to the floor, she caught the scent of blood. It turned her stomach into an ice cube.

Deep within the building there came a low rumble, and the floor shook beneath her feet. "Oh great," she said, looking up to the ceiling light fixture for confirmation. "An earthquake and I'm in the only building in Marin that's going to go down like a cracker."

The light fixture didn't show any signs of vibrating out of the ceiling, the way it should have done. Perplexed, Adele dropped to her hands and knees, pulled back the carpet, and put her ear on the wood floor. Somewhere within the structure, the low rumble sounded, but it stopped a second later, followed by a reverberating *klunk* and then metal scraping against metal.

She stood and had started toward the door when she noticed the smear on her hand.

"Blood?"

I do believe so, said Sherlock Holmes, who was sitting on the edge of the dresser. *Give it a whiff.*

She sniffed again, got back down on her hands and knees, and ran her hand through a drill of where it had been. On the back of the carpet, she discovered the spot of dark brown.

She dampened a clean white washcloth and sopped up as much of the blood as she could. The washcloth she put into a plastic bag provided by the hotel for laundry and stuffed it down into her fanny pack.

And then she remembered the stair with the sticky.

Never in her life had she driven someone else's car so fast. Usually the Beast knew how to handle itself when she got into these states, but the Citroën was nervous. It didn't like her, she was sure of that, and it didn't come outfitted with autopilot—a must in her case.

Somehow, she managed to push in the numbers on the cell phone pad and hit the send button without veering into more than one lane.

"Jesus! Where the hell are you?" Tim asked, the moment he heard her voice. "I've been trying to—"

"I'm on my way to College of Marin to return a car to a friend. The Beast is being a jerk, but I think it'll be okay now."

"What's going on?"

"I'm really freaked about Mathilde. She left the hotel early, although nobody saw her, and she didn't show up for her appointment with Jeffr—with Dr. Lavine or with Dr. Murray. I—I . . ."

She faltered, not wanting him to go officious on her, then decided she didn't care. "As a matter of fact, I let myself into her room and found a small spot of blood on the carpet. I also found blood on the stairs going up to her room. All her clothes are still there—toothbrush and everything."

"Did you talk to the manager?"

Adele sighed. "Useless. Saw, heard, and said nothing. Have you heard anything about the Saches woman?"

"She came out of surgery two hours ago. She's still in Recovery. I did what you said—smiled and waved the goddamned American flag. I might as well have been blowing feathers off a dead chicken's ass. Nobody much cared who the hell I was. They kicked me out, but I did insist she be a no-information patient."

"Wouldn't matter if you had gotten in," Adele said. "She's probably on a ventilator, so she isn't going to be talking to anybody real soon."

Adele sped up to beat a yellow light—the one directly in front of the Ross Police Department—and made it by the skin of the Citroën's bumper. "Did you track down the man with the scar?"

"Edward Reuters. He's a driver and car pool mechanic for Citadel. The manager said he hasn't shown up for work for three days. Pete Chernin is tracking him down."

Adele checked her watch. It was four after six. She hated to be late. Somewhere she still had her Girl Scout pledge of promptness signed in blood.

"Did you get samples of the blood from the rug?" Tim asked.

Adele pulled into the College Avenue lot and caught sight of Mirek coming out of the science building.

"Ayuhn. You'll get them, but I've got a few things I want to do first."

"Don't tell me," he groaned. "Just tell me the results."

"Like always."

The Beast, thoroughly ashamed of itself, started on command. On the way to Greenbrae, she delivered the "American Cars Are Disposable" speech to the dash, hoping it would sink in.

Adele pulled up in front of the modest house, secured the legs of her scrub pants above her knees with rubber bands, and changed her running shoes for a pair of dark green heels that she kept in the back of the Beast for those formal types of emergencies.

A sixty-something couple sat in the living room in front of a television, eating popcorn. Automatically she salivated at the sight of one of her three P addictions: Popcorn, Peanut butter, Potato chips. Buddha only knew what was going to happen when she smelled the aroma of fresh-popped corn. She hoped she could keep herself from drooling.

The door opened. Adele smiled, breathing through her mouth. "Hello, Irene Graham?"

"Yes?"

She held up her fake deputy sheriff's badge. "I'm Deputy Monsarrat with the Marin County sheriff's office. I know you've been questioned until you're sick of it, but I was wondering if I could bother you with a few more questions?"

The woman looked back over her shoulder at her husband, as if he would answer for her. He didn't take his eyes off the TV screen even to see who was at the door. It was boob tube brain numb at its best.

"Well . . ."

"I've found," began Adele, "that sometimes when a woman asks the questions, things that weren't touched on suddenly reveal themselves."

The woman daintily wiped the corners of her mouth and took a few steps back into the hall, holding open the door. "Well, okay, but I don't think I'll be able to add anything more. I already told Detective Robinson everything."

She led Adele through a house that had not been remodeled since it was built in the mid-sixties, to a well-lit family room. The knickknacks and family photos were abundant.

Adele sat in the La-Z-Boy next to the fireplace. "I'm sorry for dropping in like this. I promise this won't take but a few minutes."

"Oh, don't worry about it," Irene Graham said, warming to the idea of having her there. "The show was a rerun. I was getting ready to do some sewing anyway. I'm making my grandsons some vests for Thanksgiving. I found the cutest material down at Calico Corners. It's a cotton wool blend with turkeys and pilgrims on it."

Adele nodded and cleared her throat, hoping Mrs. Graham wasn't going to be a talker. She had a hard time cutting talkers off.

"May I get you some hot cocoa or coffee?" Mrs. Graham asked rising from her chair.

"Oh, thank you, but no." Adele waved her to sit down and took out her notebook. "I have another call I need to make in a few minutes, so this has to be short.

"You said you saw a priest leaving the Hightower house at two-thirty A.M. Are you sure of the time?"

"Uh-huh. I looked at the wall clock in the kitchen as soon as I saw him because it was so late and because, well, it was very strange to see a priest coming out of Alan Hightower's place."

Mrs. Graham whinnied an abrupt, high-pitched wild laugh which caused Adele to jump. It was a close relative of her own Crazy Woman laughter.

"Can you remember exactly what you were doing at the time you noticed the priest?"

"I was making myself a cottage cheese and pear salad. See, I have arthritis in my hands, and it was bothering me. I don't like taking ibuprofen on an empty stomach. I was frustrated because I couldn't cut the darned pear because of the arthritis. I *couldn't* have plain old cottage cheese . . ." She made a face. ". . . Blech! So I took a sharper knife out of the knife block, which was on the other side of the kitchen. That was when I saw this priest walking very fast down the front steps of the Hightowers'. There's a streetlight right in front of their house."

"Well!" She paused, patted the center of her chest, and looked left and right for dramatic effect. "I looked at the clock, and I thought to myself, 'What would a priest be doing at the Hightowers' at two-thirty in the morning?' "

The woman sat back. After a moment, Adele leaned forward. "What did you decide?"

Mrs. Graham looked around and shrugged. "What else? One of them was dying or dead." She held up a finger. "Except I knew that they weren't Catholics. Both Alan and Jeannette are atheists." Mrs. Graham made a sour face. "They're quite verbal about it, too."

"Where did the priest go?"

"Walked to his car and got in. That was the other thing . . ." Mrs. Graham brought herself to the edge of her chair. "What kind of priest drives a Jeep?"

Adele took a noncommittal expression and nodded. "Was there anything else about the priest that you noticed? Anything strange or slightly off?"

Mrs. Graham's eyes sparkled. She came so far to the edge of her chair, she seemed to be more in an independent crouch than a sit. "I was telling this to Harry only last night. He thinks I'm crazy but . . ."

Adele came toward her on her chair to create an air of conspiracy and intimacy. Just the girls.

"Hey—what do *men* know?" Adele finished for her.

Together they tittered in the Women's Club knowing way.

"There *was* something odd about him. Now, mind you, this is only a feeling . . . nothing I could put my finger on exactly."

Adele refrained from yelling at the woman to get on with it. "Believe me, I understand completely."

"He seemed too careful, like he was calculating every tiny movement he made . . . thinking hard about everything."

"What else?" Adele said, in a way that said to go the whole hog—pull it out of the hat.

The woman sat back and looked down into her plaid-skirted lap, thinking. There was something else, but she didn't know whether she should give it a voice. They *were* in Marin County, after all and it *was* the nineties.

"Go ahead," Adele encouraged. "Say it. Nobody is going to judge you."

Mrs. Graham looked up, startled that the woman had read her thoughts.

"It's only an impression," she said.

"That's what I asked for."

"Oh, dear, I hate to . . ."

"Trust me," Adele said, touching the back of her hand. "This is just between us women."

Irene Graham let her shoulders relax. "Well, he seemed like he might have been a little—you know . . ." She put a hand on her hip and did a flirty jiggle with her shoulders.

"Gay?" Adele asked, skeptical.

"Fruity. That's what Harry and I call it."

"What was it about him that made you think that?"

Mrs. Graham cocked her head and smiled. "I don't know exactly—it's only a feeling I got. The way he was so careful, I guess, and maybe the way he walked—like a woman."

There was a short pause and then the rubber band holding Adele's right uniform pants leg snapped. The cotton-polyester blend cuff fell over her high heel. Adele pulled her coat tight around her, completely ignoring the runaway pants leg.

"Thank you so much for allowing me to interrupt your evening," Adele said, standing to go. "You've been most helpful."

"It was no trouble at all," Mrs. Graham said. She noticed Adele's pants leg, but said nothing.

Adele said goodnight and caught sight of herself in the hallway mirror. For a moment she thought about making up some fantastic story about what a bother these latest fashions were—one leg always cold and all—but decided against it and bit extra hard on her cheek instead. She managed to keep the laughter in all the way to the sidewalk. There, she threw her head back and roared.

Mid-span Golden Gate Bridge, her phone rang, causing her to weave into the inside suicide lane. She wasn't quite used to having a phone in her car yet.

"At first I was concerned, but not to the point of calling the police or the hotel manager," Jeffrey said as soon as she said hello. "After all, I told myself, patients confuse appointment times frequently and I certainly didn't want to overreact and establish a sort of codependent pattern that might gratify her on some level and further enable the regression which accompanies the dissociation."

Adele's grin widened as she fought to make sense of his psychobabble. "You bet," she said.

"As the day progressed, I grew more uneasy during the succession of ten-minute breaks between patients. By the end of the day, when she still hadn't called, I couldn't help myself. I had to run it by you."

"Obsessing and codependency be damned, huh, doc?"

He laughed. "Correct. I'm ready to tell myself that going to the hotel to look for her is really the prudent medical course to take here."

"Well, don't waste your time. I've already been there. She's still not back. I've got the manager and Jellyroll on the lookout."

"Shit," he said. "I was hoping we could do a tad of sleuthing together. I was really getting psyched about climbing up fire escapes and looking under beds and in closets."

Adele wondered if he had any idea how close to reality he was.

She found a parking place only three blocks away from the General, which was an early Christmas gift from the Nurses' Parking God. San Francisco nurses frequently had to park long distances from their workplaces and were frequently victims of sexual assault and muggings.

Before she left the confines of the Beast, she changed back into her running shoes, threw on a lab coat she had borrowed from Grace Thompson's office, stuck a stethoscope in the pocket, brushed her hair, and applied a light spray of Aliage perfume.

Her Goodwill umbrella with the Sapporo Beer ads printed on it proved useless against the driving rain. By the time she arrived, she was soaked. That was fine—it helped create a haggard look.

When she looked in the mirrored walls of the elevator, she indeed looked like an intern who had been on duty for thirty-six hours. A med student with light blue hair and a ring in his nose gave her directions to SICU.

No one looked up when she walked through the double doors marked STAFF ONLY! except the clerk, and he only glanced for a second. Adele slumped into a chair at one of the charting desks with a groan and grabbed the chart nearest her, flipping through it trying to look like she *belonged*. The chart was for an Ahmed Nahaja. She put it down and with a bored, bitchy intern's mewl, asked who had Mrs. Saches's chart.

Without looking up, the clerk held it out to her.

Adele made a dive for it. The progress notes and the post-surgical notations all pointed to a good prognosis. The words "condition status changed from serious to fair" brought her instant relief.

Adele closed the chart and put it back on top of the pile, making note of the red letters "GG" on the binder. Her eyes searched diligently for a sign of where bed or cubicle GG might be.

At the end of the room, a white sign reading FF hung from the ceiling. Heading toward the sign, she passed a jungle of ventilators, balloon pumps, IV pumps, circoelectric beds, nasogastric suction canisters, chest tubes, urinary catheters, rectal catheters, mist machines, beeping monitors, closed-circuit TVs.

It really wasn't so far off from *Coma*.

Adele did not smile. Doctors never smiled or did much in the way of greetings in teaching hospitals. "I'm Dr. Runkle," she said in an uptight, nasal, Harvard grad tone. "Where's Ms. Saches's last ABGs?"

Instantly the nurse produced a lab slip, no questions asked.

Adele studied the numbers and, without looking up, said, "Is she awake at all?"

"I've been sedating her a lot," the nurse answered.

"I didn't ask you if she was sedated, did I?" Dr. Runkle said, in as arrogant and condescending tone as Adele could manage. God knew she'd heard the tone enough times in her career. "I want to know if she's awake. What is her level of consciousness?"

The nurse, a young Filipino, cowered. "She opens her eyes to command, doctor. She knows her name. Most of the time she sleeps."

Dr. Runkle heaved a dramatic sigh. "Get her flow sheet while I take a look at her." Adele was really getting the prick part down. "Make sure everything is up to date. I don't want to be wasting my time chasing down information."

The nurse ran in the direction of the clerk's desk, and Adele immediately turned her attention to the woman in the bed. She brought her mouth very close to Laurel Saches's ear and slipped her hand over hers.

"Laurel!"

The eyes opened.

"Laurel, my name is Adele Monsarrat. I'm working undercover with Detective Ritmann. Do you understand?"

Laurel tried to focus on her face. Her eyes rolled from side to side and closed.

"Answer me, Laurel. I don't have much time."

Laurel nodded, her hand awkwardly jerking up to her throat. "Throat hurts." The two words came out harsh and barely audible.

"That's from the tube that was in your throat during surgery," Adele said rapidly. "The pain will go away in a few days. I need to know the other person you recognized in the sketches."

"Not them."

Adele squinted. Down at the end of the room, the Filipino nurse was talking to the clerk, trying to get the chart away from him.

"Not them? What do you mean? Who was the other person you recognized besides the garage man, Ed?"

"Not sketches. Photo. Woman."

Stunned, Adele didn't care that the nurse had returned and was standing close behind her. "Give me her name, Laurel. Try to tell me who she is."

"Ellen . . ."

"I've got that chart for you, doctor," the nurse interrupted.

Adele clenched her teeth and turned on her with such fury that the woman took a step back, her eyes wide with fear. Adele's anger faltered—the last thing she needed was for the nurse to call a Code Pink on her. "Go away!" she growled. "Go take a bathroom break, for Christ's sake."

The nurse hurried off in the direction of the clerk, looking behind her every few steps to see if the insane doctor was chasing after her with a scalpel.

When she turned back to Laurel, she could see the woman grimacing in pain.

"Ellen what? What's her last name? Who is she?"

"Pain."

"Payne? Ellen Payne?" Adele looked at her. "Is that her name or are you—"

"Pain in my chest."

"I'll have the nurse take care of that in a second. Tell me her name."

Laurel kept her eyes closed, and Adele could see she was trying to remember. It was amazing she could remember anything considering what she'd been through.

"Mack. Job interview. September."

"With Yates at Citadel?"

Laurel tried to wet her lips and nodded. "Please. I need something for pain. Thirsty."

Adele looked up and grabbed the first nurse she saw. "Get the nurse taking care of this woman and tell her she needs more pain medication, stat."

"Thank you, Laurel," Adele squeezed her hand. "You're going to be okay. We're not going to let anything happen to you, so rest easy."

The Filipino nurse approached the bedside, watching Adele without blinking. She was wary.

Sure that the nurse thought her a flaming nutcase, Adele straightened, checking the name on the nurse's tag. "Dai is going to take care of that pain for you, Ms. Saches," Adele said, smiling. "Put your faith in the nurses, Laurel, they're the ones who perform the real miracles around here."

The nurse watched the doctor rush out of the unit and hoped she'd go back to whatever service she came from—psychiatric, probably—and not come back again.

She called Tim and gave him the information as she was taking the on ramp to the Golden Gate from the Marina. He, in turn, told her Detective Chernin had found Edward Reuters's car, parked near the Bay Bridge. The trunk was full of blood.

The Beast was running so smoothly and traffic was so minimal, and she was so depressed, that Adele made a trip to Trader Joe's to pick up some of their low-fat mayonnaise. According to her taste buds, it was the best, most real tasting fake mayonnaise made.

Fifteen minutes later, she exited the store with one jar of low-fat mayo and three containers of Trader Joe's Low Fat Cat Cookies—to help put her in a better frame of mind.

Timed at eight minutes, the signal in front of the store was the longest in all of Marin. Conveniently located next to a wide median strip, the location was the best deal going for Marin's homeless. Inches from the driver's window, the residentially challenged had a perfect place to hang out and beg for food, spare change, and work.

The present occupant of the Homeless Showcase was a man

with a beard down to his belt, but no hair on the top of his head. He was dressed in rags. So precisely ragged were his clothes, she came to the conclusion that he'd had them specially tailored that way.

A man in the pickup in front of her handed the ragged beggar a sandwich, which he immediately put into a cardboard box next to him. Sudden curiosity to see what else he had in the box caused her to forget where she was until the Beast's nose bumped the tailgate of the pickup.

She sighed, shut off the lights, and turned off the Beast. No sense polluting the air. Leaning her head back, she stared at the homeless man's profile, letting her thoughts run outside the car like so many bored children. She began with her dream of the night before, and then drifted to Mrs. Graham and the thought the priest might have been gay, to Laurel Saches's saying that Mathilde was Ellen Mack.

Her meandering thoughts took a turn back to the homeless man—who was walking her way. She imagined him packing up the cardboard box with the false bottom that held thousand-dollar bills and the keys to his Jaguar and his seven-million-dollar mansion, when the car behind her honked, rudely informing her the brain theater was over and the light had gone green.

It wasn't one isolated thing that made her go back to Ellis Hospital, Ward 8. It wasn't even a formed thought—just an ambiguous cloud of intuition.

Malloy greeted her without surprise. "Peace, Adele. What are you doing here?"

She joined her hands together as if in prayer, and made a slight bow before she sat down next to him in front of the monitor banks. The screens were full of mostly unexciting rhythms.

She tapped one irregular pattern snaking across the screen. "Show me this in two, three, and AVF leads."

Malloy clicked the monitor, changing the electrical views of the heart.

"Looks like Mrs. Vanderlise is having a little ST depression."

"Correct," Malloy said, "She's had some chest pain."

"Did we get a twelve lead and CCU bloods?"

"Three hours ago."

Adele knew it was useless to ask about a transfer to CCU. As a terminal cancer patient, Vivian Vanderlise's insurance wouldn't consider her a candidate for CCU. "How's her pain now?"

"Gone with two nitros. Linda has her, so I trust she's well taken care of."

Neither the ward clerk nor the off-duty nurse said anything while they watched the white pattern dance at a rate of eighty across the screen.

"I'm going to do something illegal, Malloy," Adele said quietly without looking at him. "So you'll probably want to take a break."

He turned to study her, careful not to get caught by the gold eyes and the full mouth. Her face wore the suggestion of a smile.

He opened his mouth to ask if he would get into trouble, but decided it was better not to know. Silently he stood and headed toward the employees' rest room.

Adele sat for a few minutes, keeping an eye on the hallways in the security mirrors, then she rolled her chair around to the end of the nurses' desk where the out-boxes were. The one marked "Medical Records" was jammed with the charts of discharged patients from six days past.

She spotted the one she wanted and rolled back behind the monitors. Ducking down, she made it disappear in her oversized purse.

"It's only for overnight," she said to the nurse who passed by the counter. The nurse—an L.V.N. named Nancy—smiled at her and nodded, as if she understood exactly what Adele was talking about.

"Are you okay?" Adele whispered, wiping the sweat from under Edith Hatter's sunken eyes. Linda was on the other side of the bed taking a blood pressure.

Vivian raised her eyebrows. "You still here, doll?"

"Left and came back. I forgot something."

Linda frowned, and made a notation on the flow sheet, then she lowered the head of the bed and slowed the rate on the nitroglycerine IV drip.

"Did you find what you were looking for?" Vivian asked Adele.

"Not yet."

Vivian sighed and closed her eyes. "Remember what I said," she murmured. "You'll find the men out in the fields, and the woman close to home."

"I hope you're right, Vivian, because at this point, I'm afraid I'm going to find her *in* the field—about six feet under."

FOURTEEN

NO ONE WOULD HAVE EVER GUESSED THAT THE smooth, throaty voice that answered the phone at the San Anselmo Hotel belonged to a red and pink circus tent.

"Hi. This is Mathilde's sister, Adele. The nurse? I was there earlier today, and I had another question."

There was a silence that said *Who?*

"The nurse who was there this afternoon? Do you remember?"

Nothing except some wheezy breathing. Adele imagined the tent sitting on the cot, squeezing the stuffing out of the red and pink pillows.

"You were eating a ham sandwich in the back apartment. I talked to you about Mathilde, the lady in room twenty-six?"

"Oh." The hotel manager was not moved. "Yeah?"

"Is she still AWOL?"

"Yes."

"Did she have any visitors yesterday or today?"

The silence was so long that Adele thought she might have fallen asleep . . . or gone to make another sandwich. "Hello? Are these questions too challenging or what?"

"I'm thinking."

The Beast turned onto Baltimore Avenue and her house came into view. Adele canvassed the block for Mrs. Coolidge and hunched over the steering wheel to relieve the tired muscles in her shoulders.

"A guy came looking for her night before last—around midnight. He stayed about an hour. Another guy came in a little while ago looking for her. I told him she wasn't here, so he left a note for her."

"The man who came in two nights ago—do you remember what he looked like?"

282

"Dark hair—wore it in a Marine cut. Black leather jacket. An ugly facial scar. Looked jaundiced. Either that or he had one of those fake tans—terrible skin color."

"Have you actually seen Mathilde since that time?" Adele asked, gathering her purse.

There was another long bout with thought.

"No—I mean, except when she left her key here this morning."

Adele closed the car door and walked toward her porch. "Earlier today you said you didn't see her."

"Well, no, but the key didn't get there by itself, and she had the only key."

"And what about the man tonight? What did he look like?"

"A skyscraper in a fireman's uniform."

Adele gave the tent her cell phone number. "Okay, now listen—what is your name?"

There was another pause as if the woman had to think about that too. Adele was thinking, *Please, anything but Bertha,* when the woman answered.

"Bertha. Bertha Golden."

Adele bit her lip hard. "Okay, Bertha, would you do me a favor and if Mathilde shows up, have her call me no matter what time of day or night and pass the number onto your relief clerk. I'll be back tomorrow—hopefully before the police get there."

The woman's response was instantaneous. "I can't have the police hanging around here," Bertha said in a warning, high voice. "Some of my tenants wouldn't like that."

"Oh." Adele opened the front door and flicked on the inside lights. "Well, in that case, pray that Mathilde shows up."

Nelson was happy to see Her, but not as excited to see Her after a long day as he usually was. Instead of playing the Play Dead Game, Nelson wagged his tail and resumed his game of hide-and-seek with the rabbit.

She felt a twinge of jealousy, and shrugged it off. "Want to go . . . OUT!?" she asked. That question always got a big response.

This time she had to repeat it three times before Nelson

barked a lackadaisical *Ho-hum. I guess,* and reluctantly went out into the yard, carrying Bugs in his mouth.

Maybe the rabbit companion wasn't such a good idea, Adele thought. Maybe she needed to consider keeping it out in the shed again. She put away the groceries, and was debating whether or not to eat now or wait until Tim called, when her cell phone rang.

She removed it from her purse and answered. "I was just thinking about you and some nice vegetables."

There was a long pause, and she knew at once it wasn't Tim.

"Adele? This is Jellyroll." He sounded depressed.

"Hey, Jellyroll, what's the word?"

"Nothing good. I went to the hotel. Tild hasn't shown up. I think there's a problem."

"Ditto on that, my friend."

"You think somebody got to her? You think she's okay?"

"I don't know, Jelly," Adele said. "But I don't mind telling you I'm worried."

"How about the cops? Should we—"

"Already did. They know."

Jellyroll said it for them both: "Shit."

Adele fed her children and sent them off to relax next to the warmth of the fireplace. In the background, Anita Baker's voice came soft and maudlin from the speakers.

She sat at the kitchen table with a blank piece of printer paper, her notebook, and Jane Doe's medical chart. She made a vertical column of boxes, dating each one for each day the patient was in the hospital. Next to each date box she made a second column of boxes, noting the overall picture of the patient and the results of her basic lab work for that day. A third column of boxes held the events of that day that stood out in Adele's mind.

> With Henry to MRI trailer.
> Jellyroll to visit.
> Jeff's first visit.
> Barry murder.
> Glasses fiasco.
> Burned popcorn fiasco.
> Hightower murder.
> Attack.

When she was done, she studied the columns and then her notebook. After a few minutes, she pulled out a giant sheet of banner plastic and taped it to the wall at the end of her bed.

In less than an hour, she filled the storyboard with facts, realizations, players, events, driving times, witnesses' accounts, and fourteen unanswered questions.

Switching the tape to a New Age tape called *Mothership*, Adele propped herself up with pillows and began to talk to the panel of famous sleuths who had gathered around to help her untangle the mess.

She was finishing a point with Kay Scarpetta when the shrill scream of the doorbell about knocked her off the bed.

In case it was the stolen-chart police, she threw the chart under the covers and ordered Nelson to lie on top for good measure.

Halfway down the hall, she realized she hadn't so much as brushed her hair or changed out of her uniform. She quickly stepped into the bathroom and brushed out her hair, wiped the smudges out from under her eyes, put a dab of toothpaste in her mouth and ran it over, under, and around her teeth as she opened the door. "I was wondering when you were going to g—"

Tim was bent to one side, his ear attached to Mrs. Coolidge's mouth. He waved to Adele, looking half amused and half wanting to be rescued.

"Hi," Adele said with a chilly edge. "Is something wrong, Mrs. Coolidge, or are you and this nice young man sharing whispered confidences?"

"My goodness, Adele." The old woman laughed and flapped a hand. "Don't get upset. I was asking your nice young man here if he'd talk to you about whether or not your doggie was getting enough nourishment. He came to the door tonight with a bunny in his mouth. The poor dog looked starved. Why, Queen Shredder weighs more than—"

"The rabbit is his pet, Mrs. Coolidge." She reached out and took Tim's arm, pulling him toward the house. Mrs. Coolidge, not quite ready to let her quarry go, simultaneously pulled him back toward her.

"Nelson was taking the bunny for a walk and probably decided to show him off and get treats." Adele pulled harder. "He thinks every day is Halloween. I assure you, Nelson gets more to eat than you do." She reached over and tried to pull Tim's sleeve out of the old woman's gnarled fingers. It was like pulling a child's sneaker out of a moving escalator step.

Exasperated, and irritable from want of food, Adele suddenly placed her body against him and kissed him hard on the mouth.

In his astonishment, Tim's arms automatically wrapped themselves around her, taking Mrs. Coolidge with them.

Gawping at the two of them from so close, Mrs. Coolidge eventually let go of the nice young man's sleeve and backed off the porch sputtering, "Oh well, yes, I see . . . Perhaps . . . he wanted . . ."

Adele took her chance, and pulled Tim into the house, closing the door behind them.

"I'm sorry," she said, wiping his mouth with her hand, but not meeting his eyes. "I couldn't think of any other way to get rid of her, and I'm starving." She turned toward the kitchen and more or less vaulted to the stove, busying herself with turning on the gas and preparing a skillet with olive oil. "I'm not accountable for my actions when I get hypoglycemic."

He came to the stove and turned off the gas wearing the look of a glassy-eyed male driven by The Urge. "Then let's keep you hungry."

Her neck and face turning scarlet, she sneaked a peek at him as she slid past him to the refrigerator and took out the premade salad. What had ever possessed her to do such a thing? Now he'd wonder if she was some sort of loose woman unable to control her urges. He'd probably lost any respect he did have for her, and thought he could dally with her.

The best way to deal with that, she decided as he came at her from the other side of the kitchen, was to divert his attention. From the utensil drawer next to the sink, she drew out her antique professional butcher knife and waved it at him. He stopped and stepped back. The Urge deflated.

"Cut up some green peppers for me," she said, thrusting it at him handle first. "And then some cucumbers and mushrooms."

Without losing a beat, she began extracting information from him the way a vampire sucks blood.

*   *   *

Along with the cold quinoa salad and the grilled marinated vegetables with a wild mushroom ragout, she bled a little of the information she had gathered. The tumor of suspicion forming in her gut, she kept to herself.

"Can we go over the sketches again?" Adele asked, stroking the rabbit's head as it slept on her lap.

Forty minutes later, Tim put the sketches back into an envelope. She was upset.

"Well, what did we learn from that exercise in futility?" Tim asked, smiling good-naturedly. He stood and gathered the cups, carrying them to the kitchen.

"We learned," she said, "that something is way off. There's something bothering me about them, but I don't know what."

One of the cell phones rang. They both grabbed for their own, making a sort of competition out of who could open theirs first and say hello.

He met Chernin's voice. She met static.

"Are you at the hospital tomorrow?" he asked as soon as he hung up.

"I'm on an A day," she said, saw the question in his face, and continued, "An administration day is when you push papers instead of pills. I promised to do the schedule for next month, and it has to be in by noon. I'm going in first thing in the morning for four hours."

"What's your idea of first thing in the morning?" he asked.

She looked at her watch and calculated the amount of time she needed to sleep, and how long it would take her to put together the scheduling.

"If I go in at five, I can be out by nine or ten."

He didn't know why he did what he did next. The confusion caused by the kiss? Or maybe the idea that she might somehow see something he couldn't was thrown against the rules, regulations, and normal behaviors of his profession. "I want you to go with me when I talk to Yates. I want you to feel him out."

Adele frowned. She envisioned the storyboard on her bedroom wall, weighing what she wanted—needed to do with what value would come from scoping out Phillip Yates.

"I can't," she said. "I've got some things I need to take care of."

He was surprised, then relieved, then, studying her grave expression, intrigued. "What are you doing?"

"I'm going find Jane Doe," she said, sounding more sure of herself than she felt. "You don't need me there with Yates." She nodded to his cell phone. "Was that Peter with his preliminary results on all the Ellen Macks in the western states?"

He blinked, wondering for a minute if she'd tapped into his phone. "Yep. Zippo leads so far."

"That's because Ellen Mack isn't her name."

"How do you know?"

She glanced at Tim, then back at the fire. "I don't know. I just do—it comes from years of watching people through cracks in the walls."

Nelson and Bugs took their places under her bed while she sat on top of the blue down comforter with her bowl of vinegar-soaked popcorn.

She studied the storyboard, writing things in her notebook, then biting the top of her pen, sinking her teeth into the soft plastic. It was something she did only when she was nervous.

The plastic bag next to her contained those items she'd found at the scene of Mathilde's burned car. She held up the keys and looked through the ring at the storyboard.

What do you think, Adele? Detective Kitch Heslin, her mentor from Novato PD, leaned back against the headboard on the other side of the bed and smiled.

"God, I wish you were here, old man. This one is tough."

That's why I live in a cabin in the Yolla Bolla Eel Mountain Wilderness, Kitch said. *They kept getting tougher and uglier, and I kept getting older and more tired.*

"Give me something," she pleaded.

You're too close, Kitch said, rubbing the stubble on his chin. *You need to look at the big picture. You're getting caught up in details. Work from the outside in.*

Adele traced the outline of the keys tucked into her Jogbra and continued to creep up the back steps of the San Anselmo Hotel. The black Italian leather boxing shoes kept her light on her feet and noiseless.

Crouched, she put her ear first to the door of room 26 and then to the carpeted floor. She knocked lightly, waited, and knocked again. Using the key she'd used that afternoon, she opened the door a crack at a time. When the crack was wide enough, she put her lips close to the opening and whispered, "Mathilde?"

There was no answer. She slid inside and closed the door behind her. Then she turned on the light. Things had been moved. The duffle bag was closed and sitting next to the door. The closet had been emptied of the clothes and shoes that had been there earlier in the day. The room safe remained locked.

She pulled the duffle bag onto the bed and opened it. Inside was nothing she hadn't already seen.

She returned the bag to the floor, careful to put it exactly where it had been. Then, taking out her collection of keys, she sat down in the closet and fit the smallest one into the locked safe.

Looking up at the cracked ceiling (damaged more than likely by the last earthquake), she took a deep breath, turned the key.

The hiking boots inside were clean and polished.

Adele took the right one—the one Mathilde had come in wearing—and examined every inch. With her Swiss Army knife, she pried out the insole, pushing her fingers as far into the toe as she could get. She did the same with the left, and found nothing.

"So much for *that* idea," she said, and flipped the boot back into the safe. She missed. The boot hit the rim of the opening. A faint noise came from the boot, as if something was loose inside.

She picked up the left boot and shook it close to her ear.

Pulling up the insole again, she slid the blade down between the wall of the heel and pried up the heelpiece.

A silver key lay diagonal within the hollow structure.

Good show, Ms. Monsarrat, said Mr. Holmes, quite pleased. *Now return to your house and go to sleep, perchance to dream.*

Unable to sleep, Adele went to Ward 8 around 3:30. By 7:30 she had returned Jane Doe's medical file to the out-box, completed the schedule, and hand-delivered it to nursing office.

When the automatic doors swung open, she gasped and smiled. It was one of those San Francisco Winter Surprise Days when, in the midst of icy cold, rainy gray weather, a bright, warm jewel of a day appears out of nowhere.

It was, she decided, the perfect day for a hike.

The door to apartment B swung open before she could knock a second time. Bare-chested, but with a tie hanging from his neck, Timothy Ritmann stared as if he didn't recognize her.

"My God," he said, seemingly shocked.

"Surprise." She smiled.

He shook his head as if clearing it from a hard blow. "What're you doing here?"

"I was going right by . . . I hope it's okay."

"Of course." He didn't know what to say next. He glanced behind him.

"Did you bring that blood into the lab last night?" Adele wanted to know.

"They're going to run it today." He shifted on his feet, ran a hand through his hair, and nervously looked back over his shoulder.

Her eyes followed his. Her world dimmed and stopped.

Sitting on a stool at the kitchen bar was a woman with extremely blond hair dressed in a black teddy. She was fantastically beautiful.

The sight of the wide, red mouth and huge dark eyes brought an immense sadness to Adele, which hit her in the throat like a kick from a mule. She began to shake. Instantly her mind went to her mother and Nelson and Cynthia. It would be okay, she told herself. These people loved her and the loss of this man would only be temporary. Besides, she had already begun to rationalize, he was never hers to begin with.

Tim looked into the apartment at the same time as Adele and saw not the blond woman in the teddy, but the remnants of the seven-day-old pepperoni pizza lying on the coffee table and the six empty beer cans lining the couch. He knew for certain there were a half-dozen pair of his dirty underwear somewhere near the chair, not to mention the sixteen hundred pounds of dirty laundry surrounding his bed. He thought of her tidy house, and was mortified.

"I'm really sorry," Adele said curtly. "I should have called first. I didn't . . ." She turned away, tensing her muscles to run.

Mid-step, she felt his hand wrap itself around her upper arm and pull her back before she could fly. "The place is a mess," he said, smiling sheepishly. "I swear to you that the pizza is from before I stopped eating meat. My cleaning lady got married and I haven't . . ."

He stopped short. Adele was looking at him as though he'd lost his mind. She was pale and obviously shaken. He looked back into his apartment, thinking that perhaps a piece of his soiled laundry had taken on a life of its own and was about to attack.

Then he realized Adele wasn't looking at the mess at all. Adele had seen Monique Arrowsmith.

He poured the hot water into the cups with the decaf crystals while Adele leaned against Monique Arrowsmith, rubbing her thumb against her violet glass eye.

"She's beautiful," Adele said, admiring the well-crafted mannequin.

"Not my type," Tim said, "but my mother bought ten of them when the old Proctor's Emporium closed in Los Angeles. She christened them all and gave all but two away as Christmas gifts to her children who didn't have kids or spouses. Mom kept Carolyn and Simon Scott. They're like a part of the family. We have them cleaned about every two years."

Warming her hands around the cup, Adele noticed the rest of the apartment for the first time. Masses of dirty laundry and ceiling-to-floor newspapers. Dishware where dishware usually wasn't. From the top of the desk lamp on the kitchen counter, she pried off a fork encrusted with something that had once been edible.

She watched as the blush spread to the roots of his hair, then, taking the chance, let her eyes fall to the broad muscular chest and biceps.

"You're keeping something major from me, aren't you?" he asked, taking a new shirt from its package. Together they began removing pins and plastic cuff and collar stiffeners.

She scrunched up one of her shoulders. "Maybe. I'll let you know later today when I figure out what I've got."

He put the shirt on and began buttoning the cuffs. She couldn't take her eyes off him: each simple gesture of the man dressing, she found profoundly stimulating. She looked away. "So, instead of doing laundry, you just go out and buy more clothes?"

He nodded and looked at his watch. "Don't rub it in."

"Have you ever thought of hiring a truck and—"

"Every time I walk in the door."

She stood and rotated her head so that her neck cracked. The sound made him shiver. "I've got a lot of things to do. I'd better go."

He was watching her in the mirror, tying his tie. The curve of her neck was exposed for a moment as her fingers pulled her hair up and away. The sight made him feel weak in the knees. No woman had ever made him go weak in the knees.

"Okay. Call me when you get into trouble."

"I'll call before that." She found her keys and walked to the door.

He calculated how long it would take a cleaning crew to overhaul his apartment. It would take two shifts and a pickup truck. "Hey, Adele?"

She stopped and turned back.

"Join me and Monique for dinner Monday night? I'll cook."

She gave the molded pizza on the coffee table a dubious glance. "Sure," she said. "Should I bring anything?" *Like the food?*

"Yourself—and maybe a date for Monique."

Alex McClain made a perfect United States Forest Service ranger. Conscientious. Courteous. Helpful. Nerdy.

"You're sure that no one has been in these cabins recently?" Adele asked, holding on to the armrest. The dirt road was full of rocks and deep ruts.

Ranger McClain checked his clipboard. "Yes, ma'am. The records show that the last cabin to be rented out was on October the fourteenth and fifteenth, and that was to two men who were down from Vancouver on a bicycle trip to Mexico. We don't usually have many people who want to stay out here after October," he said cautiously. "Too cold and damp for most."

He stopped his truck and got out to unlock the gate. When he got back in, he smiled and pointed out her window. "Saw a mountain lion down that trail about three days ago. She was a beauty."

She searched the area he'd pointed out with her eyes. If she hadn't been on a mission, she could have gotten excited about the prospect of seeing a mountain lion.

"So, to get in to one of these cabins, you have to register at the ranger station?"

"Uh-huh. You also have to pick up the key to the cabin. Of course, those keys get copied and passed around, and people come out here sometimes without our knowledge, but that doesn't happen during the busy season; we're out here almost every day checking on things."

They were traveling at about ten miles an hour down a dirt road through hills and woods that smelled of redwood, wild thyme, and rosemary. Ranger McClain parked the four-by-four Chevy pickup and escorted her the fifteen or so yards to the group of rustic cabins.

Mathilde said the one in which she and the child had been held hostage overlooked a bluff or a cliff. Only one of the cabins before her was on an outcropping that overlooked Stinson Beach.

"May I see this one?" she asked cautiously, not wanting to seem overeager.

Alex led the way to the front of the cabin.

"Look at this," he said, bending over a young oak that had been carelessly hacked to the ground.

She looked over his shoulder and shook her head. "Looks like somebody needed wood and didn't want to travel too far to get it."

Instead of answering, Alex sighed and pushed open the door. Warily, he entered the cabin, as though he expected to find it a shambles.

It was, to Adele's way of thinking, immaculately clean.

"Well, at least they left it in order," Alex said, surprised. He walked through, checking the bathroom and the small bedroom. "They even cleaned out the ashes in the fireplace and wiped down the toilet and the sink—that's unusual."

Adele nodded, although she was barely listening. She was busy doing a search of her own. In the bathroom she inspected the bar of travel soap on the sink, and the small bottle of shampoo left in the shower. The bedroom closet held three or four rusty hangers, a box of mothballs, and several ant stakes around the floor. In the kitchen there was nothing but two cracked cups, an enamel kettle, a rusted iron frying pan, an enamel saucepan, and a can of Campbell's pork and beans.

"It isn't much, but folks seem to love it out here," Alex said as they were leaving. "It has its charm."

He was closing the door when the nagging inside her head slapped her awake. "Would you mind if I went back in and took one last look around?" she asked.

"No problem." Alex pushed the door back open for her, and the smell of wood ashes and mothballs hit her anew.

She went straight for the bedroom, got on her hands and knees, and searched the floor. Then she flipped the twin mattress back from the box springs. Something fell between the springs and landed on the floor in the corner behind one of the legs. She pulled out the bed and reached down.

The barrette was in the shape of a tiny pink heart.

"So, did you track down Ed Reuters?" she asked, forcing her attention off the green hills rolling to the ocean.

"What the sharks didn't eat we did." Tim sat in the front seat of the Camry watching the remains of Edward Reuters's body being placed—piece by piece—inside a body bag. The coroner's deputy was calling it sea life depredation—it looked like the leftovers room in a slaughterhouse. He was suddenly very glad he was a vegetarian convert.

"The blood we found in the trunk of his car was his. Where are you?"

"Taking a nice drive down the coast at the moment. Any leads on Jane Doe? Did you get the blood results back yet?"

"Nope, but I did get in to see Ms. Saches this morning. She's sure the name was Ellen Mack. I'm on my way to Citadel. How 'bout you?"

"On my way, too," she said, forcing herself not to look down the side of the ledge she was driving along.

"You're so tight you squeak, Monsarrat," he laughed. "You don't give anything up. Do you have your peashooter on you?"

"Don't call it that," she warned. "But, yes, I do have my gun in my fanny pack."

"Want to meet for a progress report in about three hours?"

She looked at her watch and veered off to the right, the front paws of the Beast playing with the sheer drop-offs.

"No," she said.

He snorted. "Is it something I said?"

"Get the results of that blood I gave you," she said. "Will you be around later on?"

"Be more specific."

"I can't."

"You've got to give me something more than that, Monsarrat," Tim said after a pause. The coroner's deputy was walking toward him, talking on his own cell phone. "I can't hang around waiting for your call."

"Then don't hang around. If I catch you, I catch you—if not, well, you'll miss the opportunity to break this case."

He opened his mouth to tell her she was a smart-ass and found himself talking to dead air space.

Allison Davis was the twenty-one-year-old replacement for Laurel Saches. Except Allison was decidedly not a linear thinker; she was more of a budding corkscrew thinker, the type of youth who snapped her gum quietly, and had a raised inflection at the end of every sentence, Valley Girl style. The secretary pool, not to mention the gene pool, from which Miss Davis had sprung must have been somewhat shallow.

"He's not in the office right now?" Allison said, staring up into the face of the detective towering over her. "You want some, like, coffee or anything?"

Tim walked to the door of Yates's office and opened it. "No thanks, I'll get it myself."

Phillip Yates glared at the man standing in front of his desk. His jaws clenched. "You're getting to be a pest, Detective Ritmann. What do you want now?"

"Same thing I wanted last time I was here. The truth." Tim threw the photo of Jane Doe onto the desk. It slid across the ebony top. Yates stared at it and the finger began to tap.

"Who is she?" Tim asked.

"I don't know."

Tim cocked his head, and traced the outline of his bottom lip between his thumb and forefinger. "Maybe you didn't hear me, Mr. Yates. I asked you a question that if you don't answer here, you're going to answer over at my office or in court.

"Let me help you out: you saw this woman in your office about two months ago. Who is she and why was she here?"

Yates remained silent. His face gave away nothing of the panic Ritmann was sure he was feeling.

Tim put his hands on the edge of the CEO's desk and leaned forward. "Okay, then how about Edward Reuters?"

Phillip Yates blinked. "He works as a mechanic and driver for Citadel. He drives business associates around town and makes sure they . . ." The finger tapped a few times. ". . . they get to where they need to go."

In the silence that followed, Tim's clear blue eyes bored into the man. "Reuters is an ex-con. Did some time for armed robbery a few years ago, but never finished his term. I have some sources who say you went to a lot of trouble and expense to get this guy out. I understand you're still paying off the guy who you got to confess."

"Your sources are wrong, Mr. Ritmann. I know very little about this man. I simply hired him to work as a driver and a mechanic at the request of his brother, who was a long-time employee."

Tim looked away, then back at Yates. "Reuters owes you. Did you hire him to kill Laurel Saches?"

Phillip Yates began to stand, the veins in his forehead throbbing. The pitch to his voice was tight with rage. "Get the hell out of here!"

Tim leaned further over the desk and in a sudden, violent movement grabbed the man by the shirt front. "Don't make me arrest you—it wouldn't look nice on the front page of the *Chronicle*. CEO of Citadel a suspect in a multiple murder case, being led out of the building in handcuffs after refusing to cooperate with the police? How fast do you think your two kids would be thrown out of that high-priced private school up there in Pacific Heights? I doubt you'd be welcomed back at the Bohemian Club."

Slowly, he eased his grip on the shirt. Yates fell back into his chair.

"What do you want?" he spit, yanking his cuffs straight. In the recessed lights over the desk, all Tim could see was the man's belligerence.

"Start with the woman. Who is she?"

"Ellen Mack. I interviewed her for a position as my personal accountant. I didn't hire her."

"Why not?"

Yates paused, picked up his bottle of water and sipped. "She wasn't aggressive enough." The CEO relaxed a little. "She lacked imagination. I never saw her after that."

"Who referred her?"

Yates shrugged. "She answered an ad. Ms. Saches set up the appointment."

"And Ed Reuters?"

Yates waved a hand impatiently. "I told you: he's the brother of one of my long-term employees. She asked me to get him out of prison. I hired a lawyer, and then I hired Reuters. Three days ago he didn't show up for work. That's all I know."

"He tried to kill your secretary. Why?"

Yates straightened his tie. "Maybe they had a lover's quarrel?"

Tim narrowed his eyes. "Are you trying to tell me Reuters was screwing your secretary?"

"How should I know?" Yates said curtly. "Who Ms. Saches took to bed is no concern of mine."

A phone—not the one on the CEO's desk—rang close by. Yates stiffened, perceivably alarmed. On the second ring, he reached into the side drawer of his desk and pulled out the receiver of a small cell phone. He turned his back on Tim and stepped to the windows.

Yates listened for two or three minutes. Then he turned and hung up the phone. He'd gone pale.

"I—I need to terminate this meeting, Ritmann." Like a mechanical doll, Phillip sat down, his face set in fear.

"You aren't terminating anything, good buddy," Tim sneered. "I need more answers."

Yates sprang to his feet on a sudden eruption of rage. "I'm busy, you goddamned son of a bitch! You can't barge in here any time you want and harass me with this shit. I've got rights as a citizen."

Tim calmly smiled. "You're right, Mr. Yates. I should make an appointment first."

He walked to the door, closing his notebook and stuffing it into his inside jacket pocket. Opening the door, he turned.

"I want you to come in to my office so we can sort through all this shit—you and me, and maybe a couple of the other detectives who have been going over your financial records. They're confused, Yates. We need you to explain a few things. Maybe you could give all of us a crash course in money laundering and high-tech insider trading. If you don't come of your own volition, I will get an arrest warrant."

"On what charges?" Yates asked. He looked like he was about to fall down.

"Conspiracy to commit murder, to defraud, to use insider information, murder for hire, murder for profit. Conspiracy is a federal crime; so are insider crimes. Do you need more?"

The CEO turned his attention to the papers on his desk.

"Come by the office," Tim said. "It's much nicer than the jail."

FIFTEEN

ADELE PUT HER EAR AGAINST THE DOOR OF ROOM 26. The distinct sound of a shower running full blast made her bold. Again, she inserted the skeleton key, pushed the door open a half inch, and peered through the crack.

The bathroom door stood open. The smell of shampoo and soap drifted into the main room on clouds of steam that misted the windows. Over the noise of the water, a woman hummed "Heart and Soul" off key. Adele stepped inside.

The bed was a mess, a tangle of sheets and blankets spilling over the end of the iron footboard. A pair of woman's underwear was in a ball on the floor next to the bed, along with a bra and a wadded-up pair of pantyhose.

Gone was Mathilde's duffle bag. In its place, propped on the arms of the pink and black chair, was a large red suitcase. Women's clothes hung haphazardly from hangers in the closet. Red dresses, purple blouses, lavender skirts—size 14 at least. Three pair of high heels—red, purple, and green—lined the floor next to the open room safe.

On the bedside table a woman's magazine lay open to an article entitled "Ten Ways to Please Your Man in Bed." Adele shook her head, irked that the magazine trade was still selling such mindless drivel to the younger set.

The shower and the humming stopped. Adele backed out into the hall and pulled the door closed behind her. Of one thing she was sure: Mathilde was no longer in room 26. Amnesic or not, never in a million years would Mathilde ever wear purple high heels.

She crossed her arms over her chest and leaned back against the snout of the Beast. The heat from the sun-warmed metal eased the muscles of her buttocks and thighs as she lazily studied the ground floor of the hotel. Behind the partially enclosed stairway, a wide wooden door hung from a runner. The wood on the bottom edge was bright green with mold.

The door slid back with rusty squeals of protest.

The original freight elevator was the same type as the one in her aunt Ruth's bookstore on Minna Street. The door to the elevator itself had a twelve-by-twelve square of frosted glass with the fine chicken wire in the middle, the same heavy iron handle, and the same storybook keyhole.

Adele used the elevator key she'd found. The massive door opened easily, exposing a collapsible copper gate, which she slid back. Her stomach clenched. Between the concrete floor and the wooden platform was the same five-inch gap that had given birth to bouts of nightmares and panic during her childhood. Seeing the gap again gave rise to the original vision of the monster's claw reaching up to grab her leg and pull her down into Bottomless Dark Pit where little girls were tortured and made to eat worms until the end of time.

With only a small hesitation and change in pulse rate, she stepped wide of the fissure and proceeded on to the platform. A bare bulb hung from the ceiling at the end of a fabric-covered electrical wire. She reached up and pulled the short chain.

The elevator platform—that horror chamber of her youth—came to light. Years of hard use had made the wooden floor as smooth and slick as marble, and the brick shaft that surrounded it black with dirt. To one side of the gate hung two thick cables. Adele replayed the nightmare from Aunt Ruth's Minna Street store six or seven times, trying to remember what the trick was to getting the elevator going.

Unable to get the synapses moving down the proper channels, she punched in the sequence of buttons on her cell phone that had been her aunt's phone number for forty-two years.

The elderly woman answered with a warbling hello.

"Aunt Ruth? It's Adele."

"Ohhhh, Dobbie, is that you?"

Adele smiled at the old lady's use of her family nickname, which she'd carried since she was ten months old and would sit in her highchair bobbing her head like a chicken and singing,

"Dobbie dobbie dobbie . . ." to tunes she made up as she went along.

"Yes, darling, it's Dobbie. Listen, do you remember that old freight elevator in the back of your bookstore on Minna Street?"

Ruth Cramer giggled like a girl. "Oh, I remember that. What have you gotten yourself into this time?"

"I'm in an elevator exactly like it and I need to know how to make it work."

"Oh. Well, let's see. Did you close the outside door and the gate? The contraption won't work until you do."

Adele followed the memory of Aunt Ruth pulling closed the outer wooden door, then sliding the metal gate over and pushing down the lever.

"Did you do it?" Ruth asked.

"Yes. Now what?"

"There should be two cables by the door. One has a pink handkerchief tied around it to keep your hands clean."

"No pink handkerchief, but I see the cables," Adele said.

"The one closest to the wall—pull it down. That'll start the pulley and up or down you'll go. If you want to stop it, pull on the other cable."

Adele scanned the metal cables apprehensively. "What if I don't pull on the other cable? Won't it stop by itself?"

The old woman began to laugh. "Oh, it'll stop all right, dear, but you'll jar the teeth out of your head doing it."

"That's great, Aunt Ruth," Adele said flatly over her relative's Crazy Woman laughter. "Talk to you later."

Adele put away the cell phone and pulled down on the cable closest to the wall.

A deep mechanical growl and a shudder of the box sent her to her hands and knees—exactly as it had when she was a girl. Her hand again landed in something sticky and wet.

She had brought her hand up to examine it in the light when the outer door slammed open with force and a man reached in through the copper bars of the collapsible door and yanked on the cable. It came to a tooth-jarring halt.

Squat but robust, the man was dark-skinned with thick black hair and large brown eyes. "What you doing here?" he demanded in an Italian accent. "This is freight elevator for hotel and restaurant only."

He brought the elevator platform level with the ground floor. His annoyance was softened by the lovely woman with the gold eyes and the straight black hair.

"Come." He stretched his arm toward her, motioning her out. "There's rats down there. You don't want to be eaten by the rats, do you?"

Adele guessed him to be about forty, although he could have been older. Many of her Italian patients, like her African-American and Japanese-American patients, often appeared twenty or more years younger than they were.

"Nice girl like you don't want to be in cellar with rats." He inspected the outside door then cut his eyes at Adele. "How you get in here? You new at the hotel?"

Adele decided explanations would take a long time, and the man was looking her over pretty good. She knew from experience to cut it short of the invitation to coffee in the restaurant she was sure he would tell her he owned, or she'd be here all day.

She shook her head. Then she signed the beginning verses to Bette Midler's "The Rose"—the only song she knew how to sign by heart.

"Hey! You deaf?" He pronounced it "deef."

Adele smiled one of her most disarming smiles, shrugged, and headed back to the Beast. She waved goodbye and cursed all the way to San Anselmo Memorial Park, where she sat until she figured out what to do next.

Carefully wiping the blood off her hand onto a handkerchief, she relaxed, doing the breathing exercises she learned at Spirit Rock Meditation Center before it became a pickup joint for Marin's spiritually elite over-forty desperates.

The desire to find the circus tent and read her the riot act for not calling to tip her off that Mathilde had left was eclipsed by the self-disgust she felt about not staking out Mathilde's room herself.

She was going through her notebook when the phone rang and caused her to yelp.

"What do you mean she's gone?" Tim asked. "Where would she go?"

"Timbuktu?" Adele said. "I don't know yet."

"Did you check with the manager?"

"I'm gearing up for that."

"I think I need to be there," Tim said cautiously. He sure as hell didn't want to piss her off again. "I think this is bridging into police territory, kiddo."

"Let me think about it and I'll let you know." *Like sometime in another life.* "What about the blood I found in her room?"

"It's Jane Doe's."

Dumbstruck, Adele watched twin toddlers—one laughing, one crying—being pushed on the baby swings by a tired-looking woman.

The realization that Mathilde was most likely dead became hard reality in her mind. "She's dead," Adele said, instantly weighted with guilt.

"We don't know that yet, Adele. Don't count bodies before they're uncovered."

"She's dead, Tim," Adele said, her voice rising. "I should have staked out her room . . . or insisted she stay with me. I could have talked her into it. I was so completely off. I was beginning to think she was the—"

"Adele!" Tim shouted. "Shut up and stop doing the guilt bullshit. You did the best you could. Is this what you do when you lose a patient?"

His brittle, critical tone stung her into silence.

"Listen, why don't I meet you at the hotel? We can—"

"Because I'm not ready for you to horn in and take over the collection effort. Give me three hours. I'll meet you at Ted's."

"Christ! You're a pain in the ass, Monsarrat. I know exactly what you're going to do as soon as you hang up this phone, you know that, right?"

Adele fired up the Beast and pulled away from the curb.

"Stands to reason that you'd know everything," she said testily. "You're a man, aren't you?"

That the Humane Society Thrift Shop was directly across the street from the San Anselmo Hotel couldn't have been more perfect.

She picked up the dog-eared 1971 copy of a magazine called *Harvest Home* and peeked out the front window. The Italian man was sitting at one of the outside cafe tables of the restaurant smoking a cigarette, conversing with two of the waiters. It was the lull between late lunch and early dinner, and there didn't appear to be customers. Next door, the fern-covered entrance to the hotel remained empty.

Adele skimmed the magazine, flipping through the pages. The models in the advertisements wore sideburns, mustaches, long hair, and bell-bottoms. A few wore caskets.

She glanced up quickly to see one of the waiters wave and get into a red Honda CRX. The Italian man and the remaining waiter stood.

She went back to the magazine. The name of the article was "Reconstruction—Special Nose Problems in Partial Decomposition." Below that was an advertisement for "Vita-Glow!— For that lifelike glow of health!" The picture accompanying the ad was of a vital-looking corpse in a casket. She turned back to the front cover. In faint letters under the title, was the subtitle: "The Professional Journal of Licensed Embalmers."

Across the street, the waiter had disappeared, and the Italian man now sat with a glass of red wine. He lit another cigarette.

She quickly paid for the magazine—she could put it in her living room and hope the trend caught on—and left by way of the back entrance. Circling the block, Adele climbed the fence at the end of the hotel parking area.

Sliding the elevator gate closed, and with full approval from the Female Sleuth and Private Investigators Board, she lowered the movable platform to the ratty basement.

And rats there were. She didn't see them, but she could hear them scratching about. She could also smell them, rat urine being one of those permeating odors one never forgot after smelling it once—like a GI bleeder or a decomposing body.

Using the beam of her penlight, Adele searched the walls for the light switch, which was partially hidden behind a rack of unlabeled bottles of wine.

Two main cement tunnels—the longer of which went north and the shorter, east in the direction of San Rafael—accommodated a total of ten rooms. Some of the rooms were locked, some doorless altogether, some empty. The rooms in the shorter section appeared to be used mainly as storage for wine, canned foods, olive oil, and bushel baskets of garlic bulbs. In the longer section of tunnel, the rooms contained goods associated with the hotel business: crates of soaps, cleaning supplies, linens, and a laundry room.

There were several doors with security locks. Most of the locks were rusted and dusty from disuse. She took out the key with the broken tip and fit it into the first lock without success.

V. I. Warshawski appeared, whiskey in hand, and eyed the key. *New key, new lock, Monsarrat—figure it out.*

"Right," said Adele, going for the door with the only new security lock. As she touched the lock, it fell open into her hand. It had been sawed through. At her feet, metal filings littered the floor.

V.I. drank off the rest of her whiskey and soda. *Looks like somebody got impatient—or lost their key.*

"Ayuhn," Adele said, fitting the key into the broken lock. What was left of it snapped open.

Adele reached into the dark room and searched the walls for a light switch. Her hand hit something cold and slimy. Silently screaming like a banshee, she fumbled with the penlight. It flipped out of her hand in a peculiar fashion that once again reinforced Adele's belief that she had her own personal poltergeist who stalked her.

She started to explore the floor with her hands, thought of what might be on it, and felt around with her foot until she located the penlight.

The dim beam of light caught a green metal shade hanging from the center of the room. As her hand touched it, the penlight flickered twice and went out. She found the chain and pulled. Nothing happened.

Something ran over her foot, triggering instant replays of the cellar scene in *Silence of the Lambs*. Screaming into the fabric of her jacket, she felt for the bulb and gave it a twist. Electric light flooded the room.

Her eyes went to the wall by the door and followed a silver trail, which ended in an absurdly long and fat banana slug.

"How the hell did you get down here?" she whispered.

Same way you did, it answered with a distinct New Jersey

accent. *I been circling dis room for days. Take me wid ya when ya leave, will ya?*

The eight-by-eight room was dingy with years of dirt. A small alcove had been built into one wall that she imagined had once held shelves of preserves. A painted wooden chair lay on its side next to a three-legged table. Piled in the opposite corner were several cardboard boxes. The two on top were empty. The one on the bottom contained a half-dozen cotton hand towels, all of which were heavily stained. Adele took one out and held it under the light. The stains were of various shades of beige, tan, black, pink, and yellow. One corner was stiff with glue and pieces of hair. She sniffed the colored streaks, and rubbed at them with a finger.

"Like grease paint," she said as she got down on her haunches and searched the floor more closely. Under the boxes she found a sliver of thin, flesh-colored latex. Next to it was a round spot, as though something wet had been placed there and soaked into the wood. Taking a clean corner of the towel, she rubbed at the spot then brought it back to the light.

"Christ on a bike," she whispered. "What is this, a slaughter-house? This couldn't be more blood?"

It sure as shit isn't a muffuletta, Adele, said Skip Langdon, sitting next to V.I. Warshawski to watch Adele work.

Adele's heart was already going like a jackhammer when the sound of the elevator coming to life sped it up even more and propelled her toward the door. Towel still in hand, she swiped the banana slug off the wall, wrapping it as she ran.

The underneath of the platform ascended, making mechanical groans. For one moment she thought of grabbing on and hoisting herself up onto the platform, but that was only for one moment.

Well, dear, said Miss Marple, *I do think you'd better find a place to hide before the elevator returns.*

"Right-o," Adele said, her eye falling on the storage room she had just left.

Above was the sound of something heavy being dragged onto the platform. Then the door and the gate slammed shut. Adele put her shoulder to the boxes of canned tomato paste and shoved. The stack moved about an eighth of an inch.

The motor began and the platform shuddered.

Adele removed a box from the top of the stack and again tried to move the remaining boxes away from the wall. A man's shoes and cuffs were now visible. She slipped behind the stack and crouched as the shoulders and neck of the restaurant manager came into view.

Through a crack between the boxes and a drum of olive oil, she watched the Italian roll two crates of onions off the platform and toward the stacks.

Halfway across the room, he changed his mind, turned, and set the crates down closer to the elevator against the opposite wall.

"Franco?" he called out. *"Dove diavolo sei?"*

He walked past the elevator toward the tunnel. Adele stepped out from behind the stack. Had he turned, he would have seen her.

"Cosa?" the Italian called. *"Stai scherzando con la cameriera ancora? Lasciarla un po per me!"*

She stepped boldly to the platform. The Italian took a few more steps down the tunnel. The second he was out of view, she closed the elevator gate and pulled on the cable. It shuddered, rumbled, and rose.

Below, she heard the manager's footsteps running back down the tunnel.

"Franco! *Cosa? Sei pazzo? Sei sbronzo? Torna in dietro! Che cosa stai facendo?"*

The call bell went off like an old school fire alarm. When the platform was still three feet from the main floor, she reached to open the gate, then leapt upward and out. She went over the fence and down the block, turned the corner, and ran directly into a policewoman.

"Oops. Sorry. You okay?" Adele tried to smile.

The policewoman looked her up and down, trying, Adele thought, to determine if she was running or fleeing the scene of a crime. Adele jogged in place, trying to look nerdy the way some joggers did when they thought they were showing off.

The policewoman waved her away with a warning not to run on public sidewalks and to go to the local track.

Adele ran to the front of the hotel, stopping only to release the New Jersey slug in some oleander bushes.

* * *

The man at the front desk was clean-cut and wholesome in a Promise Keepers–Skinhead kind of way. His closely cropped hair and the overly bright eyes and the intense look did little, however, to cower her psychologically into walking three steps behind.

"I want to see the manager," she said.

"I'm sorry, but she's not available," he said emphatically. "What can I help you with?"

Twenty wise-ass answers came to mind, but she decided she didn't have time to fool around. Adele fished in her fanny pack and produced her deputy sheriff's badge. She flashed it, moving toward the hallway leading to the back. "I'm going to go back to Bertha's apartment and see how unavailable she is. You keep an eye out for my partner, Detective Ritmann—guy with red hair and a big gun. Send him back when he gets here, will you?"

Halfway down the hall, the smell of garlic sautéing in butter and white wine made her mouth water against her will. She passed the opening to the restaurant kitchen. Before she even looked, she knew she would see the Italian.

His whole body, but especially his hands, were engaged in some fierce activity as he raged in Italian at the infamous elevator-stealing Franco.

The moment he saw her, his mouth snapped shut, but his eyes went wide open. "Ah! You! Was that you left me down there?"

She shook her head and shrugged, hands outstretched. She kept moving toward the hotel manager's apartment. The man followed.

"Hey! hey! Come back."

She turned. To her immense enjoyment, she watched while he played out a charade of getting on the elevator and being left in the basement with the rats who apparently nipped at his toes.

Delighted with his performance, she applauded.

"*Uffa!*" he said throwing up his hands in disgust. "*Cretina!*" He went back into the restaurant kitchen bellowing for Franco.

The closer she got to the back apartment, the smells changed from mouthwatering sautéed garlic to the putrid smell of boiled liver and other organ meats. The top half of the Dutch door shook under her hand as she knocked. Fifteen seconds later, she pounded again, pressing her ear to the wood.

Nothing.

She slammed her open palm against the wood, and was ready to go again when the door swung open.

"Whose hand goes not gentle upon my door?" asked Bertha, pepperoni in hand. The red and pink dots of the tent had been changed to pink and black zebra stripes.

As soon as she saw Adele, the manager's smile faded.

"Hi," said Adele, flipping open her badge case again. "You need to answer lots of questions."

The tent held up her free hand. "Hey—wait. I thought you were her sister. Nobody said anything about you being a cop."

"Yeah, well, I don't believe in upsetting any apple crates until I have to."

"I don't want to get involved in this," Bertha said, still holding up a hand.

"Well, okay, but before you make up your mind for sure that that's the stand you want to take, let me inform you that if you *don't* cooperate, the Sheriff's Department won't have any choice except to assume you're somehow involved with the murders—"

"Murders!?" Bertha choked. Her face and chins turned bright red. "What murders?"

". . . and," continued Adele, "you could be charged with being an accessory before and after the crimes and punished as a co-murderer." Adele lifted her eyebrows. "Sound exciting?"

Bertha cleared her throat with a nervous gurgle. "How long is this going to take?"

"Longer than it will take to eat that pepperoni." Adele pointed at the eight-inch sausage.

The tent looked at the pepperoni as if she didn't know how it got there. She suppressed a belch and made a sour face. "Okay, come on in. Close the door behind you."

The kitchen was cramped, but then again, Adele figured that any room Bertha was in would feel that way. Seated at the kitchen table, she watched Bertha make the real-life equivalent of a Dagwood sandwich. Large slice of Jewish rye on the bottom, heavy layer of mayonnaise, thick slices of onion, thicker slices of pepperoni, salami, more rye.

"Why didn't you call me when she checked out?" Adele asked.

Bertha cleared her throat, keeping her eyes on what she was doing. "Because I didn't know she checked out until this morning when she called in and said she had already vacated the room and wasn't coming back. She said she'd talked to you a few minutes before and not to call you."

Down went another layer of mayo, mustard, six slices of provolone, ham, tomato, lettuce, dill pickle, more rye.

"Are you sure it was her?"

The tent shrugged, and stuffed a slice of ham and provolone into her mouth. The corner of the ham slice flopped on her chin like the tail of a fish as it went down a pelican's distensible pouch.

"I think so. It sounded like her. I'm not a voice expert, but she has one of those low, husky voices."

"Why did she have a key to the elevator?"

Bertha blew breath through her nose in an angry snort. "Now *that* pissed me off!" Sandwich making was momentarily suspended as she waved a hand angrily. "She said she lost the one I gave her. Now I've only got two left and Angelo at the restaurant has one of those."

Returning to her task, Bertha laid on olives, mozzarella, mayo, salt, lemon pepper, a layer of crumbled potato chips, feta cheese, and a roof of rye. The edible superstructure threatened to fall over as Bertha braced the leaning tower of food with two shish kebab skewers.

"But why did she have a key at all?" Adele asked.

"I sometimes rent spaces down there for short-term storage to the hotel tenants." She made a precise cut between the skewers with a serrated meat carver. "She had some boxes she wanted stored. Paid for a full month up front—just like her room."

"There isn't any chance she might have given you an address to send her refund money to?"

Bertha shook her head. "She said to keep the money." Bertha pulled back one of the skewers and picked up half the sandwich, squeezing the ends together like an accordian. "There wasn't but two days' refund left anyway. It's not like we're talking about hundreds of dollars."

The sandwich was hoisted to the open mouth of the tent, as a weightlifter hoists his barbell. Bertha was salivating, swallowing rapidly in anticipation—Mrs. Joyboy waiting for the King Crab commercials.

Unaware of what she was doing, Adele opened her mouth slightly, watching the end of the humongous ship of food sail between those small white teeth.

All at once, the woman's words registered. Adele jumped out of her chair. Her coffee spilled onto the table. "*What* did you say?"

Lips firmly around the prow of the sandwich, all of Bertha froze except her eyes, which widened.

Adele grabbed for the sandwich to push it back down to the plate. Bertha pulled away in a protective gesture.

"Please," Adele pleaded. "Repeat what you just said about the refund."

Bertha put the sandwich into reverse. It came out from the mouth of the whale as whole as Jonah. "She didn't want it back and—"

"No, I mean about paying a month in advance and only having two days of refund."

Bertha's mouth flapped once . . . twice. "What about it?"

"How can that be if she checked in two days ago?"

"Two days?" Bertha hooked up a corner of her mouth. "She checked in three and a half weeks ago. Paid cash. I thought she was going to leave sooner, to be honest with you, but then she got into that accident, and she ended up staying." The sandwich floated, came back to the mouth.

Adele sat back down, and mopped at the spilled coffee with a pink paper napkin. She watched as Bertha's lips again closed around the sandwich. When it lowered to the plate, a good third was missing.

The down time while Bertha chewed gave her time to think. When the pudgy hands with the pink nails wrapped themselves around the sandwich again, Adele asked her next question quickly.

"What name did she give when she checked in?"

Bertha smiled, but there was impatience behind it. "Ellen Mack. Said she was an accountant who was trying out a job at some company in the city."

"Did she have anyone with her?"

"Nope."

The sandwich was jerking closer toward the toothed cavern. Adele could not take her eyes off it. "Did anyone ever visit or call her?"

"Never before the other day when the Marine type came by."

"But if you knew her name was Ellen, then why did you call her Mathilde?"

"*I* didn't," Bertha said irritably. "You did. She told me a nurse named Adele was going to come by and that you knew her by her middle name."

"But didn't you . . ."

The middle of the sandwich disappeared. There was only one bite left of the first half.

". . . recognize her photo from the papers or on TV?"

Bertha shook her head, and wiped her fingers free of mayonnaise. "Nmphoo. Ahm nndt eeee mdit."

Adele held up a hand. "Save it. I can't understand a word you're saying."

While she waited for termination of mastication, Adele noticed that Bertha was beginning to look more and more like a pelican. It was unnerving, to say the least.

"I don't read the papers or watch TV," the woman said after clearing her mouth with a sip of Coke. "I keep the TV on for company, but I never watch or listen to it. It's like my invisible guest."

Adele's mind skimmed over Bertha's reference to invisible guests; that was a subject better left undiscussed for the time being.

"But it's been posted in every store and on telephone pole in Marin County for a week. How could you not see—"

"Look at me!" Bertha opened her arms, filling the kitchen with her hugeness. There was no rancor in her voice, but there was a trace of despair. "I never leave this place—I can't fit into a car. It takes me thirty minutes just to go relieve myself."

Adele looked at her, considerably sobered and saddened by the woman's speech. "What do you do?" she asked quietly. "I mean, how do you live?"

"I order my groceries, and get my books from the mobile library."

The big woman was silent, no longer eating. "Did Ellen do something wrong?"

"We don't know," Adele said. "Neither does she. She's been amnesic the entire time she was in the hospital. I'm surprised she remembered the hotel. Did she remember you?"

Bertha hesitated in picking up the rest of the sandwich and tilted her head—as best she could. She stared at her, wearing an odd expression. "What *are* you talking about, girl?"

Adele took a deep breath. Somehow, she knew that whatever was coming was going to be significant. "What do you mean?"

"Ellen has been here at the hotel. She wasn't suffering from any amnesia that I know of." Bertha raised her eyebrows. "Granted, she had weird hours, but unless she was away on business, I saw her every night since the night after the accident.

"She'd bring me dressing supplies and I wrapped her hands. I couldn't believe they let her out of the hospital with those burns. That left hand was bad."

"You wrapped her burns?" Adele's lower lip hung down a bit. "At night?"

"Well, morning, really. About oh three hundred hours she'd come down and—"

"Did she ever talk to you about herself? Tell you anything about her personal life, or where she came from?"

Bertha shook her head. "Tight as a clam. I asked where she was from, and she said she was from a lot of places. When I asked if she was married or had any kids, she said no, and that she traveled around a lot. Vague answers."

Adele swallowed. "On the day the man with the scar came here to see her, what do you remember about that that was unusual?"

The rest of the half disappeared, and the woman thought while she chewed. "Just that he looked terrible when he came back downstairs. Like he'd gotten some mighty bad news." Bertha pressed her finger over some crumbs that had fallen on the tabletop and licked at them absentmindedly. "Come to think of it, I never saw Ellen after that, but I know she was here, because of the key, and because all her stuff was here."

"How long did the man with the scar spend up there?"

Bertha removed the skewer from the second half and circled the sandwich with her fingers. "Mmm, maybe an hour or so."

"I'm going to ask you to stretch for this one," Adele said.

"It's okay." Bertha pulled the sandwich up to her mouth and shrugged. "My body is gone, but my memory is still with me."

"During the time he was up there, did you hear the freight elevator?"

"Oh, Lord, I wouldn't have noticed that," Bertha said, angling for the best bite approach. "I don't pay any attention to the elevator anymore. Angelo and Franco go up and down on that thing a hundred times a day."

"What about her room? Did the cleaning woman find anything today when she cleaned?"

"Not with *that* one," Bertha snorted. "I would have loved to have had her in my barracks. Neat as a pin. Bridget barely had to do anything."

Adele looked at her watch, got up suddenly and stepped over the Saint Bernard. "I gotta go," she said. "But I'll be back."

One street over, parallel with the hotel, Adele and Tim sat at Ted's Bar and Grill digesting each other's news and the Caesar salad they'd split. Ted's had had its day of fame back in the eighties and was waiting for a rerun. Except the loyal patrons who had been wild party animals in the eighties were now the very crowd who were placing the joint into the "bunch of old farts" category.

Adele sipped her gin and tonic, savoring the slightly oily taste of an olive she'd pilfered from the garnishes. "No responses from other law agencies on her ID?"

Tim wagged a pen between his fingers as he finished going over her notes. "It's too early for that." He drank off his coffee and laid cash down on top of the check. On top of that he placed his water glass.

"Ready?" he asked, standing and tying the belt of his raincoat. He felt in his pocket for the plastic bag that held the blood-smeared hand towel she'd given him and held her chair.

"Where are we going?"

"We're off to see the woman behind the curtain."

Walking back to Tim's car they passed three antique shops in a row. In one window display, a mannequin who was probably from the same mold as Monique Arrowsmith was bent over a trunk overflowing with vintage clothes. Hanging from her stiffened fingers was a pair of eyelet bloomers.

Adele stopped dead in her tracks and stared. The homeless beggar from outside Trader Joe's popped into mind. She grabbed Tim's arm.

"We need to detour for a second. Come on."

"Where?"

"We're going to visit a tent. Just go along with whatever I say, okay?"

Inside the registration office, Bertha sat on the army cot drinking a Diet Coke and reading *The New York Times*. Introductions made, Adele got to the point.

"What about the boxes Mathilde had in storage?"

"The only thing she had in there that she took with her was a wooden case with a handle. After she called and said she wasn't coming back, I had Angelo saw the lock open and haul whatever was left to the thrift store. It wasn't much except a couple of boxes of junky clothes."

"What kind of clothes?" Tim asked.

"Oh, there was a uniform, and a policeman's hat and a black jacket with like a priest's collar and some dungarees and work boots."

The mountain swayed, gaining momentum, until she rocked herself to her feet and waddled to the desk. It seemed unbelievable that such small structures of support bone could hold up the mountain of a body.

"I took out a leather jacket and a weird pair of glasses to give to my nephew." Bertha opened the desk drawer and produced the iridescent glasses.

Adele reached over and took the glasses, turning them over in her hand. "Do you still have those boxes?"

Bertha shook her head. She was still breathing in wheezy gasps. "Angelo took them across the street to the thrift shop. They'll sell to the kids around here."

"What about the wooden case you mentioned?" Tim asked. "What did it look like?"

"It was about sixteen inches tall and two feet wide. Had lots of drawers," Bertha said. "Looked heavy."

"A makeup case," Adele said, "I used to do volunteer nursing at San Francisco American Conservatory Theater during their big productions. The makeup artists all used them."

"Okay, Bertha." Tim wrote his cell phone number on the back of his card and handed it to her. "Deputy Monsarrat and I have to meet someone right now, but call this number if you hear from Ellen Mack again. And try to find out where she is."

Bertha read the card and looked back at the detective. "Yes, sir. If I'd known the cops were looking for her, I would have let you know earlier." She tapped the card against the back of her pudgy hand and chuckled.

"The really ironic part is that she was one of the best renters I've ever had—except losing the elevator key. She paid in advance, was quiet, neat, and never complained."

"Yeah," Adele said, slapping her knees and getting up. "You can never tell about those nice, quiet types, can you?"

Through the back door, Adele saw not two, but twenty boxes stuffed with clothes, old teapots, curtains, Etch-A-Sketches, deflated footballs, lamps, pillows, picture frames, and wooden spoons with the handles burned to nubs.

"They open at nine," Tim said. "We need to be here before they open."

Adele frowned. "*You* can be here. I have to work."

"Call in sick."

"Yeah, right," she said, headed for his car again. "You don't understand the nurse-slave mentality, darling. Want to hear a true story that puts nursing into perspective for the normal person?"

He opened the car door and waited for her to slide in. "Don't you dare call me normal."

"There was a nurse who lived in some east coast state that was being hit with a horrible hurricane and flood," Adele began as soon as he was in the car. "She called in to the nursing office from the Red Cross shelter where she and her children had been evacuated and told them she couldn't come to work because she didn't have transportation and her house was under water.

"Well, of course the nursing supervisor insisted she come to work anyway or be fired. The nurse pleaded with the supervisor to understand her situation. She refused and fired her on the spot.

"That night, the nurse called the supervisor back and told her to turn on the TV. There, on the six o'clock news, was the tape of the nurse and her children being airlifted from the roof of her house, while her car floated away down the river.

"They rescinded the firing, but they refused to accept that she had a good enough reason for not coming to work that day and docked her sick pay."

Tim shot her a disbelieving glance.

Adele held up her hands. "I swear it's a true story. I've got vet bills, and doggie shrink bills and special order doggie food to pay for . . . not to mention rent, so don't talk to me about calling in sick, pal."

The Land of Oz was a dimly lit bar located on a strip known as the Miracle Mile between San Rafael and San Anselmo. The regulation bar smell of cigarette smoke, booze, and old urine almost knocked her over. The place was jammed.

When her eyes adjusted to the dark, Adele could see the heads of animals mounted on the wall behind the bar. "What the hell is this?" she shouted over the noise of other people shouting over each other.

Tim finished paying for their nonalcoholic beers. "You've lived in Marin all your life and you've never been to the Land of Oz?" he yelled over the noise. "Shit, that's bordering on being underprivileged."

She gave her surroundings another hairy eyeballing. "I'd call it fortunate. Why are we here?"

Tim held up a finger and led her to an even darker, though quieter back room that was half the size of the front room. They found an empty table lit by a red lava lamp and sat down.

"We're making a contact: an ex-con who owes me a big favor."

Adele sipped her beer and played with a corner of the label.

"I gave her some information to check on."

"You mean, she's a snitch?"

Tim pursed his lips and glanced around before he answered. For a moment his blue eyes went narrow, sharpening their focus on her. "You don't ever want to use that word out loud, Adele." Despite the look in his eye, his voice was kind. "And don't use your real name."

Adele nodded. "Okay. What information did you—"

A frizzy blonde, beer in hand, bumped into their table, spilling their beers and knocking over the lava lamp. Both Adele and Tim rescued their beers.

"There she goes again!" laughed the blonde. She had one of those wheezy, cigarette-rough voices that made Janis Joplin famous. She smiled down at Adele. "Sorry. I forget how to walk after the fifth beer," she said, her light blue eyes evaluating her—sizing her up. "I need gravity wings to keep me upright."

Adele guessed the freckle-faced woman to be about thirty, although she might have been older if judged on the look behind her eyes. "It's okay. Did you hurt your hip?"

The woman looked at Tim and then back at Adele. "Yeah," she said, sliding into the chair next to Adele and pulling it so close her thigh rubbed against hers. "I'm wounded. I better sit down."

Tim reached past Adele and righted the lava lamp. "Faye, meet Detective Monique Arrowsmith. Detective Arrowsmith, meet Faye Kreigor."

Faye held out a small plump hand and shook Adele's long and narrow one. "You're too cute to be in law enforcement," she said, and pulled the thinnest cigarette Adele had ever seen out of a pack. "Why'd you decide on that?"

"I don't mind breaking fingernails?" Adele said.

The woman chuckled and lit her cigarette without taking her eyes off Adele. "I've never seen gold eyes before. How'd you come by those?"

Before Adele could answer, Tim cleared his throat and leaned forward, speaking low. "Forget it Faye. She's straight."

Faye snapped her fingers and sighed, but still didn't take her eyes off Adele. "Damn it. The best-looking ones are either taken or straight." She put her arm over the back of Adele's chair. There was an amusement behind her stare. "Don't suppose you'd want to try a little adventure on the other side of the fence, would you?"

Adele flushed under the frankness of the woman's stare and shook her head. "No thanks, but thanks for the offer."

The blonde let up on the press of her thigh into Adele's hip. She set her beer on the table and folded her hands, looking out at the room. "Timothy, me lad," she said in an Irish brogue, "I love ya, darlin', but I won't be owin' you nothin' after this one."

"And how's that, Faye?" Tim said, taking another swig of his beer. Adele noticed he also stared out at the crowd.

"You got a monster by the tail, darlin'." Faye lowered her voice, and made a dramatic change in attitude. All amusement was gone from her eyes, replaced by a hard expression. The muscles of her jaw clenched as she spoke.

"She changes her name and ID like you change your socks. Nobody knows her real name, but people in the business call her the Invisible Chameleon. Some say her name is Paula Greene, some in L.A. say it's Ellen Mack, others know her as Nancy something or other.

"She's the highest-priced, most infamous hit woman in the business anywhere." Faye took a drag off her cigarette and turned her head to the side, blowing the smoke away from Adele and Tim.

"She's a genius at setting up murders or accidents—sort of like in 'Mission Impossible.' As a killer, she's like a machine— no mistakes, everything clean and neat. Cross her, get in her way, and you're dead. She's an equal opportunity biller. Age, race, gender—she doesn't care. She always works alone, and she never fucks up. That's how the law boys recognize her work: she's too good."

She leveled her gaze at Tim. "Nobody messes with her, Timothy. Nobody. Not even the mob. She's not just bad news, she's the worst news you'll ever have."

"How long has she been in operation?" Tim asked.

Faye lowered her chin onto the hand cupped around the top of her beer bottle and shrugged. "Long time. She started out as a specialty makeup artist in Hollywood, then got into the stunt-woman thing for a while. She got mixed up with the Mafia, then disappeared and nobody heard anything about her."

"How do you know for sure the woman in the photo is the same person?"

Faye laughed, shook her head, and took a pull on her beer. "You got to learn to trust your sources, Timothy."

Tim gave her a questioning look.

She shook her head again. "What I do for you I do because I owe you, but I'm not willing to take a bullet in the head for you. Some things you don't tell anybody. Besides, nothing I tell you is going to lead you to her. She moves around—Europe, Asia, South America. She can't be caught."

"How much does she get a hit?" Adele asked.

"Shit, I dunno what she gets now. Somebody out of Chicago paid her fifty thou a few years ago to take out his wife so it couldn't ever be tracked back to him. It worked. The guy's still around."

"Somebody has to be close to her. A mother, or a boy-friend . . ." Adele trailed off at the sight of Faye's smirk.

"Nope. No personal ties, or, if she does, it's someone who doesn't have a clue who she really is." Fay laughed. "Like maybe a non-English-speaking blind person living in a hut in Siberia or something."

Adele had an instant mind movie of Mathilde living in a garret in some Venetian back alley apartment with a young, at-tractive waiter who thinks her name is Jane Doe and she works sales for Fuller Brush.

"What you're saying is she's a psychopath," said Adele.

"Say it in plain English, girl," Faye said, laughing. "The bitch is a cold-blooded killer."

"What's this?" Adele beamed.

Vivian was sitting up in the patient lounger, reading a copy of *Variety*. Her putty gray color had changed to a lighter shade of putty, with a splash of pink on her lips and cheeks.

The woman looked over her bifocals, and removed them, careful not to disturb the oxygen cannula in her nose. "They couldn't kill a tough old bird like me, so they decided to prop me up and let me fool people into thinking I'm half-alive."

She gave Adele's sleuthing outfit a once-over. "Track your woman down?"

"Not yet, but I'm starting to get the idea she's flown the coop."

"Why are you looking for her?"

"Murder."

"Oh my." Surprised, but not shocked, the older woman stared at Adele for a few seconds. "I was thinking in terms of a runaway wife. Murder is a different story. Women who murder, run to a friend or a lover . . . maybe a relative."

"None of the above. This woman doesn't allow herself to have personal contacts."

"You mean she's inhuman," Vivian said, touching her bottom lip with the earpiece of her glasses. "One must be either a god or an animal to live without human connections." Vivian clucked her tongue. "Poor thing. She must be terribly hurt."

"I don't think so, Vivian," Adele said. "I think you can stop at the inhuman conjecture and leave it at that."

From thirty-six thousand feet, Arizona looked dry and uninteresting. Her thoughts ran to D. B. Cooper, which made her smile—a rare event for her mouth. It was the element of outwitting someone and getting away with it that thrilled her. It always had.

During the years her mother withheld food and clothing and kept her locked in the cage, she'd turned the desperate need for food and warmth into an adventure. Even on those rare occasions when she'd been caught sneaking food, and was crammed into a refrigerator kept for the purpose of punishment, she mentally thrived on the thought that she had—for a few moments anyway—won.

After a time, the game of not being caught turned into something more serious: it supplied her with a reason to survive. She had led two lives—that of the cipher who existed inside a cage, and that of the superchild who existed by her own wits. The art of deception and paying attention to detail, which had begun out of necessity, made her rich. The actual act of murder was merely part of the game, a simple task in exchange for money.

The money had been quite satisfactory this time. Two hundred fifty thousand was more than adequate, even though there had been complications.

The woman and the two kids. Hysterical woman. She'd had to kill them sooner than she wanted. She should have killed the smaller child, too, instead of using her to persuade the father to hand over Yates's program.

The car accident. Her momentary loss of control and the photographs in the papers. She shuddered, leaning back into the plush cushion of the seat.

Then there'd been Reuters thinking he could play a blackmail game—with *her*, the Invisible Chameleon? But, she had to admit, it had worked beautifully, using the fool's clothes and his likeness to kill Yates's secretary. And the touch of leaving a spot of her own blood on the carpet was good. It would serve to confuse them and put them off track for a while—at least until the fat lady sang and spilled her guts about changing dressings at strange hours. And then—she smiled—then they would think they had her.

She reclined in the plush first-class seat and inspected her hands. Barry and Hightower had been easy disguises and even easier kills. Yates liked her work and had promised more.

That was how it went. People got a taste for it . . . for getting away with something. It was as addictive as a drug or gambling, but on a much higher order.

The stewardess stopped to check if she wanted anything; they were due to land in twenty minutes. She turned away and looked out the window again until the woman went away. Only when she was sure no one was around her did she reach under the seat and pull out the boot. With her penknife, she pried up the insole and removed the heel section.

She stared inside the empty heel, her breath coming faster. A minute passed before she moved to put away the boot.

Control. She had to get control of herself. Pulling the blanket up over her head, she traveled back into the cage to think. When she had regulated the rate of her heart and respirations, she began to plan.

SIXTEEN

THE LANDING BETWEEN THE SEVENTH AND EIGHTH floors turned into a dance floor for Cynthia and Dr. Dhery. The scene resembled a dance contest from the thirties, where one partner held up the other while he or she slept. The nurse was doing a slow waltz while Dr. Dhery snored on her shoulder.

"What the hell are you doing, Cynthia?" Adele asked as soon as they'd come into view.

"Shhhh." Cynthia glowered at her. "The artist sleeps."

Adele snorted. "The artist?"

"It's a brilliant concept," Cynthia said. "Sleep deprivation visual art. He's channeled his artistic talents from writing to drawing. Instead of charting, he's begun to draw word pictures of how the patient is doing. Pictorial medicine. It's going to revolutionize our way of documenting medicine forever. He's so talented, Adele—it's like watching the birth of a Picasso or a—"

"Christ on a violin, Cynthia!" Adele looked at her friend—dressed in scrubs, with a physician draped over her—and suddenly had the feeling she'd been thrown into a Fellini movie. "Have you completely lost what was left of your mind?"

"No." Cynthia sniffed, offended Adele didn't understand the beauty of his artist's soul. "Not at all. It's brilliant. No more dreary charting—just beautiful pictures to study. Each patient will have a complete set of physician and nurse art depicting—"

"This is the idea of a sleep-deprived madman," Adele said, walking past the odd couple. "I hope he hasn't actually had a chance to try this out."

"Oh, yes," Cynthia said, rather offhandedly. "He had his debut last night. All his patients' charts on Ward Eight. Look at them and then tell me you think it's the work of a madman and not a genius."

"Don't be late for report," Adele said over her shoulder. "And please put your dance partner away somewhere where people can't trip over him."

Adele held Mr. Gonzales's chart away from her and squinted at the tricolored progress note/sketch the same way she might look at a pen-and-ink at an art gallery. She had to admit the arrangement of written words and numbers was interesting and pleasing to the eye. Lab values floated like so many dead fish at the top of the page, while blood pressures and temperatures were interspersed with the lung sounds and kidney function results to create an underwater motif. It was almost appropriate, she thought, seeing how Mr. Gonzales was a near-drowning victim.

The focal point of the word sketch was the prognosis—done all in black. The word "P O O R" had little shrouds surrounding each letter and a row of coffins underlining the word.

Unable to look at any more examples of Dr. Dhery's artistic brilliance, Adele closed the chart, wondering if the senior partners would find the hidden meaning behind the conceptual charting, and send the young physician either to a psychiatrist for some professional help, or to art school.

Report was long and dreary. Besides being in charge, Adele was also assigned to six patients, all of whom were presently stable, but, like Vivian Vanderlise, were walking time bombs waiting for any opportunity to explode into full-blown congestive heart failure, kidney failure, pulmonary edema, stroke, massive coronary, or just plain old death.

The staff were equally unstable, but not physically. It was a dismaying thought that the most normal of the crew were Tina and Cynthia.

Skip's patient load of four stable and four unstable patients guaranteed that she would have to listen to his whining and complaints all shift, and Abby's intolerance of Skip meant there would be catfights and backbiting to referee. Adele had barely finished morning rounds when Abby pulled her aside, into the women's bathroom.

"He keeps asking me to do his vital signs," Abby complained in a low voice. "Why can't he take care of his own patients? I have as many sick patients as he does. And he's not answering his call lights. I . . ."

Adele closed her eyes and counted to ten. Abby was one of the tightly wound, anal-retentive nurses: she would have to do the Flattering Lies with a Touch of Guilt routine.

"Skip gets easily overwhelmed, Ab. You are the most capable nurse I have today. I'm counting on you to keep it together for me on the battlefield. Can you do that? Can you bite your tongue and help the poor bastard hold up his end? Just for this shift?"

Abby picked at one fingernail and sighed. "He's so *use*less, Adele. Why don't they fire him? I mean . . ."

"I know, Abby, but you've got to give him a little credit." Adele faltered, trying to come up with that little credit. "Um. He does do a good job at—um, lifting the heavy patients."

Ms. Vanderlise's light went off, saving her from more mewling.

Both Vivian and Dr. Murray smiled at her when she came into the room. "I'm sending Vivian home this morning, Adele," Dr. Murray said. "Would you set that into motion for us?"

Adele blinked. "But . . . she's not ready to go home."

"Yes, we're aware of that, Adele, but Vivian wants to go home. She's going to have a home health nurse look after her."

Adele was torn. She was a proponent of allowing patients to go home to die, but this wasn't just any patient, and the possibility they could give her another year of life by continued treatments at the hospital was good. "But what about monitoring and—"

"It's all right, doll," Vivian said. "I want to go home so I can be near my things and my cats. Whatever will be, will be."

"But why not give it one more week? By that time we'll have your medications regulated and . . ."

Vivian Vanderlise took the nurse's hand and held it. "Humor me, doll. I'm a fussy old lady who wants to gamble with life in the comfort of my own home."

Kneeling next to the chair, Adele studied the woman's drawn face with an unrelieved seriousness. "Okay. As soon as Dr. Murray writes the discharge order, I'll have Tina call Registration and Pharmacy. Shall I call someone to come and pick you up?"

"It's already done," Vivian said, and let go of her hand. "What you can do is bring me some towels. This big lug . . ." She jabbed Dr. Murray in the midsection with her elbow. ". . . said I could have a shower."

"Okay, then," Adele said, feeling like a kid at a party where the pony ride had been canceled. "I'd better find some towels before we run out."

"Come and visit me," Vivian said. "Do you play Scrabble?"

"I love Scrabble."

"Great. I'll teach you how to play."

Adele smiled. "Challenge accepted."

She was cautious, suspicious, and clearly doubting the wisdom of Tim's insistence that he go through all the donated boxes. Policeman or not, she couldn't have him making a mess after the volunteers had worked so hard to put the donations in order.

"If you could tell me what you're looking for, Officer Ritmann?" said Gwen. The woman's delicate thin hands darted about in accompaniment to her words.

"It's Detective Ritmann, ma'am. There are two boxes which were brought over yesterday by Angelo from the restaurant across the street. Do you remember what you might have done with them?"

"That was Rose." Both hands flew up and settled, each hand on an opposite shoulder. "Rose worked yesterday until noon and then Mary worked from noon until four. I was at home baking for the church supper. But if you could tell me what it was in the boxes that you want, perhaps I can find something similar in the shop that—"

"That won't be necessary, ma'am. You see, the boxes that were brought in contain evidence in a case I'm working on."

Gwen looked uncomfortable. Her hands once again bolted up and apart. "You don't mean that you would have to con—confis . . ."

"Confiscate them? Yes. That's what I have to do. I'll give you a receipt, and when they're no longer considered evidence, you can have them back." Which, Tim thought, with the way this case is going, might be in about fifty years.

Tim could tell by the way Gwen McLaughlin's blue-veined

hands fluttered to her chest, then hovered there like ailing butterflies, that he needed to take charge. He pointed to the back room, his body following his finger. "The donations from yesterday are back here?"

"Wait." The butterflies flew up wildly in alarm. "I need to call Rose and find out . . ."

Tim stopped. "Is Rose the manager?"

"Yes. I can't let you go back there. That's for employees only. We don't let anyone except—"

"Gwen." Tim was careful not to threaten or use profane language. "This is police business. We aren't going to take into custody anything that isn't absolutely necessary to this case. Call Rose. Or, if you'd like, I can call a San Anselmo police officer to supervise the operations. Would a uniformed police officer make you feel more comfortable?"

"Yes," said Gwen. Tears had formed at the corners of her eyes. The hands were trembling as she wiped them away. "Yes, it would."

"May I use your phone?"

Gwen looked flustered again. "Well, Rose says the phone is strictly for employees. We can't let . . ."

Tim took out his cell phone and dialed San Anselmo police for an officer to assist in collection of evidence.

When Officer Rothschild arrived five minutes later, Gwen grabbed his arm, putting the five-foot-seven-inch man between herself and Tim. "Thank God you're here, officer. This detective . . ." She said the word as though the very idea of him being a detective was absurd. ". . . wants to take away boxes of donations."

Her hands balled into small fists—butterflies changed to heavy wasps. "The humane society isn't going to like this. The money we make from our donations goes to feed all the poor starving animals at the shelter. This man said—"

"It's fine," Officer Rothschild interrupted gently. "Detective Ritmann will give you a receipt. I'll stand right here and make sure he takes only the evidence he needs."

Her fists shot open, as though they'd had the wind knocked out of them. Gwen looked from the officer to Tim, "conspiracy" written between the deep wrinkles of her face.

"I need to call Rose," she said, backing toward the phone. "Rose isn't going to like this."

"What the hell is this?" Dr. Wortz, one of the senior surgeons, was holding a patient's chart open to one of Dr. Dhery's progress notes, turning it upside down and then sideways.

The words and numbers were arranged in the shape of a noose. Among his other health problems, the patient was suffering from depression and frequently voiced a threat to kill himself.

Before the tornado of outrage began, Adele went to Vivian Vanderlise's room, closed the door, and didn't come out until she was sure the storm had passed.

The 911 call diverted and Gwen properly reprimanded, Detective Ritmann was lost in the boxes of "junk." He'd become engrossed with the manner of things people discarded: brand new pots and pans, clothing from the seventies, dish sets, silverware, paintings by amateurs, broken toys, naughty lingerie, a dildo ($2.98), nubs of pencils and erasers, motherboards from ancient computers (free), eight-track tapes, ant farms, broken keyboards.

Only when he opened the box with a half-full bag of kapok, and a cop's uniform jacket on top, did he snap out of the state Adele tagged the Goodwill Stupor.

Thirty-four-year-old runner Bjorn Hunt had been airlifted off an isolated Mount Tam trail in poor conditions. After wandering off the trail and coming up hopelessly lost, dehydration and twelve hours of exposure to freezing rain and wind had won Mr. Hunt last place in the Tamalpa Running Club's All Men Midnight Chance Race. It also won him a bed in Ward 8.

Rather than listen to the protests of the nurses under her supervision about taking on a new admission in the middle of the morning, Adele took him.

"You're lucky, pal," Adele said, removing the rectal thermometer. "Your temp is almost up to ninety-five-point-six."

The muscular man closed his eyes, too tired and sick to speak.

"Is the heating blanket warm enough?"

A nod.

"I did the same thing about three years ago, so don't feel bad. I'll warn you, though—you'll never go on any runs after midnight again."

Another nod.

"You want me to shut up and let you sleep?"

Two nods.

Using his side table as a temporary desk, Adele filled in the vital signs flow sheet, then began her charting. The clean, unmarked sheet of paper called to her to make a small drawing in the corner—a landscape made by lines of numbers and descriptions of the patient's physical state.

She set her pen on the corner. "Just a small one," she said to the sleeping patient.

He half opened his eyes and nodded.

"You sure?"

The patient nodded again.

She was describing his lung sounds—fine rales in the bases, with decreased inspiratory breath sounds all fields—in the shape of rolling hills and a bright moon, when Tina appeared in the doorway.

"Dr. Lavine is on line three," she said, "He sounds like he needs a shrink."

Adele took the flow sheet and went out to the nurses' desk.

"Oops!" she said, picking up the phone. "I forgot to call you last night—I'm really sorry."

"Are you harboring some hostility for me, Adele?" Jeffrey asked.

"Not really, no . . . But, well, okay, maybe a little bit for not waiting for me to mature."

"Have you found out where Mathilde is?" he asked. He did not drop the ardently serious tone.

"Jeffrey, you're never going to believe this one."

"Is she dead?"

"I thought so, but now I'm not so sure."

He let out a sigh of relief. "That's positive at least."

"Well . . ."

"I detect uncertainty. Can you talk now?"

Adele looked down one hall where at least five call lights

were blinking, then she looked behind her where Abby, Cynthia, and Tina were all waiting to tell her something of dire importance. At the end of the hall behind them, Skip waved his arms over his head and whistled for help.

"Not really. The embittered crowds are battering down the doors right now. How about if I call you later?"

"That's what you said day before yesterday."

Tina stepped in front of her and mouthed dramatic, angry words without sound.

"I'll try extra hard," Adele said, turning her back on the unruly gang of angry children. "And if I don't talk to you today, definitely tomorrow."

"I'll call you after my one P.M. appointment," the psychiatrist said. "But verify one thing—she wasn't really amnesic, was she?"

"I'm afraid not—emphasis on the 'afraid.' "

He exhaled a sigh of disappointment and groaned. "I should have known."

"Don't feel too bad, Jeffrey, she fooled us all."

Adele hung up the phone and glared at the lot of them bearing down on her for support, direction, and soothing. If she'd had teats filled with the juices of human compassion and understanding, she would have offered them suck.

"Okay, children," she said, opening her arms, "I succumb to your needs. Lay it on me one at a time."

It was one of those modest Marin mansions nestled on the ridges of Mount Tam, overlooking a valley of redwoods. On the outside it was redwood shingle that had been weathered over the years of rain and sun, and gone from honey gold to brown to ash gray.

The housemaid ushered Adele into the foyer and asked her to follow her down a steep set of stairs and into the master bedroom, which took up the better part of the downstairs. In the beautiful four-poster, Vivian Vanderlise lay propped up by numerous large pillows. The old woman's skin was almost translucent where it stretched over the high cheekbones and under the rheumy blue eyes.

Overall, it seemed to Adele that she did not look well, but she did seem happier than when she had been at Ellis. Vivian patted the bed next to her.

"Take a load off, doll."

Adele sat down facing her, but Vivian indicated she needed to turn around and rest her back against the pillows so as to face the end of the bed.

"Take a gander at the view," Vivian clucked, her false teeth not quite keeping up. "I paid a lot for it, so you may as well enjoy it." With a bony arthritic finger, Vivian pointed over her shoulder.

Adele turned and gasped. The entire wall was a window overlooking a forest-covered ridge and hills that rolled on forever. To the left, the bay, the Golden Gate, and the skyline of San Francisco could be seen, while to the right, the peaks of Tamalpais were outlined in the twilight. Early evening fog was coming in at a sleepy pace over the ridge, making it appear that they were in some fantastic, futuristic dreamscape.

"No wonder you wanted to come home," Adele whispered.

"Yes, I love this room." Vivian's voice was dreamy. "I'll be perfectly content to die right here looking out at that."

"It's sort of like having one foot in heaven already," Adele said.

Vivian looked at her and smiled that crooked smile that was her trademark. "Why, that's exactly how I think of it."

The maid came in carrying a tray of crackers, cheeses, and fruit. "I'm having a highball, doll," Vivian said. "What's yours?"

Adele asked for tea and engaged in a short disagreement with Vivian who wanted her to "let her hair down" and have a martini. Vivian cut a slice of apple and nibbled at it, while Adele spread Brie on a water cracker.

"So I'm dying to know about this woman you're tracking," Vivian began. "Tell me all about it."

"I don't know very much about her. She came into the hospital amnesic from an accident in which a child died, and then she disappeared."

Vivian sat up patting her sternum. "Oh. I know. That woman on the boob tube . . . the missing person. I read about it in the *Chronicle*. She looked vaguely familiar—but I say that about all the milk carton kids and the post office most wanted posters too, so you can't trust my judgment."

"As it turns out, she might not have been amnesic at all," Adele continued, taking a bite of the cracker. "She disappeared as soon as she was discharged, and now we've got indications that she could have done some heinous things."

Vivian paused in her chewing. "Murder?"

Adele nodded. "Many, apparently."

"You don't seem sure," Vivian said.

Adele squeezed her lips together and wiped the corners of her mouth. "I took care of her. She didn't seem like the type to murder—she seemed more suited to the victim role."

Vivian startled her with a short, loud burst of laughter. "There is no type, doll. Everyone has an Achilles' heel. Everybody is capable of murder—people do it all the time. There are some people who kill and don't even think twice about it. I've met them in Hollywood and New York—rubbed shoulders with them—rubbed more than shoulders with some."

The maid came in with Adele's tea and set it on a butler's table by the bed. Adele sipped, holding it in her mouth before she swallowed.

"Is she affiliated with a group?" Vivian asked, sucking on the end of her stirrer.

"She used to work for the mob in Los Angeles, but apparently moved on and works on her own."

Vivian's invisible eyebrows lifted. "I know some of those guys. Maybe I could make a few calls."

"I doubt it would turn up much. No one knows much about her."

Vivian jerked herself upright with sudden enthusiasm. "Oh, come on, doll. I need something to keep me occupied. Dying is so goddamned boring."

Adele took another sip of tea and settled back into the pillows. "This is a woman who started out in L.A. as a specialty makeup woman and then went into stunts. She worked for the mob apparently—"

"Ellen Mack," Vivian said, holding up her lime wedge between two painted fingernails.

"Christ on a bike!" Adele jerked forward, astonished. "You *know* her?!"

"Yes, I think so. I saw this woman in action when the big guns at Stallion Studios decided they wanted to make a couple of reunion episodes of 'Moon Alley' before the cast started dying off. We'd already lost Freddie Burelle, and they figured we'd all go sooner than later, so they got one of the studios. It so happened that there were a couple of action movies being filmed on the lot, and during breaks I'd visit other sets.

"She was a splendid special effects makeup girl. She could make up a person to look completely different—men to women, women to men, white to black, black to Hispanic, cuts, bruises, broken noses—she could do it all."

Vivian took a sip of her drink. "She wasn't as good as a stunt gal as she was with the putty and glue, but she wasn't chopped liver either. I watched her do an action scene. She was like a fly, jumping and falling.

"When I heard she'd gotten in with the mob, it didn't surprise me at all. I never met her face to face, but I consider myself fairly intuitive. There seemed to be too much going on in secret behind her eyes. She wasn't a very warm person. As I remember, she was a loner."

"I've been told she can't be trapped," Adele said. "She's without a—"

"Achilles' heel?" Vivian finished for her.

"Exactly."

Together they looked out at San Francisco Bay—that sometime dark glass, sometime chest of jewels.

"Now," Adele said, settling in, "tell me every intimate detail you know about Cary Grant, Clark Gable, and Jimmy Stewart."

Walking to her car in the dark, Adele felt she was being watched. She whirled around in a circle, piercing every direction, including up in the branches of the trees, with her penlight. She checked inside the Beast, back and front, and, indulging her fantasies, opened the hood to make sure no wires had been tampered with, and tried the brakes for patency.

On the way home, she watched the rearview mirror, but saw nothing to confirm her suspicions. Taking the Tiburon entrance onto Highway 101, she scrutinized every car she passed or that passed her.

At once, everything seemed to be a threat—the car behind her, the one on her right, the walkways over the freeway—all potential places from which someone could aim and shoot.

When she turned onto Baltimore Avenue from the east end,

and her headlights caught Mrs. Coolidge squatting in the lantana bushes under her bay window, she was almost relieved.

"Anything I can help you with, Mrs. Coolidge?" Adele called as she stepped from the Beast.

Mrs. Coolidge straightened from her squat and waved. "I think I've found something you'll be interested in, Adele."

"A nice young man is buried under my lantana bushes?"

Mrs. Coolidge looked at her blankly. "There is?"

"What did you find to interest me, Mrs. Coolidge?"

Mrs. Coolidge crooked her finger, beckoning her to come closer, and handed her her flashlight.

Adele crouched down and peered through the lattice under the house. Three feet from the lattice, in a nest of her favorite scrub dress, which had been missing for weeks, was a gray tabby and five tiny kittens. An automatic coo escaped her throat followed by a groan. The place was turning into a menagerie. "As soon as I catch them I'll bring over a few, Mrs. Coolidge. You can start your own zoo with Queen Shredder reigning over them."

Inside the house, Nelson began to howl.

"This is sort of a minor point, Mrs. Coolidge, but what brought you to the wayward conclusion that you needed to look under my house?"

Mrs. Coolidge gulped some air. "Oh, well, I saw a workman over here earlier, and I thought that maybe you were having sewer problems, and I wanted to make sure that it wasn't a problem with the sewers backing up, because then I would have to be careful about an overflow at my house, because we all go into the same sewer main, you know, and . . ."

Adele stopped, house key poised. She turned her full attention to Mrs. Coolidge. "What workman?"

"Why, the sewer workman. I was cleaning up some of the doggie doodie on my lawn, and I noticed him over here working. He had one of those hard hats on, and I thought maybe—"

"Did you talk to him?" Adele stepped closer to her.

Mrs. Coolidge sensed the tall, gold-eyed woman's impatience and took a step back. "Well, yes—yes, I did. I like to keep track of what's going on in the neighborhood, you know, so I thought I'd ask what he was doing—to make sure there wasn't any hanky-panky business going on. He seemed like a nice, young—"

"What did he tell you?"

"That your sewer was backed up, and that he was going to check the ground for overflow."

"Was he driving a municipal water van or truck?"

Mrs. Coolidge grew flustered. "Well, let's see, I think he was . . . but . . ." She tittered. "Oh, you're making me so nervous, I can't think. He might have been driving a car, but I can't be sure. He said—"

"What did he look like?"

"He . . . looked like . . . a nice young man. It's nothing you should be worried—"

Adele gripped her hands together, to keep them from the woman's neck. "How tall, what color hair and eyes did he have?"

"He was as tall as you. He had on a hard hat. I don't know about his hair. And he wore sunglasses. He said his name was Don."

"How long did he stay and what did he do?"

"My goodness, Adele, what—"

"Tell me!" Adele was practically on top of the woman. "How long did he stay around my house and what did he do?"

"Well, I don't know how long he was here before I saw him, but he only stayed for a few minutes longer. He looked under your house and then he went around to the back. I didn't see what he did back there, because I—"

"That's fine, thank you, Mrs. Coolidge. Next time you see a stranger around my house when I'm not here, I'd appreciate it if you'd call the police. As a matter of fact, if you see anything suspicious going on over here, call the cops."

Maybe it was the way Mrs. Coolidge's eyes lit up that made Adele think twice about what she'd said. "Obviously you have to be prudent in your judgment of when to call . . ." Adele amended. "I mean, you shouldn't call if a UPS driver tries to deliver a package or anything like that."

"Oh, no no no." Mrs. Coolidge giggled, breathlessly. "Of course I wouldn't call for anything like that. How silly."

Adele gave the woman a last look and immediately regretted her directions. She sighed and let herself into the house, wondering if she had any whole milk or a stray can of cat food at the back of her pantry. If she was going to become a receiving center for the animal homeless, she needed to be prepared.

She was making broccoli-barley soup for her and Nelson's dinner when the phone rang the first time: her mother was frantic about Thanksgiving and cooking for a vegetarian dog and his friend.

The second time the phone rang, it was Cynthia calling from work with the news that her creative genius had been warned by the senior partners and the chart police to unleash his artistic talents at home or on the sides of buildings, but not at the hospital.

The third call came as she was crawling around under the house, leaving a bowl of milk and cat food mush for the mother cat. In her attempts to get to the phone, she scraped her back, banged her head, and almost broke her neck when she slipped on a patch of wet grass.

"Catch you at a bad time, doll?" Vivian's voice sound weak. "I can call back some other time."

"No, just hanging out under the house." She washed her hands and sat down to chop carrots for a salad. Nelson walked into the kitchen. Bugs, curled up like a kitten, dangled from his mouth. Gently, he placed the rabbit in her lap and licked off where he'd drooled on the animal's neck.

"How are you?" Adele asked. "You sound tired."

"Hell, I've been tired since I hit eighty. I've got some information for you. Your bird lives part-time in Germany. When she does her job, she arranges it so nothing can be traced to her. My friend of dubious affiliations said the big boys leave her alone, and she leaves them alone."

Adele waited until the woman finished coughing to ask, "No personal ties? Mother? Siblings?"

"The mother was murdered in her L.A. apartment some years back. It was a horrible story." Vivian shivered. "The woman had her face cut off while she was still alive. No part of it was ever found. She bled to death."

Adele grimaced. "Did they ever find out who did it?"

"Nobody was ever caught, although the cops thought it was part of a drug gang thing. The papers played out the story that she'd done a bad deal and withheld some money, and the drug lords had mutilated her to warn anyone else who might be thinking of cheating them." Vivian sighed. "No one ever really knew who did it."

Adele looked around at the three large windows over the sink and immediately got up and closed the blinds.

"There weren't any brothers or sisters that my friend knew of," continued Vivian. "I don't know about the father, but she got married at seventeen to a Hispanic boy who died within the year when an electric fan 'accidentally' fell into his bathtub."

The hairs on the back of Adele's neck did a little jig. She took the rabbit off her lap and went into the living room to lower the blinds in the bay window. "Thanks for the info," Adele said. "Is there anything I can do for you?"

"Let me beat you at Scrabble some afternoon." The woman laughed. "Come over for cocktails this week, why don't you?"

"Sounds wonderful to me. That room of yours is like an oasis. Can I bring anything? Bread, cheese, wine?" *A couple of kittens?*

The spoon had just made it to Adele's lips when the phone rang again. She picked it up and was about to say hello when she heard the whoosh of white noise that generally meant a long-distance call.

"Hello?" She waited.

There was a shuffling as if someone were taking a hand off of the mouthpiece. For a half a second, she heard background sounds like a crowd in a large open place. Then there was a click and, then, the dial tone.

Four seconds later, the phone rang again.

"Don't hang up!" she said.

"I wasn't going to," Tim said. "What kind of a hello is that?"

"Oh, nothing. I thought you might be my aunt Ruth; she always hangs up if you don't answer halfway through the first ring. What's going on?"

"We think Jane Doe went to Miami," Tim said. "I've notified Miami PD, the sheriff's office, and Miami FBI. They're going to work together to hook her up."

Adele licked her lips, which had gone dry. "How do you know she went to Miami?"

"The notation on the paper you found in her room? It correlates with a flight time out of Oakland to Miami. A flight attendant on American recognized Jane Doe as one of the first-class passengers."

"Thank God," Adele breathed.

"What?"

"Mrs. Coolidge said there was somebody from the sewer department at my house looking around today. I called Muni water and sewer, PG and E, cable—none of them sent anybody to this address."

Tim took a deep breath. "I don't like this, Adele. Why don't I come spend the night? I'll sleep in the living room."

"Get serious, but thanks for the offer. I can protect myself."

"Well, what about dinner? At least let me—"

"I'm having dinner as we speak. I'd invite you over, but I've got things to do."

"Like what?"

She thought about telling him about the nurses' march on San Francisco meeting and decided not. "Tim. I've got a mother. I don't need another one."

"Just tell me this: are you sleuthing?"

"Timothy . . ." She drew his name out in a teasing, warning tone.

"Okay, okay."

"What about the blood from the storage room floor?"

"Reuters's."

"What about the towel? What was all the stuff—the paint and the hair?"

"Lab said it was theater makeup. High quality. She probably used the kapok to pad the clothes she used in her various disguises."

Both of them were silent for a minute.

"It's her, Adele. I know you don't want it to be."

She sank wearily to the couch. "Okay. So it's her. Now what?"

"Now, sport, we wait."

The wait was not long. Forty-one minutes later the phone rang again. She answered on the third ring, heard the long-distance echo, and said hello twice. Again, there was nothing except the whooshy white noise. When she heard the hand uncovering the mouthpiece, she spoke quickly.

"Mathilde? Don't hang up. I'm not tapped, I promise. Talk to me. I want to know you're okay."

"Be careful." The low, husky voice was shaking. "Be very careful. You have something of m—"

What came next, Adele played over a hundred time in her head. The gasp, the noise of confusion, and the click of the broken connection.

"She called," Adele said in a steady voice. She didn't want to give away the relief she felt.

"When?" Tim stopped in the middle of his living room holding a dusty piece of underwear.

"Five minutes ago." Adele took a deep breath. "I was walking out the door. I thought it was you calling back."

"Okay," he said, stuffing the underwear into the jumbo black plastic bag that held about twenty-five pounds of trash and dirty laundry. "What did she say?"

"She told me to be careful and that I have something, and then she hung up, or the phone was disconnected. It sounded more like the phone was disconnected."

"Do you have your gun?"

"In the back of my jeans."

"I'm bringing you my Walther. I want you to borrow it. Where are you?"

"I don't want your Walther, Timothy. I know the Colt backwards and forwards. I don't know the Walther."

"I'll introduce you. It's a semiautomatic. The Colt is a single shot. You can't—"

"I'm in the Beast on my way to a meeting," she said. "I'll be okay, so chill out."

"Did you check to make sure nobody's following you?"

Despite the urge not to, Adele looked in her rear- and side-view mirrors. "No. I'm the only one on the road and—"

"What road?"

She waited a second. "The Corte Madera–Mill Valley Hill."

"I'm three minutes away from the Mill Valley side. Why don't I—"

"No, Timothy."

"Goddamn it, Adele!" he exploded. "Are you *trying* to get yourself killed? What is that going to prove? That you've got bigger balls than the rest of the guys?"

"Well, Timothy, if I *do* get myself killed, I'm sure David Takamoto will be glad to tell you whether or not I did have larger balls than any of the boys in blue. Make sure you tell David that you want to—"

In the rearview mirror, a flash of headlights drew her attention. Her heart began to pound. There wasn't so much as a fringe of road to pull off on. She pressed the gas pedal.

". . . see Monsarrat's world-famous balls. I've got to go now; the battery on my cell phone is getting weak. I'll talk to you—"

The headlights flashed again—much closer. Adele estimated the car to be traveling at double her speed. Considering the profusion of sharp curves, anyone traveling that fast definitely had a purpose for doing so—like life, death, or a teenager trying to impress his friends.

"Adele!"

She looked at the phone, forgetting for the moment who she'd been talking to. Then she remembered, and hit the end button. Checking her seat belt, she patted the Beast's chest and floored it.

At 3 A.M. her phone rang, startling all three of the bed's occupants.

The dog raised its head, the rabbit's ears twitched. The human flew straight up then out of bed, Colt in hand. Her back pressed against the wall, she aimed at the door, then the windows, and finally the closet.

The phone rang again.

Sagging in at the middle, Adele let the gun drop to her side and wearily picked up the phone. "Who is this?" she said, her voice rough with sleep.

"Adele!" Tim whispered. "They got her."

"Who got who?"

"The FBI picked up Jane Doe at Miami International. She was waiting to board a flight for San Francisco—no disguise, nothing. It's like she *wanted* to be caught. Hell, she still wore the damn bandages on her hands—didn't even try to run. It was like taking candy from a dentist. She's being held on a California no-bail warrant for multiple one eighty-sevens at Miami county jail."

Adele dropped to the bed, daubing at the sleep drool still wet on her chin.

"Adele, you awake?"

"I don't get it," she groaned. "Why would she let herself be caught now?"

"Maybe she was tired of running. These people live stressful lives."

Adel shook her head. "Yeah, except psychopaths don't get tired of the game, and they don't really have a lot of stress."

"This one did," Tim said. "We'll find out more when they bring her back. I've sent Pete to get her. They're scheduled in SFO around one in the afternoon. When are you working?"

Adele yawned. "Tomorrow. I mean, today. Another administration day. I have to go on from seven to nine for a budget meeting, and then go back at three and work until nine."

"How about if I bring lunch over to your place around noon?"

She fell back on the bed. "Sure."

"Don't take it so hard, Adele," he said. "She needs to be taken out of the game. This woman killed a couple of kids. I mean—"

A sound—he refused to believe it was coming from that delicate creature he found so alluring—vibrated the earpiece of his phone in the slow, rhythmic breathing pattern of sleep.

The budget meeting was more infuriating than anything else. In management double-talk, the administrator outlined for the group of nurse-managers the new policies that needed to be implemented throughout the hospital. He suggested introducing the money-sparing but patient-unfriendly tactics "gently" to the staff.

Those present were reminded that the business concerns of Ellis Hospital were always to come before the safety and welfare of the patient.

Adele was grateful that she'd brought her minicorder, so as to catch the whole thing on tape. As soon as she had a chance, she was going to run it by Jimmy Olson, dba Joe Rickey, at the *Pacific Intelligencer*.

* * *

She was working in the window seat. A stack of completed EVERY PATIENT DESERVES AN R.N. signs lay to one side of the seat, the blank ones to the other. The white Camry pulled up and parked behind the Beast.

Getting out of the car, Tim waved, held up two white packages in each hand, and mouthed the word "Lunch?"

She waved him in, watching as he strode up the walk and onto the porch. It hit her, as it sometimes did—the masculinity of him, his frame, the way he walked, the sight of his eyes—that she was more in love with him than she realized. Her breath caught in her throat, and as he opened the front door, she forced herself to breathe. He was only a man, after all . . .

She savored the last bite of her all-time favorite sandwich: a veggie with provolone on a sourdough roll, extra mayo and onions, but hold the mustard and pickles.

Tim was still working on his first half, his tie flung over his shoulder. He looked over at her, and abruptly stopped chewing.

"Jesus Christ!" he said, eyes wide in shocked disbelief. "Where's the rest of your sandwich?"

She shook her head, the sides of her mouth fighting back the grin.

"Where the hell did it go? You didn't eat that whole thing . . ." He paused and looked around. "*Did* you?"

Caught between embarrassment and amusement, Adele smiled and nodded. "Yes, I did."

"Christ, if I'd know you were *that* hungry, I'd have brought you two of them and a few pounds of potato salad." He pushed the untouched half of his sandwich toward her. "Here, go for it." He jerked his hand away quickly. "Let me get my fingers out of the way first. The human vacuum cleaner has jaws."

Adele eyed the sandwich half and shook her head. "No, that's okay—I'm stuffed," she lied. She could have easily eaten two more of the sixteen-ounce sandwiches. Midcycle Madness was upon her—that time of month when her hormones diddled her appetite into believing it belonged to Forty-niner Kevin Greene. If Tim knew the amount of sugars, salt, carbohydrates, and starches she could put away during those five or six days, she was sure he'd hit the sidewalk running and never look back.

Adele looked at her watch. "I've got a few more signs to

make and then I've got to get ready for work, and run to Mill Valley to see a locksmith about a key. I'll meet you at your office in an hour."

Adele got up and brought their plates to the sink. She looked out at the azalea bushes that had grown over the narrow path along the side of her house. "I still can't believe it's Mathilde."

The motto on the last sign read NURSES ARE THE PATIENT'S ONLY ADVOCATES!!! She stared out the window, thinking of an appropriate picture she could sketch under the words, when a Hummer came around the far corner of the street, jerked, backfired, jerked, bucked again, and stalled in front of the church next door.

She could hear the labored whine of the starter as the driver tried two, three times to get it going again. On the fourth try, the car belched out a plume of blue smoke, lurched forward with such violence that it caused the driver's head to jerk forward and hit the steering wheel, and knocked off his sunglasses. It stalled again.

She could see the driver's mouth as it formed one syllable words while his hand hit the steering wheel. There were several more attempts at starting the mechanical offspring of a Loomis armored truck and a rhinoceros, but to no avail.

A minute later, a young man of perhaps thirty emerged, kicked the side of the car and checked out his surroundings. When he saw her, he made the universal sigh for phone. She nodded and pointed to the front door.

"Sorry," he said, smiling sheepishly as he stepped onto the porch. "I've got triple-A. May I use your phone?"

She opened the door. He passed into the house, saying something she couldn't quite hear about having the "damned thing serviced," when the bottom of her world fell out.

SEVENTEEN

HE MOVED FASTER THAN ANY HUMAN SHE'D EVER
seen. In a movement so quick she couldn't comprehend what
had happened until it was over, the young man hit her in the
small of her back with both hands clenched together in one big
fist. The impact sent her tumbling back over one of the signs,
feet going over her head. On her way to the floor, he relieved her
of her Colt.

"You're stupid," the young man said in Mathilde's voice as
he—she put on a pair of kid gloves.

Adele put her hands under her and tried pushing herself up.
The boot crushed down on the back of her head, smashing her
face into the hardwood floor. When she came to, she was
choking. Blood from her broken nose dripped down the back of
her throat, making it difficult to breathe.

The sound of growling forced her to open her eyes. In the
kitchen, she could see a portion of Nelson's face—teeth bared,
ears back. He was almost unrecognizable, as though some Eocene
ancestor had taken over his body.

Seeing Her hurt, smelling Her blood, Nelson was, in fact,
filled with impulses as savage as the coyote or the wolf. His
bark turned ferocious. Mixed with guttural noises, it was a
sound Adele had never heard from him before.

A vise grip around the back of her neck lifted her to her feet,
let go, and wrenched her arm behind her. Like a hot knife
through her shoulder, the pain was so great she fought to keep
from losing consciousness again.

"Lock him up, or I'll make you kill him," Mathilde said.

Gasping, Adele touched the dog's raised hackles with a shaking hand, then retched. Blood from her nose and throat spattered

over the floor and carpet. "Bedroom," she said in a strangled whisper. "Lock in there."

The pressure on her arm let up, and a wave of nausea *went* over her. Taking Nelson by the scruff, she stumbled to the bedroom, but the dog could not be made to leave her side.

Mathilde reached around Adele to push him, and the dog lunged at her arm, his teeth bared. Mathilde jumped back and raised the gun.

Adele's panic went beyond her pain. "No!" she screamed. "Don't hurt him! Please!"

The gun floated in Adele's vision, suspended for an eternity, then fell to where it had been—aimed at her heart. Somewhere in the midst of the confusion and the pain, Adele sensed the woman's reluctance to hurt the dog. Out of the jumble of gray matter came a fact from psych training: there were people who would think nothing of strangling a newborn, but could not bear to cause an animal a moment's discomfort. Summoning her voice, she commanded Nelson into the room.

"Who are you?" Adele whispered as she was pushed back to the kitchen.

"You don't know me," said the voice behind her ear. "Give me the key."

"What key?"

The woman jammed the muzzle of her gun tight against Adele's temple and brought her face so close to hers, they were almost touching. Only that close could Adele see the barely visible line between where the skin stopped and the flesh-colored latex began at the hairline.

"Don't play games or you'll wish you were dead sooner than you're going to be. I want the key—where is it?"

The muzzle shoved harder into her temple, making her sick again. "Fanny pack," Adele said quickly.

"Get it!"

Adele was half pushed, half carried forward, the gun digging into her head. Unable to look down, she unzipped the pack by feel, and found the plastic Baggie with the three keys.

Mathilde shook the key out onto the floor, pushed them around with her toe, and suddenly let go of Adele.

Adele staggered backward two or three steps, tripped over one of the signs again, and fell, banging her head on the floor.

There was a fleeting thought about how the signs had proved more deadly than her gun, followed by a faraway but distinct sound.

It was a sound no one would have recognized unless they lived with Nelson. In the past she would have punished him for it. Now, it was the most beautiful noise in the world—that of a ninety-pound dog jumping through the screen of the bedroom window.

Tim turned up the radio and rapped out the rhythm of "Run-around Sue" on the steering wheel of the Camry. Songs of the sixties and seventies. He shook his head. They sure didn't make sounds like that anymore.

He sipped his double espresso from Rulli's and checked the clock tower outside Ellis Hospital: 12:29. He looked at his car clock: 12:26. Still singing along, he reset the time. He'd turned onto Sir Francis Drake Boulevard from Bon Air Road when his phone went off.

"Erin Middleton has arrived," said Peter Chernin. "She's scared."

"Oh dear, my heart is breaking," Tim snorted sarcastically. "She's killed babies for money, Chernin, so don't get too dewy-eyed over her."

"She says it isn't her we're after, Tim. She keeps saying that she was trying to save the kid in the car. That she'd taken the kid from her sister."

"And I've got a golden bridge I want to sell you, detective. Get real. The woman is a killer. What's with you? You're usually brutal. What, she get to you on the plane or something? You've been watching too many women's prison movies, bud."

Peter Chernin hesitated. "The sister is her identical twin. Her story matched exactly what your informant told you last night, except the junkie mother had twins—split them up at birth. Kept her sister, and sold the one we have—Erin—to a couple in Maine by the name of Middleton."

"I don't believe I'm hearing this. You going soft on me, Chernin? Listen, stay away from her until I get there. That's an order."

"Three positive IDs came in from Freeport, Maine, this morning," the detective continued. "A teacher, a church pastor, and a Freeport PD sergeant. She's an aerobics instructor up there.

"She's been gone for a week. Wouldn't tell anyone where she was going." Detective Chernin stopped to take a breath. "I believe them, Tim."

Tim took his foot off the gas pedal, a bad feeling starting in the pit of his stomach. He reached for the bottle of Mylanta II in his glove compartment. "Yeah, sure you do, Pete. I think you need to go look at the evidence. Make sure to pay special attention to the Deveraux kid's postmortem photos. See you in fifteen."

"Put your hands behind your back," Mathilde said. Her knee was in the small of Adele's back; a gloved hand was clamped over her mouth.

The cold steel of handcuffs cut into her wrists.

"You scream, and I'll smash your head in. Now stand up."

Adele stood, wobbling awkwardly. She was facing the bay window. The sign she'd been making had fallen so the slogan side faced the street. It would have been funny, had she not been sure she was going to die.

Her brain was scrambling around like a chicken on ice skates, thinking of a way to stall, at the same time trying to prepare for her death. All she could think of was how much she would miss Nelson, her mother, Tim, and Cynthia. Except she wouldn't miss them at all—Adele looked into the ice cold steel gray eyes staring into hers—she'd be dead.

"You must not have understood me," Mathilde said evenly. "I want the key you took out of my boot heel."

Beyond Mathilde's left ear, she watched Nelson bound onto Mrs. Coolidge's front porch, throwing himself against her screen door, barking like a wild beast. Mentally Adele thanked her landlord for the Duopane glass in all the windows. You couldn't hear a bulldozer through them, if it'd been on the front lawn.

"I don't—"

Stars—black ones on an all-white background—blotted out her vision as the butt of the gun smashed into her jaw. While she spun around in a full circle, she felt her temporal mandibular joint pop twice, as she sank to her knees then hit the floor again.

Losing consciousness, she wondered if she would feel the initial force of the bullet as it entered her heart.

Over the years, listening to the police radio had become an involuntary awareness. Like breathing was an involuntary reflex. Without having to think, the voice of the dispatcher coming across with a suspicious circumstance report wafted in and out of his mind like so much Muzak.

And, like Muzak, when a tune played that he particularly liked, Tim's mind shook him to attention so he could sing along. His mind was shaking him now, as he waited for the light to turn.

He heard the address where a suspicious circumstance was in progress. It was an address he knew.

He grabbed his mike and did a sharp U-turn at the same time. "Larkspur PD dispatch, this is one K thirty-six. I'm ten sixty with an ETA of three. I'll handle the suspicious circ."

He fished around the back seat until his hand found what he needed. Sticking the blue flashing light on his roof, he went over another median strip.

"The resident at that address is a witness in an active case of mine," he continued. "Have your unit continue in for backup, code two."

Adele remained on her stomach, breathing in the dust off the floor. The pain in her shoulder, jaw, and nose had eased off, but the handcuffs had cut off the circulation to her hands, and that bothered her more than anything.

Kitch Heslin sat in the back of her mind shaking his head, disgusted. *She was right,* he said. *You're stupid. You have something that belongs to a psycho killer, known far and wide as the Invisible Chameleon, who has killed—in your own words—"lots of people" and never been caught—and you hear she's been apprehended somewhere over the rainbow, so you think you're safe and open the door for a total stranger who stalls conveniently in front of your house?*

"Okay, okay, so she's right," Adele whispered to the floor. "I'm stupid. Gloat about it after I'm dead."

Kitch rocked once and held up a finger. *Use your available means—the brain and what you have left of the body.*

Her mind worked through the fog on two tracks: the physical—

call up Gavin's combat training—and the mental—her nurse's training in psych on how to deal with psychopaths.

The noise of the medicine chest being ravaged had not been particularly comforting as she came to. If this woman was as good as the snitch said she was, she would eventually find the key. Even now, she could hear her unscrewing tops of things in the refrigerator, and ripping open packages from the freezer. Out of the corner of her eye, she could see that the wall thermostat was hanging by the wires.

Whatever the key was to, Adele figured, it must be important.

Footsteps approached. Ice cold water was dumped over her head followed by the vise grip on her neck jerking her to her feet again. The shock of the water had brought her out of the lingering fog back to reality

"So this is the famous nurse Adele," Mathilde said, without a change in expression.

"Mathilde—?"

"Shut up! You've taken my key, and I want it. If you want to play games, I can promise I'll take out every person close to you. Your mother first, then the shrink, then the cop, then the nurse friend. I can do them all in one day—probably all within four hours. Want to test me? I enjoy challenges."

Adele shook her head. "I gave it to the cops. It's in evidence."

Mathilde gave her a look that made her shudder inside. Pursing her lips, she shook her head.

It was the second in which Adele knew she had to take the gamble.

Tim parked the car on Holcomb Avenue and walked around the corner to Baltimore. Through the bushes that separated the side yard of the church and Adele's house, he searched and listened for anything that seemed off. Other than the distant barking of a dog, there was nothing to indicate suspicious activity in progress.

Not taking any chances, Tim crouched and crawled below the bay window and then onto her porch. The blinds were closed on the door, but the high horizontal window that looked into the living room was parallel with his eyes. Straightening slowly, he looked inside.

*   *   *

Adele brought her knee up sharply between the woman's legs. From her ex-husband's combat training, she knew men were not the only ones who could be rendered useless by a sharp hit to the groin.

The natural reaction she expected—that of a woman bending over so that she could get in a nice solid head-butt or a knee to the nose—didn't happen. Instead, the woman had seen it coming, and raised herself on her toes enough so that the contact was nothing more than a mild bump.

When she raised up, Mathilde caught a brief glimpse of someone from the bay window. Quickly she pulled Adele to the floor, ripping open her blouse as they fell. Cupping one of Adele's exposed breasts, Mathilde straddled her, pressing her mouth hard against Adele's.

Before Adele could yell out, Mathilde took her tongue and bottom lip between her teeth, cutting into them so that she could not move.

Tim stumbled off the porch, not feeling the floorboards or the sidewalk. His heart was pounding so much that his whole body shook. It was like being hit in the gut with a two-by-four.

Slowly, the anguish filtered up to his chest so that he found himself out of breath. He could barely keep his feet going to the car, one foot in front of the other.

Fuck! Fuck! How could this happen? I thought I knew her. I thought we were so close to . . .

He stopped, unable to remember where the car was parked. He saw it halfway down Holcomb.

Where the fuck did this guy come from? What a fool to think I could ever have interested her. Of course it would have to be the shrink—that Jeffrey. Why the fuck didn't I see it coming?

The fucking jerk could never give her what I can. He comes waltzing out of her past and bingo, she's fucking him in broad daylight on her living room floor ten minutes after I leave the house?

Tim got in his car and immediately pulled around the corner onto Baltimore. He'd check for cars he didn't recognize. Look for out of state plates or . . .

The Hummer parked at a slight angle to the curb in front of

the church caught his attention immediately. The rental plate gave it away as the car that belonged to the jerk she was fucking.

He stepped on the gas, and squealed onto Magnolia Avenue. His mind was ablaze with confusion. In the distance of a block, his detective's intuition—that same sense that got him to where he was—kicked in.

At William Street, one block away, the Camry made the corner with a half inch to spare the redwood that divided the street in two. The Toyota people would not have believed the vehicle could have made such a maneuver at that rate of speed.

"The games have to stop now, nurse," Mathilde said calmly. Coldly. "Where is my key?"

Adele was a survivor. She lived by her wits. That's why what came out of her mouth next surprised her as much as it did Mathilde.

"It is was up your ass, you'd know," Adele said, then she relaxed, waiting to receive the blow—or the bullet. The damage, she'd decided, would be less if she let her muscles go slack.

Mathilde did not strike her. Instead, she studied Adele, her eyes telegraphing an incredible concentration. The gun pressed into the notch of her throat as she was pushed against the front door. The blinds crumpled noisily under her weight.

"What is it?" the woman asked. "What do you want?"

"I want to know who you are."

"That doesn't matter."

"Yes it does—to me."

"We haven't met," the woman said finally.

"But—" Her eye caught the movement on the side porch. A familiar beige raincoat. Her heart caught for a beat.

"My twin," the woman said, "The best trackers in the world can't find me, and Goody Two-shoes shows up out of nowhere. Thinks she's going to 'save' me by making me give up my day job."

She took a few steps back away from the bay windows and pulled Adele into the kitchen. "Erin has done nothing more than provide me with a perfect fall guy. It'll cool things off for a long time. I'll give her your regards when I see her next."

Tim came into her line of sight. He was holding the .380 Walther close to his chest. The side door opened an inch.

Adele didn't know if she could keep the woman talking. She was getting impatient—getting ready to kill her.

"How did you know she wouldn't give you away?"

"She's stupid and soft. She thinks we're going to be the next Walton family."

"What about Reuters? Why did you—"

"He had the erroneous notion he could blackmail me."

Mathilde was getting bored. Adele could tell by the way her eyes got colder. Tim had one shoulder through the side door, pushing himself against the washer and dryer an inch at a time.

Adele spoke urgently to distract her. "One more thing . . . please."

Mathilde's eyes narrowed almost imperceptibly. The pupils opened. On some level, Adele thought, she was aware of something—the way an animal had instincts about invisible dangers.

"You were at the hotel. The manager said she wrapped your hands at night and that there were terrible burns . . . I don't understand . . ."

Mathilde straightened, pressing the gun into her sternum. She was getting ready to kill her. This was the style.

"Detail is what convinces district attorneys and gets people convicted. I made up my hands to look burned. On sight even a surgeon couldn't have told the difference—it was a perfect connection between the murders and my sister."

"You mean you'll . . ."

From across the room, Tim leveled his gun at the woman's head.

"Enough of this shit," she said. "Where's the key?"

The words were barely out of the woman's mouth when the muscles of her arm contracted just enough. At that instant, Adele realized she had seen Tim in the glass of the dish cupboards. She pushed the muzzle back into her sternal notch so hard, Adele blanched.

"Put the gun on the table, or I'll kill her," the woman said in the same way she might have said, "Lovely day today."

"You shoot me, Mr. Cop, and she dies. Slide the gun across the table, and put your hands over your head."

Tim put the gun on the table where they had eaten Safeway

sandwiches less than an hour ago and slid it across. Adele could see the grip of the gun hanging off the edge.

Tim slowly put his hands over his head.

Without letting up on the pressure on the gun, the woman turned Adele around, took Tim's gun from the table, and pushed her next to him. Then she ordered Tim to face the wall.

"Perfect." The muzzle of the gun moved from Adele's throat to the back of Tim's head.

At the first touch of the barrel, his body was already tightening for a quick move. He could bring his arm up sharply, drop straight down, rotate and grab for her gun wrist, but as quickly as he readied himself for it, he stopped.

It was too risky. There were too many things to interfere; this was a pro, she'd be ready for it and would probably try to shoot him from above. And there was Adele to consider. He didn't want to do anything to get her hurt.

"Tell me where the key is or I kill him."

Adele looked into the eyes of a killer, and knew the woman wasn't bluffing.

"It's in the drain of the bathtub," Adele said. "Hanging by plastic thread from the drain cover."

The woman shoved Tim forward, the gun still held to his head.

"Let's make sure," she said. "If it's not there, he's a dead man."

Deena Mae Coolidge looked nervously out her kitchen window, wondering where the police were. She wanted them to take the dog away with them when they went. She was sure the animal was sick.

She had managed to get him to stop barking and hurling himself against her back door, but he would not stop pacing nervously around the door, whining. He'd refused to touch the marble-sized balls of ground sirloin she'd put in front of him, snarling when she held it to his nose.

The thought that the dog might be rabid (she doubted the woman ever took the poor thing to a vet) crossed her mind. Thank the Lord she'd locked Queen Shredder in the bathroom or God only knew what sort of mayhem would have taken place.

A blood-curdling yeowl, filled with all the horrors of hell, came from the next room. Queen Shredder was feeling left out and a bit indignant.

At the sound of the she-cat, Nelson's gastrointestinal tract shivered and bucked.

"Does doggie need to make doodie?" Mrs. Coolidge asked, fanning the air, pushing the noxious odor further around the kitchen.

Nelson sensed the woman's anxiety, and got more excited. He scratched at the door and gave a test yelp.

Mrs. Coolidge read it as "That was only a preview, lady. Keep me inside another second and your kitchen floor will never be the same."

"Doodie? Need to make doodie?"

Nelson yelped, barked, yelped again. *Helloooo? SOS!*

"Of course you do," Mrs. Coolidge said, fighting her way into her sweater. "Now what did I do with that umbrella?"

Nelson began to bark ferociously, and, knowing it had worked its magic on humans before, passed more gas.

Carefully, they all walked, one careful step at a time, back into the kitchen. Adele first, then Tim, the gun still held to his skull.

She and Tim had been arranged side by side for execution, when the kitchen side door crashed against the wall of the pantry, sending a shower of glass over the three of them.

A long howl, and the body of a dog flew through the air as though it had been shot from a cannon.

Nelson hit both Adele and the woman with the gun sideways, so that they fell into Tim.

The woman recovered instantly and with the agility of an athlete kicked Nelson away, swung the gun around, and leveled it at Tim's chest. In the fraction of a second that the trigger was squeezed, Adele spontaneously lunged for the gun.

The bullet struck her somewhere on the left side of her body and her white cotton blouse exploded in red polka dots. The searing fire of metal tearing through her flesh, blotted out any awareness of her knees being smashed backward.

Adele floated to the floor, seeing as she fell Tim's shirt tear, and then his chest open up like a red rose in a time-lapse film. A spatter of his blood fell on her lips, warm and salty.

She landed on top of him, her eyes seeking his face. His eyes, like those of all the dead people she'd ever seen, were partially opened but unseeing.

There was a stillness wherein she felt herself losing consciousness, trying to concentrate on the sounds around her. The woman was gone: that much she sensed. Outside, Nelson barked. There was a high, warbling scream, and a sudden squall of voices.

She moved her ear against the open hole in Tim's chest to listen for a heartbeat, but heard nothing except the whooshing sound in her head.

Through the white and blue spots taking over her vision, she searched for Nelson, could not find him, and gave herself over to the oncoming darkness.

EIGHTEEN

CYNTHIA POSITIONED THE PATIENT SO AS TO TAKE the pressure off her new hip. Mrs. Coolidge sucked in a breath. "For goodness' sake, be careful! You're so *rough*! I want that other nurse! Why can't I have that other nurse? He's so much nicer than the female nurses."

Cynthia tilted her head. "What other nurse?"

"You know—that nice young man." Mrs. Coolidge's eyes gleamed.

"You mean Skip?" a sickly smile crept slowly across the nurse's mouth. "You like him?"

"Oh yes. He's so . . ." Mrs. Coolidge sighed, bringing her hands together between her ample breasts. ". . . virile yet sweet."

The nurse burst out laughing. Never in his weird, sexually ambiguous, whiny life had Skip Muldinardo fit the description of virile. Maybe when he was a newborn he might have been considered sweet.

Perhaps if she told Skip that he had an adoring fan, she could dump Mrs. Coolidge on to him in exchange for one of his lighter patients. Mrs. Coolidge could fill Skip's fantasy of a surrogate mother, and he'd be the nice young man the old bag was desperately seeking. Both were whiners and nonstop talkers. The match was perfect.

Deena Mae Coolidge was driving her nuts with her constant yammer about the "terrible young man" who had pointed a gun at her and pushed her down into the street as he ran from Adele's house. That was only the lead-in to the long, drawn-out diatribe about how she lay in pain, hip smashed, in the cold wet gutter, screaming until the neighbors heard her over the barking of the dog. Cynthia thought it would drive her insane to have to hear it again.

"Let me go find Skip," she cooed. "We'll see what we can work out."

Cynthia found the nurse in 802B, standing on one foot, suctioning Tim Ritmann's endotracheal tube and reciting recent football scores. The detective had not regained consciousness since the shooting except for a brief few minutes in the Emergency Room, when his one and only question had been about whether or not Adele was alive.

"How's he doing?" Cynthia asked, lightly touching Skip's shoulder.

"Okay," Skip said. "He's not responsive, but everything else is stable. He's only got the one chest tube left. Niesman is going to try weaning him off the respirator pretty soon."

Cynthia nodded, recalling her own brush with death not all that long ago. Suspended in a limbo of unconsciousness for several days, she remembered how reluctant her psyche had been to wake up.

"You're a lucky man, Timothy." Cynthia kissed his forehead. "If Adele didn't have such great muscles in her upper arm, you'd be dead. Those biceps of hers slowed that bullet down big-time."

"How is Adele?" Skip pushed an extra breath of oxygen before hooking Tim back on the ventilator. "I haven't had time to stop in and say hello."

"She's healing—sort of." Cynthia bit her lip, a worry flitting around her stomach. Adele was okay physically, but emotionally she wasn't quite present and accounted for. Her spirit was hiding—or still too injured to get up and run. One thing for certain: if Tim didn't survive, Adele would blame herself. His death would leave a scar so deep, she'd never come out of it.

"Listen, Skip, who's your least favorite patient?"

"The angina in 812B. He's a pain in the ass."

"You mean Mr. Rendridge? He's cute."

"Cute?" Skip flipped his hand in a way that reminded Cynthia of the Castro district boys. "I can't stand him. He's one of those self-important stockbroker yuppies who thinks the world is his office. I haven't been able to pry him off of his cell phone. He's laying there clutching his chest, buying and selling stocks between the morphine doses."

"How about if I take him off your hands?"

Skip's eyebrows shot over the black rims of his Coke-bottle glasses. "Sure. What's the catch?"

"You get to take Mrs. Coolidge—she thinks you walk on water."

"Mrs. Coolidge?" Skip seemed surprised. "Why don't you want her? She's a nice old lady."

"Because all she does is talk about *you*. She thinks you're the sweetest, most understanding man in the world. Nothing anybody does for her compares with your superb care."

"Oh yeah?"

Skip's lopsided smile reminded her of a thirteen-year-old boy's after being told there were naked girls right around the corner.

"Want to switch?" she asked casually. "I'll help you out with Tim, too."

"Sure." Skip tossed the used suction catheter into the trash. "I'd love to take the old girl."

A *Harold and Maude* fantasy involving Skip and Mrs. Coolidge crossed her mind. It made her want to throw up.

The florist's shop that was Adele's room held almost as many people as flower arrangements, not to mention cards, which lay in two tall piles on her bedside table.

Against medical advice, Adele had moved from her bed to the chair by the window. To further fly in the face of her medical advisers, she'd listened to her own body instead of catering to what someone else thought best for her. Twenty-four hours after the surgery to repair her arm and nose, she'd begun exercising her lower body. The day she was discharged, she was planning on going for a one- or two-mile run and increasing that by a mile a day until she was up to eight or ten.

Vivian Vanderlise sat in a wheelchair, talking to Adele's mother, while Jeffrey and Dr. Dhery sat on the bed discussing the concept of art in medicine. Henry Williams perched on the arm of Adele's lounger, doing range of motion on her hand and wrist, while Mirek Dvorak took her blood pressure and pulse on her uninjured arm.

Grace Thompson, the head nurse of Ward 8, entered, did a double-take at the three-ring circus and frowned.

"Good God!" she bellowed in her proper British accent.

"What, may I ask, is going in here? Ward Eight allows only two visitors at a time, and . . ." She moved toward the nearest bank of vases—bachelor buttons, peonies, and gardenias—Adele's favorite flowers. ". . . no flowers or plants in the patient's room." She sneezed and backed away.

"Here," said Martha Monsarrat, handing the nurse a handkerchief. "Cover your mouth. My daughter and Ms. Vanderlise are in weakened conditions."

Grace glanced at the handsome, large-boned woman and then the offered linen hanky. "No, thank you," she said curtly, "However, I insist you take this *foliage* with you when you leave."

"The flowers stay, Grace," Adele interjected wearily, in a voice lower than her normal one. "There are no other patients in the room, and *I'm* not allergic to flowers."

The head nurse had opened her mouth to restate her objection when Jeffrey Lavine spoke. "You know there *was* a study done by, ah . . ." The psychiatrist paused to think, his chin in his hand.

"Jameson and Jameson?" Rymesteade Dhery spoke up.

"Yes, yes, that's right, by Jameson and Jameson, the famous psychologists, who proved that flowers and plants, ah . . ."

". . . absorb the damaging negative fragments in the air and replace them with healing ions," Dr. Dhery finished.

"Right." Jeffrey nodded in total agreement. "And that the patients whose rooms were filled with flowers and plants healed more quickly and got back to work sooner."

Cynthia, who'd caught the last portion of Dr. Lavine's speech, bent over to give Adele a kiss. "Not only that, but flowers and plants emit certain psychic vibes which cleanse the chakras and aural rings."

"Aural rings?" Jeffrey and Grace asked in unison.

"Oh yes," Cynthia said. "That's essential."

Henry nodded. "Boss lady? This girl here—she need all the essential 'gredients for healing she can get."

Grace closed her eyes and sighed in a very British, old-school way. "For God's sake, all right, but the visitors *must* go."

"You said two visitors were allowed," Adele protested.

The boss lady made a dramatic sweeping gesture with her

arm. "And what do you call this?" she said. "It looks like the morning crush at Victoria Station."

"Only two of these people are visitors," Adele argued. "Surely you can't call Dr. Lavine or Dr. Dhery visitors."

Grace sputtered. "Well, I . . ."

"Cynthia and Mirek are my nurses, and Henry is here to do range of motion. That leaves two visitors. My mother and Ms. Vanderlise. Which means that you'll have to leave, Grace."

A young girl dressed in the pink and white uniform of the candy striper knocked quietly. "Hi," she said shyly, her eyes targeting the only person in the crowd wearing a hospital gown. "Are you Adele Monsarrat?"

Adele nodded.

"I'm Nikki from the Volunteer's Pets for Patients program?" The girl winked at Cynthia. Cynthia winked back.

"It's time for your pet visit."

"My pet what? Ouch! Stop pinching!" Adele glared at Henry.

"The new hospital administration–approved program?" the young girl said. "You know, the pet-a-pet-for-health thing?"

"The pets," Mirek said to the room in general. "They come to see the patients and make them happy. They get well better."

"This is nonsense!" Grace's jowls did a little dance when she stamped her foot. "I will not allow some filthy fleabag to come into my ward. It's ludicrous. Animals carry diseases that could—"

"New treatment modality," Dr. Dhery said. "Latest discovery of . . . ah . . ."

"Them Jameson and Jameson brothers," finished Henry.

Nelson bounded into the room, dragging the volunteer by his leash. At the sight of his best two-legged friend, he dropped his Mickey rug and laid his head on her lap. Adele clutched him, hiding her face in his fur.

"This is outrageous!" raged Grace. "Who approved this? Who gave permission to . . . ?"

"Oh, shut up, doll!" Vivian piped up. "You sound like a Shakespearean lunatic with a broom handle stuck up her ass."

Before she stormed from the room, Grace looked from one face to the other, all of them—including the damned animal— grinning crazily like a modern-day version of the Merry Pranksters high on love and hallucinogenics.

* * *

Twelve days into December, Cynthia and Adele sat holding hands next to Timothy Ritmann's hospital bed. Adele never moved her eyes from his face. Tim slept the senseless sleep of the heavily sedated. She examined the area of his lip where the endotracheal tube had rubbed the flesh raw, and applied a daub of antibiotic ointment.

The ventilator had been removed, along with wound drains, chest tubes, oral airway, nasogastric tube, and one of his three IVs. The doctors assured her he would recover completely— well, almost completely. He would have to be careful. He would get pneumonia easily and be more prone to spontaneous pneumothoraxes.

That she expected. What she hadn't been prepared for was his sunken, hollow cheeks and the dark circles under his eyes. Not that she hadn't seen worse. Almost every night she dreamed of his chest opening like a rose, spewing rivers of blood. It robbed her of sleep and appetite, until she, too, wore the same haunted, emaciated look.

The day she was discharged from the hospital she talked Peter Chernin into selling her a Walther .380. As soon as she exercised the stiffness out of her arm, she planned on taking the gun to the firing range and working with it until she was as good on that as she was with the Colt.

Cynthia stared around the hospital room, which now looked suddenly bleak and cold. "I can't believe she pulled off such a major deception. It's almost inhuman."

"Deception is a professional killer's stock in trade," Adele said. Her voice was still an octave lower than usual. "It's what she counts on to keep her in business."

Adele reached over and took Tim's hand, massaging his fingers, doing range of motion on his wrist and elbow. "We probably aren't going to put everything together until we find her—if we ever do."

"And probably not even then," Cynthia interjected.

"Probably. Thank God Erin had the presence of mind to ignore her sister's orders to wait for her in that Miami hotel, or she'd be dead, too, and we'd never know what the hell happened."

The timing mechanism of the IV pump clicked. Adele took a

shaky breath and let it out. Cynthia slipped her arm around her friend's shoulders.

"Don't let's talk about it, Del. Why don't we go for a run or something? We can go up Shaver Grade to your church and hang out. I'll treat you to dinner at Pier Six and then we can go to my house and watch the video of the nurses' march again."

Adele's gaunt, bruised face unnerved her. No longer did the nurse broadcast that confident, don't-mess-with-me attitude. There was a torment beyond the gold eyes that Cynthia found unbearable to see.

"I could watch that tape a hundred times, ya know?" Cynthia said, speaking faster now. "I love the part where you're marching backward at the front of the line, all bruised up, yelling at them to hold their banners high? Remember, Del? And all those nurses dressed in uniform—like they were ready for battle?

"Your speech was the best, though. Where did you get that idea about health care being DOA without nurses, and the—"

Adele covered her face with her hands. Her body shook.

Cynthia stopped and stared at her best friend. Her throat ached. Taking her into her arms, Cynthia pressed her face into Adele's hair. "Adele? What can I do? I am so sorry this happened. I'd do anything to change it, but you're so far away, I can't reach you."

Unable to speak, Adele shook her head. She wanted to explain that it wasn't what had happened that scared her—it was what had almost happened. It was the fact that the killer was still out there, and that she would always have to watch her back. Never again would she enter a darkened room, or run on an isolated trail, without fear of a bullet smashing into her chest or head.

"I need to talk about it, Cyn," she said. "Otherwise I'll start to pretend it didn't really happen. The other night I woke up trying to remember the name of the horror movie I'd seen about the cop, the dog, and the nurse."

"All right, so talk about it. I don't know anything except the crumbs that Boxer Takamoto and Pete Chernin gave me." Cynthia gently pressed down a piece of tape that had peeled away from the bandage on Adele's arm. "Pete said that Erin and Ellen were born to a junkie who sold Erin to a childless couple from Maine. Ellen stayed with her mother."

Gingerly, Adele dabbed at her swollen nose and stared out the window. "Right. Ellen grew up in a living hell with a tripped-out sadistic addict, and Erin was raised like a normal kid—until her adoptive parents made the mistake of telling her she had a twin sister. After that, locating and reconnecting with Ellen became an obsession."

"Which she did, right?"

Adele nodded. "Ellen had created a name for herself in the film industry by the time she was twenty-one, so Erin found her in L.A. with minimal effort. However, the loving reconciliation that she was hoping for didn't quite come off. Ellen told her to get lost in no uncertain terms."

Adele got up and walked over to the window. She found a shaft of sun and turned her back to it, letting it warm her. "But hope springs eternal. Erin never lost faith that her sister would come around and they'd be reunited. She kept track of her as much as she could."

"Did Erin know what her sister was?" Cynthia asked. "The killing, I mean?"

"She says she did," Adele said, looking over her shoulder and back out at the sky. "I mean, when you add the known facts together—the abusive upbringing, a young husband accidentally killed in his own bathtub and then their mother mutilated and allowed to bleed to death—and add that to what she'd heard through rumor, it wasn't hard to draw a conclusion."

Abby McGowan came into the room carrying an armful of linens. Shocked at the change in Adele, the nurse stared until Cynthia cleared her throat.

"Hey," Abby said finally, looking away, "since you guys are just slumming, do you think you could put a fresh pull sheet under Mr. Ritmann for me? I've got a new admit coming up in four-point leather restraints, and I don't even have the bed ready for him yet."

Abby laid a fresh pull sheet and some clean pillowcases on the counter. "When are they going to let you come back to work?"

Adele took a pillowcase from the pile of clean linen. "Next week. They'll let me do charge with a light patient load for a couple of weeks, then it's back to the grind."

Abby patted her back, not daring to let her gaze wander to the once pretty face, now disfigured by a purple, swollen nose and blackened eyes. "We miss you. It'll be good to have you back before Skip and I kill each other."

Adele squeezed the nurse's arm in thanks. For the next few minutes, she and Cynthia removed the pillows from the bed, arranged cornstarch powder, a couple of warm moist washcloths, and the new linen. With Cynthia on one side of the bed, Adele on the other, they rolled the detective toward Cynthia, while Adele used the washcloth to wipe down his back and buttocks.

"Tell me the rest." Cynthia worked the knot on Tim's gown, her thumb knuckles cracking.

"Erin says she went partly on a twin's inner connection and partly on information she paid for in order to find her twin at the San Anselmo Hotel. How she really found her . . ." Adele shrugged. "Who knows?"

The man's muscular legs and buttocks were thinner, but the shape of his body was still amazingly well preserved. Adele rinsed out the washcloth with one hand and handed it to Cynthia to clean under his arms and his genitals.

"I'll bet Ellen wanted to kill her on the spot," Cynthia said.

"Probably." Adele nodded, smoothing down the clean pull sheet. "But she probably figured a clone could be useful, so she had Erin stay put at the hotel, keep a low profile, and went ahead with her plans. She must have flown into San Diego, rented a car in Escondido, driven to L.A., and persuaded Mrs. Deveraux into taking the kids and going with her."

"But why Mrs. Deveraux?"

"She knew too much—at least as much as what earned the rest of the victims a bullet."

Cynthia removed the soiled gown and placed a fresh one over him. "Ellen must have told the woman her husband was in trouble or something in order to get her to take the kids and go."

"Probably." Adele nodded. "But of course, instead of going to him, they went to their graves. The other child she used to bribe Deveraux into giving her whatever evidence he had that he was using to blackmail Yates." She shook cornstarch powder over Tim's back and spread it around. The warmth of his muscles seeped through her fingers and into her arm.

Cynthia watched for a minute. "But after she got what she

wanted and killed Mr. Deveraux, why didn't she kill the kid then? You think she had a moment of conscience?"

"I guarantee you it wasn't conscience. It might have been a way to keep Erin occupied until she was done with the job." She shook her head. "I don't know, Cyn, but I'm sure there was a good reason for it, because she went out of her way to keep the kid—the whole thing with staying out at Steep Ravine instead of the hotel."

"Then Erin took the kid because . . . ?"

"Because she realized Ellen was probably going to kill her." Adele rolled Tim carefully over the bump of linen, so that he now faced her. She studied him, letting her finger slide lightly over his lips and jaw. "Erin might have been obsessed with her sister, but not enough to allow an innocent child to be murdered. She says she put a couple of sleeping pills in Ellen's food, waited until she fell asleep, and ran. On her way out she grabbed the first pair of shoes she touched, which unfortunately turned out to be Ellen's boots."

"The ones with the key in the heel?"

Adele nodded, folding pillows behind Tim's back and hips. Together they arranged his legs and hips in a position of comfort, and covered him with a clean sheet. Taking a pocket comb from his bedside cabinet, Cynthia ran it through his hair.

"The accident threw a big hairy wrench into the plan," Adele said, washing her hands at the sink. "Erin doesn't remember any of it, and I suppose I believe her up to a point. She probably really did try to save the child, freaked out when she couldn't, and tried to run away.

"Faking amnesia seemed the best way to deal with everything. She sure as hell wasn't going to give away anything that might lead the cops to the only blood relative she had left."

"The ties that bind," Cynthia said. "Are stronger than the sense of justice."

Adele sat down at the foot of the bed and rested her feet on the edge of the bed extender that had been added to accommodate the detective's six-foot-four-inch frame. For a time she seemed lost in thought as she watched Cynthia finish grooming Tim's hair.

"I'll bet Ellen never went anywhere without a disguise after Erin's photo got plastered all over the papers and TV," Cynthia said finally. She opened her bottle of Calistoga water and waited for the fizz of carbonation to dissipate a little before she drank. "The twins must have been in communication while Erin was in the hospital."

"Oh yeah," Adele said not looking up from the floor. "The first thing Erin did when she was admitted to the ward was insist she not be disturbed at night, remember?"

Cynthia nodded. "That way she could call Ellen without fear of being caught?"

"You got it." Adele paused. "Remember the night of the popcorn fire when I found Erin on the stairwell?"

Cynthia rolled her eyes. "How can I forget?"

"She was headed back to the hotel to have a last go at talking Ellen out of killing any more people. Unfortunately for Alan Hightower, she was a little late."

"So, what role did Reuters play in this movie?"

"Being the ex-con he was, he put all the pieces together and thought he could make some money. I'm sure he recognized Erin's photo as someone he'd seen visiting Yates a few weeks before. He probably showed the picture around, found out she was the Chameleon, and figured that she was Yates's hired shooter, using the hospital as a cover.

"Problem with Reuters was that he was more greedy than he was bright." Adele bent forward to watch a gull pass by outside the hospital window. She held it in her sight as long as she could.

"The night he broke into Erin's room, he started out telling her that he wanted to help her out of the jam she was in. Erin, thinking Reuters might really be a friend of Ellen's, told him who she was and that Ellen was at the hotel. That's when I popped in and spoiled their little tête-à-tête.

"As soon as his testicles returned to the lower half of his body, Reuters must have hot-footed it over to the hotel."

"What an idiot," Cynthia said, testing one of Tim's shed hairs for strength. "Did he actually think he was going to get away with blackmailing the Chameleon?"

Adele attempted a smile. "Like I said, I don't think he was too long on brains. There's no telling what happened after he arrived at the hotel, but I'd guess that when Ellen told him to go fuck himself, Reuters got rough and pulled his knife on her—

thus the blood on the carpet that, without running subtyping tests, showed up to be Erin's type.

"After Ellen killed him, she made herself up to look like him and walked out, making sure the manager saw her leave.

"Pushing the hypothetical envelope, I'd guess that she then contacted Yates, who took the news about Reuters with some amount of distress, although he was probably more worried about Laurel Saches having a touch of conscience and talking to Tim.

"Knowing that Tim was on his tail, and that Saches was a weak link, Yates got scared, threw in more monetary incentive, and provided Ellen with the time Ms. Saches's ferry docked at the Ferry Building."

Adele spread her hand out over her bandaged arm and pressed slightly, as if she had a sudden pain there and wanted to ease it out.

"So she dressed up like Reuters to kill Laurel Saches."

"Yeah," Adele sighed. "Except she missed the mark. It probably irked her to no end."

"Anal-retentive," Cynthia said, blowing into the now half empty bottle of water. For some unknown reason, the sound made them both smile.

"Precision with detail is probably a more accurate description," Adele continued. "Especially when you look at the thought that went into setting up her twin. Encouraging Erin to do an hour of vigorous exercise before bed so she'd have low potassiums—corresponding perfectly to the dates the victims were murdered. Having the hotel manager bandage her fake wounds."

"Jesus," Cynthia breathed, picturing this. "So everybody would think Erin had sneaked out of the hospital at night and killed those people?"

"Right," Adele said, hugging her legs. "And just as hard as Ellen tried to indicate her sister, Erin tried to protect Ellen. That whole story about the man at the farmhouse, and then, when we showed her all the sketches, she pointed out the man with the glasses, knowing that Ellen never used the same disguise more than twice. Saying the man with the glasses and Reuters were the same person put even more of a spin on things."

"So that's what the whole thing with the flight to Miami was about?"

"Yeah. Ellen had her sister leave her things in the room at the hotel—I assume to make anyone who came looking for her think she was still there—and put her on a plane to Miami, where she was to wait in a hotel until she got there.

"Ellen purposely left a notation of the flight in room twenty-six, knowing that eventually someone would find it, trace the flight, and then track Erin down to the hotel where they would find her body and think the Chameleon had committed suicide."

"But why did Ellen hang around at all?" Cynthia asked. "It would seem to me she'd want to be gone ASAP."

"Housekeeping," Adele said. "She had to get rid of Reuters and his car and finish off Laurel Saches."

"And the boot?"

"That, too. She must have discovered the key was missing sometime after she disposed of Reuters, but before she went after Saches.

"Of course Erin told her that I was the one who'd found the boot at the accident site, and that I had a connection with the cops and did PI work from time to time. She probably thought I'd found the key and kept it." Adele stretched her back and stood. She walked to the head of Tim's bed and looked down at the man.

"What about Phillip Yates?"

Adele's mouth cracked in a queer smile. "Remember the pager I found out at the accident site?"

Cynthia nodded.

"The only calls received were traced to a cell phone registered to Leslie Normac. The clerk at the store who sold the phone gave a description then positively ID'd a photo—it was Yates. It was enough cause to get search warrants for everything connected to him: computer records, his house, all his files." Adele sighed with a shudder, as if she were shedding a heavy burden. "Nothing much has been turned up yet—at least not enough to nail him, but I take some pleasure in the thought that although he's still with us, I'm sure looming in the forefront of his worry center is the knowledge that there's a warrant for his arrest for conspiracy to commit murder just waiting for the right piece of evidence to be discovered."

"Where's Erin now?"

"At Jellyroll's apartment," Adele said. "The sheriff released her once they sorted out her involvement and deemed her an un-witting withholder."

Adele looked out the windows again. The sun was about to sink behind Mount Tam. Shreds of clouds showed lavender and purple against the orange sky. "I can't stand the fact I was taken in."

"Oh, come on, Del. Erin played the role to the hilt. I took care of her too—hysterics, tears, going on about how the kid could have been *her* child, and all that crap? Shit, she had everybody convinced she was the innocent victim—even Jeffrey believed her. She could've won the Oscar for that performance. I mean, who outside Hollywood would have come up with an identical evil twin story?"

Adele made a face indicating a tough call. "I never thought I'd say it, but thank God for Mrs. Coolidge and Nelson."

". . . and your big arms," Tim mumbled sleepily.

"Hey, you." Adele went to the side rail and leaned over, taking his hand.

"Yo Timothy." Cynthia rubbed his shoulder. "Talk to us, baby."

The man opened his eyes and stared first at Cynthia and then at Adele. "You look like hell," he said, focusing on Adele's bruised face.

"Oh yeah?" Adele put her hand on her hip. "Well, let me tell you, pal, your own reflection ain't all that pleasant either."

With his free hand, he reached out to touch the bruises on her face and nose. "You okay?" His tone turned soft.

"Yeah," she smiled. "How about you?"

He tried to take a deep breath, winced, and let the air fizzle out. "They tell me I'll live to eat more tofu."

"Good," Cynthia said, laughing. "Because Pete and Enrico bought you a gift certificate at Veggie Haven for ten free soy burgers."

"And you don't have to be afraid to go home," Adele said. "The four of us put our life savings together and talked a cleaning service into shoveling out your apartment. Even the landlord didn't recognize it when they were done."

"Yeah," said Cynthia. "He thought it looked so nice, he raised your rent."

Tim's smile faded, and he closed his eyes again. His hand

went to his chest, tentatively probing, investigating. "They didn't get her, did they?" he whispered.

Adele gripped his hand tighter. "No. No, they didn't."

"Yates?" he asked hopefully.

"Nothing—yet."

There was a silence for a minute or two while they stared at each other, just happy to be alive and in each other's presence.

"The key?" he asked. "What the hell was it to?"

Adele shook her head. The same question had eaten at her since the moment Ellen had pulled the thing out of her shower drain and pocketed it with a look of relief, even joy.

"I wish I knew," she said finally. "Whatever it was, it was important enough to kill for."

EPILOGUE

Zurich, Switzerland

AN ELEGANT, PRISTINE CITY: THE ONLY PLACE IN the world she felt completely comfortable. It was a vast relief to be away from the chaos and filth of the United States.

She crossed onto Paradeplatz from Bahnhofstrasse and headed toward the building with the glass front. The alpine wind rearranged her hair and gave motion to the lapel of her cashmere coat, so that it stroked her chin. The moment she passed through the brass doors, warm air penetrated her clothes and crept up the insides of her legs under her skirt.

What took Emil's attention as she came toward him across the circular marble lobby was the confidence that surrounded her like a second skin. She was set apart from other women by the odd exactness of her movements. Her bearing, her clothes, the makeup, her look—everything fitting together as in a precision timepiece. He studied her face. The light hair, cut so as not to detract from the wide gray eyes. Her lips, he remembered from before, had been unsmiling, full, and sensuous.

He invited her to sit down, first in German, and then in English. She slid into the chair across from him, and handed him her identification over the brass plaque: SAFETY DEPOSIT BOXES.

The fluid grace with which the man moved drew her notice to his hands, which were small but perfectly manicured. With curious detachment, she watched him in much the same manner as one might observe strangers in a park.

He studied the photo and compared it to her. "Very beautiful," he said, closing the passport. His smile was inviting, without being flirtatious.

Her eyebrow arched, and she held the blue eyes with hers only long enough to acknowledge the invitation.

Peter pushed the signature card across the polished wood of the desk and removed a gold Flèche pen from his jacket. When he handed it to her, the tips of their fingers touched.

He was aware of the intensity of her gaze as he verified her signature with the one on the permanent signature card. When he turned his eyes on her this time, he did not smile. This woman would never require him to smile.

A slight nod from him brought the guard to her side.

"I have an appointment with Monsieur Eber in thirty minutes to discuss my accounts." She held her hand out to him. He took it in his and gave it a polite shake. "Please tell him I am in the safety deposit vault and will be up to see him directly."

He made a slight bow. "Of course, Miss Conroy."

He watched her walk away, still feeling the cool of her hand.

There was something behind the eyes, he thought, something untouched.

Behind the guard, she twisted the flat silver key over and over in her hand. She had gone to some trouble to reclaim the key, not because of the minor nuisance of having the lock drilled out and replaced, but because it was hers and someone had taken it from her. No one took anything away from her anymore.

The cold of the steel vault prompted her to pull her coat tight around her. The guard—a gray, stern man—searched for the box, muttering to himself. After a moment he raised his pass key and fit it into one of the two locks on the front of the compartment.

He held out his hand for her key.

Ignoring his outstretched hand, she reached past him and fit the key into the second lock. The thick door swung open. She pulled out the wide metal box, gripping it close to her chest as she followed the guard to a private cubicle the size of a small closet.

When the guard's footsteps faded, she locked the door and switched off the light. With the box still clasped to her chest, she got down on the floor and crawled under the small counter where she was engulfed by silence and total darkness. Several minutes passed before she set the box down and lifted the top.

She closed her eyes and breathed in the odors. Mold. Her perfume. Formaldehyde. Dust.

Slowly, she let her fingers search down the sides of the box and then over the contents until she found the familiar contours of the nose, the leathery hollows of the eyes . . . the hard, tight mouth.

Her mind reconstructed the face so that the mouth became soft and smiling, speaking loving words, and the eyes, large and gray, looking at her with kindness instead of cold hatred.

When she felt at peace, she rested her chin on her knees and rocked until everything was swept away, leaving only the vast, open nothing of the dark.

Monsieur Eber kissed her hand at the top of the stairs and excused himself from accompanying her to the door; his arthritis was terrible this time of year.

At the entrance of the bank, she paused, and unfolded her coat when she perceived him—suddenly there, behind her.

"Allow me," Emil said, taking the coat from her and holding it open, waiting. His hands smelled faintly of cologne.

Wordless, she nodded.

He wondered what had taken place with the old banker. It had obviously been positive. There was a flush on her cheeks and an aliveness in the eyes that had not been there before.

"I am going to take lunch," he said impassively. The rich satin lining of her coat slid easily over her arms. "Would you care to join me?"

Her eyes shifted momentarily to his hands, his chest, his neck, and finally his face.

He didn't flinch under the cold gray eyes. He deflected the intensity of her gaze with his own scrutiny of her. His hand touched the small of her back through her coat, exerting the slightest pressure.

She drew up the collar of her coat, regarded the city through the door, and took a step toward it.

If you enjoyed this Adele Monsarrat thriller,
don't miss her debut!

PULSE

Adele, a dedicated nurse in a big-city hospital where anything can happen and usually does, takes a sweet, new, young nurse under her wing. When her protégée dies after a minor operation, Adele is the first to suspect murder. When the killings get bloody, Adele begins to investigate with the help of a handsome medical examiner. But Adele's investigation could send her on a one-way trip to the morgue.

PULSE
by Echo Heron

Published by Ivy Books.
Available wherever books are sold.

PANIC

by ECHO HERON

The daughter of a prominent San Francisco doctor and senatorial candidate suddenly dies—apparently killed by a deadly virus that soon infects the girl's father and Adele Monsarrat's friend. But this virus kills selectively, and Adele suspects the murderer is all too human.

Published by Ivy Books.
Available in a bookstore near you.

*Now, at a time when the spotlight is turned on
health care and what goes on in hospitals,*

Echo Heron

has written

TENDING LIVES
Nurses
on the Medical Front

a compelling collection of real-life medical
dramas experienced by nurses throughout
the country.

Each nurse has a chapter, every chapter written
in his or her own voice. Their experiences range
from inspiring to tragic to downright funny. And
the stories are charged with the issues that affect
nursing care today.

TENDING LIVES

is a moving, inspiring book about a noble profession.

Published by Ivy Books.
Available in bookstores everywhere.